The
Thirteen-Gun
Salute

The

Thirteen-Gun

Salute

WITHDRAWN

Patrick O'Brian

Thorndike Press • Chivers Press
Waterville, Maine USA   Bath, England

This Large Print edition is published by Thorndike Press, USA and by Chivers Press, England.

Published in 2002 in the U.S. by arrangement with W. W. Norton & Company, Inc.

Published in 2002 in the U.K. by arrangement with HarperCollins Publishers Limited.

U.S. Hardcover 0-7862-1937-8 (Famous Authors Series)
U.K. Hardcover 0-7540-1821-0 (Windsor Large Print)
U.K. Softcover 0-7540-9200-3 (Paragon Large Print)

The text of this Large Print edition is unabridged.
Other aspects of the book may vary from the original edition.

Cover illustration by Geoff Hunt.

Set in 16 pt. Plantin by Al Chase.

Printed in the United States on permanent paper.

British Library Cataloguing-in-Publication Data available

Library of Congress Cataloging-in-Publication Data

O'Brian, Patrick, 1914–
  The thirteen-gun salute / Patrick O'Brian.
    p. cm.
   ISBN 0-7862-1937-8 (lg. print : hc : alk. paper)
   1. Great Britain — History, Naval — 19th century — Fiction.
  2. Maturin, Stephen (Fictitious character) — Fiction.
  3. Aubrey, Jack (Fictitious character) — Fiction.   4. South
China Sea Region — Fiction.   5. Large type books.   I. Title.
PR6029.B56 T45 2002
  823'.914—dc21   2001054089

to
Richard Ollard

The sails of a square-rigged ship, hung out to dry in a calm.

1 Flying jib
2 Jib
3 Fore topmast staysail
4 Fore staysail
5 Foresail, or course
6 Fore topsail
7 Fore topgallant
8 Mainstaysail
9 Maintopmast staysail
10 Middle staysail
11 Main topgallant staysail

12 Mainsail, or course
13 Maintopsail
14 Main topgallant
15 Mizzen staysail
16 Mizzen topmast staysail
17 Mizzen topgallant staysail
18 Mizzen sail
19 Spanker
20 Mizzen topsail
21 Mizzen topgallant

Illustration source: Serres, Liber Nauticus.
Courtesy of The Science and Technology Research Center,
The New York Public Library, Astor, Lenox,
and Tilden Foundations

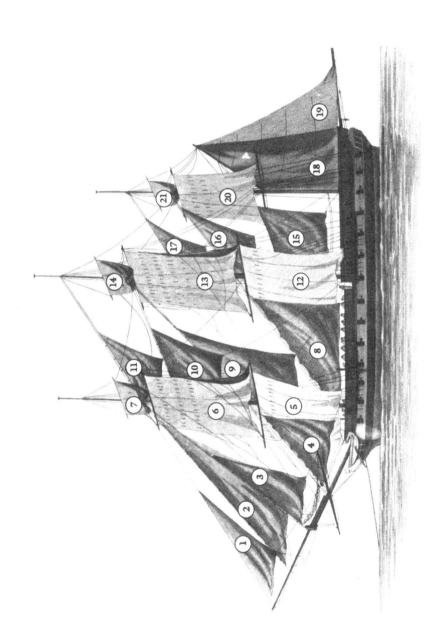

Chapter 1

In spite of the hurry, many wives and many sweethearts had come to see the ship off, and those members of her company who were not taken up with sailing her on her difficult course close-hauled to the brisk south-east breeze, watched the white flutter of their handkerchiefs far across the water until Black Point hid them entirely, shut them right out.

The married men on the quarterdeck of the *Surprise* stepped back from the rail with a sigh and clapped their telescopes to. They were all sincerely attached to their wives, and they all — Jack Aubrey, her commander, Captain Pullings, a volunteer acting as his first lieutenant, Stephen Maturin, her surgeon, and Nathaniel Martin, his assistant — they all regretted the parting extremely. Yet it so happened that from a variety of official delays and other causes they had all had an unusually long spell of domesticity; some had found their consequence much reduced by the coming of a baby; others had suffered from occasional differences of opinion, from relatives by marriage, smoking chimneys, leaks in the roof, rates, taxes, the social round, insubordination; and turning they now looked to the clear south-west, the light-blue sky with a fleet of white rounded clouds marching over it in the right direction, the darker blue sea drawn to a tight line high on the horizon, and beyond that horizon endless possibilities even now, in spite of their late and inauspicious start.

It would be an absurd exaggeration to speak of a feeling of escape or holiday; but underlying the regret there was a sense of a return to a simpler world, one in which the roof, or what passed for it, was not expected to be universally waterproof, where chimneys and the poor-rate amounted to little, where a settled hierarchy, independent of moral or intellectual merit, did away if not with difference of opinion then at least with its more candid expression, a world in which there were no morning calls and in which servants could not give notice; a world devoid of most comforts, complex enough in all conscience, and not without its dangers, yet one whose complexity was as who should say more direct, less infinitely various; and above all a world that they were used to. Jack Aubrey, by a mere count of days, must have spent more time afloat than ashore; and if the formative years of his youth were given greater value, an impartial observer might have set him down as nine-tenths marine, particularly as his strongest emotions had all been known at sea. To be sure, love and an encounter with the law at its most unjust had marked him deeply by land, but these feelings, powerful though they were, could not equal those he had known as a sailor in number or intensity. Quite apart from the extreme perils of storm and shipwreck natural to his calling, he had fought in more great fleet battles and in more single-ship actions than most officers of his time. He had boarded many and many an enemy and it was at these times that he felt most wholly alive. Ordinarily he was not at all aggressive — a cheerful, sanguine, friendly, good-natured creature, severe only in the event of bad seamanship — but when he was on a Frenchman's deck, sword in hand, he felt a wild and savage joy, a fullness of being, like no other; and he remembered every detail of blows given or received, every detail of the whole engagement, with the most vivid clarity.

In this he was quite unlike his friend Maturin, who disliked violence and who took no pleasure in any battle whatsoever. When he was obliged to fight he did so with a cold efficiency, but never without an apprehension that had continually to be mastered, disliking both the occasion and the recollection of it.

Martin, the surgeon's mate, was no berserker either, perhaps in part because he was a clergyman (though unbeneficed and for this occasion 'unreverend' too, since he had left his cloth behind for the voyage, the immensely long voyage, perhaps a circumnavigation, sailing as Maturin's assistant) but quite certainly because he could feel no anger, no fighting anger, until he had been seriously attacked, and not a very great deal even then — only a wild, indignant sense of defence. Indeed there were probably as many attitudes towards battle in the ship as there were men, and as many kinds of courage; yet though the variation might run from Awkward Davis's dark lethal subhuman fury to Barret Bonden's simple delight in the excitement, the immense excitement, there was nobody aboard the *Surprise* who could possibly have been called shy. With very few exceptions they were all professional fighting seamen. Some had originally come from blue-water privateers, some from inshore smugglers and some from men-of-war; but they were a hand-picked crew (because of his peculiar circumstances Jack Aubrey had had his choice of large numbers) and now they had been together long enough, with a good deal of foul weather and some very hard fighting, to have formed a distinct community with a great sense of their ship and a great pride in her.

A somewhat anomalous community however in a ship that looked so very like a man-of-war, for not only did it contain no Marines, no uniformed officers and no midshipmen, but people walked about at ease, even with their hands in their pockets; there was a certain amount of laughter in the forecastle in spite of the parting; and the quartermaster at the con, wiping a tear from his cheek and shaking his grey head, did not scruple to address Jack directly: 'I shall never see her like again, sir. The loveliest young woman in Shelmerston.'

'A lovely young woman indeed, Heaven,' said Jack. 'Mrs Heaven, if I do not mistake?'

'Why, sir, in a manner of speaking: but some might say more on the porcupine-lay, the roving-line, if you understand me.'

'There is a great deal to be said for porcupines, Heaven: Solomon had a thousand, and Solomon knew what o'clock it was, I believe. You will certainly see her again.'

But the *Surprise* herself was anomalous

too. Although she looked so very like a King's ship she was in fact only a letter of marque, a private man-of-war licensed to cruise upon the enemy; yet she was no ordinary letter of marque either, since government was paying her expenses to go to the South Seas, there to harry the French and American whalers and fur-traders and any enemy war-ship that might be within her capacity. This would normally have brought her much nearer the status of one of His Majesty's hired vessels, particularly as her people were exempted from impressment; but it so happened that the administration's real aim was to enable Dr Maturin to look into the possibility of independent states arising in Chile and Peru — of their being helped to arise — thus weakening the Spanish empire. Since Spain was at this time England's ally the aim could not possibly be avowed, nor the payments, nor indeed anything to do with the whole potentially embarrassing affair.

This however did not worry the Surprises to the least degree. The hands knew that they had their precious exemption and that they had succeeded in remaining on the books, the highly selective books, of the most extraordinarily successful privateer afloat, one whose recent list of prizes had enabled even the humblest seamen she carried to play ducks and drakes with gold pieces if they chose. Several of them and several of their shipmates had so chosen throughout the unexpectedly long period of refitting before the South American voyage, and they were now paupers once more, though very cheerful paupers, since what had happened before might very well happen again — was almost certain to happen again — and even a short cruise, let alone one into the South Sea, might bring Captain Aubrey back with so many prizes at his tail that the port of Shelmerston would be choked for the second time.

Yet rather more of them, particularly the two- and two-and-a-half-share hands, had listened to their captain's advice. Captain Aubrey was remarkably good at giving financial advice: he cried up thrift, caution, small returns (the Navy Five per cents were the very utmost limit of what he would approve), perpetual vigilance and strict economy. It was known throughout the maritime world that although Lucky Jack Aubrey had quite certainly earned his nickname at sea, making at least three fortunes before the last astonishing stroke, he had also been spectacularly unfortunate by land. At certain periods he had been extravagant, maintaining a racing stable and cutting a figure at Brooks's; at others he had been credulous, believing in projectors and their schemes; and generally speaking disaster had attended upon his undertakings. It was therefore perfectly clear to an objective eye that no one had less right to give advice. Yet among seamen, Aubrey's handling of a ship, his behaviour when he brought that ship into action, his list of victories and his list of prizes outweighed a certain want of practical management; and his words, always very kindly intended, always adapted to the means and the understanding of his hearers, had great influence, rather as Tom Cribb's on a point of foreign politics might have done, and some of the Surprises, all of them married men with children, retired from the sea. But none, except a sailmaker's mate who was married to the daughter and sole heiress of a carrier, had retired very far, and the seven new inns or ale-houses called the Aubrey Arms and with those arms (azure, three sheep's heads erased, proper) on their sign-posts, now scattered about the country were all within easy reach of the strand — and, it must be admitted, of the publican's smuggling brothers, uncles, cousins, nephews, and even God preserve us grandchildren. Yet the prudent and uxorious amounted to so small a proportion of the frigate's people that even when they were added to the paupers they hardly took away from the second anomaly, which was that the *Surprise* was also a ship largely filled with men who were sailing away under no compulsion on the part of authority, poverty or want of employment, men who had considerable sums at home and who were setting out on this prodigious voyage for something more — something less definite than gain and more important. With such a multiplicity of characters the 'more' was necessarily somewhat shapeless, though some obvious part of it had to do with going far foreign, seeing new countries, cutting capers on Tom Tiddler's ground and perhaps picking up gold and silver, sailing in a happy ship, sailing away in war-time from the strong likelihood of eventual impressment and forced service under officers of a very different character — it was not the fighting that the Shelmerstonians disliked, nor even the hard lying and short commons, but the often unnecessarily harsh discipline, the hazing, the starting and sometimes the direct oppression. And although there was not a heart that did not delight in spoil — a sack of doubloons would make any man chuckle — a real and vehement desire for it was rarely a prime ingredient.

There were some men of course whose 'more' was eminently clear. Jack Aubrey did not give a damn for money: his sole aim was reinstatement in the service and restoration to the list of post-captains in the Royal Navy, with his former seniority if possible. All this had been semi-officially and conditionally offered after his cutting-out of the *Diane*; and it had been absolutely promised him after his election to parliament, or rather after his cousin had given him the pocket borough of Milford. But at last, at very long last, Aubrey had grown less sanguine, less confident in promises; his brief acquaintance with the House and his fellow-members had told him a great deal about the fragility of the administration and therefore of its undertakings; he did not for a moment doubt the present First Lord's word, but he knew that in the event of a change of ministry this word, this purely personal, verbal word, would not necessarily bind Melville's successor. He also knew — and this was a fresh though not entirely unforeseen development — that the Regent was by no means favourable to him. It arose partly from the fact that the Regent's naval brother, the Duke of Clarence, was both one of Jack's most fervent advocates and one of the Regent's most outspoken critics — the brothers were scarcely on speaking-terms; furthermore several strongly independent Whiggish admirals also said that Aubrey absolutely *must* be reinstated; and then by way of completing things Jack had made one of his rare adventures into literature. On hearing that in the course of a drawing-room the Regent's mistress Lady Hertford had been rude to Diana Maturin, his cousin by marriage and his best friend's wife, he said angrily and in rather too public a place, 'Birds of a feather, birds of a feather; fowl in their own nest, all tarred with the same brush. Dryden put it very well, speaking of another great man's mistresses: he said — he said — I have it. He said *false, foolish, old, ill-natured and ill-bred.* Aye: there's no beating Dryden. *False, foolish, old, ill-natured and ill-bred* — nothing more ill-bred than being uncivil at a levee or a drawing-room.'

It was his former shipmate Mowett who had told him the quotation and it was his present shipmate Maturin who told him that the words had reached the royal ear. Stephen had the news from his friend and close colleague Sir Joseph Blaine, the head of naval intelligence, who added, 'If we could tell who was in the backgammon room at the time, we might possibly be able to put a name on the worm in the apple.'

A worm in the apple there was. Some time before this two singularly well-placed French agents, Ledward of the Treasury and Wray of the Admiralty, had concocted a charge against Jack Aubrey: with Wray's intimate knowledge of naval officers' movements and Ledward's of the criminal world the accusation was so cleverly framed that it convinced a Guildhall jury and Jack was found guilty of rigging the Stock Exchange, fined, pilloried, and of course struck off the Navy List. The charge was false and its falsity was proved by a discontented enemy agent who betrayed Ledward and his friend, giving unquestionable evidence of their treachery; yet neither had been arrested, and now both were known to be in Paris. Blaine was sure they had been protected by some remarkably influential friend, probably some very high permanent official: this man (or possibly this small group of men), whose identity neither Blaine nor his colleagues could make out in spite of all their pains, was still active, still potentially very dangerous. And since at least part of Wray's plot had been directed against Aubrey out of personal malevolence, it was almost certainly this shadowy protector's influence that lay behind the odd official delay and reluctance that had met any proposals in favour of the now obviously innocent Aubrey up until the moment he became a member of parliament.

'The worm is still with us,' said Blaine. 'He must be reasonably conspicuous from his office; it is very probable that he has an unorthodox attachment for Wray; and if very delicate enquiries tell us that a distinguished man with ambiguous tastes — and even the greatest care cannot conceal these things from servants — was in the backgammon room on Friday, why, then, we may pin him at last.'

'Certainly,' said Stephen, 'if we accept that the only man present willing to carry ill-natured gossip was the worm in question.'

'Very true,' said Blaine. 'Still, it might give some slight hint or indication. But in any case, I do beg you will urge our friend to be discreet. Tell him that although the First Lord is an honourable man the present complexion of affairs is such that he may be physically incapable of fulfilling his promises; he may be excluded from the Admiralty. Tell Aubrey to be very cautious in his certainties; and tell him to put to sea as soon as ever he can. Tell him that quite apart

from obvious considerations there are obscure forces that may do him harm.'

Jack Aubrey had little notion of his
friend's mathematical or astronomical abilities and none whatsoever of his seamanship,
while his performance at billiards, tennis or
fives, let alone cricket, would have been
contemptible if they had not excited such a
degree of hopeless compassion; but where
physic, a foreign language and political intelligence were concerned, Maturin might
have been all the Sibyls rolled into one, together with the Witch of Edmonton, Old
Moore, Mother Shipton and even the holy
Nautical Almanack, and no sooner had Stephen finished his account with the words 'It
is thought you might be well advised to put
to sea quite soon. Not only would it place
those concerned before a fait accompli but
it would also — forgive me, brother — prevent you from committing yourself farther
in some unguarded moment or in the event
of provocation,' than Jack gave him a
piercing look and asked 'Should I put to sea
directly?'

'I believe so,' said Stephen.

Jack nodded, turned towards Ashgrove
Cottage and hailed 'The house, ahoy. Ho,
Killick, there,' in a voice that would quite

certainly reach across the intervening two hundred yards.

He need not have called out so loud, for after a decent pause Killick stepped from behind the hedge, where he had been listening. How such an awkward, slab-sided creature could have got along by that sparse and dwarvish hedge undetected Stephen could not tell. This newly-planned bowling-green had seemed an ideal place for confidential remarks, the best apart from the inconveniently remote open down; Stephen had chosen it deliberately, but although he was experienced in these things he was not infallible, and once again Killick had done him brown. He consoled himself with reflecting that the steward's eavesdropping was perfectly disinterested — the true miser's love for coins as coins, not as a means of exchange — and that his loyalty to Jack's interests (as perceived by Killick) was beyond all question.

'Killick,' said Aubrey, 'sea-chest for tomorrow at dawn; and pass the word for Bonden.'

'Sea-chest for tomorrow at dawn it is, sir; and Bonden to report to the skittle-alley,' replied Killick without any change whatsoever in his wooden expression; but when he had gone a little way he stopped, crept back to the hedge again and peered at them for a while through the branches. There were no bowling-greens in the remote estuarine hamlet where Preserved Killick had been born, but there was, thcre always had been, a skittle-alley; and this was the term he used — used with a steady obstinacy typical of his dogged, thoroughly awkward nature.

And yet, reflected Stephen as they paced up and down as though on a green or at least greenish quarterdeck, Killick was nearly in the right of it: this had no close resemblance to a bowling-green, any more than Jack Aubrey's rose-garden looked like anything planted by a Christian for his pleasure. Most skills were to be found in a man-of-war — the *Surprise*'s Sethians, for example, with only the armourer and a carpenter's mate to help them, had run themselves up a new meeting-house in what was understood to be the Babylonian taste, with a chain of great gilded S's on each of its marble walls — but in the present case gardening did not seem to be one of them. Certainly fine scything was not. The green was covered with crescent-shaped pecks where the ill-directed blade had plunged into the sward: some of the pecks were bald with a yellow surround, others were bald entirely; and their presence had apparently encouraged all the moles of the neighbourhood to throw up their mounds beside them.

It was the most superficial part of his mind that made these reflexions: below there was a mixture of surprise and consternation, largely wordless. Surprise because although he thought he knew Jack Aubrey very well he had clearly under-estimated the measureless importance he attached to every aspect of this voyage. Consternation because he had not meant to be taken literally. This 'sea-chest for tomorrow at dawn' would be exceedingly inconvenient to Stephen — he had a great deal of business to attend to before sailing, more than he could comfortably do even in the five or six days allotted — but he had so phrased his words, particularly the discourse that preceded the direct warning, that he could think of no way of going back on them with any sort of consistency. In any case, his invention was at a particularly low ebb; so was his memory — if he had recalled that the frigate was already fully victualled for her great voyage he would have been less oracular. He was in a thoroughly bad state of mind and temper, dissatisfied with the people in his banking-house, dissatisfied with the universities in which he meant to endow chairs of comparative anatomy; he was hungry; and he was cross with his wife, who had said in her clear ringing voice, 'I will tell you what, Maturin, if this baby of ours has anything like the discontented, bilious, liverish expression you have brought down from town, it shall be changed out of hand for something more cheerful from the Foundling Hospital.'

Of course in theory he could say 'The ship will not sail until I am ready', for absurdly enough he was her owner; but here theory was so utterly remote from any conceivable practice, the relations between Aubrey and himself being what they were, that he never dwelt on it; and in his hurry of spirits and the muddled thinking caused by ill-temper he hit upon nothing else before Bonden came at the double and the Goat's and the George's post-chaises were bespoke, express messengers sent off to Shelmerston, London and Plymouth; and even if Maturin had spoken with the tongues of angels it was now too late for him to recant with any decency at all.

'Lord, Stephen,' said Jack, cocking his ear towards the clock-tower in the stable-yard, a fine great yard now filled with Diana's Arabians, 'we must go and shift ourselves. Dinner will be ready in half an hour.'

'Oh for all love,' cried Stephen with a most unusual jet of ill-humour, 'must our lives be ruled by bells on land as well as by sea?'

'Dear Stephen,' said Jack, looking down on him kindly, though with a little surprise, 'this is Liberty Hall, you know. If you had rather take a cold pork pie and a bottle of wine into the summer-house, do not feel the least constraint. For my own part, I do not choose to disoblige Sophie, who means to put on a prodigious fine gown: I believe it is our wedding-day, or perhaps her mother's. And in any case Edward Smith is coming.'

As it happened Stephen did not choose to disoblige Diana either. They had recently had a larger number of disputes than usual, including a quite furious battle about Barham Down. The place was too large and far too remote for a woman living by herself; the grass was by no means suitable for a stud-farm — she had seen the aftermath from the meadows: poor thin stuff. And the hard pocked surface of the gallops would knock delicate hooves to pieces. She would be far better off staying with Sophie and using Jack's unoccupied downs — such grass, second only to the Curragh of Kildare. This led on to the inadvisability of her riding at all while she was pregnant and to her reply 'My God, Maturin, how you do go on. Anyone would think I was a prize heifer. You are turning this baby into an infernal bore.'

He regretted their disagreements extremely, particularly since they had grown more — not so much more acrimonious or vehement as more spirited since their real marriage, their marriage in a church. During their former cohabitation they had quarrelled, of course; but very mildly — never a raised voice nor an oath, no broken furniture at all or even plates. Their marriage however had coincided with Stephen's giving up his long-established and habitual taking of opium, and although he was a physician it was only at this point that he fully realized what a very soothing effect his draught had had upon him, how very much it had calmed his body as well as his mind, and what a shamefully inadequate husband it had made him, particularly for a woman like Diana. The change in his behaviour, the very decided change (for when undulled by laudanum he was of an ardent temperament) had added an almost entirely new and almost entirely beneficent depth to their connexion; and although it was in all likelihood the cause of the heat with which they now argued, each preserving an imperilled independence, it was quite certainly the cause of this baby. When Stephen had first heard that foetal heart beat, his own had stopped dead and then turned over. He was filled with a joy he had never known before, and with a kind of adoration for Diana.

The association of ideas led him to say, when they were half-way to the house, 'Jack, in my hurry I had almost forgot to tell you that I had two letters from Sam and two about him, all delivered from the same Lisbon packet. In both he sends you his most respectful and affectionate greetings —' Jack's face flushed with pleasure '— and I believe his affairs are in a most promising way.'

'I am delighted, delighted to hear it,' said Jack. 'He is a dear good boy.' Sam Panda, as tall as Aubrey and even broader, was Jack's natural son, as black as polished ebony yet absurdly recognizable — the same carriage, the same big man's gentleness, even the same features, transposed to another key. He had been brought up by Irish missionary priests in South Africa, and he was now in minor orders; he was unusually intelligent and from the merely temporal point of view he had a brilliant career before him, if only a dispensation would allow him to be or-dained priest, for without one no bastard could advance much higher than an exorcist. Stephen had taken a great liking to him at their first meeting in the West Indies, and he had been using his influence in Rome and elsewhere. 'Indeed,' Stephen went on, his vexation of spirit diminishing as he spoke, 'I believe all that is needed now is the good word of the Patriarch, which I trust I may obtain when we touch at Lisbon.'

'Patriarch?' cried Jack, laughing loud. 'Is there really a Patriarch in Lisbon? A living Patriarch?'

'Of course there is a Patriarch. How do you suppose the Portuguese church could get along without a Patriarch? Even your quite recent sects find what they call bishops and indeed archbishops forsooth necessary. Every schoolboy knows that there are and always have been Patriarchs of Constantinople, Alexandria, Antioch, Jerusalem, the Indies, Venice, and, as I say, of Lisbon.'

'You astonish me, Stephen. I had always imagined that patriarchs were very, very old gentlemen in ancient times, with beards to their knees and long robes — Abraham, Methusalem, Anchises and so on. But you have Patriarchs actually walking about, ha, ha, ha!' He laughed with such good humour and amusement that it was impossible to preserve a sullen or dogged expression.

'Forgive me, Stephen. I am only an ignorant sailorman, you know, and mean no disrespect — Patriarchs, oh Lord!' They reached the gravel drive and with a graver look he said, but not nearly so loud, 'I am amazingly glad at what you tell me about Sam. He does so deserve to get on, with all his studying, his Latin and Greek and I dare say theology too — yet none of your bookworms neither — he must weigh a good seventeen stone and as strong as an ox. And his letters to me are so amiable and discreet — diplomatic, if you know what I mean. Anyone could read 'em. But, Stephen,' lowering his voice still farther as they walked up the steps, 'you need not mention it, unless you see fit, of course.'

Sophie had liked what she had seen of Sam, and although his relationship to her husband was obvious enough she had made no fuss of any kind: the begetting of Sam was indeed so long before her time that she scarcely had much ground for any sense of personal injury, and righteous indignation was not in her style; nevertheless Jack felt profoundly grateful to her. He also felt a corresponding degree of guilt when Sam was fresh in his mind; but these were not obsessive feelings by any means, and at present he was required to grapple with a completely different problem.

By the time he walked into the drawing-room with freshly-powdered hair and a fine scarlet coat there was no remaining hint of guilt in his expression or his tone of voice. He glanced at the clock, saw that it would be at least five minutes before the arrival of his guests, and said, 'Ladies, I am sorry to tell you that our time ashore is cut short. We go aboard tomorrow and sail with the noonday tide.'

They all cried out at once, a shrill and discordant clamour of dissent — certainly he should not go — another six days had always been understood and laid down — how was it possible that their linen should be ready? — had he forgotten that Admiral Schank was to dine on Thursday? — it was the girls' birthday on the fourth: they would be so disappointed — how could he have overlooked his own daughters' birthday? Even Mrs Williams, his mother-in-law, whom poverty and age had quite suddenly reduced to a most pitiable figure, hesitant, fearful of giving offence or of not understanding, universally civil, painfully obsequious to Jack and Diana, almost unrecognizable to those who had known her in her strong shrewish confident talking prime, recovered something of her fire and declared that Mr Aubrey could not possibly fly off in that wild manner.

Stephen walked in, and Diana at once went over to him as he stood there in the doorway. Unlike Sophie she had dressed rather carelessly, partly because she was not pleased with her husband and partly because as she said 'women with great bellies had no business with finery'. She plucked his waistcoat straight and said, 'Stephen, is it true that you sail tomorrow?'

'With the blessing,' he said, looking a little doubtfully into her face.

She turned straight out of the room and could be heard running upstairs two at a time, like a boy.

'Heavens, Sophie, what a magnificent gown you are wearing, to be sure,' said Stephen.

'It is the first time I have put it on,' she replied, with a wan little smile and tears brimming in her eyes. 'It is the Lyons velvet you were so very kind as to . . .'

The guests arrived, Edward Smith, a shipmate of Jack's in three separate commissions and now captain of the *Tremendous*, 74, together with his pretty wife. Talk, much talk, the hearty talk of old friends, and in the midst of it Diana slipped in, blue silk from head to foot, the shade best calculated to set off the beauty of a woman with black hair, blue eyes, and an immense diamond, bluer still, hanging against her bosom. She had genuinely meant to make a discreet, unnoticed entrance, but conversation stopped dead, and Mrs Smith, a simple country lady who had been holding forth on jellies, gazed open-mouthed and mute at the Blue Peter pendant, which she had never seen before.

In a way this silence was just as well, for Killick, who acted as butler ashore, had recently been polished: he knew he must not jerk his thumb over his shoulder towards the dining-room in the sea-going way and say 'Wittles is up', but he was not yet quite sure of the right form: now, coming in just after Diana, he said in a low, hesitant tone that might not have been heard if there had been much of a din, 'Dinner is on table sir which I mean ma'am if you please.'

A pretty good dinner in the English way, a dinner of two courses with five removes, but nothing to what Sophie would have ordered if she had known that this was to be Jack's last at home for an immense space of time. Yet at least the best port the cellar possessed had come up, and when the gorgeously-dressed women left them, the men settled down to it.

'When they are making good port wine,

and the better kinds of claret and bur-gundy,' said Stephen, looking at the candle through his glass, 'men act like rational creatures. In almost all their other activities we see little but foolishness and chaos. Would not you say, sir, that the world was filled with chaos?'

'Indeed I should, sir,' said Captain Smith. 'Except in a well-run man-of-war, we see chaos all around us.'

'Chaos everywhere. Nothing could be simpler than carrying on a banking-house. You receive money, you write it down; you pay money out, you write it down; and the difference between the two sums is the cus-tomer's balance. But can I induce my bank to tell me my balance, answer my letters, attend to my instructions promptly? I cannot. When I go to expostulate I swim in chaos. The partner I wish to see is fishing for salmons in his native Tweed — papers have been mislaid — papers have not come to hand — nobody in the house can read Portuguese or understand the Portuguese way of doing business — it would be better if I were to make an appointment in a fort-night's time. I do not say they are dishonest (though there is a fourpence for unex-plained sundries that I do not much care for) but I do say they are incompetent, vainly struggling in an amorphous fog. Tell me, sir, do you know of any banker that really understands his business? Some modern Fugger?'

'Oh, Stephen, if you please,' cried Jack, for both Edward and Henry Smith, the sons of an Evangelical parson they much admired, were spoken of as Blue Lights in the Navy (prayers every day aboard and twice on Sunday), and although their fighting qualities took away from any sanctimonious implication the words might possess, it was known that they were very strict about coarse words, oaths and impropriety. Both brothers, Blue Lights or not, had been steadily kind and attentive to him in his recent disgrace, at considerable risk to their naval careers, and he did not wish his guest to be offended.

'I refer to the Fuggers, Mr Aubrey,' said Stephen, looking coldly at him. 'The Fuggers, I repeat, an eminent High Dutch family of bankers, the very type of those who understood their business, particularly in the time of Charles V.'

'Oh? I was not aware — perhaps I mistook your pronunciation. I beg pardon. But in any case Captain Smith is brother to the gentleman I told you about, the gentleman who is setting up a bank just at hand. That is to say another bank, for they have offices all over the county, and one in town of course. You know his other brother too, Henry Smith, who commands *Revenge* and who married Admiral Piggot's daughter: a thoroughly naval family. Poor Tom would have been a sailor too, but for his game leg. A most capital bank, I am sure; I am making some pretty considerable transfers, Tom Smith being so conveniently near. But as for your people, Stephen, I did not like to see young Robin lose fifteen thousand guineas in one session at Brooks's.'

'I am not to cry up my own family's bank,' said Captain Edward Smith, 'but at least I think I can assert that there is no chaos in Tom's concern, or as little as can be imagined in sublunar affairs. Letters that come in are answered the same day, fourpences do not pass unnoticed, and Tom's notes are honoured all over the country, even in Scotland, as readily as those of the Bank of England.'

'He plays a fine game of cricket, too, in spite of his poor leg,' said Jack. 'He has a man to run for him when he bats, and he bowls a most diabolical twister. I have known him since I was a boy.'

'I beg your pardon, sir, for not recognizing you before,' said Stephen. 'I have had the pleasure of seeing your brother quite often on board the *Revenge*, and if I had not been so bemused I should have made out the likeness directly.'

It was indeed very marked; and in the drawing-room Stephen contemplated upon the possible extent of family likeness: in this case the two brothers were both typical naval officers of the kind Stephen liked best — men with weather-beaten faces, good-looking, capable faces, whose open, friendly expressions quite lacked the self-consciousness, self-satisfaction and morgue sometimes to be seen in soldiers; they were both physically very much alike, and Edward Smith had exactly the same rueful, kindly laugh and movement of his head as Henry.

Mrs Williams had turned to him for support. 'Surely you, sir, who have known Mr Aubrey so long, can make him understand how wrong it is to fly off in this wild manner, with the girls' birthday so near at hand and Parliament about to be summoned any day?'

'Why, ma'am,' said Captain Smith, with this same chuckle and inclination of the head, 'with the best will in the world to serve you, I am afraid that is more than I can undertake to do.'

And it was more than any of the others could undertake to do. When Jack Aubrey spoke in his service tone of voice, Sophie, Diana and Stephen knew perfectly well that he could and would fly off in that wild manner: Stephen in particular had often seen him do so. When there was some naval advantage to be gained by losing not a minute, where weather-gage, chase, engagement or escape were concerned, vessels under Aubrey's command were liable to slip their cables and fly off beyond recall, leaving liberty-men, comforts, and even the Captain's sacred coffee behind, to say nothing of unfulfilled social obligations. Stephen was aware that nothing could change this state of affairs; he had been aware of it all along; and that was why he was now standing on the quarterdeck of the *Surprise*, staring morosely into the offing, a victim of his own over-emphatic persuasion.

Another five or six days would have made things so much easier. Yet on the other hand Jack was in fact much safer afloat: with the opening of parliament just at hand he might have made another blunder, or what was far more likely, this obscure adverse influence might easily have fixed one upon him, either by provocation through a third party or by pure invention. No. Upon the whole Stephen was glad to be at sea. His affairs might still be in some disorder, but Jack had arranged for the purser to put off from Plymouth and join the ship off the Eddystone: Standish would bring many things, including letters, and the pilot-cutter that brought him out would carry letters back again. And then there was always their pause in Lisbon. With all its disadvantages — vexing to an already exacerbated spirit deprived of its habitual balm but trifling in sum — the great voyage that he and Martin had so looked forward to as natural philosophers had actually begun, a voyage that had an even greater importance for Maturin from the point of view of political intelligence. There was a considerable pro-French party in the South American possessions, and this party was also much in favour of slavery: Stephen was as strongly opposed to the French, in the sense of the imperialist, Bonapartist French, as he was to slavery, which he hated with all his being, just as he hated other forms of tyranny, such as that of the Castilians in Catalonia.

Jack Aubrey's other shipmates, above all those who had been with him since his early commands, were also quite used to his abrupt departures. Yet although they were not spiritually disconcerted by the frigate's leaving Shelmerston with a large variety of ropes dangling disgracefully, open pots of paint lying about on deck, part of her starboard blackstrake scraped bare and part tarred and lamp-blacked, while all the officers' washing was still ashore, they were physically much affected, since all this horrible, unseamanlike confusion must be reduced to order without the loss of a moment. They were all on deck, and now that Penlee Head was well astern they, and virtually the whole of the ship's company with them, were exceedingly busy. Exceedingly busy, but not in the least put out or surprised: all the more knowing old hands knew that Jack Aubrey rarely or never put to sea in this tearing hurry unless he had had private intelligence ('And who off of, mate? Who off of?' would ask the oldest and most knowing of them all, tapping the sides of their noses) of an attackable enemy or a glorious prize within the next few hundred miles of sea; and for this reason they flew about their duties with an even greater zeal than unqualified devotion would have required.

Tom Pullings, a captain by courtesy but in fact only a commander in the Royal Navy, and a commander who, like so many of his rank, had no ship to command, was sailing once again as a volunteer, and at present he occupied the quarterdeck with the Captain. Davidge was in the waist with the carpenter and a large number of powerful hands, stowing the frigate's many boats; West and the bosun were on the forecastle apparently playing cat's cradle with an improbable amount of cordage, while hands crept round them, above them, outboard of them, each a thorough-going seaman intent upon his business.

All these officers had been aboard the *Surprise* in her last spectacularly successful cruise, which had been intended as a mere trial run in home waters, a preparation for this present long voyage, and all had done well out of it; Davidge and West were present chiefly because they felt committed to Aubrey, but partly because they would like to do even better (both had had very heavy debts to pay out of their prize-money) and because, it being generally understood in the service that Aubrey would sooner or later be reinstated, they rather hoped they might regain the Navy List in his wake. Pullings' prime motion was plain devotion to Jack, helped a little by a certain developing shrewishness in Mrs Pullings (unimaginable to those who had only seen her as a timid country-mouse several years and four stout children ago), who more and more frequently asked him *why* he had no ship when scrubs like Willis and Caley were provided for and who had written a letter, neither very wise nor very well spelt, to the Admiralty, pressing his claims.

Much the same kind of attachment had brought and kept Jack Aubrey's regular followers aboard — his followers in the naval sense, his coxswain, his steward, his bargemen, and a considerable number of hands who had sailed with him all this war and sometimes a part of the last, like old Plaice and his cousins and a dreadful man called Awkward Davies, an uncommonly powerful, clumsy, violent, drunken and ill-tempered creature who had haunted him voyage after voyage in spite of all that could be said or done. For these men there was also the fact that being aboard a man-of-war run Navy fashion was the natural and proper way of life, as natural as their loose trousers and comfortable roomy frocks. Wearing long togs to astonish friends and relations ashore was gratifying to the mind, and so was screeching and hallooing around the streets of Gosport or kicking up Bob's a-dying from Wapping to the Tower; but apart from fun of that sort, the land's main function was to provide marine stores — it was not a place for real existence. Then again following the sea was what they were used to, and they liked what they were used to, a regular life with no changes of any kind, no mad interferencc with the steady succession of salt pork on Sunday and Thursday, salt beef on Tuesday and Saturday, with banyan-days between; the sea itself could be relied upon to provide all the variety that could possibly be desired.

Obviously this attachment to the frigate and her commander and to the ordered pattern of naval life was unevenly spread among the ship's company. There were some recently-entered hands, taken on during the *Surprise*'s journey from the Baltic, whose devotion was primarily to Mammon. They were thoroughly able seamen — they would never have been aboard otherwise — but they did not yet form part of the crew. The real Surprises, that is to say those who had sailed in her time out of mind and the men from Shelmerston who had fought in her last two actions, looked upon these Orkneymen with distant reserve, and Jack had not yet made up his mind how to deal with the situation.

A glance at the vane showed him that the breeze had backed far enough; and the sky said that in all likelihood it would go on backing until at least sunset. The gangways and the forecastle were reasonably clear, and after a considering pause he said, 'Captain Pullings, I believe we may attend to the foretopsailyard at last.'

In the present violent putting to sea, earlier than all expectation, both watches were strangely mingled, with duties and stations far out of the ordinary run; and it so happened that most of the Orkneymen were on the forecastle, gathered round their leader Macaulay. Pullings gave the orders loud and clear, the bosun piped them in the shorthand of the sea, and the hands on the forecastle instantly clapped on to the falls, Macaulay at their head.

A slight pause, and then, throwing his weight on the rope, he sang out

'Heisa, heisa,'

followed by his mates in perfect unison,

'Heisa, heisa,
Vorsa, vorsa,
Vou, vou.
One long pull
More power
Young blood
Ha ha ha hough.'

45

They sang on a scale unknown to Jack, with intervals he had never heard; and the last line, a falsetto shriek as the blocks clashed together, quite astonished him.

He looked aft, where Stephen would ordinarily be leaning over the taffrail gazing at the wake. No Stephen. 'I suppose the Doctor has gone below,' he said. 'He would have liked that. We might ease off again and ask him to come on deck.'

'I doubt we might get a short answer,' said Pullings in a low voice. 'He is sitting there with so many papers he might be paying off a first-rate, and he roared at Mr Martin just now like a bull.'

As far as devotion was concerned, Nathaniel Martin's was directed more towards Maturin than Aubrey, and Stephen's snappishness had quite wounded him — a snappishness that Martin had scarcely known in him before, but that seemed to be growing sharper and more frequent.

There was to be sure some excuse for it on this occasion, since a moderate lee-lurch had sent Martin staggering from one piled chair to another, upsetting and mingling four carefully-separated heaps of paper, while the draught he let in spread them over the cabin deck like a whitish carpet.

Their presence arose from the fact that

the British government was not alone in wishing to change the state of affairs in the Spanish and even Portuguese possessions in South America: the French hoped to do the same, and well before London's tentative contacts with the potential rebels in Chile, Peru and elsewhere, the French had carried their much more ambitious (and much more avowable) plans to the verge of action. They had equipped a new frigate that was to cruise upon Allied merchantmen and particularly South Sea whalers while at the same time landing agents, arms and money on the coast of Chile. It was this frigate, the *Diane*, that Jack Aubrey had cut out from St Martin's just before she sailed, and in her he had captured all the French agents' information and instruction, all their correspondents' views of the various local situations, all the names of French sympathizers and of those whose loyalty had been or could be purchased. All this was encoded according to four separate systems, and it was these systems that Martin had upset, together with their substrata of Maturin's involved private business — university chairs, annuities, settlements and the like. All the French papers would have to be sorted all over again, then read in clear, digested and committed to memory, with perhaps some of the more forgettable points re-encoded for future reference. Ordinarily the great bulk of this work would have been done by Sir Joseph's department, but in this instance both he and Stephen agreed that they should keep the existence of the whole mass of papers to themselves.

Martin retired to the orlop, where by the light of a battle-lantern he finished entering the ship's medical stores in a book and then wrote labels for the bottles and boxes in the medicine-chest, a new, particularly massive affair with two locks.

From these he went on to check their surgical instruments, the grim saws, retractors, artery-hooks, gags, leather-covered chains; and then the more massive substances such as portable soup, stored in flat wooden cases of thirty-six slabs apiece, lime and lemon juice, plaster of Paris for healing broken limbs in the oriental manner (much favoured now by Dr Maturin), and neat square bales of lint, each marked with the broad arrow. He was turning over the last (already attacked by rats) when Stephen joined him. 'Everything seems to be in order,' said Martin, 'except that I have not been able to find more than this single case-bottle quart of laudanum, instead of all our usual five-gallon carboys.'

'There is only that one quart,' said Stephen. 'I have decided to employ it no more, except in the greatest emergency.'

'It used to be your panacea,' observed Martin, his mind drifting away to the builders at home: were they attending to the roof at this moment? He doubted it: he would send a note to Mr Huge by the Plymouth pilot-boat.

'I am no more infallible than Paracelsus, who used antimony for a great many years,' replied Maturin. 'There are grave objections to the frequent exhibition of laudanum, I find.'

'Yes, yes, of course,' said Martin, clapping his hand to his forehead. 'I beg your pardon.'

There were indeed very grave objections. Padeen, Stephen's Irish servant and loblolly-boy, often in and about the sick-berth and the medical stores, had become deeply addicted to laudanum, the alcoholic tincture of opium. Stephen, late in discovering the fact, had done what he could, but what he could do was not enough; and at the time he was disabled. Padeen deserted the ship when she touched at Leith, and being unable to get his opium by fair means — he was illiterate, barely comprehensible in English, and he knew the substance only by the name of tincture — had taken it by force, breaking into an apothecary's house by night and tasting till he found it.

This had happened in Edinburgh, far from Stephen's knowledge until the very end; but all the talent of the Scottish bar could not disguise the fact that a capital offence had been committed or that the big wild Papist at the bar was guilty of it. Padeen was sentenced to death, and it had required all the force of Jack Aubrey's influence as member for Milford to have the hanging commuted to transportation. Padeen had been sent, with many hundred more, in the next convoy to Botany Bay; but at least he carried an earnest recommendation from Dr Martin to the surgeon of the ship and the medical officer in the colony and one from Sir Joseph Banks to the Governor of New South Wales.

'I beg your pardon,' said Martin again. 'How my mind came to . . .'

A hail on deck, the distant reverberation of running feet, the perceptible rotation of the deck and the dying away of the complex sound of a ship in motion relieved him from his embarrassment. 'It is stopping,' he said.

'We are lying up,' said Stephen. 'Let us go above, having first locked the chest and dowsed the light.'

They climbed quite nimbly up the dim, familiar ladders — seamen in this if in nothing else — and emerged blinking into the brilliant light of day; and there was the Eddystone a mile to the north-westward, with the mainland rather hazy beyond it and four ships of the line close hauled for the Sound.

'Are you not amazed, Doctor?' asked Davidge, the officer of the watch.

'Certainly,' said Stephen, looking at the lighthouse with the ring of surf at its foot and the halo of gulls over its head. 'As noble an erection as could well be conceived.'

'No, no,' said Davidge. 'The decks, the brasswork, the squared yards, all fit for an admiral's inspection.'

'Nothing could be neater, or more trim,' said Stephen; and still gazing at the lighthouse he saw a pilot-cutter, obviously bound for the frigate and obviously receiving signals from her and replying to them.

'Thank God I have my letters prepared,' he cried, and ran down to his cabin. By the time he had actually found the letters and brought them on deck, direct hailing had replaced the signals, and he heard the cutter being desired to come under the ship's lee and to pass up the parcels first.

'I told you I mean to carry out a chain of observations for Humboldt, did I not?' said Jack, breaking off his conversation with the pilot. 'A chain right round to the Pacific. There is an improved dipping-ncedlc in one of those cases, together with a very delicate hygrometer of his own invention, a better azimuth-compass than anything I possess, and a Geneva cyanograph, as well as spare thermometers graduated by Ramsden. The pilot says they can go into a man's pocket, with a shove; but I shall not trust them to anything but a whip: in any case there is the post.'

The cutter came alongside, Mr Standish, the frigate's new purser, beaming up at his friends. 'Now just you sit there, sir,' said the pilot, guiding him to a coil of rope, 'and stay quiet while the valuables are got aboard.'

The mail-bag came first, and Jack, sorting its meagre contents, said, 'A bundle of letters for you, Doctor, and a parcel, as heavy as one of the girls' plum-puddings: post paid, I am happy to say.' This was followed by a number of little cases, Standish's violin, and an object that looked like a telescope but that was a rolled-up chart showing Humboldt's maximum and minimum sea-temperatures over a vast stretch of ocean all placed successively in a net attached to a whip from the yard-arm, which gently rose and gently fell to the traditional cry of Two — six, two — six, the nearest thing to a shanty (apart from the bowline-haul) countenanced by the strictly Royal Navy members of the crew.

The quartermaster unhooked the last and waved his arm; the pilot turned to Standish, said, 'Now, sir, if you please,' and guided him to the rail, helped him to mount upon it and balance there, grasping a shroud, and said 'Just spring across to them steps at the top of the rise; spring easy before she falls.' With a boat-hook he pulled the cutter as close to the ship as was right in this choppy sea and right under the steps.

The *Surprise*, stored for a very long voyage, was low in the water, yet even so some twelve feet of wet side rose from the sea-level; and the steps, though wide, were startlingly shallow. Stephen and Martin stood immediately above him, by a gangway stanchion, leaning down and giving advice: Standish was the only man belonging to the ship who knew less about the sea than they (he had never left the land before) and they did not dislike sharing their knowledge.

'You are to consider,' said Stephen, 'that the inward slope of the ship's flank, the *tumblehome* as we call it, makes the steps far less vertical than they seem. Furthermore, when the ship rolls *from* you, showing her copper, the angle is even more advantageous.'

'The great thing is not to hesitate,' said Martin. 'A determined spring at the right moment, and the impetus will carry you up directly. I am sure you have seen a cat fly up a much steeper wall, only touching once or twice. Impetus; it is all impetus.'

The two vessels wallowed companionably for a while.

'Leap, leap!' cried Martin at the third upward rise.

'Stay,' said Stephen, holding up his hand. 'The roll, or heave, is wrong.'

Standish relaxed again, breathing hard. 'Come on, sir,' said the pilot impatiently as the boat rose once more. Standish gauged the distance and gave a convulsive spring; he had much over-estimated the expanse of water and he struck the side with great force, missing the steps entirely and falling straight back into the sea. The pilot instantly shoved off, to prevent the next surge from crushing him between the cutter and the ship. Standish came to the surface, spouting water; the pilot lunged with his boat-hook, but missing his collar, tore his scalp. Standish sank again, and the cutter, no longer anchored to the *Surprise,* drove before the wind. 'I can't swim,' roared the pilot, and Jack, looking up from his precious hygrometer, cyanograph and the rest, grasped the situation at once.

Flinging off his coat, he plunged straight over the side, striking the purser as he rose again and driving him down breathless a good four fathoms, into quite dim water. This however gave time for entering ropes to be shipped and for a line with a man-harness hitch to be passed down, so that when Jack — a practised hand — brought Standish's head clear of the water, the purser could be hauled aboard and the Captain could walk up the steps of his ship at his ease.

He found Standish sitting on a carronade-slide and gasping while the surgeons examined his wound. 'Nothing at all,' said Stephen. 'A mere superficial tear. Mr Martin will sew it up in a trice.'

'I am most exceedingly obliged to you, sir,' said the purser, standing up and fairly pouring blood from the superficial tear.

'My dear sir, I beg you will not think of it,' replied Jack, shaking his bloody hand. Leaning over the rail he called out to the pilot, who was clawing up into the wind, 'All's well', and ran below, where a furious

Killick was waiting with a towel, a dry shirt and trousers. 'And these here woollen drawers, sir,' he said. 'You done it again — you are always a-doing of it — but this time you will catch your death, without you put on these woollen drawers. Who ever heard of dipping his bare arse off of the Eddystone? It is worse than the North Pole: far worse.'

Standish had been led right aft to be stitched in a really good light, and they were swabbing his blood from the deck, the slide and even the metal of the carronade. Opinion among the foremast hands was quite strongly against the purser.

'A pretty beginning,' said Awkward Davies, who like many other Surprises had been rescued by Jack Aubrey but who very much disliked sharing this distinction. 'Nothing could bring worse luck.'

'He has ruined the Captain's fine pantaloons with his nasty blood,' said a forecastleman. 'It never comes out.'

'Now he is being sick,' observed old Plaice.

'Mr Martin is handing him below.'

Standish and his perfectly proper, indeed absolutely called-for, expression of gratitude having disappeared, faintly belching, Jack returned to the quarterdeck and said to

Stephen, 'Let me show you my splendid hygrometer. Here are spare blades, at the side of the case, do you see — uncommon neat. And wonderfully sensitive, much more so than the whalebone kind. Should you like to breathe upon it? What a piece of luck poor Standish did not bring it over in his pocket. That would have damped its spirit, I believe.' Jack laughed heartily, showed Stephen the cyanoscope, and walked him away to the taffrail, where he said quietly, 'I wish you had been here a little while ago. The Orkneymen sang out in a most surprising manner. I had never heard them before, what with the refitting, the coppering, the quarter-davits, and they being kept busy in the hold; but before we get under way again I think it can be repeated, and I should like you to tell me what you make of their cadences.'

The *Surprise* had been lying to all this time, although the pilot-cutter was now no more than a speck beyond the Eddystone and the ships of the line had altered course to enter the Sound; and many a questioning glance had been cast at her captain. He now walked forward and said, 'Mr Davidge, I am not quite pleased with the foretopsailyard; pray let it be eased off and settled a trifle more snug. Then we may get under way again, setting the foretopgallant: the course south-west by south. I should like to see it done by Macaulay and his mates,' he added, 'with the after-guard tailing on.'

The usual crics, pipes and running feet, and then after a moment's pause that out-landish song:

> Heisa, heisa,
> Vorsa, vorsa,
> Vou, vou.
> One long pull,
> More power,
> Young blood.
> More mud.

'I believe they may have it from the Hebrides,' said Stephen. 'It is not unlike the seal-singing of those parts; or indeed some I have heard in the far, far west of Ireland, on Belmullet, where the phalarope lives.'

Jack nodded. He was considering the fact that 'more mud' had replaced the wild shriek, and that the blocks had not clashed together with the haulers' zeal. He would go into that with Stephen later, and ask him whether it was a deformation of Gaelic. Or Norse? An expression of opinion? In any event, it had a strange beauty. For the moment there was the foretopgallant to be set.

More orders, more piping, more running feet: hands racing aloft. The cry 'Let fall, let fall,' and the topgallant billowed loose; they sheeted it home and the Orkneymen clapped on to the halliards. The sail rose, filling round and taut as the yard moved up and the men sang

> Afore the wind, afore the wind
> God send, God send
> Fair weather, fair weather,
> Many prizes, many prizes.

The naval Surprises might not hold with shanties in general but they thoroughly approved of this one, above all its sentiment; and with ship swinging to the true south-west by west and gathering speed, all those forward of the quarterdeck repeated

> Many prizes, many prizes.

Chapter 2

Fair weather, fair weather bore the *Surprise* right out beyond the chops of the Channel, to the lonely waters Jack preferred for priddying the decks and making all ship-shape and man-of-war fashion before he turned south for Portugal. It was not that as a letter of marque he feared any pressing of his hands, nor incivility on the part of any considerable King's ship; for in the first place he had his protection from the Admiralty and in the second those few senior officers in the home or Mediterranean fleets who might have offered to treat the *Surprise* as a common privateer — obliging Aubrey to lie to, to come up under their lee, bring his papers aboard, justify his existence, answer questions and so on — knew that now he was a member of parliament he was likely to be restored to the list. But on the one hand he preferred to avoid the invitations of even the well-inclined (apart from intimate friends) and the slight awkwardness of their reception of him as a mere civilian; and on the other he would as soon do without the nuisance of the busy unrated vessels of the smaller kind commanded by lieutenants or even by master's mates. They could be dealt with, of course, but it was a time-wasting bore, an irritation.

The frigate therefore sailed into a vast unfrequented pool, traversed by whales and creatures of the deep and by young boobies in the season of the year, but by little else: its centre lay far to the south of Cape Clear in Ireland, and here, if the day should prove as peaceful as they hoped, the Surprises meant to carry on with their titivating and above all to deal with the piebald blackstrake. The weather was ideal: a dying air from the south-west and the remains of a long easy southern swell, but barely a ripple on the surface. It was one of those early mornings when there is no horizon, when sea and sky blend imperceptibly in a nameless band of colour that strengthens to pale blue at the zenith; and many hands thought they might have a little fishing over the side before they started on the blackstrake — this was a most promising time for codlings.

But before that they were to have breakfast; and presently eight bells, the bosun's call, the general hurrying about and banging of mess-kids told Stephen that they were in the act of taking it. His own would come soon, when Jack smelt the coffee, the toast and the frying bacon. Aubrey had stayed up until the middle watch, studying Humboldt's observations and working out the best form to record his own, and now as usual he was sleeping right through the din that followed eight bells — nothing but a change of wind, the cry of 'Sail ho!' or the smell of breakfast would wake him.

Had he been sailing alone as captain of the *Surprise* he would have enjoyed no less than three apartments of his own, the great cabin right aft, a noble room flooded with light from the stern-window that stretched across almost its whole width, and just forward of that much the same amount of space divided down the middle into the coach on the larboard side and the bed-place on the starboard. But since he was not alone he and Stephen shared the great cabin and Stephen had the coach to himself. As the frigate's surgeon, Maturin also had a cabin below, a stuffy little hole which, like those of the other officers, opened on to the gunroom: he used it on occasion, when Jack, the other side of the frail partition, snored beyond all bearing; but at present, in spite of a steady volume of sound, he was sitting there with his papers, chewing a few coca-leaves.

He had woken not long since from a most

unusually explicit and vivid erotic dream; they had become increasingly frequent of late, with the laudanum dying even in its remotest lingering effects, and the vehemence of his desire quite distressed him. 'I am becoming a mere satyr,' he said. 'Where should I be without my coca-leaves? Where indeed?'

He reached out for the letters the pilot had brought and read them again. The bank regretted that it appeared to have no trace of the vouchers mentioned in his esteemed communication of the seventh ultimo; it would be obliged if Dr Maturin's verbal instructions to Mr McBean might be confirmed in writing, a necessary formality without which the business could not proceed; it was concerned to say that the requested dispatch of guineas to Mrs Maturin had not yet been able to be effected, the premium for gold now having risen from five to six shillings in the pound and Dr Maturin's direct written consent, naming this increased sum, being required for the transaction; and awaiting the favour of his further instructions it begged to have the honour of remaining his most humble obedient etc. 'Buggers,' said Stephen, using a word that he had quite often heard aboard but that rarely came to his mind as a term of reproach. A little surprised at himself, he took up the small heavy parcel that had been delivered at the same time. He had recognized the hand when first he saw the address, and in any case the sender's name was written on the back — Ashley Pratt, a surgeon and fellow member of the Royal Society who had for some time laid himself out to be agreeable. Stephen could not like him. It was true that Sir Joseph Banks thought highly of Pratt and often entertained him; but Sir Joseph's judgment of a plant or a beetle was more to be relied upon than his judgment of a man; his general kindness sometimes led him into acquaintances that his friends regretted and his general obstinacy confirmed him in them. Stephen had seen something of an obsequious, bullying fellow named Bligh, a naval officer alas, whose government of New South Wales had ended in very great discredit for everyone concerned; yet Banks still countenanced the man. Stephen was fond of Sir Joseph and he thought him an excellent president of the Society, but he did not feel that judgment was his most outstanding quality — indeed Stephen disliked almost everything he had ever heard about the management of the colony, generally looked upon as Banks's child. And though Pratt was a fashionable and no doubt fairly able surgeon, Stephen would never trust him with a popliteal aneurism, having seen what he had done to a patient in Barts. However, it was benevolent in Pratt to send him this present, a peculiarly strong magnet or combination of magnets designed to extract splinters of cannonball from wounds, particularly from wounded eyes: Pratt had praised the device at their last meeting.

'It might answer, especially if one could direct the force, and make out the path of entry. If Jack is not stirring in seven minutes' — looking attentively at his watch — 'I shall call for coffee and breakfast by myself: perhaps a lightly boiled egg. Perhaps *two* lightly boiled eggs. In the meantime I shall put Pratt's object in the medicine-chest.'

Emerging from the medicinal smell of his part of the orlop, he became aware both of the eddying smell of coffee (which had in fact roused the Captain) and of a confused noise and excitement on deck. As he reached the gunroom door he met Standish, recognizable by his bandaged head; he was carrying a cup of tea and he cried, 'Doctor, they were quite right. The Captain has hit the very place. Come and see. You can make her out even from the quarterdeck.'

They climbed two ladders and they

reached the quarterdeck, Standish still carrying his cup of tea unspilled, and there in that golden morning were all the officers at the leeward rail — leeward, but only just, so gentle was the moving air. West, as officer of the watch, was dressed with some formality; the others were in trousers and shirt; they all, like the hands along the gangway and on the forecastle, were gazing fixedly to the north-east; and the dew dripped on them from the yards and rigging.

Martin took the telescope from his one eye, and offering Stephen the glass he said with a beaming smile, 'Just below where the horizon ought to be. You can make her out quite clear when the haze shifts. I never said good morning,' he added. 'How rude I am — greed reduces man to a very brutal state, I am afraid. Forgive me, Maturin.'

'So you think she is a lawful prize?'

'I have no notion at all,' said Martin, laughing happily. 'But everyone else seems sure of it — all the seasoned mariners. And what small part of her ballast is not silver is pure double-refined gold in bars.'

'Masthead, there,' called Jack, drowning any conversation around him. 'What do you make of her now?'

It was Auden, a middle-aged experienced Shelmerstonian, who was up there; and after a moment he replied, 'No. She's not one of ours. I'll take my davy on that, sir. It is my belief she is a Frenchman. Most uncommon massy yards. She is gathering her boats as quick as ever they can pull. A very guilty conscience there, I fear. Oh, conscience does make cowards of us all.'

Standish looked up at the masthead with some surprise, and Stephen said, 'Auden is what would be called a lay-preacher among the Sethians, I believe.' He then returned to his examination of the distant vessel. On this sea so calm that whole stretches were glassy and even the smallest air made ripples, it was easy to hold a telescope still; and now that the sun was gaining strength — warm, even hot through their shirts — the air grew so clear that he could distinguish the flash of the separate oars as the boats raced home, and even, he thought, the net of silver fishes passing up the side.

'Good morning, gentlemen,' said Jack, turning. 'Have you seen the snow?'

He spoke in perfectly good faith; he had not the least intention of astonishing the poor unfortunate landlubbers; but he had so often felt put down by their literary remarks that now it quite pleased him to see the look of utter stupidity on all three faces.

He was less pleased however when

Standish, the first to recover his wits, replied, 'Oh yes, sir; and I was thinking of going to fetch my greatcoat.' Pullings frowned; West and Davidge looked away; this was not the tone in which a new-joined purser should answer the Captain; the mere fact of having been pulled out of the sea did not warrant this degree of familiarity.

Jack said, 'Snow is the term we use for vessels of that kind, which carry a trysailmast abaft the main.' Turning to Stephen he said, 'Auden, who understands these things if any man does, swears she is not a West-Country smuggler or privateer. So I think we must look a little closer; the breeze may strengthen with the sun. Poor souls, they had a fine bank of codlings about half a mile astern, and they were hauling them in hand over fist when first they saw us.'

'They would never be innocent fishermen, at all?'

'With yards like that, and all built for speed? And pierced for five guns aside, her decks full of men? No. I believe she is a French privateer, and probably new off the stocks. Captain Pullings, we have sweeps aboard, have we not?'

'Yes, sir,' said Pullings. 'I arranged it myself at Dock: they come out of the old

Diomede, and they just happened to be laying by.'

'Very good: capital. It would scarcely be worth sweeping at this point, unless she starts doing so, for I am reasonably confident' — touching a wooden belaying-pin — 'that we shall have a breeze from the southwest in time; but let them be cleared away and the ports made ready. In the meanwhile, Mr West, let us take advantage of what little air may see fit to move. Doctor, what do you say to breakfast?'

It was most unusual for a ship as large and heavy as the *Surprise* to use sweeps, so unusual that the little oar-ports were deeply encrusted with generations of paint, and had to be opened by the carpenter with a heavy persuader and a fid; but since so much of the forenoon had passed without a breath of air she ran them out at four bells — dinner was to be taken watch by watch — and began to creep across the smooth surface like some vast long-legged inefficient water-creature. The snow instantly did the same.

'Will you take your stand by the cooper, sir, you being quite tall?' said Pullings to Standish; and seeing his questioning look he added, 'There is an old saying in the service, when very hard work is to be done, "the gentlemen hale and draw with the mariners". Presently you will see the Captain and the Doctor take their spell.'

'Oh, certainly,' cried Standish. 'I should be very happy — I should like to have an oar in my hand again.'

The gentlemen haled and drew with the mariners, and although for the first quarter of a mile there was some confusion, with one monstrous crab sending half a dozen men tumbling into their shipmates' laps, they soon found their rhythm; and once she had gained her impetus the long cumbrous sweeps moved the ship along so that the water ran whispering along her side. There was no lack of zeal, advice — 'Stretch out, sir, and keep your eyes in the boat' — and merriment: it was a pretty example of a good ship's company at work, and when the log was heaved it showed that the *Surprise* was making two knots and a half.

Unhappily the snow made three or even more. She was much lighter; her people were far more accustomed to sweeping; and being so much nearer the surface they could use their oars with greater effect. At the end of his first spell of rowing Jack fixed her with his come-up glass, which showed him that the chase was gaining; and in an hour this was evident to every man aboard — even in that light-filled immensity of sea and sky a mile could still be made out. The laughter died away, but not the determination, and with grave, set faces the rowers lunged forward, dipped and pulled hour after hour, their reliefs stepping in at the first sound of the bell so neatly that barely a stroke was lost.

The sun was well past the zenith, the snow had merged with the horizon, almost hull-down, far, far ahead, and there was silence aboard, apart from the rowers' grunting heave, before the longed-for air began to breathe from the south-southwest. It rounded the upper sails first and rippled the sea quite far ahead; already the ship had a fresh life, and when the topgallants were drawing Jack cried, 'Lay on your oars.' With anxious delight he and all the ship's company listened to the breeze in the rigging and the bow-wave shearing on either side.

Topsails filled and then courses, and with the yards exactly trimmed Jack had the sweeps brought inboard; many a man stood bending and cherishing his arms and legs or rubbing the small of his back, but a moment later they ran eagerly and fairly nimbly aloft to spread the cloud of sail the frigate was used to. The strengthening breeze had settled half a point west of its origin; she had it well abaft the beam and she was able to set a most imposing array of royals and skysails, as well as weather studding-sails from top to bottom, spritsail, spritsailtopsail and a host of staysails, an array so beautiful that Standish, coming up for fresh air from tepid mutton soup and his first encounter with the larger kind of weevil called bargemen and seeing all this with the sun shining through and across all its curves, convexities and infinite variety of brilliantly lit or delicately shadowed white, cried out in admiration.

'Lord, sir,' he said to Pullings, 'what more than Gothic glory!'

'I dare say you are right, sir,' said Pullings. 'But we shan't keep it long, I doubt. See how she has started to pitch and roll.' So she had, and with something less than her usual well-bred air and long easy buoyant motion: rarely had she been so deep in the water. 'It is a swell coming up from the south-west, and it is sure to bring us half a gale.'

'Are we overtaking the snow?' asked Standish, peering forward at impenetrable canvas. 'We must be going at an amazing speed.'

'Close on nine knots,' said Pullings. 'And

since it was us brought by the wind, we have gained maybe a mile or so. Yet so deep-laden — twelve months' stores and more — the barky cannot do her best, nor nothing like it. With a breeze like this I have seen her run twelve knots off the reel; and at that rate we should have been alongside the snow half an hour ago. But now, in course, she has the wind too, and she may be drawing away a trifle. Most remarkable rapid for a snow: such yards I have rarely seen. Was you to go into the bows with this glass, you could see her plain; and was you to look hard you would see she has set save-alls, too.'

'Thank you,' said Standish absently: his eyes were fixed on the rail as it rose, rose, rose still, hung for an instant and then began its inevitable, deliberate, vertiginous fall.

'Mark you,' continued Pullings, 'if it comes on to blow like the Captain says and I am sure he is right, then we shall have the advantage; for we are the taller ship, and a heavy sea will not wrong us as it will wrong the snow. Hold up, there: over the rail, sir, if you please.'

When Standish had finished this first bout Pullings told him there was nothing like a good vomit — better than bleeding or rhubarb or blue pill — he would soon get used to the motion — and called two amused hands to lead him below. He could barely stand, and his face had turned a yellowish green — his lips were curiously pale.

Standish did not reappear that day, nor would any man at all subject to queasiness have done so, for the half-gale reached them even sooner than they had hoped, and Stephen, deep in his papers though he was, noticed that the *Surprise* had grown unusually skittish and that the whole sound of the ship had changed: a far greater volume, a far greater urgency. Closing a file and tying its original black French tape around it — poor thin stuff, compared with Dublin tape: a man could hang himself with Dublin tape — he leant back in his chair; and as he did so he saw Jack Aubrey look cautiously through the door.

'Should you like to see the chase?' asked Jack. 'She is a pretty sight.'

'I should like it of all things,' said Stephen, getting up. 'Jesus, Mary and Joseph, how my back hurts.'

'The sight of the prize will cure it, I am sure.'

The deck — the world in general — now had a very different appearance. The great spread of canvas had shrunk to courses, reefed topsails and spritsail; the deck itself was canted some twenty degrees and the bow-wave flung high white and wide to leeward. A few sparse clouds were racing over the bright blue sky and dark banks had gathered far in the south, but the air was still flashing clear and filled with light — a slightly pinkish light already, the glorious sun so low.

'Clap on to the line,' said Jack, leading him forward; and as Stephen edged along the weather gangway many a hand took his elbow, passing him to a sure hold and telling him to watch out, to take great care; and behind their kindness to him there was a certain grim ferocity.

Pullings was waiting for them in the bows. He said, 'She has not altered course, no not by half a point since first we seen her; she must surely be running for the Cove of Cork, or a little south.'

Jack nodded, and over his shoulder he called, 'Duck up.'

The spritsail puckered and turned, and to his astonishment Stephen saw the chase right ahead, almost within gunshot, very, very much closer than he had expected. She was a black, low ship, all the blacker for her great foaming wake, brilliant white in the sun; and she seemed all the lower for the great breadth of her yards, the dun sails drum-tight upon them as she raced along. Jack had given him his telescope and as Stephen listened with half his mind to the sailors' remarks about double and even triple preventer-stays — extraordinary speed for a snow, even one so well handled — *Surprise* shockingly handicapped — trim not at all that could be wished, by any means: distinctly by the head — he gazed at the men gathered at the snow's taffrail, and they steadily watching the *Surprise*, never moving, though the spray often swept across their faces. The glass was exceptionally good and the air so perfectly clear that he distinguished a kittiwake as it moved along the side of the snow, the bird too faintly tinged with pink. He had directed the telescope at the two guns, probably ninepounders, pointing through the snow's chase-ports when his mind as it were leapt to attention and he instantly returned to the man, to the third man from the left: he focussed with even greater sharpness and there was not the least possible doubt. He was looking at Robert Gough.

Gough too had been a member of the United Irishmen: he and Maturin had agreed that Irishmen should govern Ireland and that Catholics should be emancipated:

on everything else they were opposed and had been from the beginning. Gough was one of the leaders of that part of the movement which was in favour of French intervention whereas Maturin was wholly against it — he was against violence and he was even more against importing or in any way helping the new kind of tyranny that had arisen in France, the horribly disappointing sequel of that Revolution which Maturin and most of his friends had welcomed with such joy. When the rising of 1798 was put down with revolting cruelty and with the help of swarms of informers, native, foreign and half-bred, their lives were equally in danger, but since then all similarity had vanished. Gough, with the survivors of his school of thought, had become even more committed to France, whereas Maturin, once he had recovered from the stunning shock, which had coincided with the loss of his sweetheart, had observed the development of an exceedingly dangerous dictatorship, entirely replacing the generous ideas of 1789 but at the same time profiting from them. He had seen the treatment of the Catholic church in France, of the Italian sympathizers in those unfortunate regions overrun by the French, and of the Catalans in his own Catalonia; and well before the end of the Revolutionary War he had seen that this whole system of pillage and oppression, this whole series of police-states must, before everything else, be brought to an end. And everything he had seen since, the subversion of countless states by brute force, the imprisonment of the Pope, the universal bad faith, had confirmed his diagnosis, strengthening him in his conviction that this tyranny, far more intelligent and invasive than anything that had been known, must be destroyed. The freedom of Ireland and of Catalonia were dependent upon its destruction — the defeat of French imperialism was a necessary condition for all the rest.

Yet there was Gough, just over the water, eager for another French landing; and Stephen had the absolute certainty that he was on a mission to Ireland. If the snow were taken Gough would be hanged: the tyranny would be by so much the weaker. But at this all Stephen's old loathing for informers rose up with overwhelming force, his utter revulsion from anything and everything to do with them and the result of their betrayals, the torture, the floggings, the melted pitch on men's heads, and of course the hangings. He could not bear the slightest hint of a connexion between himself and such people; he could not bear being connected in any way whatsoever with the taking of Gough.

He heard Pullings say, 'I have had the bow-guns cleared away, sir, in case you would like to try a random shot before it gets dark.'

'Well, Tom,' said Aubrey, considering the range with narrowed eyes and stroking the larboard chaser, a beautiful brass long nine, 'I have been thinking of it, naturally: and with luck we might knock away a spar or two and kill some of her people, though the distance is so great and the ship is behaving more like a rocking-horse than a Christian. But I do hate battering a prize, particularly a small one. Apart from anything else it takes so much time, what with repairing and towing and perhaps having to send her in with a prize-crew we have to wait for. No. What I should like best would be to range up alongside and offer her a full broadside if she don't strike: nobody but a mad lunatic would refuse — we carry five times her weight of metal. Then without any slaughter or repairing or fuss we carry her into the nearest port and so proceed to Lisbon, where we are likely to be uncommon late in any case, after such a run.'

'To be sure,' said Pullings, 'there is not

much likelihood of our losing her tonight, with the moon so near the full; and to be sure, we have the weather-gage — could not have it more. But I was only thinking that if we do not check her in some way, at this pace it will be a great while before we can show her our broadside clear and close; and by then we may have run almost the whole length of the Irish Sea; and beating into a south-wester off Galloway is tedious work.'

They discussed a variety of possibilities; and then, breaking off, Jack said, 'Where is the Doctor?'

'I believe he went aft some minutes ago,' said Pullings. 'How dark it has grown.'

Maturin had indeed gone aft, aft and below to the orlop, where he sat on a three-legged stool by the medicine-chest, staring at the candle in the lantern he had brought with him: he was more likely to be alone here than anywhere in the ship, alone and in silence, for although there was the ship's own voice and the tumultuous roar of the sea echoing down here in a general confusion of sound, it was an unceasing noise and could be set aside in time, forgotten, quite unlike the spasmodic cries and orders, the footsteps and clashing that would break in upon his thoughts if he were to sit in the coach.

He had long since accepted that Gough was now of no real importance and that in view of the disastrous outcome of all the attempted French landings hitherto it was extremely unlikely that they would in fact ever launch another, whatever promises Gough might be carrying. His loss would not weaken Bonaparte's machine to any perceptible degree. Yet although Maturin could and did look upon this as axiomatic, it in no way affected his determination not to be associated with Gough's arrest and his mind had now been turning for some considerable time on possible ways of dealing with the situation.

Yet so far his mind had produced little; it turned and turned, but the turning, though arduous, was sterile. Some great man had said, 'A thought is like a flash between two dark nights': at present Stephen's nights were running into one uninterrupted darkness, lit by no gleams at all. The coca-leaves he chewed had the property of doing away with hunger and fatigue, giving some degree of euphoria, and making one feel clever and even witty; he certainly had no appetite and he did not feel physically tired, but as for the rest he might have been eating hay.

There was of course Pratt's magnet. A ship's compass would deviate from the north in the presence of a magnet and the helmsman would be misled: the ship would wander from her true course. But how much would the compass deviate, and how near was the required presence? He knew nothing whatsoever about either point. Nor did he know the ship's position, except that she was in the Irish Sea; and in such a state of general ignorance he could not form any useful opinion about the danger of casting her and his friends away on some rocky shore.

He put the instrument into his pocket and made his way to the quarterdeck, stopping to put the lantern on its hook in the coach. Although the light coming through the companion should have warned him, he was still astonished by the brilliance of the moonlit night. Though the colours were subtly different it might almost have been day; there was not the least question of his failing to recognize the four men at the wheel, Davis and Simms, old Surprises, and Fisher and Harvey, from Shelmerston, or the quartermaster at the con, old Neave. Nor was there the least question of his approaching the binnacle and observing the variation of the compass as he moved the magnet, for not only did West, who had the watch, at once come over and ask him whether he had not turned in, but it was perfectly obvious that the ship was not steering by compass at all. The wind had now increased to a stiff gale, and at the last change of watch the *Surprise* had taken another reef in her topsails and forecourse and had furled the spritsail, so there, right ahead, lay the chase; and it was by the chase that the frigate was steering, her bowsprit pointing directly at the long moonlit wake, both ships tearing through the sea with extreme urgency.

'The distance seems about the same,' observed Stephen.

'I wish I could think so,' said West. 'We had gained a cable's length by two bells, but now she has won it back and even more. Still, the tide will change against the wind in an hour or so, and that should chop up a nasty head-sea for her.'

'Has the Captain gone to bed?' asked Stephen, cupping his hands to make his voice, curiously hoarse and weak at present, carry over the roar of sea and wind.

'No. He is in the cabin, pricking the chart. We had a very fine fix with Vega and Arcturus just now.'

That, of course, would be the simplest way of dealing with at least one side of his ignorance. If he were to walk into the cabin there he would see the ship's position marked on the chart with all the accuracy of an expert navigator. Doing so would not be elegant however; and as well as being inelegant it would be in direct contravention to his particular morality, the private set of laws which for him separated the odious practice of spying from the legitimate gathering of intelligence.

'I beg your pardon,' he said, having missed everything of West's last remark but for the fact that he had spoken or rather bellowed something about fire.

'I was only saying they must be burning heather or furze over there in Anglesea,' said West, pointing to a distant orange serpent on the starboard beam.

Stephen nodded, reflected for a moment and then crept backwards down the companion-ladder meaning to walk forward along the waist. Most of the starboard watch were sheltering under the break of the quarterdeck, and Barret Bonden left the group to shepherd him along past the double-breeched guns and under the double-griped boats on the skid-beams, past the galley and so by the hooked steps in the *Surprise*'s broad top-tackle scuttle to a place as nearly comfortable, safe and dry as so bleak a station could afford.

It was quieter here in the bows, in the lee of the foremast and the topsail-sheet bitts, and they talked for a while about the progress of the chase, the snow there before them clear and sharp, a mile ahead, tearing along and throwing the water wide. Bonden knew the Doctor was upset, and in case it should be something to do with this prize, with the frigate's relatively poor performance, or with what a landsman might consider the Captain's want of enterprise, he very delicately offered a few points for consideration: at the beginning of a very long voyage, no captain would risk masts, spars and cordage unless he were up against an enemy man-of-war, a national ship, or at least a very important privateer; at the beginning of a very long voyage the ship, low and sluggish with all her stores, could not be driven really hard, as she could be driven when she was riding light and homeward-bound, with supplies only a few days ahead — the Doctor would remember how the barky wore topgallants in a close-reef topsail breeze, and not only topgallants but foretopmast and lower studdingsails too, when they were chasing the *Spartan* on their way home from Barbados. If they were to do that now, the barky would fall to pieces, and they would have to swim home, those that were not provided with wings.

Bonden observed with regret that he had been on the wrong lay altogether, that this was not what the Doctor had been fretting about. So with a few general remarks about taking great care when he came aft — a hand for the ship and a hand for himself — he left him to his own reflexions, if indeed that was the word for the anxious hurry of spirits, going over and over the same ground while the frigate and her chase sailed perpetually over the same troubled moonlit sea, neither making any perceptible progress in a world with no fixed object.

Yet there was this new factor: Jack Aubrey did not regard the capture of the snow as of the first importance. Might it therefore be suggested to him that they turn about and hurry south for their rendezvous in Lisbon?

No, it might not. Jack Aubrey knew exactly how far he was allowed or rather required to endanger the ship for the sake of the prize; and where his professional duty was concerned it would be as useful to offer him a bribe as a piece of advice.

'Why, Stephen, there you are,' cried Jack, suddenly emerging from behind the bitts and Bonden's little sailcloth screen stretched between them. 'You are as wet as a soused herring. The tide is on the turn; it will cut up quite a sea presently and you will get wetter still, if possible. Lord, you could be wrung out like a swab even now. Why did not you put on oilskins? Diana bought you a suit. Come and have a mug of broth and some toasted cheese. Let me give you a hand round the bitts: wait till she rises.'

A quarter of an hour later Maturin said that he would digest his broth and toasted cheese in the orlop, where he had a number of urgent tasks.

'I am going to turn in until the end of the watch,' said Jack. 'You might be well advised to do the same: you look quite done up.'

'Indeed, I am somewhat out of order. Perhaps I shall prescribe myself a draught.'

He had every reason to be out of order, he reflected, sitting there by the medicine-chest on his stool. His very remote and tentative words about other commanders, in other circumstances, abandoning some hypothetical chase had been quite useless; or even, if Jack had caught any faint hint of their drift, worse than useless. His only plan, that of diverting the ship's course, was one of those easy phantasms that look well enough until they are examined; in this case it would be practicable only in dark and covered weather, when the compass alone commanded, and if it could be done discreetly. Though admittedly the ship's position was right; she could be made to turn well to the west of her present position without coming to any harm: not that in itself the fact was of any consequence.

Out of order he was, and restless he was: the changing tide had worked up a considerable sea, not as fierce as had been hoped, because the wind was slackening, but still so rough that the bows were impossible for any length of time. He therefore paced the length of the upper deck between the cabin door and the foremost gun on the weather side. Each watch saw him pass to and fro, and in each watch some of the simpler hands said they had never known the Doctor worry so about a prize, while their more gifted mates asked them 'was it likely that a gent with a gold-headed cane and his own carriage should worry about a little ten-gun privateer snow? No. It was the toothache he had, and he was trying to walk it off; but that would not answer — it never did — and presently he would take a comfortable draught, or perhaps Mr Martin would draw the tooth.'

It was at five bells in the graveyard watch, with the situation, as far as he could tell, quite unchanged, that Stephen finally returned to the orlop, unlocked the medicine-chest and took out his bottle of laudanum. 'No,' he said, drinking his modest dose with deliberate composure, 'the only concrete and feasible solution I have been able to devise is worthless. I shall have to await the event and act accordingly; but in order to act with any effect I must have at least some sleep and I must overcome this dispropor-tionate distress.'

He climbed the ladders for the last time, walked into the coach, and threw off his sodden clothes. Killick, who had no right to be up at this hour, silently opened the door and handed him a towel, then a dry night-shirt. He picked up the heap of clothes, looked sternly at the Doctor, but changed what he was going to say to a 'Good night, sir.'

Stephen took his rosary from its drawer: telling beads was as near to superstition as intelligence-work was to spying, but al-though for many years he had thought pri-vate prayer, private requests impertinent and ill-mannered, the more impersonal, almost ejaculatory forms seemed to him to have quite another nature; and at this point a need for explicit piety was strong on him. Yet the warmth of the dry nightshirt on his pale soaked shivering body, the ease of the swinging cot, once he had managed to get into it, and the effect of his draught were such that sleep enveloped him entirely before his seventh Ave.

He was woken by the sound of gunfire and by the roar of orders immediately overhead. He sat up, staring and collecting himself; a thin grey light was straggling through the companion, and he had the impression that the glass was being strongly hosed with water. The sea had gone down. Another gun, right forward.

He stepped out of the cot, stood swaying, and then put on the clean shirt and breeches lying on the locker. He was hurrying towards the companion-ladder when Killick roared out 'Oh no you don't. Oh no you don't, sir. Not without this here' — a long, heavy, smelly tarpaulin coat with a hood, both fastened with white marline.

'Thank you kindly, Killick,' said Stephen, when he was tied in. 'Where is the Captain?'

'On the forecastle, in the middle of the catastrophe, carrying on like Beelzebub.'

At the foot of the ladder Stephen looked up, and his face was instantly drenched — drenched with fresh water, with teeming cold rain so thick he could hardly draw breath. Bowing his head he reached the mizen-mast and the wheel, the rain drumming on his hood and shoulders. The decks were full of men, exceedingly busy, apparently letting fly sheets, most of them unrecognizable in their foul-weather gear; but there seemed to be no very great alarm, nor was the ship even beginning to clear for action. A tall sou'westered figure bent over him and looked into his face: Awkward Davies. 'Oh, it's you, sir,' he said. 'I'll take you forward.'

As they groped their way along the larboard gangway, scarcely able to see across the deck for the downpour, the squall passed over, still blotting out the north-east entirely but leaving no more than a remnant of drizzle over the ship and the sea to the south and west. There was Jack in his oilskins with Pullings, the bosun and some hands, still streaming with water amidst what looked like an inextricable tangle of cordage, sailcloth and a few spars, among which Stephen thought he recognized the topgallantmast with its cheerful apple-green truck.

'Good morning, Doctor,' cried Jack. 'You have brought fine weather with you, I am happy to see. Captain Pullings, you and Mr Bulkeley have everything in hand, I believe?'

'Yes, sir,' said Pullings. 'Once Mr Bentley

has roused out his spare cap, there are only trifles left to be done.'

'At least the decks will not need swabbing today,' said Jack, looking aft, where the rain-water was still gushing in thick jets from the scuppers. 'Doctor, shall we take an early pot, and what is left of the soft-tack, toasted?'

In the cabin he said, 'Stephen, I am sorry to be obliged to tell you I have made a sad cock of it, and the snow has run clear. Last night Tom wanted to have a long shot at her, in the hope of checking her speed. I said no, but this morning I was sorry for it. The squall had flattened the sea, and with the breeze dying on us she was drawing away hand over fist: so I said "It is now or never" and cracked on till all sneered again. We came within possible range and we had a few shots, one pitching so close it threw water on to her deck, before a back-stay parted and our foretopgallant came by the board. She has run clear away, going like smoke and oakum, and in this dirty weather there will be no finding her again. I hope you are not too disappointed.'

'Not at all — never in life,' said Stephen, drinking coffee to hide his intense satisfaction and gratitude.

'Mark you,' said Jack earnestly, 'she is

very likely to be taken by one of our cruisers. She altered course eastwards when she saw us coming up so fast, and now she is hopelessly embayed in the Firth. She will never get out with this wind, and it may last for weeks.'

'Does not the same apply to us?'

'Oh no. We have much more sea-room. Once we have head-sails we can make a short leg to the south-east to be sure of weathering the Mull, go north about past Malin Head, gain a good offing, a very good offing, and then hey for Lisbon. Come in, Tom. Sit down and have a cup of coffee, cold though it be.'

'Thank you, sir. The immediate work is done, and we can hoist jib and foretopmast staysail whenever you choose.'

'Very good, very good indeed: the sooner the better.' He swallowed his coffee and the two of them hurried on deck. A moment later Stephen, finishing the pot, heard Jack's powerful voice at its strongest: 'All hands, there. All hands about ship.'

Chapter 3

'Bonden,' said Jack Aubrey to his coxswain, 'tell the Doctor that if he is at leisure there is something to be seen on deck.'

The Doctor was at leisure; the 'cello on which he had been practising gave a last deep boom and he ran up the companion-ladder, an expectant look on his face.

'There, right on the beam,' said Jack, nodding southwards. 'You can catch the breakers at its foot as clear as can be on the rise.'

'Certainly,' said Stephen, watching Malin Head fade and faintly reappear in the thin rain; then, feeling that something more was expected of him, 'I am obliged to you for showing it to me.'

'It will be your last glimpse of your native land for about sixteen degrees of latitude and God knows how many of longitude, for I mean to make a great offing if ever I can. Should you like to look at it with a tele-scope?'

'If you please,' said Stephen. He was fond of his native land, even though this piece of it looked unnaturally black, wet and uninviting; but he could not wish the spectacle prolonged, particularly as he knew from personal experience that part of this province was inhabited by a tattling, guileful, tale-bearing, noisy, contemptible, mean, wretched, unsteady and inhospitable people, and as soon as he decently could he clapped the glass to, handed it back, and returned to his 'cello. They were to attempt another Mozart quartet in a few days and he did not wish to disgrace himself in the presence of the purser's far more accomplished playing.

Left alone Jack continued his habitual pacing fore and aft. He must have covered hundreds and hundreds of miles on this same quarterdeck in the course of all these years and the ringbolt near the taffrail where he turned shone like silver; it was also dangerously thin. He was glad to have seen Malin Head so clear. It proved that Inishtrahull and the Garvans, upon which many a better navigator than himself had come to grief, especially in thick weather with no sight of the sun by day or any star by night, were all safely astern. After a measured mile for good luck, he gave the orders that would carry the ship as nearly due west as the south-west wind would allow; and he found to his pleasure that she needed it only half a point free to run happily at seven knots under no more than topsails and courses, though a moderate sea kept striking her larboard bow with all the regularity of a long-established swell, throwing her slightly off her course and sweeping spray and even packets of water diagonally across the forecastle and the waist.

This, and the taste of salt on his lips, was a deep satisfaction; yet at the same time he knew that the frigate's people were upon the whole low-spirited, disappointed and out of humour. He thought it very probable that some of the more dismal hands might already be using the words 'an unlucky voyage or 'a Jonah aboard', which could become very dangerous indeed if they got a firm hold on the ship's collective mind, always inclined to fatalism — even more dangerous in a ship with no Marines, no Articles of War, no recourse to the service as a whole, a ship in which the Captain's authority depended solely on his standing and his standing on his present as well as his past success. This he had not learnt from listening to their conversation nor from reports brought by confidential hands like Bonden or Killick or the equivalent of the master-at-arms or the ship's corporal — he hated a tale-bearer — but from having spent most of his life afloat, some of it as a fore-mast-jack. His gauging of the ship's mood was for the most part unconscious — faintly recorded impressions of dutifulness rather than zeal, lack of coarse humorous remarks forward, the occasional wry look or contentious answer between shipmates, and the general want of tone — but though it was largely instinctive it was surprisingly accurate.

'There is little hope of any consolation in these waters unless we chance on an American,' he reflected, 'but at least for the rest of the month we shall have regular blue-water sailing, tack upon tack every watch until we reach the westerlies; plenty to keep them busy but not too much; and then presently we shall see the sun again.'

Far out into the Atlantic, long tack upon long tack, every day having the same steady routine from swabbing the decks at first dawn to lights out, its unchanging succession of bells, its wholly predictable food, nothing in sight from one horizon to another but sea and sky, both growing more agreeable, and the habit of sea-life exerted its usual force; cheerfulness returned to almost its old carefree level and as always there was the violent emotion and enthusiasm of the great-gun practice every evening at quarters — practice carried out with the full deadly charge and the ball directed at a floating target.

While the *Surprise* was making her westing Jack spent more in barrels of powder than ever he would have made in prize-money if the snow had been taken. He justified this to his conscience (for no one else, least of all Stephen, questioned the expense) by an appeal to the frigate's very high standards of rapid, accurate fire, by the fact that all hands were somewhat rusty and the Orkneymen (some of whom had come aboard with crossbows) had very little notion of combined disciplined practice at all; but he knew very well that the thunderous roar, the stabbing flame in the smoke-cloud, the screech of the recoiling gun, the competition between watch and watch, and the ecstasy when a raft of beef-cask two hundred yards away flew suddenly to pieces in a flurry of white water and single staves flung high did a great deal towards restoring the general tone and bringing the *Surprise* back towards the state of a happy ship, the only efficient fighting-machine, the only ship that it was a pleasure to command.

Only in a few exceptional cases did this

state arise spontaneously, as when a good set of foremast hands happened to enter upon a dry, weatherly ship with efficient warrant-officers — the bosun was often a most important figure where happiness was concerned — a decent group of seamanlike officers, and a taut but not tyrannical captain. Otherwise it had to be nursed along. The lower deck had its own way of dealing with really worthless hands, turning them out of their messes and leading them a horrible life; but there were others, stronger characters, men of some education, who could cause serious trouble if they chanced to be both awkward and discontented. In the *Surprise* at present, for example, there were eight Shelmerstonians serving before the mast who had had commands of their own, while there were more who had been mates and who understood navigation.

The same applied, in rather a different way, to the wardroom or gunroom as the case might be. An ill-fitting member of that small society could upset the working of the whole ship to a remarkable degree; and the small failings that would not matter at all during a passage to Gibraltar might assume gigantic proportions in the course of a long commission — a couple of years blockading Toulon, for example, or three on the African station. And Jack was wondering whether he had been very wise in appointing Standish purser, almost entirely on the basis of the man's excellent violin-playing and the recommendation of Martin, who had been acquainted with him at Oxford, and in spite of Standish's want of experience.

Except for that excellence, Jack had rarely been more mistaken in a man: the modesty and diffidence that the penniless, unemployed Standish had brought aboard were now no longer to be seen; and the assurance of a monthly income and a settled position had developed a displeasing and often didactic loquacity. He was also, of course, incompetent. As Jack said in his letter to Sophie, 'I had supposed anyone with common sense could become a tolerable purser; but I was wrong. He did make an attempt at first, but as he is seasick every time we hand topgallants and as he can neither add nor multiply so as to get the same answer twice, he soon grew discouraged and now he leaves everything to his steward and Jack in the Dust. He is not without his good points. He is perfectly honest (which cannot be said of all pursers) and it was most gentlemanly in him not to let anyone know that he was a strong swimmer after I had pulled him out of the sea. And he listens attentively, even eagerly, when Stephen and Martin explain the ship's manoeuvres to him, and the difference between the plansheer and the spirketting; but apart from these lectures (and it would do your heart good to hear them) when he is quiet, he talks, he talks, he talks, and always about himself. Tom, West and Davidge, who have had no more education than can be picked up aboard ship and who are not much given to reading, are rather shy of him, he being a university man, and Martin is wonderfully charitable; but this cannot last, because as well as being incompetent as a purser, he is also sadly foolish.'

Jack paused, remembering an incident during his most recent dinner with the gunroom, when he heard someone, in the midst of Standish's long anecdote, say, 'I did not know you had been a schoolmaster.'

'Oh, it was only for a short time, when my fortunes were low. That is a recourse we university men always have — in case of temporary embarrassment, you can always take refuge in a school, if you have a degree.'

Delightful task, to teach the young idea how to shoot,' observed Stephen.

'Oh no,' cried Standish. 'My duties were of a far higher order: I took them through

Lily and the gradus. Another man came in and taught them fencing and archery and pistol-practice and that kind of thing.'

Jack returned to his pen. 'But it is the music that particularly distresses me. Martin is not a gifted player, and Standish perpetually puts him right — shows him how his fingering is at fault and his bowing, and the way he holds his instrument, and his notion of the tempo, and his phrasing. He has already offered Stephen a few hints and I think that when he grows bolder he may do the same kind office by me. I was very much mistaken in supposing I could play second fiddle to such a man and I shall have to find some decent excuse. The music is indeed celestial (how such a man can so lose himself in it and play so well is beyond my comprehension) but I do not look forward to this evening's bout at all. Perhaps there will be none. The sea is getting up a little.'

Jack paused, re-read the last page and shook his head. Sophie disliked fault-finding; it distressed her, and she had heard a very great deal of it when she was a girl. And fault-finding in a letter might well sound harsher than by word of mouth. He balled up the sheet and threw it into the waste-paper-basket, a mine of interest to Killick and those members of the crew who shared his confidence, and as he did so he heard Pullings cry 'Stand by to hand foretopgallant,' followed immediately by the bosun's call.

There was no music that evening apart from some quiet rumbling over familiar paths by Aubrey and Maturin — an evenly-shared mediocrity — and an hour or so of their favourite exercise, which was improvisation on a theme proposed by one and answered by the other, which sometimes rose well above mediocrity because of their deep mutual comprehension, in this field at least. Standish sent his excuses — regretted that indisposition prevented him from having the honour, etc — and Martin in his double capacity of assistant surgeon and early acquaintance sat by the wretched purser's side, holding a bowl.

There was no music when they reached the westerlies either, for they were blowing briskly with a little north in them, so briskly that the *Surprise* went bowling along under close-reefed topsails with the wind on her quarter at nine and even ten knots, wallowing at the bottom of her long roll and pitch in a way that did her little credit.

This splendid breeze held day after day, only slackening when they were approaching the Berlings. Martin led Standish on deck to view them that evening — cruel jagged rocks far out in a troubled ocean and under a troubled sky, the horizon dark. The purser clung to the rail, looking hungrily at these first specks of land since Malin Head: his clothes hung loose about him.

'I hope I see you in better trim, Mr Standish,' said Jack Aubrey. 'Even at this gentle rate we should raise the Rock of Lisbon by dawn, and if we are lucky with our tide you may eat your dinner in Black Horse Square. Nothing sets a man up like a good square meal.'

'But before that,' said Stephen, 'Mr Standish would be well advised to eat a couple of eggs, lightly boiled and taken with a little softened biscuit, as soon as ever his stomach will bear them; then he may have a good restorative, roborative sleep. As for the eggs, I heard two of the gunroom hens proclaim that they had laid this morning.'

They did indeed raise the Rock of Lisbon a little before the dawn of a brilliant sparkling clear morning with warm scented air breathing off the land; and at the same time they passed HMS *Briseis*, 74, a cloud of sail in the offing, obviously homeward bound from Lisbon and making the most of the stronger breeze out there. Jack struck his topsails as in duty bound to a King's ship and *Briseis*, now commanded by an amiable man called Lampson, returned the salute, at the same time throwing out a signal whose only intelligible word was Happy.

But they were not lucky with their tide: breathing the warm scented air was certainly a delight to those that longed for land, but it prevented the *Surprise* from crossing the Tagus bar and she was obliged to anchor all through slack water and well beyond before the pilot would consent to take her in.

In this lakelike peace Standish, who had eaten his two eggs the evening before and had spent a calm night, spent his time eating first three pints of portable soup, thickened with oatmeal, and then a large quantity of ham; this recovered his spirits wonderfully, and although he was still feeble he gasped his way into the maintop, where Stephen and Martin were to explain the operation of getting under way.

Below them on the quarterdeck the pilot finished his account of how the *Weymouth*, relying on her own knowledge of the river, had been wrecked on the bar — just over there, three points on the starboard bow, not quite a mile away — with the words 'And all for the sake of the pilot's fee.'

'That was very bad, I am sure,' said Jack. 'Were the people saved?'

'A few,' said the pilot reluctantly. 'But those few were all horribly disfigured. Now, sir, whenever you please to give the word, I believe we may proceed.'

'All hands unmoor ship,' said Jack, raising his voice to the pitch of an order, though every man had been at his station these ten minutes past, angrily willing the pilot to stop his prating, to stash it, to pipe down; and instantly the bosun sprung his call.

'See,' cried Stephen, 'the carpenter and his crew put the bars in the capstan — they *ship* them, pin them and swift them.'

'They bring the messenger to the capstan: the gunner ties its rounded ends together. What are they called, Maturin?'

'Let us not be too pedantic, for all love. The whole point is, the messenger is now endless: it is a serpent that has swallowed its own tail.'

'I cannot see it,' said Standish, leaning far out over the rail. 'Where is this messenger?'

'Why,' said Martin, 'it is that rope they are putting over the rollers just beneath us in the waist, a vast loop that goes from the capstan to two other stout vertical rollers by the hawse-holes and so back.'

'I do not understand. I see the capstan, but there is no rope round it at all.'

'What you see is the upper capstan,' said Stephen with some complacency. 'The messenger is twined about the lower part, under the quarterdeck. But both the lower and the upper part are equipped with bars: both turn: both *heave*, as we say. See, they undo the deck-stoppers, or dog-stoppers as some superficial observers call them — they loosen the starboard cable, the cable on the right-hand side — they throw off the turn about the riding-bitts! What force and dexterity!'

'They bring the messenger to the cable — they bind it to the cable with nippers.'

'Where? Where? I cannot see.'

'Of course not. They are right forward, by the hawse-holes, where the cable comes into the ship, under the forecastle.'

'But presently,' said Stephen in a comforting tone, 'you will perceive the cable come creeping aft, led by the messenger.'

John Foley, the Shelmerston fiddler, skipped on to the capstan-head; at his first notes the men at the bars stepped out, and after the first turns that brought on the strain, three deep voices and one clear tenor sang

Yeo heave ho, round the capstan go,
Heave men with a will
Tramp and tramp it still
The anchor must be weighed, the anchor
  must be weighed

joined by all in a roaring

Yeo heave ho
Yeo heave ho

five times repeated before the three struck in
again

Yeo heave ho, raise her from below
Heave men with a will
Tramp and tramp it still
The anchor's off the ground, the anchor's
  off the ground

'There is your cable,' said Martin in a
very much louder voice, after the first few
lines.

'So it is,' said Standish; and having stared
at it coming in like a great wet serpent he
went on, 'But it is not going to the capstan
at all.'

'Certainly not,' said Stephen in a screech
above the full chorus. 'It is far too thick to
bend round the capstan; furthermore, it is

loaded with the vile mud of Tagus.'

'They undo the nippers and let the cable down the main hatchway and so to the orlop, where they coil it on the cable-tiers,' said Martin. 'And they hurry back with the nippers to bind fresh cable to the messenger as it travels round.'

'How active they are,' observed Stephen. 'See how diligently they answer Captain Pullings' request *to light along the messenger,* that is to say pull along the slack on that side which is not heaving in —'

'And how they run with the nippers: Davies has knocked Plaice flat.'

'What are those men doing with the other cable?' asked Standish.

'They are veering it out,' answered Martin quickly.

'You are to understand that we are *moored,*' said Stephen. 'In other words we are held by two anchors, widely separated; when we approach the one, therefore, by pulling on its cable, the cable belonging to the other must necessarily be let out, and this is done by the veering cable-men. But their task is almost over, for if I do not mistake we are short stay apeak. I say we are short stay apeak.' But before he could insist upon this term, better than any Martin could produce, and reasonably accurate, a voice from the forecastle called 'Heave and a-weigh, sir,' whereupon Jack cried 'Heave and rally' with great force. All the veerers ran to the bars, the fiddler fiddled extremely fast, and with a violent, grunting yeo heave ho they broke the anchor from its bed and ran it up to the bows.

The subsequent operations, the hooking of the cat to the anchor-ring, the running of the anchor up to the cat-head, the fishing of the anchor, the shifting of the messenger for the other cable (which of course required a contrary turn), and many more, were too rapid and perhaps too obscure to be explained before Jack gave the order 'Up anchor' and the music started again; but this time they sang

We'll heave him up from down below
Way oh Criana
That is where the cocks do crow
We're all bound over the mountain

to the sound of a shrill sweet fife.

The ship moved easily, steadily over the water — the tide was making fast — and presently West, on the forecastle, called 'Up and down, sir.'

'He means that we are directly over the

anchor,' said Stephen. 'Now you will see something.'

'Loose topsails,' said Jack in little more than a conversational voice, and at once the shrouds were dark with men racing aloft.

He gave no more orders. The Surprises lay out, let fall, sheeted home, hoisted and braced the topsails with perfect unity, as though they had all served together throughout a long commission. The frigate gathered way, plucked the anchor from its bed and moved smoothly up the Tagus.

'If you can bring her to one of the moorings in the middle reach in time for me to have dinner in Black Horse Square, you shall have an extra five guineas,' said Jack as he handed the ship over to the pilot.

'By three o'clock?' said the pilot, looking at the sky and then over the side. 'I believe it may be done.'

'Even earlier, if possible,' said Jack. He was an old-fashioned creature in some ways, as his hero Nelson had been; he still wore his hair long and plaited into a clubbed pigtail, not cut in the short modern Brutus manner; he put on his cocked hat athwartships rather than fore and aft; and he liked his dinner at the traditional captain's two o'clock. But tradition was now failing him; naval habits were beginning to ape those of the land, where dinner at five, six, and even seven was becoming frequent; and at sea most post-captains, particularly if they had guests, dined at three. Jack's stomach was even more conservative than his mind, but at present he had trained it to hold out with tolerable good humour until half past two.

The hands had their dinner (two pounds of salt beef, one pound of ship's bread and a pint of grog) as soon as the ship was over the worst of the bar; the members of the gun-room had theirs at one (it smelt to Jack like uncommonly good roast mutton) and when Belem was clear on the larboard bow they came on deck, rosy and comfortable, to view the tower and Lisbon itself, white in the distance beyond.

Jack went below to see whether a biscuit and a glass of madeira would quieten the wolf within, and there he found Stephen with an almanack and a small paper of calculations.

'I dare say you are working out when we shall pick up the trades,' he said. 'Will you join me in a glass of madeira and a biscuit? We had a very early breakfast.'

'With all my heart. But the trade winds I leave to you entirely: what I am looking for is the saint's day upon which my daughter will most probably be born. These things cannot be foretold to the day nor even to the week, so I shall have to spread my offerings pretty wide; but on the most likely, most physically orthodox day, what clouds of incense will go up! What mounds of pure beeswax! And in looking through this almanack I see that it was on Saint Eudoxia's day, when the Ethiopian Copts so strangely celebrate Pontius Pilate, that Padeen would have been hanged but for your great kindness. I shall have a Mass said for his intention as soon as we get ashore.'

'It was no great kindness I do assure you. When I went they looked very grave because they thought I wanted a sinecure or a place at court for a friend, but when I said it was only a man's life they cheered up amazingly, laughed, told me the weather had been delightful these last days, and gave me the paper out of hand. But tell me, why are you so sure that Diana is going to be brought to bed of a girl?'

'Can you imagine her being brought to bed of anything else?'

Jack could perfectly well imagine it, but he had so often heard Stephen speak of his future delight in the company of this little hypothetical daughter that he only said, 'The pilot tells me there are no other men-of-war in the river, which is just as well —

there is always a certain amount of awkwardness. He also tells me that the post office is shut today, which is an infernal bore. Have you any idea of what to order for dinner?'

'Cold green soup, grilled swordfish, roast sucking-pig, pineapple and the little round marchpane cakes whose name escapes me with our coffee.'

'Stephen, you will deal with the quarantine-officer, will you not?'

'I have prepared a little douceur in this purse, which I must remember to transfer to the fine clothes Killick is laying out for me. And that reminds me, I must look out for a servant to replace Padeen at last. Killick will wither quite away if he has to go on looking after us both.'

'I think any newcomer would wither away even quicker under the effect of his ill-will. He has grown so used to it since poor Padeen was sent away that he looks upon you as his own property, and he would resent anyone else. The only thing he would bear would be some lumpkin to stand behind you at dinner; with the best will in the world he cannot stand behind both of us at the same time and it drives him distracted. But why are you putting out fine clothes? It is only a tavern dinner at João's.'

'Because I must call at the palace and ask for an audience with the Patriarch. On the way back I shall look in at my bankers' correspondent.'

The dinner at João's had passed off very well, for although the port was in the Portuguese taste, somewhat thin, sharp and even astringent, the coffee was the best in the world; Dr Maturin's reception by the Patriarch himself had been kind and gracious beyond expectation; and now he was walking towards what English sailors called Roly Poly Square, where his bankers' Lisbon correspondents had their place of business. He was conscious of a sense of positive well-being; the sun shone upon the broad river and its countless masts; and he was happy for Sam. But he had a feeling that he was being observed. 'Those criminals, intelligence-agents and foxes who last, who survive to have offspring, develop an eye in the back of their heads,' he reflected; and when he had finished dealing with his letter of credit and some other matters he was not surprised at being accosted on the doorstep by a decent-looking man in a brown coat who took off his hat and said, 'Dr Maturin, I presume?'

Stephen also took off his hat, saying,

'Maturin is indeed my name, sir.' But he showed no inclination to stop, and the other, hurrying along beside him, went on in a low urgent tone, 'Pray forgive me, sir, for this want of ceremony, but I come from Sir Joseph Blaine. He is just arrived at the Quinta de Monserrate, near Cintra, and he begs you will come to see him. I have a carriage close at hand.'

'My compliments to Sir Joseph, if you please,' said Stephen. 'I regret I am not at leisure to wait upon him, but trust I may have the pleasure of a meeting at either the Royal or the Entomological society when next I am in London. Good day to you, sir.' He said this in so decided a tone and with so very cold a look in his pale eyes that the messenger did not persist, but stood there looking wretched.

'Damned villain,' said Stephen as he crossed the square and began to walk down the Rua d'Ouro. 'To come without even a pretence of credentials, supposing that I should hurry off into the hills and beg Taillandier to cut my throat' — Taillandier being the principal French agent in Lisbon, and usually much more professional in his methods.

'Hola, Stephen,' called Jack from the other side of the street. 'Well met, shipmate.

Come and help me choose some taffeta for Sophie. I want some so fine it will go through a ring. I am sure you understand taffeta, Stephen.'

'I doubt there is a man in the whole of Ballinasloe that understands it better,' said Stephen. 'And if there is blue taffeta to be had, I shall buy some for Diana too.'

They walked back to the quay carrying their parcels, and since Jack, not knowing how long they would be, had not taken his own gig ashore, they were about to hail a boat when a party of the *Surprise*'s liberty men, gathering about the launch true to their hour, caught sight of them the whole breadth of the square away and roared out, 'Never waste your money on a skiff, sir. Come along o' we.'

Jack went along o' they in the democratical corsair fashion quite happily, though he was just as glad that there were no serving officers in their formal barges to watch him: though in fact, apart from their first free, uninhibited invitation the Shelmerstonians were as prim and mute as any long-serving man-of-war's men throughout the crossing.

It was clear that Jack was right in saying that Killick regarded Stephen as his own property. He at once took him down to the coach and made him take off his fine English broadcloth coat, crying out in a shrill nagging tone, 'Look at these here great slobs of grease, so deep you could plough a furrow in them: and your best satin breeches, oh Lord! Didn't I say you was to call for two napkins and never mind if they stared? Now it will be scrub-scrub, brush-brush for poor bloody Killick all through the night watches; and even then they will never be the same.'

'Here is a box of Portugal marchpane for you, Killick,' said Stephen.

'Well, I take it kindly that you remembered, sir,' said Killick, who was passionately fond of marchpane. 'Thank you, sir. Now when you have put on these here old togs — they are quite clean and dry — there is Mr Martin as would like to have a word with you.'

For once the word, which was a serious, private one, did not have to be uttered at the masthead or in the remotest corner of the hold, for Stephen and Martin were both fluent in Latin, and in spite of Martin's barbarous English pronunciation they understood one another very well.

Martin said, 'Standish has asked me to approach you, who know Captain Aubrey best, to learn whether you think he would be likely to entertain a request to resign the pursership. He says you told him there was no cure for seasickness —'

'So I did, too.'

'— and although he is very fond of the sea he is extremely unwilling to face a repetition of what he has already suffered, if the Captain will release him from his obligations.'

'I do not wonder at it. In his case the prostration was as severe as anything I have ever seen. But I do wonder at the suddenness of his decision. He followed our explanation of the unmooring with the liveliest interest; yet he was perfectly aware of what he had undergone and of what in all likelihood he was to undergo again.'

'Yes. It struck me too; but he was always a strange, versatile creature.'

'I believe he suddenly threw up a living in the Anglican church, to the astonishment of his friends.'

'That was not quite the same, however. To have the living he was required to subscribe to the Thirty-Nine Articles, and the thirty-first describes Masses — forgive me — as blasphemous fables and dangerous deceits. When he came to that he said he could not put his name to it, picked up his hat, bowed to the company, and walked off. He was much attached to a Catholic young woman at the time, but what influence that had upon his action I do not know. We never discussed it: we were not at all intimate.'

Stephen made no comment; after a moment he said, 'If Captain Aubrey releases him, what will he do? Unless I mistake he has no money at all.'

'He means to wander about as Goldsmith did, disputing at universities and the like, and playing his fiddle.'

'Well, may God be with him. I do not think there will be any objection to his leaving the ship, splendidly though he plays the violin.'

They looked at one another, and Martin said, 'Poor man, I am afraid he has made himself much disliked aboard. He was not at all like this at Oxford. I believe it was loneliness after the university and all that wretched schoolmastering.'

'On some it acts like a poison, making them unfit for the society of grown men.'

'That was what he felt. He was afraid he was no longer good company. He bought a jest-book: "It is my ambition to set the table in a roar," he said. But upon my honour I think the seasickness is the true causa causans, though it is possible that some sharp reflexion in the gunroom may have precipitated his decision.'

'In any event, it is honourable in him to feel so bound to Captain Aubrey that he will not leave without permission.'

'Oh yes, he has always been perfectly honourable.' There was a long pause, and Martin said, 'Do you know when the post office will open in the morning? We spent so long in the Irish Sea that the packet is sure to have come before us: perhaps two packets. I long to hear from home.'

'It opens at eight o'clock. I shall be there as the bell strikes.'

'So shall I.'

So they were, and little good did it do them. There was nothing whatsoever for Martin and only two letters for Dr Maturin. Jack had a couple from Hampshire, and according to their usual habit they read them at breakfast, exchanging pieces of family news. Stephen had scarcely broken the seal of his first before he cried, with a passion rare in him, 'Upon my word, Jack, that woman is as headstrong as an allegory on the banks of Nile.'

Jack was not always quick, but this time he instantly grasped that Stephen was talking about his wife and he said, 'Has she taken Barham Down?'

'She has not only taken it, she has bought

it.' And in an undertone 'The animal.'

'Sophie always said she was very much set upon the place.'

Stephen read on, and then said, 'But she means to live with Sophie until we come home, however. She is only sending Hitch-cock and a few horses.'

'So much the better. Stephen, did she tell you the kitchen boiler at Ashgrove blew up on Tuesday?'

'She is doing so at this minute — the words are before me. Brother, there is much to be said for living in a monastery.'

The next letter did nothing to reconcile him with his lot. It was written in that curiously ungracious business style which his bankers had brought to a state of high perfection: the person who signed it asserted that he was, with great respect, Stephen's humble obedient servant, but he either ignored questions or gave irrelevant answers, and where quite pressing matters were concerned he had a way of saying 'these instructions will be carried out in due course'. The nearest he could bring himself to an apology for the loss of a paper or certificate was 'it is regretted that if the document in question ever reached our hands, it has temporarily been mislaid; any inconvenience that may possibly have been caused is deplored'; the general tone was contentious, the advice on financial matters was so hedged with reservations as to be valueless, the language was both inflated and incorrect. 'Oh for a Fugger, oh for a literate Fugger,' he said.

'Two letters for the Doctor, sir, if you please,' said Killick, coming in with a sneer on his naturally rather disapproving face. 'This here delivered upside down, at the *starboard* gangway, by a parcel of lobsters. T'other by a genteel Lisbon craft with a violet awning and handed up decent.'

Killick had studied the seals with some care; the first he recognized, the English royal arms impressed in black wax, the second, a violet affair, he could not make out at all. But they were both important seals and naturally he was concerned to find out what the letters contained. Lingering at a suitable distance he heard Stephen cry, 'Give you joy, Jack! Sam is made: he is to be ordained by his own bishop on the twenty-third.'

For Jack the word 'made' was ringed with haloes. In the service it had two meanings, the first (a very great happiness) being commissioned, the second (supreme happiness) being appointed post-captain. Yet the world in which he had been brought up and which still clung about him most tenaciously looked upon Papists with disfavour — their loyalty was uncertain, their practices foreign, and Gunpowder Plot and the Jesuits had given them a bad name — and although he could without much difficulty accept Sam as some kind of an acting monk or monk's assistant, Sam as a full-blown Popish priest was quite different. But he was extremely fond of Sam, and if the promotion gave Sam joy . . . 'Well I'm damned,' he exclaimed, all these emotions finding expression in the words. 'What is it, Mr West?'

'I beg pardon, sir,' said West, 'but the port-captain is coming alongside.'

Jack being gone, Stephen opened his second letter. It was from the embassy and it asked him to call at his very earliest convenience.

'Here is your second-best coat, sir,' said Killick. 'I have made a tolerable good job of t'other, but it is not dry yet, and this will serve in a dark old church. The launch is going over the side this minute.'

So it was too, to judge by the rhythmic cries and the time-honoured oaths and crashes; and when Stephen, neat and brushed, with a fresh-curled wig and a clean handkerchief, came on deck, the Irish, Polish and north-country English Catholic members of the ship's company who were going to Padeen's Mass had already taken their places. They were in shore-going rig — wide-brimmed white sennit hats, Watchet-blue jackets with brass buttons, black silk neckerchiefs, white duck trousers and very small shoes — but with no ribbons in the seams or coloured streamers: a sober finery. Maturin bowed to the port-captain, took his leave of Aubrey, and went down the side scarcely thinking of steps or entering-ropes, his mind being so far away. They pulled across to the shore, and leaving the launch with two boat-keepers they moved off in no sort of formation, gazing at the strangely-dressed Portuguese until they came to the Benedictine church; here, once they had passed the holy water, they might all have been at home, hearing the same words, the same plainchant, seeing the same formal hieratic motions and smelling the same incense they had always known.

The Mass over, they lit candles for Padeen and walked out of the cool, gently-lit timeless familiar world into the brilliant sunshine of Lisbon, a very recent city and to many of them quite foreign.

'Good day to you, now, shipmates,' said Stephen. 'You will never forget the way to the boat, I am sure; it is right down the hill.'

He walked up it towards the embassy, his mind turning back more and more rapidly to worldly things.

The porter looked a little doubtfully at his second-best coat — somewhat rusty and threadbare in the full light of the sun — but he sent in his card and the first secretary came hurrying. 'I am so sorry that His Excellency is not in the way this morning,' he said, taking Dr Maturin into his office, '— pray take a seat — but I am to say that the invitation to Monserrate may be accepted with perfect confidence, and that an escort will be provided if it is desired. A coach too, of course.'

'I should be most grateful for a carriage of some kind; yet perhaps a well-paced horse would be quicker and less conspicuous, if one can be spared.'

'Certainly.'

'And may I beg you to have a message carried down to the ship?'

'Alas, my dear Maturin,' cried Sir Joseph from the steps of the Quinta, 'I am afraid you have had a terribly hot ride.' Stephen dismounted; the horse was led away; and Sir Joseph went on, 'Can you ever forgive me? I was so confused, so weary, so muddle-headed by the time I arrived that I sent

Carrick off empty-handed. My letter to you is still in my pocket. I will show it to you. Come, walk in, walk in out of the sun and drink some lemonade or East India ale or barley-water — anything you can think of. Tea, perhaps?'

'If it is agreeable to you, I had as soon sit on the grass in the shade by a brook. I am not at all thirsty.'

'What a beautiful idea.' And as they walked along, 'Maturin, why do you carry your hat in that curious way? If I were to walk bare-headed in the sun, or even with a small bob-wig, I should be struck down dead.'

'There is an insect in it that I shall show you when we sit down. Here is a perfect place — green leaves overhead, sweet-smelling grass, a murmuring brook.' He opened his folded hat, took out a pocket-handkerchief and spread it on the ground. The creature, quite unharmed, stood there gently swaying on its long legs. It was a very large insect indeed, greenish, with immense antennae and a disproportionately small, meek, and indeed rather stupid face.

'Bless me,' said Blaine. 'It is not a mantis. And yet —'

'It is *Saga pedo*.'

'Of course, of course. I have seen him figured, but never preserved nor even dried, far less alive and swaying at me. What a glorious animal! But look at those wicked serrated limbs! Two pairs of them! Where did you find him?'

'On the side of the road just outside Cintra. *She,* if I may be pedantic. In these parts the females alone are seen: they reproduce parthenogenetically, which must surely ease some of the tensions of family life.'

'Yes. I remember from Olivier's paper. But surely you do not mean to let her go, so rare?' The saga was walking confidently off the handkerchief and into the grass.

'I do, though. Who is without superstition? It seems to me that letting her go may have a favourable influence upon our meeting; for I assume that it is no trifling matter that has brought you to Portugal.'

Blaine followed the saga until it vanished among the grass-stems, then turning resolutely away he said, 'No, by God. A little while ago the heavens fell on our heads: opened and fell on our heads. The Spanish ambassador called at the Foreign Office and asked whether there was any truth in the report that the *Surprise* had been fitted out and sent to encourage rebels or potential rebels, "independentists", in the Spanish

South American possessions. Oh dear me, no, he was told; the *Surprise* was merely a privateer, one of many, going to cruise upon United States whalers and China-bound ships and any Frenchmen she happened to meet. This absurd report must have arisen from a confusion with a perfectly genuine French expedition designed for that very purpose, an expedition that had been frustrated by our capture of the *Diane*, which was to carry the agents — an expedition that could be substantiated, if any substantiation against such very grave and indeed monstrous charges were required, by the production of documents seized aboard the French frigate. The Spaniard may not have been wholly convinced, though he was certainly shaken; he said he should be very glad to see any evidence, particularly that inculpating those who had been in correspondence with the French, our common enemies; he expressed some surprise that the substance of these documents had not been communicated to him before; but that was easily accounted for by the extreme slowness of British official procedures.'

Blaine took off his shoes and stockings, shifted a little forward on the grass and dangled his feet in the stream. 'Oh what a relief,' he said. 'Maturin, I have had a most hellish journey from Corunna — sleeping in the coach — jolting over vile roads — eight and even ten mules scarcely enough sometimes — the heat, the dust, the dreadful inns — wheels coming off, axles breaking — brigands, large desperate isolated bodies of French and their unpaid mercenaries — our own army pushing us off the road on to byways, blind alleys, mountain tracks — a furious French advance that came very near to cutting us off — goat's milk in the coffee, goat's milk in the tea — but above all the perpetual hurry, perpetual weariness and heat — the flies! Forgive me again for being so stupid about Carrick; forgive me if my account of the situation is out of sequence, patchy, disordered — a clear mind is wanted for such complexity, not one that has just been trundled over rocks and deserts that would be a disgrace to Ethiopia.'

'No doubt there were good reasons why you did not take the packet or one of the Admiralty yachts.'

'Two excellent reasons. The first, that although the packet did in fact reach Lisbon long before me, there was no guaranteeing that it would not be windbound for a month, whereas once I was on Spanish soil I could be sure that perseverance would get me to Portugal within certain limits of time, if I survived. The second, that purgatorial though the journey was, I preferred it to a voyage by sea. I am most horribly seasick, and I should certainly have lost essential elements in my grasp of the situation.' He sat stirring his feet in the water and rehearsing the order of events in his mind, and presently he said, 'You will already have perceived that this most damaging information can have reached the Spaniards only through one of the very few men who knew about your mission, almost certainly the man who protected Wray and Ledward and allowed them to get out of the country. Warren and I suspected that the report would be sent, and that is why I particularly insisted upon your calling at Lisbon.'

'I had imagined that to be your motive. In the same way I had understood from the beginning that our journey to South America was also intended to counteract Buonapartist influence there; and your earliest reference to the *Diane* made it even more certain. From my own, personal point of view this conflict with the French was of the first importance.'

'Of course it was; and will be again, in the same region, I hope. But for the moment we must utterly demolish the report and dis-

131

credit the source of information. The *Surprise* must carry on with her voyage, ostentatiously privateering and avoiding all contact with the supporters of independence.'

There was a pause, and Stephen observed that Blaine was looking at him with a quizzical eye, his head cocked on one side; but he made no observation and after the cool breeze had wafted through the leaves for a while Blaine went on, 'But although you and Aubrey will not be fully employed in that hemisphere, I trust that if you agree to my plan you will be even more so in another. The French have learnt, probably through this same source, Ledward's protector, that except on paper we are extremely weak in Java and the East Indies in general. They have therefore sent a mission to the Sultan of Pulo Prabang, one of the piratical Malay states in the South China Sea, urging him to become their ally and to build and equip vessels large enough to capture our East Indiamen on their way to and from Canton, thus cutting the Company's throat. The Sultan's dominions lie almost directly across the Indiamen's route; he has a splendid harbour, forests of teak and everything that is desirable; and a hardy population of seafaring Malays who have hitherto confined themselves to native craft and to piracy on a modest scale — Chinese junks, the occasional Arab dhow. The French have sent shipwrights, tools, materials, guns and treasure. Their official envoy is Jean Duplessis, something of a nonentity; the man who will really conduct the affair is Ledward. He spent much of his youth in Penang and I am told that he speaks Malay like a native — at all events I know he held an important post there under the Company and that he is an unusually able negotiator. The French have sent Wray too, more with the idea of getting rid of him than for any use he is likely to be: once he had ceased to be of value to them in Paris he was treated with great neglect and contempt, whereas Ledward always retained a certain position.' Blame stopped to collect his ideas again, but shaking his head he went on, 'Do you mind if we go back into the house? If I were given a good pot of tea, a good pot of brown London tea, I believe it might clear my wits.'

'Sure, I only wished to be outside to release my saga,' said Stephen, 'and if I might be indulged in a glass of white wine I should happily watch you drink your tea. In a place designed by Beckford you should be able to rely on an honest brew.'

'Did you ever read Vathek?'

'I tried, on the recommendation of men whose taste I respected.'

Sir Joseph drank his tea and Stephen his wine in an immensely long cool gallery on the north side of the house, with a flight of windows looking out on to gardens, lawns with three different streams flowing through the grass, copses, and on the rising ground beyond a noble wood, while the gallery's opposite wall held a great number of large pictures, mostly of the last age and mostly allegorical. In this sweep of space the two men sitting in English armchairs with a little table between them looked minute: they could speak without the least fear of being overheard.

'Of course,' said Blaine, 'we plan a counter-mission, and we have a capital man to take charge of it. His name is Fox, Edward Fox: he was my guest once at the dinner of the Royal Society Club and afterwards you heard him read a paper on the spread of Buddhism eastward and its subsequent relations with Brahmanism and the Muslims.'

'Certainly. A man of unusual parts.'

'Yes. Of most unusual parts; and yet he has never been appreciated at his full value. Always acting, temporary appointments — always moved on to some other administration. Perhaps there is some fault of manner . . . a certain unorthodoxy . . . a certain bitterness from want of recognition. But there are undoubtedly remarkable abilities, and he might have been made for this particular undertaking. He is, by the way, a friend of Raffles, the Governor of Java, another interesting man.'

'So I am told. I have not met the gentleman, but I have seen some of his letters to Banks: they think of founding a zoological society.'

'Fox too was in Penang at one time, and it is from him that I have my information about Ledward in that respect.' A long silence followed; the room was so still that a turtle-dove could be heard a great way off. 'But naturally,' continued Blaine, draining his pot, 'we have to get our envoy there before the French have converted their man and signed their treaty. It can certainly be done, given equal diligence, because although they have a start, Fox and all other authorities assure me that with potentates of the Sultan's kind these things are never concluded without discussions lasting a month or two, and because, since we control the Sunda Strait, the French have to go very, very much farther round. It can be done: I mean they can be frustrated, undermined, done in the eye, and I will tell you how I think we should set about it. I have said how essentially important it is that this report about South America should be scotched, have I not?'

'You emphasized it as strongly as possible.'

'Very well, then. Now according to my plan the *Surprise* will carry on with her avowable activities under her second in command and her present ship's company — the authorities' confidential arrangement for her hire will continue in force — and you and Aubrey will take the envoy to Pulo Prabang in the *Diane*, which has been bought into the service. We had meant to wait until there was a victory that could be announced together with the news of Aubrey's reinstatement — a question of saving official face — but now it is agreed that the country's interests will be better served by openly, publicly, almost ostentatiously reinstating him and giving him this command. What more convincing proof that you are neither of you going to Peru?'

Stephen nodded.

Blaine went on, 'But that is not all. Let us suppose that the *Surprise* makes her way into the Pacific in Captain Pullings' able hands — his name has come back to me —

and there, having done what she ostensibly set out to do, she sails to some given rendezvous; and then let us suppose that the *Diane*, having dealt with the situation in Pulo Prabang, joins the *Surprise* at this rendezvous, so that you can return by South America, thus being enabled to make at least some of the discreet contacts that we had planned. What do you say to that, Maturin?'

Stephen looked at him for some moments with an expressionless face; then he said, 'It is a grandiose scheme. I am in favour of it. But I cannot answer for Aubrey.'

'No. Of course you cannot. Yet an answer must we have within two days, no more. Clearly, I do not know Aubrey as well as you, not by a thousand miles; but I have little doubt of what he will say.'

Chapter 4

Jack Aubrey's answer was yes, as Stephen had known very well it would be; but with what tearings of heart, what anxious self-questioning did he produce it at length, well on in the eleventh hour; and what sad, longing, perhaps guilt-stricken looks did he direct at the *Surprise,* already under sail far down there in the Tagus as he rode away, leaving his shipmates low-spirited, disappointed and in some cases even bereft. Some had been angry at first; many had said they had always known it would be an unlucky voyage; but no man had accepted Jack's offer to give him his wages and pay his passage home, and they had derived increasing comfort from the fact that it was the *Diane* that they personally had cut out, their own *Diane,* in which he was to sail, and that the two ships were to meet at a given rendezvous — a rendezvous made all the more solid and palpable by the Captain's wine and cold-weather clothes, which remained on board, together with crate after crate of the Doctor's books.

Not only the hands but the officers took

the parting hard. Pullings was devoted to Jack and the others had the greatest respect for him; and although they attributed less importance to Aubrey's private personal luck than did the foremost hands, it did not leave them indifferent by any means; furthermore, they knew very well how much easier it was to command a fierce, turbulent crew when there was a legendary figure aboard — legendary for courage, success and good fortune. However, Stephen was able to assure Pullings that he was virtually certain of a command if he brought the *Surprise* home safely; and both West and Davidge felt that in such a case they would have much better chances of reinstatement.

Since Aubrey was to travel to his new ship by land and with the utmost haste he was unable to take any followers apart from his steward and coxswain, and the deserted, uncomplaining look of those he left behind was one of the hardest things about the whole operation.

Yet it was clear to him — it was clear to everyone concerned — that this was still another of those naval occasions on which there was not a moment to be lost; and in a way it was just as well, since the incessant activity, and the extreme difficulty of travelling fast through Portugal and north-western Spain in a time of armed occupation and massive destruction, with the tide of war only just receding and liable to come flooding back at any time, took Jack's mind from his deserted ship and shipmates. But nothing, travel, guilt, extreme discomfort, could take away from the deep glow in his heart: if he could stay alive for the next couple of weeks or so, he would be gazetted and he would have a command — the charming promises would become infinitely more solid realities: changing from what his mind believed to what his whole person knew as a living fact. The fact, however, could not be mentioned, nor the glow acknowledged; even the inward singing must be repressed.

They travelled in a variety of hired coaches and carriages, sometimes drawn by an improbable number of animals but always, however many or however few, running as fast as ever they could be induced to run. That is to say Sir Joseph, Standish, whom Jack had offered a lift after their explanation, the baggage, the musical instruments and the large number of documents Stephen needed travelled so, with Killick and Bonden (no great horsemen) sitting with the driver or up behind, except in the blinding rain of Galicia, when Sir Joseph made them come inside. Jack and Stephen rode: there were great numbers of lost, stolen, strayed cavalry horses from the various armies to be had and each travelled with a remount and a groom, pushing ahead in the evening to attend to supper and bed.

It was hard going, on and on, always on and on, passing wonders without ever a pause — never so much as a glass of wine in Oporto itself — mud in the north, mud axle-deep, and once a band that tried to stop the coach but that scattered in the face of determined professional pistol and carbine fire. Yet for Blaine it was nothing like such hard going as it had been on the way down: now he had a guide perfectly accustomed to the language and the manners of the people, familiar with the road and most of the towns, widely acquainted, so that they stayed at two country houses and one monastery as well as the best inns the country afforded. He was also now part of a formidable armed party, including powerful sailors capable of dealing with most situations, such as freeing a bogged wheel by means of a tackle seized to a stout tree, the fall running along a dry bank, so that all hands could bowse upon it. Indeed the travelling itself was almost pleasant and the evening was very much so: on his way down Sir Joseph, spending public money, had not exactly stinted himself, but he had a certain conscience, whereas Stephen, once he had overcome a reluctance to part with copper, flung gold about like jack-ashore, and Aubrey had never been less than lavish whenever he had anything to be lavish with. Having travelled like kings all day, they ran dinner and supper into one regal feast in the evening, and after it Standish would play to them.

Sir Joseph was devoted to music; he appreciated Standish's playing at its true worth, and Stephen hoped that he might deal with the situation by finding the unhappy man some harmless minor position under Government. But this was not to be. One evening in Santiago Standish was playing a brilliant Corelli partita entirely from memory — not a hemidemisemiquaver of all the multitude out of place — when Jack, who had drunk a great deal of the thin, piercing white wine from the landlady's own vineyard, was obliged to tiptoe to the door. He opened it with the utmost precaution and a bulky officer in the uniform of the First Foot Guards fell into the room. He was covered with confusion — apologized most profusely for listening — fairly worshipped good music — Corelli, was it not? — congratulated the gentleman most heartily. When the music was done they invited him to stay and drink port with them. His name was Lumley; he was in charge of the regiment's depot in Santiago — they had already noticed a number of battered guardsmen creeping about the muddy streets — and as it so often happens in cases of this kind they found they had a large number of acquaintances in common. When the others had gone to bed he shared a last pot with Stephen, who gave him a discreet account of Standish and his position. 'Do you think he would be my secretary?' asked Colonel Lumley. 'The duties would be very light — my clerks do most of the paper-work — but I should give a great deal to have such a violin at hand.'

'It seems to me quite probable,' said Stephen, and he might have added, 'Indeed, I believe the poor man would accept any work that would keep him alive rather than go aboard ship again, and in the Bay of Biscay at that', if he had not thought it liable to influence even a very benevolent employer; and Colonel Lumley had, at least in these circumstances, the kindest face. Instead he observed, 'So probable that I am sure it is worth making the offer.'

The offer was made and accepted. The party set off as soon after dawn as the ostlers could be roused from their straw, with Standish standing by the stable gates in the drizzle waving until they were out of sight. His happiness, his relief, his sense of reprieve affected thcm all, even Bonden and Killick, who imitated post-horns on the back of the coach and made antic gestures at the passing peasants and soldiers most of the morning; but the mounting south-south-west wind veering to south-west with heavy rain damped their ardour, and presently Sir Joseph made them get inside again, where they sat stiff, mum and genteel until at last the gasping mules brought the carriage down through Corunna to the port.

Here Jack and Stephen were waiting for them on the quay, beside the *Nimble*, the cutter that was to carry Sir Joseph and his party home.

'This could not be better,' said Jack as he heaved the coach door open against the blast. 'It is almost sure to strengthen, and even if it don't we may well see Ushant by Thursday evening.'

In the last grey twilight Blaine looked at the streaming, shining quay, the streaming, shining mules drooping their heads under the rain, the uneasy surface of the harbour, the steeply-chopped white water beyond, where the tide was ebbing against the Atlantic rollers. He made no reply, but took Jack's arm and staggered across the brow into the cutter, his eyes half-closed.

Stephen settled with the coachman and his carbine-bearing companion, paid the grooms, telling them they might keep the horses, and so in his turn crossed the brow. The baggage had long since been whipped across by a line of seamen, and as soon as Stephen was aboard they cast off fore and aft, filled the jib and stood for the open sea.

The two-hundred-ton *Nimble*, fourteen guns, was one of the largest cutters in the Royal Navy, and for those accustomed to doggers, hoys, galliots and smacks in general she seemed a behemoth, particularly when she had topgallants and even royals spread on her tall single mast; but for the rest of the world, especially those used to rated ships, she might have seemed designed for dwarfs. Even Maturin, who was rather a small man, stood bent, with bowed head, in the cabin. Yet as it so often happened in the Navy, she was commanded by one of the tallest officers the service possessed: he came in, having seen his cutter well clear of the land, and stood there, a pink-faced, smiling, anxious young man in a lieutenant's coat.

'You are very welcome, gentlemen,' he

said again. 'May I offer you a little something to stay you before supper? Sandwiches, for example, and a glass of sillery?'

'That would be delightful,' said his
guests, to whom it was clear that the sandwiches had already been cut and the wine
put over the side in a net to cool.

'Where is Sir Joseph?' asked the captain of
the *Nimble.*

'He turned in at once,' said Jack, 'because, says he, *prevention is better than cure.*'

'I hope it answers, I am sure. Lord Nelson's coxswain told me the admiral used to
suffer most cruelly for the first few days, if
he had been ashore for a while. Stubbs' —
directing his voice through a scuttle — 'light
along the sandwiches and the wine.'

'The bubbly stuff is all very well,' said
Jack, looking at the light through his glass,
'but for flavour, for bouquet and for quality,
give me good sillery every time. Capital
wine, sir: but now I come to think of it, I do
not believe I caught your name.'

'Fitton, sir. Michael Fitton,' said the
young man with a shy, expectant look.

'Not John Fitton's son?' asked Jack.

'Yes, sir. He often spoke about you, and I
saw you once at home when I was a boy.'

'We were shipmates in three commissions,' said Jack, shaking his hand. '*Isis*, *Resolution*, and *Colossus*, of course.' He looked down, for it was on the gun-deck of the *Colossus*, not three feet away from him, that John Fitton had been killed during the battle of St Vincent.

At this moment Sir Joseph, whose cupboard opened into the cabin, called out in a choking voice for his servant, and when the hurrying to and fro was over Stephen said, gazing about, 'So this is a cutter. Well, I am prodigiously glad to have seen a cutter. Pray why is it so called?'

At another time Jack might have replied that Stephen had seen cutters by the score, by the hundred, every time he came into home waters, and very often elsewhere, and that the rig had been carefully explained to him so that he should not confuse a cutter with a sloop; but now he only said, 'Why, because they go cutting along, you know. Skilfully handled' — smiling at young Fitton — 'they are the fastest craft in the Navy.'

'Should you like to see over her, Doctor, when it is raining a little less?' asked Fitton. 'She is remarkably large and elegant for a cutter — nearly seventy feet long — and although some people might say she wanted headroom, she is much broader in the beam than you would think: twenty-four feet, but for a trifle. Twenty-four feet, sir, I do assure you.'

After supper Jack and the captain of the *Nimble* fell to a close discussion of the sailing of cutters, both with fore-and-aft and with square rig, in order to get the best out of them by as well as large; and although from time to time they remembered that Stephen was there and tried to make the question clear to him, he soon went to bed. He was in fact quite tired — he had reason to be — but before he went to sleep he reflected for a while on diaries, on the keeping of diaries. The *Nimble* was now pitching to such an extent that Killick came in and took seven turns about him and his cot to prevent him from being tossed out or being flung against the deck-head, but even without the constriction it would have been impossible to make one of his habitual entries — cryptic entries, because of his strongly-developed sense of privacy, and selective entries, because of his connexion with intelligence.

'Today I should have recorded no more than the weather, the helleborus foetidus when we stopped to mend a trace, and the handsomely expressed gentlemanly gratitude of the men, the wholly uneducated men, to whom we gave the horses. When first I met Jack I should have been very much more prolix. Or should I? I was terribly low in those days, after the obvious, inevitable failure of the rising, the infamous conduct of so very, very many people, and of course the loss of Mona; to say nothing of the intolerable miseries in France and the destruction of all our sanguine generous youthful hopes. Lord, how a man can change! I remember telling James Dillon, God rest his soul, that I no longer felt loyalty to any nation or any body of men, only to my immediate friends — that Dr Johnson was right in saying that the form of government was of no consequence to the individual — that I should not move a finger to bring about the millennium or independence. And yet here I am, hurrying through this wicked sea in an attempt however slight at bringing about both, if the defeat of Buonaparte can be considered the one and Catholic emancipation and the dissolution of the union the other. When I am at the Grapes I shall look at the diary of that year and see what in fact I said. Shall I remember the code?'

At breakfast Michael Fitton said, 'Today, Doctor, if the rain stops, you will see the *Nimble* in all her glory: she is almost directly before the wind, with topsail and single-reefed square mainsail, and at the last heave she ran off eleven knots and the best part of a fathom.'

'Yes,' said Jack, 'and you will scc the extraordinary merits of a running bowsprit. When she pitches like this' — the table took on a forward slope of twenty-five degrees, their hands automatically securing the toast — 'the bowsprit does not stab into the sea and snap off short or at the very least check her way.'

'How can this be achieved, for all love?'

'Since a cutter's bowsprit has no steeve, since it is horizontal, it can be run in on deck,' they told him kindly, and promised that he should see it directly.

But they were mistaken. The rain continued steadily, sweeping in vast grey swathes from the south-west, over a grey sea mottled here and there with white; and although in the dim afternoon of Thursday Jack dragged him on deck to look at Ushant, a faint white-ringed blur on the starboard bow, he could not be induced to go forward to see the bowsprit nor even to climb a little way up the shrouds to view the remote ships of the Brest blockade; and the next day, when the *Nimble* was racing up the Channel, the breeze had hauled so far forward that she now wore her fore-and-aft mainsail, foresail and jib; her bowsprit was therefore run out, and it remained run out until the end of their voyage — a most remarkably fine passage that brought them into Portsmouth late on Friday afternoon, quite a warm day for May, and with no more than an intermittent drizzle.

Sir Joseph, whose policy of lying motionless and eating very large quantities of dry bread had worked well after the first horrible hours, set off for London as soon as he had taken tea and muffins at the Crown; he said to Jack, 'I presume orders will be telegraphed down to Admiral Martin as soon as I have made my report; and I have little doubt that officially or unofficially I shall see you both early next week.'

They accompanied him to his post-chaise, and as they walked back Stephen said, 'I have been thinking, brother. Diana will be in a very delicate condition by now, and if we suddenly appear, it may shock her extremely.'

'Oh,' said Jack, who had been on the point of sending for horses, 'I suppose it might. Pen a discreet, diplomatic note hinting that you might be in the neighbourhood presently, and we will send it by Bonden or Killick or both in a chaise.'

'A chaise, with Bonden and Killick getting out of it, would be sure to cause alarm — dreadful apprehensions of bad news travelling with such speed and ostentation. A boy on a mule would be much more suitable.'

The boy on a mule set off with a note — *My dear, pray do not be alarmed or in any way concerned if you should see us presently: we are both perfectly well and send our love* — and the men were about to set off to gaze at the *Diane* from a discreet distance when they ran into the Port Admiral, a cheerful soul, who insisted on their cracking a bottle: 'I am seventy-four today; you cannot refuse me.' A number of other sea-officers were in the hall and he invited them too. Some were very well known to Jack, among them three post-captains; like many other post-captains they made up for their solitary state at sea by being unusually loquacious by land. The Physician of the Fleet was also there, together with one of the medical men from Haslar; and they too were very conversible. Talk flowed, bottles came and went, time passed, passed. But at length the landlord's son came and stood by Stephen: 'Oh, Dr Maturin, sir,' he said when Stephen paused in his account of the Basrah method of setting broken bones, 'there is a coach outside with some ladies asking for you.'

'Jesus, Mary and Joseph,' muttered Stephen, darting from the room.

Diana was at the near-side window. She leant out and cried, 'Oh Maturin, my dear, what a monster you are to terrify innocent women like this.' Inside the coach behind her Sophie's voice rose to a high squeak, 'Is not Jack there? You said Jack would be there.'

Diana opened the door and offered to jump out, but Stephen took her elbows and lifted her down. 'My dear, you are a fine size,' he said, kissing her tenderly. 'Sophie, will you come in and see Jack and Admiral Martin and a number of other sailors? They are drinking port in the Dolphin room.'

'Oh Stephen,' called Sophie, 'pray bring him out and let us all go home together at once. I do not want to lose a minute of him. Nor of you either, dear Stephen.'

'Sure you are right, for the moments are few: we must be in town on Tuesday, I do believe.'

In fact it was on Sunday evening that a message came from the Port Admiral requiring *Captain* Aubrey to wait upon the First Lord in Arlington Street at half-past five o'clock the next day. Yet if the reprieve had been longer they could scarcely have said any more, all of them having talked incessantly since the coach started moving back to Ashgrove Cottage from the Crown.

'Arlington Street,' said Jack in a hoarse whisper. 'His private house. I am heartily glad of it. Because had it been the Admiralty I should have been in a fine quandary — report in uniform and be presumptuous or report in civilian clothes and be incorrect. However I shall take uniform as well, in case I have to go on. Sweetheart, it has not gone to wrack and ruin all these years?'

'Neither the one nor the other, my dear, only the epaulettes are a little tarnished. Killick and my mother and both the girls have been blowing on your best and dry-scrubbing it with soft brushes to get the smell of moth-balls out since yesterday morning. But I am afraid it will be much too big; you have grown pitifully thin, my poor darling.'

Pitifully thin or not, Jack Aubrey still made the post-chaise heel well over as he stepped into it, having kissed his family all round except for George, who had been wearing breeches for quite some time now.

They struck into the main London road at Cosham and bowled along at a splendid rate under a blue, blue sky with billowing, flat-bottomed white clouds travelling in the same direction, but at a far more stately pace. 'Remarkable fine horses,' observed Jack. 'And a most uncommon pretty day.' He whistled and then sang *From Ushant to Scilly, 'tis thirty-five leagues* right through.

Since there had been no rain on Saturday or Sunday the hedges all along the busy road were white with dust, but only a little way beyond them there was a living green in the wheat, oats and barley, in the various leys, and in the woods and copses with leaves coming to their glory under the brilliant sky that it would have lifted the heart of any man, let alone one who might expect such an end to his journey.

Most of the summer migrants had arrived and there were still some passing through to northern parts; the countryside was therefore rich in birds, and as they changed horses at a village some way beyond Petersfield Stephen heard no less than three separate cuckoos at once. He shook his head, remembering the extreme pain that call had caused him at an earlier time, but almost at once his mind was taken off by the sight of a wryneck, a bird he had much more often heard than seen. He pointed it out to Jack with the usual result: 'There is a wryneck.' 'Where?' 'On the young elm to the right of — it is gone.'

Wrynecks, the progress of Jack's daughters in learning and deportment under Miss O'Mara, and the albatrosses of the high and even moderate southern latitudes occupied the next stage, but after that Jack became more and more silent. There was so very much at stake and now the moment of decision was so very near — hurrying and even racing nearer every minute. He grew exceedingly uneasy in his mind.

'I shall feel better after dinner,' he said to himself as the chaise turned off the Strand, rolled down into the Liberties of the Savoy and came to a halt at the Grapes, their accustomed inn.

Mrs Broad made them heartily welcome. Killick, travelling up on yesterday's night-coach, had given her warning, and she provided them with a dinner that would have soothed any reasonable man; but at this point Jack Aubrey was not a reasonable man. His mind was fixed on the possibility of unacceptable conditions or even downright failure and he ate mechanically, drawing no benefit from his food whatsoever.

'It is my belief the Captain has been called out, and is going to meet some gentleman in Hyde Park,' said Mrs Broad to Lucy, for Castlereagh's duel with Canning and some other slightly less notorious encounters were still very much in the public mind. 'He never even touched the pudding.'

'Oh Aunt Broad, what a terrible thing to say,' cried Lucy. 'But sure I never saw a man look so grim.'

Yet not so grim when he knocked on the door in Arlington Street as the St James's clock struck half past five, for now the action was engaged; the time of waiting was over; he was on the enemy's deck at last.

He gave the servant his card, saying, 'I have an appointment with his lordship.' 'Oh yes, sir, this way, if you please,' said the man, and led him to a small room opening directly off the hall.

'Captain Aubrey,' said Lord Melville, rising from behind his desk and stretching out his hand, 'let me be the first to congratulate you. We have sorted out this wretched business at last: it has taken far longer than I could have wished for — far, far longer than you can have wished, I fear — but it is done. Sit down and read that: it is a proof-sheet of the Gazette that is now printing off.'

Jack looked at the sheet with a fixed, stern expression. The ringed-round lines ran *May 15. Captain John Aubrey, Royal Navy, is restored to the List with his former rank and seniority, and is appointed to the Diane, of thirty-two guns.* He said, 'I am deeply sensible of your kindness, my lord.'

Melville went on, 'And here is your appointment to the *Diane.* Your orders will be ready in a day or two, but of course you already know the essence of the matter from Sir Joseph. I am so glad — we are so glad — that you are able to undertake this mission, with Dr Maturin to keep you company, for nobody could be better qualified in every way. Ideally, no doubt, you would bring those evil men Ledward and Wray back with you, but Mr Fox, our envoy and a man of great experience in Oriental concerns, tells me that this could not possibly be done without injuring our subsequent relations with the Sultanate. The same, and I say it with the deepest regret, applies to their frigate, the' — he looked into a folder on his desk — 'the *Cornélie.* Yet at least I most sincerely hope that the mission will frustrate and confound them, bringing them to utter and permanent discredit. And ideally you would be able to choose many of your own officers and midshipmen, but as you know time presses most urgently and unless you can catch the tail of the south-west monsoon Mr Fox may arrive to find the French in possession of a treaty. If you have any friends or followers within immediate reach, well and good — but this is a matter you will discuss with Admiral Satterley. I have made an appointment for you at nine tomorrow morning at the Admiralty, if that is convenient.'

'Perfectly so, my lord,' said Jack, who had recovered during Melville's steady, practised flow and who was aware of a grave — happiness is too slight a word — emotion filling his whole heart; though even now he found that he was crushing his appointment, grasping it with enormous force and ruining its folds. He smoothed it discreetly and slid it into his pocket.

'As for hands, Admiral Martin will I am sure do his very best for you, both because their lordships command it and because he has a great liking for you and Mrs Aubrey; but there again you know the difficulties he has to contend with. And lastly, as for Mr Fox, I had thought of arranging a dinner, but Sir Joseph thought it might be better, less formal, if you and he and Maturin were to invite him to Black's, to a private room at Black's.' Jack bowed. 'And speaking of that,' said Melville, glancing at the clock, 'I trust you will eat your mutton with us this evening? Heneage is coming and I can imagine his disappointment at missing you.'

Jack said he would be very happy, and Melville continued, 'There, I believe that is all I have to say as First Lord: the admirals will deal with the purely service aspects. But speaking as an ordinary mortal, may I say that my cousin William Dundas is bringing in a private bill on Wednesday to allow him to win some land from the sea. There is likely to be a very thin House, perhaps not enough for a quorum, so if you were to look in, and if you were to approve what he says — though it would diminish your watery realm by nearly two square miles — why, we should take it very kindly.'

No one but a man far more obtuse than Maturin would have had to ask the result of the interview as Jack came running upstairs, his papers in his hand.

'He did it as handsomely as the thing could be done,' he said. 'No humming and whoreing, no barking about the wrong bush, no God-damned morality: just shook my hand, said "Captain Aubrey, let me be the first to congratulate you" and showed me these.' Then, having chuckled over the Gazette again, observing that it would make poor Oldham, the post-captain who had stepped into his seniority, look pretty blank tomorrow, he gave Stephen a minute account of the conversation, the subsequent dinner — 'it went down remarkably well, considering; but I believe I could have ate a hippopotamus in my relief' — and the truly affecting behaviour of Heneage Dundas. 'He sends his very kindest wishes, by the way, and will look in tomorrow in case you have a free moment while he is in town. Lord, how pleased I was with the whole thing, and how pleased Sophie will be. I shall send an express. But,' he went on after a hesitant pause, 'I do rather wish Melville had not asked me for a vote, not just at that time.'

'A professional deformation, I suppose: politics and delicacy can rarely go together,' said Stephen, looking at the appointment again. 'But will I tell you something, brother? This is a most wonderfully auspicious date, so it is. On this same fifteenth of May, a Saturday if I remember but in any event just forty days before the Flood, Noah's grand-daughter Ceasoir came to Ireland with fifty maidens and three men. They landed I believe at Dun-na-Mbarc in the County Cork; she was the first person that ever set foot on an Irish strand, and she was buried at Carn Ceasra in Connaught, beside which I have often sat, watching the blue hares run.'

'You astonish me, Stephen: I am amazed. So the Irish are really Jews?'

'Not at all. Ceasoir's father was a Greek. And in any case they were all drowned in the Flood. It was not for close on three hundred years more that Partholan arrived.'

Jack reflected upon this for some little while, looking at Stephen's face from time to time; and then he said, 'But here I am prating away eternally about my own affairs; and I have never even asked what kind of a day you spent. Not a very pleasant one, I fear?'

'It is quite mended now, I thank you; your news would have mended anything. But I was put out, I confess. Indeed, I flew into a passion. I went to my bank and there I found that the dogs had carried out almost none of the instructions I had left with them nor those I had sent from Lisbon: there were even some small annuities still unpaid because of trifling informalities in my initial order. Then when I desired them to send a considerable sum in gold down to Portsmouth as soon as we were aboard they observed that gold was exceedingly hard to come by; that if paper money really would not answer they would do their best for me but that I should have to pay a premium. I pointed out that in the first place I had deposited a very much larger sum in gold with them, that it was absurd to expect me to pay for metal that was my own, and eventually I carried my point, though not without the use of some very warm expressions, such as the nautical *lobcock* and *bugger.*'

'Quite rightly applied too. I am sure I should never have been so moderate. Stephen, why do you not change to Smith, the brother of the Smith we dined with just before we left? For my part I shall never desert Hoare's because sooner or later they do everything I ask and because they treated me so well when I had no money at all; but still I do have an account down there with Smith because it is so convenient, particularly for Sophie. In your place I should cashier your lobcocks out of hand and place everything with Smith.'

'I shall do so, Jack. As soon as that gold is aboard the *Diane* I shall write them a letter in which every legal requirement is fulfilled three times over — I shall have it drafted by a lawyer. Come in.'

It was Lucy, sent to know what the gentlemen chose to eat for supper: Mrs Broad thought a venison pasty and an apple pie would be very lovely. Stephen agreed, but Jack said, 'Heavens, Lucy, I could not eat another thing today. Except perhaps for some of the apple pie, and a little piece of cheese. And Lucy, pray ask Killick to step up, if he is below.' A moment later Killick appeared, his eyes starting from his head, and Jack said, 'Killick, jump round to Rowley's, will you, and get a new pair of epaulettes. Ship them first thing tomorrow morning and have a hackney-coach waiting at half past eight. I have an appointment at the Admiralty. Here is some money.'

'So it's all right, sir?' cried Killick, his shrewish face suffused with triumph. He held out his hand and said, 'If I may make so bold. Give you joy, sir, give you joy with all my heart. But I knew it would be — I said so all along — ha, ha, ha! I told 'em all, it will be all right, mates. Ha, ha, ha! That'll learn the buggers.'

'Speaking of food,' said Stephen, 'will you come to Black's and dine with Sir Joseph and me and Mr Fox tomorrow at half five? That is to say, in your dialect, at half past four?'

'If I am through with the Admiralty by then, I should be very happy.'

'This is not an invitation, Aubrey; you are still a member, and must pay your share.'

'I know I am, and very handsome it was in the committee to write to me so; but I had sworn never to set foot in the place until I was reinstated. And the Gazette will be out tomorrow, ha, ha. I shall pay my scot with the greatest pleasure.'

In order to be through with the Admiralty by dinner-time, Jack Aubrey had first to get there, and at one point this seemed to present insuperable difficulties: a little after midnight Killick was brought back to the Grapes on a shutter, drunk even by the strict naval standards, being incapable of speech or movement, however slight. He had been tumbled in the mud; someone had plucked out a handful of his sparse pale hair; he had been partially stripped; his money had been taken away from him; he had no new epaulettes and those which he had carried as a pattern had disappeared.

Rowley did not live over his shop and no amount of hammering at the door could therefore rouse him, and the rival establishment was far over beyond Longacre, directly away from Whitehall. However, by dint of a great expense of spirit on Jack's part and of effort on that of the coach-horse he did arrive, very hot but properly dressed, in time for his appointment at the Admiralty; and there, in that familiar waiting-room, he had time to grow cool again and to relish the sensation of being in uniform once more. Sophie had been quite right: his white breeches and his blue coat were loose about the middle, where his paunch had been; but the coat and high stiff collar still sat perfectly well on his shoulders and neck, sustaining them in the most agreeable manner. There were few other officers there, and those few only single-epauletted lieutenants, who did not presume to say anything more than 'Good morning, sir,' to his 'Good morning, gentlemen', so presently he took up *The Times*. He opened it at hazard, and there leaping out of the page before him there stood the column from the Gazette, which, he found, could not be contemplated too often.

'Captain Aubrey, if you please, sir,' said the ancient attendant, and a moment later Admiral Satterley, having greeted Jack most cordially, with the kindest congratulations, explained the *Diane*'s present situation. 'She was given to Bushel for the West Indies and she was to sail next month. He has been offered the Norfolk Fencibles, which suits him tolerably well — his wife has an estate there — and which has this advantage, seeing we are so pressed for time: he can take almost no followers with him. He has a full gunroom and some capital warrant officers: the midshipmen's berth is short of experienced master's mates, however. I believe his stores are pretty well completed, but his complement was still sixty or seventy hands short when last I heard. Here is a list of his officers: if there are any alterations you wish to make, I will do what I can in the short time we have at our disposal; but in your place I should not make any sweeping changes. They have not been together long enough under Bushel to feel any jealousy at his suppression, and they all know who took the *Diane* in the first place and who has a natural right to her. But you study the list while I sign these letters.'

It was an informative list, with each officer's age, service and seniority. They were young men, upon the whole, with James Fielding, at thirty-three, the oldest and most senior of the lieutenants: he had been at sea for twenty-one years, ten of them with a commission, but most of his service had been in line-of-battle ships on blockade and he had seen very little action, missing Trafalgar by a week — his ship the *Canopus* was sent off to water and take in provisions at Gibraltar and Tetuan. The second lieutenant, Bampfylde Elliott, obviously enjoyed a good deal of influence, having been made well before the legal age; but he had seen almost no sea-service as an officer, since a wound received in the action between the *Sylph* and the *Flèche* had kept him ashore until this appointment. The third was young Dixon, whom he knew; and then came Graham, the surgeon, Blyth, the purser, and Warren, the master, all men who had served in respectable ships. The same applied to the gunner, carpenter and bosun.

'Well, sir,' said Jack, 'I have only two observations to make. The first is that the third lieutenant is the son of an officer with whom I disagreed in Minorca. I say nothing against the young man, but he is aware of the disagreement and he takes his father's part. It is no doubt natural, but it would not make for a happy ship.'

'Dixon? His father's name was Harte until he inherited Bewley, as I recall,' said the admiral, with a look that was not easily interpreted. Perhaps it was knowing, perhaps inwardly amused, conceivably disapproving; in any event Satterley was obviously aware that Aubrey was one of those who had made a cuckold of Captain Harte at Port Mahon.

'Just so, sir.'

'Have you any other officer to suggest?'

'I am somewhat out of touch, sir. Might I

have a word with your people and see whether one of my own young men is available?'

'Very well. But he will have to be within hand's reach, you know. What is your second observation, Aubrey?'

'It is about the surgeon, sir: Mr Graham. I am sure he is a very able man, but I have always sailed with my particular friend Dr Maturin.'

'Yes, so the First Lord told me. Mr Graham's appointment or removal, of course, rests with the Sick and Hurt Board, and although we could induce them to offer him another ship, it was thought that under the circumstances Dr Maturin should travel either as though he were taking up an appointment in let us say Batavia or as physician to the envoy and his suite, or even, if as I understand pay is of little consequence to the gentleman, as your guest.'

It was as well that Jack Aubrey walked into Black's quite a long time before his rendezvous with Stephen and Sir Joseph, for this was the height of the London season and the place was crowded with country gentlemen. But Tom the head porter, disengaging himself from a group with the usual country-gentleman's enquiries, emerged from his box and shaking Jack's hand said,

'I am right glad to see you again, sir. The club was not at all the same,' and a surprising number of members, some of whom he hardly knew, came up and congratulated him upon his reinstatement. It is true that some of them said they had always known it must be so, while others told him that *all was well that ended well,* yet still the sense of friendliness and support were extremely grateful, and although by now he was pretty well aware that the winning side was most widely applauded when the victory had become evident, he was much more moved than he would have supposed.

Sir Joseph and Stephen came up the steps together and Sir Joseph said, 'May I give you joy of your Gazette, or has the tide already risen higher than you can bear?'

'You are very good, Sir Joseph: many, many thanks. No, the tide cannot rise too high for me; I find I have a splendid appetite for the kindness of those I respect.'

They went upstairs and sat at a window in the Long Room, drinking sherry and watching the crowded street. 'I am just come from Westminster,' observed Jack, 'and do you know it took me nearly half an hour, there was such a press.'

'Was there anything afoot in the House?' asked Blaine.

'Oh no. It was just a string of private members' bills: very few people. I only went to see Dacres take his seat. So few people it was only just legal, and poor fellow he was in a sad bate, since he has to post away to Plymouth this evening. Yet even so three members asked me whether I would take sons or nephews as midshipmen. And when I go tomorrow I dare say the same thing will happen. It is astonishing how eager people are to get rid of their boys. Though perhaps not really so very astonishing, when you consider.'

'What did you reply?'

'I said I should be very happy, so long as the boy was thirteen or fourteen and had been at a mathematical school for at least a year; and provided he already knew enough about the sea to be some use. A new command with a ship's company you know nothing about and no schoolmaster is no place for little boys; they are much better off in a ship of the line, where at least they can act as ballast.'

'Your guest has arrived, Sir Joseph,' said a servant, and a few minutes later Blaine brought Mr Fox upstairs, a tall slim man, well dressed in the modern way — short unpowdered hair, black coat, white neck-cloth and waistcoat, shoes and breeches with plain buckles — rather good-looking, self-possessed, perhaps forty. He paid a particularly obliging attention to Sir Joseph's introductions and this favourable first impression was strengthened when they sat down to dinner in the smallest of the private rooms, a charming little octagon with a domed ceiling, and he said how happy he was to meet Captain Aubrey, whose capture of the *Cacafuego* in the last war had raised him to a pitch of enthusiasm exceeded only by the cutting-out of the *Diane*, and Dr Maturin, of whom he had heard so much from Sir Joseph. 'To a natural philosopher, sir, the islands of the South China Sea must present a vast wealth of nondescript plants and birds. Was you ever there?'

'Alas, sir, it was never my good fortune to sail farther east than the coast of Sumatra. But I hope to do better this time.'

'I hope so too, upon my word. I have a friend in those parts who is a great naturalist and he assures me that even the larger mammals are hardly known with any degree of certainty, that the Dutch scarcely knew anything of the interior of Java or Sumatra — were concerned only with commerce and took no scientific interest in the country at all — were in no way natural philosophers. He has wonderful collections and he spends what time he can spare from his official duties increasing them — but I am sure you know of him: Stamford Raffles, the Lieutenant-Governor of Java.'

'I have never had the happiness of meeting the gentleman, but I have seen his letters: Sir Joseph Banks has shown me several, some with dried specimens and admirable descriptions of plants and some with what seem to me most judicious suggestions for a living museum of natural history, a Kew on the faunal plane.'

'You would like him, I am sure. He is possessed of the most brilliant talents and an extraordinary fund of energy. I met him years ago in Penang when I was a member of the legislative council and he was in the Company's service: he worked all day and he read all night and between times he collected anything from tigers to shrew-mice. A great linguist, too. He was of the utmost help to me when I was enquiring into the spread of Buddhism — the arrival of Mahayana Buddhism in Java.'

'Dr Maturin and I were present when you read your paper at Somerset House,' observed Sir Joseph, and both Stephen and Jack, who had seen it in the *Proceedings*, took the opportunity to return Fox's civilities. The talk flowed steadily, and Fox spoke of naval affairs and naval politics as they were seen from the shore — spoke intelligently, with a great deal of information. It moved on to the *Surprise*'s unfortunate voyage, carrying Mr Stanhope to see another Malay sultan some years before, the voyage that had very nearly brought Stephen into the naturalist's Paradise beyond the Sunda Strait.

'Yes,' said Fox, 'I remember that mission well, one of Whitehall's less brilliant ideas — it would have been far better left to us: Raffles would have dealt with it on the spot, and poor Mr Stanhope would have been spared all that weary voyage and his fatal illness. It was absurd to send a man of his age; though to be sure, the King's representative, the Crown by proxy and entitled to a thirteen-gun salute, if I do not mistake?'

'Quite right, sir,' said Jack. 'Envoys have thirteen guns.'

'Entitled to a thirteen-gun salute, then, has to be a man of great family or' — smiling round the table — 'of towering parts.'

'He was a most amiable companion,' said Stephen. 'We studied the Malay language together, when he was well enough, and I remember his delight at the verb: no person, no number, no mood, no tense.'

'That is the kind of verb for me,' said Jack.

'Did you make much progress?' asked Fox.

'We did not,' said Stephen. 'Ours was a deeply stupid book, written by a German in what he conceived to be French. When Mr Stanhope's oriental secretary joined us in India he was as helpful as could be and I did acquire some rudimentary notions; but the voyage was too short. This time I mean to do better, and I hope to find a Malay servant from some East-Indiaman.'

'Oh,' cried Fox, 'there I can be of service, if you wish. My Ali has a cousin Ahmed who is out of a place, or about to be out of a place, a well-trained intelligent young fellow who was with a retired Straits merchant, Mr Waller: he died a little while ago. I should have taken him myself, but with my suite I shall have no room. If you wish I will tell Ali to send him round. I am sure Mrs Waller will give him a good character.'

'That would be very kind indeed; I should be most obliged to you, sir.'

'Speaking of suites,' said Jack, 'I do not know that it would be in order to discuss practical arrangements at this point, but before I go down to Portsmouth I should like to hear Mr Fox's views on numbers and messing, so that the carpenters and joiners can get to work at once; for there is not a moment to be lost.'

'Yet if Sir Joseph and Dr Maturin do not mind, perhaps we might deal with the question straight away,' replied Fox. 'For as you so rightly say, we cannot spare a minute. I have been in ships that try to beat into the north-east monsoon, having missed the south-west, and it is terribly wearing to the spirit, as well as being fatal to success in a case like ours.'

While these arrangements were being worked out, Stephen and Blaine, who were side by side, exchanged views on the wine they were drinking with their lamb, a delightful St Julien, and about other wines from the Médoc — the extraordinary variations in their price — the pitiful nonsense of most talk on the subject.

'So although I shall leave with only a secretary and a couple of servants,' said Fox, summing up, 'when we touch at Batavia, Raffles will find me two or three imposing but largely ornamental figures who, together with their servants, will counterbalance the French mission; and obviously I shall need room for them.'

'Pulo Prabang,' said Stephen after a pause. 'The name has been reminding me of two things ever since I first heard it, and now they are coming to the surface of what I facetiously call my memory. The first is that in your lecture, sir, you spoke of it as exhibiting some of the very few remains of Buddhism in the country of the Malays.'

'Yes,' said Fox, smiling. 'It is an exceedingly interesting place from many points of view, and I long to see it. The Sultan is of course a Mahometan, like most Malays; but like most Malays he is also far from zealous. And as one usually finds in those parts, he and his people retain many other pieties, beliefs, superstitions — call them what you please — and he would never, never disturb the Buddhist sanctuary at Kumai. Nor would anyone else: that would be the height of folly, sacrilege, and what is perhaps even more to the point, ill-luck for ever. The man who told me about the temple thought he could make out Hinayana influences, which would make it unique. Geologically the island is of great interest too, being the site of two ancient volcanic eruptions that have left vast and remarkably perfect craters, one by the sea, where the Sultan has his port, and the other high in the mountains. The second is now a lake, and by it stand the temple and the sanctuary. My informant says that the few monks come from Ceylon, but as our conversation was in French, a language neither of us spoke at all well, I may be mistaken; perhaps it was their rite that came from Ceylon. At all events I am quite sure Raffles said that the orang-utang and the rhinoceros were to be seen; and I believe he mentioned the elephant.'

'What joy,' said Stephen. 'And that brings me to my second point. Surely Pulo Prabang is the place to which van Buren retired when we took Java, is it not?'

'Van Buren? I do not think I recall the name.'

'Cornelius van Buren. Some people put him on a level with Cuvier; some even higher. In any case there is no greater authority on the spleen.'

'The anatomist? Of course, of course. Forgive me, my wits were astray: I am afraid I do not know what happened to him, but Raffles will certainly tell us.'

From the anatomist they went on to those who supplied anatomists with what Blaine pleasantly described as their raw material: resurrection-men, hangman's assistants, Thames watermen. 'There are also those who are on what is called the smothering-lay, men who entice benighted youths or countrymen who have had their pockets picked to a kipping-ken, and when they are

178

asleep, lay another mattress on them and lie upon it themselves, two or three together.'

From wicked men in general they passed to traitors in particular and then quite abruptly to Ledward; and both Jack and Stephen were astonished at Fox's passionate hatred of the man, the more so as their recent talk had been light, almost trifling. Fox was so moved that he spoke grossly — obviously an unusual thing with him, and oddly grating — turned pale and ate no more until the cloth was drawn and port and walnuts were on the table, and when the coming and going of servants necessarily changed the subject.

He recovered fairly soon, however; and they sat long over their wine, the decanter twice renewed and the dinner ending very cheerfully. He declined their invitation to go with them to a concert of ancient music — to his great regret he could not tell one note from another — thanked them handsomely for the pleasure, the very great pleasure, of their company and for his excellent dinner, and so took his leave.

While Jack was talking to a friend in the hall of the concert-room Stephen said to Blaine, 'There was another point I thought of raising but did not: I should have mentioned it to you long before. I trust I am right in supposing that there is no question of hierarchy, no question of relative rank, where the envoy and I are concerned?'

'Oh no. None whatsoever. It is perfectly understood that although Fox will ask your advice if any difficulties should arise, he is not required to follow it; on the other hand you are under no obligation to follow his recommendations either. There is nothing but a consultative nexus. He is in Pulo Prabang to conclude a treaty with the Sultan. You are there to observe the French; though naturally you will communicate any intelligence that may come into your possession and that may help him in his task.'

'Stephen, a very good morning to you,' said Jack, looking up from his letter. 'I hope you slept well?'

'Admirably well, I thank you. Lord, how I love the smell of coffee, bacon, toasted bread.'

'Do you remember a very horrible midshipman called Richardson?'

'I do not.'

'Spotted Dick they used to call him in the *Boadicea*: he had more pimples than were quite right even in the Navy. We saw him again in Bridgetown, Admiral Pellow's flag-lieutenant. He had quite lost them by then.'

'So we did too. A mathematician, as I recall. What of him?'

'He is on the beach, so I sent down to ask whether he would like to be third in the *Diane*. And here is his letter, overflowing with delight and gratitude. I am so glad. Now do you remember Mr Muffitt?'

'The captain of the *Lushington* Indiaman when we had our brush with Linois on the way back from Sumatra?'

'Well done, Stephen. He has made the Canton voyage God knows how many times and he knows the South China Sea intimately well, which I do not. I wrote to ask his advice and here' — waving another letter — 'he invites me down to Greenwich. He has retired from the sea, but loves to watch the ships go up and down the river.'

Mrs Broad came in to say good day and to bring more bacon and a dish of Leadenhall sausages, three of which Stephen instantly devoured. 'No one would think,' he said indistinctly through the third, 'that I had had a good dinner yesterday, and an excellent supper.'

'The club's port was the best I have drunk for years,' said Jack. 'Fox stood it remarkably well: never a tremor as he went downstairs, which is more than could be said for

Worsley and Hammond and some other members. What did you think of him?'

'Sure my first impression was good, and he is certainly an intelligent, knowledgeable man; but this impression did not last quite as well as I could have wished. He laid a great compliment on his speech, as though he wished us to love him; and perhaps he talked a little too much, as barristers so often do. But then until you know a man well it is hard to know how much to put down to nervousness, and it is a nervous thing to be outnumbered three to one. Sir Joseph, who is better acquainted with him, rates his abilities very high — likes him too, I believe. And it was pleasant to hear him speak with such generous enthusiasm of his friend in Batavia, Raffles.' He rang for more coffee, and pouring Jack a cup he went on, 'Few men like to be trampled upon, but it seems to me that some go too far in avoiding it, and try to assume a dominating position from the start or at least as soon as the first civilities are over. Dr Johnson said that every meeting or every conversation was a contest in which the man of superior parts was the victor. But I think he was mistaken: for that is surely wrangling or hostile debate, often self-defeating — it is not con-versation as I understand it at all, a calm amicable interchange of opinions, news, information, reflexions, without any striving for superiority. I particularly noticed that Sir Joseph, indulging in several of his masterly flashes of silence — rather prolonged flashes — remained quite obviously the most considerable man among us.'

Jack nodded and breakfasted on: he had now reached toast and marmalade, and when he had emptied the nearer rack he said, 'Years ago I should have thought he was a great man and excellent company. But I have grown more reserved since then — a cantankerous old dog rather than a friendly young one — and although he may indeed be a great man I shall not make up my mind till I know him better. You did not hear us arranging his accommodation in *Diane*? He has exactly Mr Stanhope's ideas of the importance of an envoy, the direct representative of the Crown. We shall mess separately, except for particular invitations, though the extra bulkheads will make clearing the ship for action a longer, more complicated affair. And, by the way, you have not told me how you prefer to travel, as physician to the envoy and his suite or as my guest.'

'Oh as your guest Jack, if you please. It would be so much simpler, and they can always ask for my services, if they need them.'

'I am sure you are right,' said Jack. 'Stephen, I am away to Buckmaster's in five minutes: my uniform no longer fits. Will not you come with me? You could do with a decent coat.'

'Alas, brother, I am taken up this morning. I have an interesting, delicate operation with my friend Aston at Guy's; and you will be at the House in the afternoon. But let us meet in the evening and go to the opera if Sir Joseph will lend us his box. They are playing La Clemenza di Tito.'

'I shall look forward to it,' said Jack. 'And perhaps tomorrow we will take a boat down to Greenwich.'

Stephen's operation went well, although throughout its not inconsiderable length the patient cried 'Oh God, oh Jesus, oh no no no, no more for God's sake. Oh God, oh God, I can't bear it,' the rapid flow of words broken by screams, for the frailty of his teeth and the state of his nose forbade the efficient use of a gag; and this Stephen found unusually tiring, so instead of calling on Sir Joseph Banks at Spring Grove as he had intended he sat in an easy chair by the window in his room at the Grapes and looked first for van Buren's essay on the spleen in primates (the zoological primates) in the *Journal des Sçavans* and found that it was indeed dated from Pulo Prabang. Then he searched back among those diaries he had preserved — some had been taken, sunk or destroyed — and he found that of the year in which he first met Jack Aubrey.

He had not used this particular code for a great while and at first it offered some difficulty; but in time he was reading fluently enough. 'Yes,' he said, 'even as late as that I was stunned entirely, I find — no feelings at all but sorrow, and even that a dull grey: music the only living thing.' He read on, going faster now and catching the mood of his former self not so much from the entries as from all the associations they brought back to vivid present life. 'Sure I have changed from the man who could speak such words to Dillon,' he said, 'but it is rather a recovery from an enormous blow, a reversion to a former state, than an evolution. The change in Jack is in fact more considerable, for even the most prescient eye could scarcely have seen the present Captain Aubrey in the wilful, indeed wanton, undisciplined Jack of those days, somewhat profligate and so impatient of restraint. Or do I exaggerate?' He turned the pages, running through his first contacts with naval intelligence — dear John Somerville, the fourth generation of a family of Barcelona merchants, a member of the Germandat, the Catalan brotherhood struggling against the Spanish, the Castilian, oppression of their country — the Catalans' hatred for the French armies that had burnt Montserrat and ravaged towns, villages, and even remote isolated mountain farms, destroying, raping, murdering — the Germandat's total refusal when in 1797 the Castilians deserted their English allies and joined the French — the appalling successes of Buonaparte's campaigns and Stephen's realization that the only hope for Europe was an English victory, which must be won at sea; and that this victory was a necessary condition for both Catalan autonomy and Irish independence. The diary recorded his connexion with Somerville after his early days in the *Sophie* and with Somerville's English chief, one of Blaine's best agents until his horrible death in France: recorded it in much too much detail, and though to be sure the code never had been broken some of the entries made him shudder even now. What insane risks he had run before he came to understand the true nature of intelligence!

Lucy brought him abruptly back to the present by knocking at the door and saying in a voice that showed neither pleasure nor approval that there was a black man downstairs with a letter for Dr Maturin.

'Is he a seaman, Lucy?' asked Stephen, his bemused mind turning to some one of the black members of the *Surprise*'s crew, now thousands of miles away.

'No, sir,' said Lucy. 'He is more like a native.' And leaning forward she added in a low tone, 'He has black teeth.'

'Pray bring him up.'

It was Fox's Ahmed; and although his teeth were indeed quite black from the chewing of betel, his face was only a moderate brownish yellow. At this juncture it wore an anxious expression, and he stood there bowing in the doorway, holding the letter in both hands. He was wearing European clothes and in many parts of the town, particularly down by the Pool or Wapping, he would have passed unnoticed; but the Liberties of the Savoy was not one of them. In fact legally it was not part of London or Westminster at all, but of the Duchy of Lancaster, and culturally it was a self-contained village, with no notion at all of natives, nor even of people from the Surrey side.

'Ahmed,' said Stephen, 'come in.' The

letter was a friendly note from Fox, saying how much he had enjoyed their dinner and enclosing a testimonial from Mrs Waller, who gave Ahmed an excellent character but said that he found England a little *cold* and *damp* in the winter, that he would probably thrive better on his *native heath* and that in any case she was obliged to reduce her household. 'I see,' said Stephen. 'Ahmed, how much English do you speak? And has Ali explained the situation to you?' Ahmed said he spoke little but understood more: Ali had explained everything. And on being asked when he could leave his place said, 'Tomorrow, tuan,' bowing again.

'Very well,' said Stephen. 'The wages are fifteen pounds a year: if that suits, bring your things here before noon. Can you manage your chest?'

'Oh yes, yes, tuan; Ali so kind with cart.' Ahmed bowed again and again, backed slowly to the door and even down the first few stairs, smiling as brilliantly as his dim teeth would allow.

'Now I shall have to calm Killick and Mrs Broad,' reflected Stephen. '*He* is likely to grow more shrewish than usual, and *she* is certain to think of human sacrifices and heathens running amuck: a difficult interview I foresee.'

★ ★ ★

It was indeed heavy going at first. 'Bears I have borne, sir, and badgers . . .' said Mrs Broad, her arms folded over a formal black silk dress.

'It was only a very small bear,' said Stephen, 'and long ago.'

'. . . and badgers, several large badgers, in the out-house,' continued Mrs Broad, 'but them black teeth fairly curdle the blood in your weins.'

Yet it being Dr Maturin, and since Mrs Maturin was quite used to black teeth in India, some days' trial were eventually conceded; and before the end of those days the Grapes' blood was flowing quite normally: Ahmed, always clean, sober, meek and obliging, passed in and out exciting no adverse comment, whereas by contrast Killick ashore was often something of a nuisance, always noisy and frequently drunk; and when at the end of their stay in London a cart came to carry them and the baggage to the Portsmouth coach Mrs Broad, Lucy and Nancy shook Mr Ahmed by the hand as well as Mr Killick, and wished him a prosperous voyage and a happy return; they would be very pleased to see him again.

Jack and Stephen had left earlier by post-chaise, and when they were clear of the town, the horses stepping out briskly, Jack said, 'I wish Tom Pullings were with us. He does so love riding in a chaise and four.'

'Where will he be by now, do you suppose?' asked Stephen. 'If they picked up the trades well north of the line, they might be somewhere near Cape San Roque: I hope so, I am sure. I hate to think of the *Surprise* rolling her masts out and spewing her oakum in the doldrums.' He shuffled among the papers on the seat beside him. 'Here are my orders — Admiralty orders, I am happy to say, so that if by any improbable chance we take a prize there will be no iniquitous admiral's third — and here is what Muffitt sent me this morning — most obliging of him — extracts from his logs in the South China Sea these twenty-five years past and more, charts, remarks on typhoons, currents, variations of the compass and the setting-in of the monsoons. It is extremely valuable, and it would be even more so if the Indiamen did not keep as close as they could to an established course from Canton to the Sunda Strait: they could hardly do otherwise in a sea that as far as anyone can tell is nowhere more than a hundred fathom water and generally less than fifty. A shallow, unexplored sea with volcanoes all round and therefore sudden unexpected shoals. It is not blue-water sailing at all, and as he frankly told me down at Greenwich they often prefer to lie to at night, or even anchor, which is easy enough in such modest depths.'

'A very sensible precaution too. I wonder everyone does not adopt it.'

'Why, Stephen, some people are in a hurry: men-of-war, for instance. It is no good carrying your pig to market and finding . . .' He paused, frowning.

'It will not drink?'

'No, it ain't that neither.'

'That there are no pokes to be had?'

'Oh well, be damned to literary airs and graces — it is no good hurrying as we have been hurrying these last few days and carrying your ship half way round the world, cracking on to make all sneer again, if you are going to balance your mizen all night once you are past Java Head. Lord, Stephen, I am quite fagged with running about London so. Pillar and post ain't in it.' He yawned, made some indistinct remarks about time and tide, and went to sleep in his corner, going out like a light — his usual habit.

He was bright awake however well before the chaise reached Ashgrove, and he gazed out at his plantations, now in finer leaf than when last he saw them, and at the rather stunted shrubs along the drive, with delight. He was expected, for the clash of the new iron gate could be heard a great way off, and with even greater delight he saw his family in front of the house, the children waving already. But as he jumped out he saw with concern that in spite of her welcome Sophie looked thoroughly upset, her smile constrained, her whole attitude anxious. Mrs Williams was looking very grave. Diana was taken up with telling Stephen about a horse. The children seemed unaffected.

'A dreadful thing has happened,' said Sophie as soon as she had him alone. 'Your brother — my brother, since he is yours, and I love him dearly' — Sophie, when moved, had a way of talking very quick, her words tumbling over one another — 'I mean dear Philip of course has run away from school and he declares he will go to sea with you.'

'Is that all?' cried Jack with great relief. 'Where is he?'

'On the landing. He dared not come down.'

Jack opened the door and hailed, 'Ho Philip, there. Come down, old fellow.' And when he came, 'Why brother, how glad I am to see you.'

'Give you joy, sir,' said Philip in a trembling voice.

'That is kind in you, Philip,' said Jack, shaking his hand, 'and it grieves me all the more to disappoint you. But this won't do, d'ye see? I cannot take my own brother as a youngster in a new command where I know none of the people and they know nothing about me. All the fellows in the midshipmen's berth and everybody else for that matter would put you down as a favourite at once. It would not do; upon my word it would not do. But do not take it too hard. Next year, if you mind your mathematics, Captain Dundas will take you in the *Orion*, I promise, a ship of the line. He has plenty of squeakers of your age — do not take it too hard.'

He turned away, because Philip was almost certainly going to cry, and Sophie said, 'There was a message from the Commissioner, asking you to call as soon as you could.'

'I shall write him a note at once. And another inviting poor Bushel of the *Diane* to dinner tomorrow. Or would that put you out, my dear?'

'Not in the least, my love.'

'Then please tell Bonden to stand by, dressed like a Christian, to go down with

Dray as soon as the letters are wrote.'

Jack knew very well that the Commissioner would have to confer with the Master Shipwright to put the Navy Board's order into just the right shape and indeed to start the urgent work even before the order had a formal existence: the highly-skilled confidential joiners who were to fashion places for the treasure had already come down — treasure which, combined with the envoy's less tangible offerings, would outweigh anything the French could provide; at least that was what the ministry hoped.

He had never met Captain Bushel, and his invitation was necessarily formal; but he put it in as friendly a manner as he could, hoping that it might make the supersession slightly less painful.

It appeared to have no such effect, however. Bonden brought back a note in which Captain Bushel regretted that a previous engagement prevented him from accepting Captain Aubrey's invitation: he ventured to suggest that Captain Aubrey should come aboard tomorrow at half past three o'clock. Captain Aubrey would understand that Captain Bushel, having introduced the officers, should prefer to leave the ship before his successor was read in.

The note came when Captain Aubrey

was deep in a very earnest game of speculation, the children hooting and roaring steadily. Philip had recovered his spirits; his niece Caroline was particularly kind in guiding his play, and his eyes sparkled as he piped his bids. At the moment Jack only took notice of the refusal and then carried on with his plot for undermining George, who had little notion of the laws of probability. But later he reflected that Bushel must be rather a pitiful fellow to resent his displacement to such a pitch. The previous engagement might possibly exist, but the total lack of any formal compliments or thanks for the invitation was churlish, while the appointing of a time was most incorrect, and the failure to offer a boat to take him out was shabby in the extreme. It would be perfectly in order for Jack to choose his own date and his own hour: he was senior to Bushel by several years. But although he had never been superseded himself he knew it was generally a most disagreeable process; perhaps so disagreeable in this case that it justified a high degree of resentment. 'Anyhow,' he said, 'I shall follow the scrub's directions.' And in a more inward voice, scarcely a whisper to his most private being, he said, 'Indeed, I should do anything short of slaughtering

Sophie and the children to be in my place again.' For although he had been gazetted and although his name was on the list, it was the symbolic and for the sea-officer quasi-sacramental reading-in that would pass the ring and marry him to the Navy once more.

They drove down all four in Diana's coach, with Killick and Bonden up behind — a sight that would have made London stare but that was usual enough around Portsmouth, Chatham and Plymouth — for after Jack had done his business with the Commissioner and had taken possession of the *Diane* they were to dine at the Crown and the women were to be shown the ship.

The Commissioner and Master Shipwright deeply relished anything in the secret line; they were as brisk and co-operative as could be — the confidential joiners' work would be masked by the alterations necessary for the envoy and his people — and when Jack said he was going across to the *Diane* the Commissioner immediately offered his own barge to take him.

The frigate was lying conveniently near at hand, just this side of Whale Island, and it was clear that Captain Bushel was still removing his belongings: boats were plying to and fro.

'Pull round her, will you?' said Jack to the coxswain, for there was still some time to go. 'Pull easy.'

He gazed at her with intense concentration, shading his eyes from the bright sunlight. Trim, shipshape, prettier than he had remembered her: she must have a good first lieutenant. A trifle by the stern, perhaps, but otherwise he could not fault her.

Two leisurely circuits and he looked at his watch again. 'Larboard,' he said, to avoid the awkwardness of the coxswain calling out *Diane* when her nominal captain was still aboard.

Up the side: man-ropes but no ceremony. He saluted the quarterdeck and every hat came off in reply, a simultaneous flash of gold.

'Captain Bushel?' he said, advancing with his hand held out. 'Good afternoon, sir: my name is Aubrey.'

Bushel gave him a limp hand, a mechanical smile, and a look of hatred. 'Good afternoon to you, sir. Allow me to name my officers.'

They came forward in turn: the first lieutenant, Fielding; the second, Elliott. 'My third, Mr Dixon, has been removed, and is to be replaced as I understand it by a person of your choosing,' said Bushel. Then the solitary Marine officer, Welby; Warren the master, a fine looking man; Graham the surgeon; the purser Blyth. They all looked gravely and attentively at him; and as he shook their hands he did the same by them. The little knot of midshipmen were not introduced.

As soon as it was over Bushel called out 'My barge'. It was in fact already hooked on to the starboard main-chains, with white-gloved side-boys waiting by the gangway stanchions, and in a moment the farewell ceremony was in train. With a rhythmic stamp and clash the Marines presented arms, all the officers attended him to the side, and the bosun and his mates sprung their calls. In some ships the crew cheered their departing captain: in this case the Dianes only stared heavily, some chewing on their quids, others open-mouthed, all completely indifferent.

When the barge was at a proper distance Jack drew his order from his inner pocket and handing it to the first lieutenant said, 'Mr Fielding, be so good as to have all hands called aft, and read them this.'

Again the calls howled and twittered: the ship's company came flocking aft along the gangways and in the waist and stood there, silent, waiting.

Jack withdrew almost to the taffrail, looking down at this strangely familiar quarterdeck, which he had last seen flowing with blood, some of it his own. In a strong voice Fielding cried 'Off hats', and to the bareheaded crew he read 'By the Commissioners for executing the office of Lord High Admiral of Great Britain and Ireland et cetera and of all His Majesty's plantations et cetera. To John Aubrey, esquire, hereby appointed captain of His Majesty's ship the Diane. By virtue of the power and authority to us given we do hereby constitute and appoint you captain of His Majesty's ship the Diane willing and requiring you forthwith to go on board and take upon you the charge and command of captain in her accordingly, strictly charging and commanding the officers and company belonging to the said ship subordinate to you to behave themselves jointly and severally in their respective employments with all due respect and obedience to you their said captain, and you likewise to observe and execute as well the general printed instructions as what orders and directions you shall from time to time receive from us or any other your superior officers for His Majesty's service. Hereof nor you nor any of you may fail as you will answer the contrary at your peril. And for so doing this shall be your warrant. Given under our hands and the seal of the office of Admiralty on this fifteenth day of May in the fifty-third year of His Majesty's reign.'

Chapter 5

'Amen,' said Captain Aubrey in a strong voice, echoed by two hundred and nine other voices, equally strong. He rose from the elbow-chair draped with a union flag, laid his prayer-book on the small arms-chest — decently covered with bunting like the carronades on either side — and stood for a moment with his head bowed, swaying automatically to the enormous roll.

On his right hand stood the envoy and his secretary: beyond them the forty-odd Royal Marines, exactly-lined rows of scarlet coats, white trousers and white cross-belts. On his left the sea-officers, blue and gold in their full-dress uniforms, then the white-patched midshipmen, six of them, four quite tall; and beyond, right along the quarter-deck and the gangways, the foremast hands, all shaved, in clean shirts, their best bright-blue brass-buttoned jackets or white frocks, the seams often adorned with ribbon. The Marines had been sitting on benches, the officers on chairs brought from the gun-room or on the carronade slides, the seamen on stools, mess-kids or upturned buckets. Now they stood in silence, and there was silence all around them. No sound came from the sky, none from the great western swell; only the flap of the sails as they sagged on the roll, the straining creak and groan of shrouds and dead-eyes and the double breeching of the guns, the working of the ship, the strangely deep and solemn call of penguins, and the voices, far forward, of the pagans, Mahometans, Jews and Catholics who had not attended the Anglican service.

Jack looked up, returning from whatever ill-defined region of piety he had inhabited to the anxiety that had been with him since he first saw Inaccessible Island that morning, far nearer than it should have been, in the wrong place, and directly to leeward. Three days and nights of heavy weather with low driving cloud had deprived them of exact observation; both he and the master were out in their reckoning, and this comparatively fine Sunday found them twenty-five miles south-east of Tristan da Cunha, which Jack had intended to approach from the north, touching for fresh provisions, perhaps some water, perhaps snapping up one or even two of the Americans who used the island as a base when they were cruising upon Allied shipping in the South Atlantic. A very slight anxiety at first, for although he had lain in his cot much later than usual — a long session of whist with Fox, and then half the graveyard watch on deck — and although Elliott, disregarding orders, had not sent to tell him until long after it had been sighted, the gentle air from the west was then quite enough to carry the ship clear of Inaccessible and up to the north-west corner of Tristan, where boats could land; and according to his reading of the sky the breeze would certainly strengthen before the afternoon. Yet even so, after hurrying through divisions he ordered church to be rigged on the quarterdeck rather than on the comparatively clement upper deck, so that he might keep an eye on the situation.

It was while they were singing the Old Hundredth that the breeze died wholly away, and all hands noticed that in the subsequent prayers the Captain's voice took on a harder, sterner tone than was usual on these occasions, more the tone for reading the Articles of War. For not only had the breeze failed, but the great swell, combined with the westerly current, was heaving the ship in towards that dark wall of cliffs somewhat faster than he liked.

He looked up from his meditations, therefore, said to his second lieutenant (the first being tied to his cot with a broken leg), 'Very well, Mr Elliott: carry on, if you please,' glanced at the drooping sails, and walked to the starboard rail. At once the pattern broke to pieces. The Marines clumped forward and below to ease their stocks and their pipe-clayed belts; the seamen of the larboard watch repaired, in a general way, to their stations, while the younger, more vapid starbowlines, particularly the landsmen, went below to relax before dinner; but the older hands, the able seamen, stayed on deck, looking at Inaccessible as intently as their captain.

'Well, sir,' said Mr Fox at his elbow, 'we have done almost everything that should be done in a sea-voyage: we have caught our shark — indeed a multiplicity of sharks — we have eaten our flying fishes, we have seen the dolphin die in glory, we have sweltered in the doldrums, we have crossed the Line, and now as I understand it we behold a desert island. And wet, grey and forbidding though it looks, I am glad to see solid land again; I had begun to doubt its existence.' He spoke in this easy way, standing by the Captain's side on a particularly sacred part of the quarterdeck, because church was now being unrigged: the bosun's mates were folding the perfectly unnecessary awning, and for the moment the quarterdeck, poised between two functions, no longer called for formality, secular or divine.

'Desert it is, sir,' said Jack, 'and likely to remain so. Its name is Inaccessible, and as far as I am aware nobody has ever succeeded in landing upon it.'

'Is it like that all round?' asked Fox, looking out over the grey sea. 'Those cliffs must be a thousand foot sheer.'

'It is worse on the other three sides,' said Jack. 'Never a landing-place: only a few rock-shelves and islets where the seals haul out and the penguins nest.'

'There are plenty of them, in all conscience,' said Fox, and as he spoke three penguins leapt clear of the water just by the mainchains and instantly dived again. 'So clearly we are not actually to set foot on our desert island. By definition, Inaccessible could not be our goal,' he went on.

'No,' said Jack. 'You may recall that yesterday evening I spoke of Tristan itself. If you look forward, just to the west — to the left — of the cliff, you can make out its snowy peak among the clouds, rather more than twenty miles away. It is quite clear on the top of the rise. And there is Nightingale away to the south.'

'I see them both,' said Fox, having peered awhile. 'But do you know, I believe I shall go and put on a greatcoat. I find the air a little raw. If there were any wind it would be mortal.'

'This is mid-winter, after all,' said Jack with a civil smile. He watched Fox walk off to the companion-ladder with scarcely a lurch in spite of the most uncommon roll — clear proof not only that he had an athletic frame and an excellent sense of balance but that he had been at sea without a break for some ninety degrees of latitude: never a sight of land since they cleared the Channel, Finisterre, Teneriffe and Cape San Roque all having passed in dirty weather or in darkness. Fox disappeared and Jack returned to his anxiety.

This had been an anxious voyage even before it began, with great difficulty in manning the ship in spite of Admiral Martin's good will, and the *Diane* had had to sail twenty-six hands short of her complement. Then there had come the heart-breaking weeks of lying windbound in Plymouth, eventually putting to sea in search of a wind the moment the weather allowed him to scrape past Wembury Point, but leaving so fast that he had had to abandon his surgeon and four valuable hands, they not having responded to the blue peter within the prescribed twenty minutes.

It was when they sank the Lizard at last, with a charming steady topgallant gale on the starboard quarter but with the plan of their voyage hopelessly disrupted, that Jack decided to go far south, keeping well over on the Brazil side for the current and the south-east trades to carry them down as quickly as possible to the forties, with their strong and constant westerly winds, leaving out the Cape of Good Hope altogether. He had long had the possibility in mind, and he had conned over Muffitt's logs, observations and charts. Now the shortage of hands seemed less disastrous, for given a moderately favourable run the *Diane*'s provisions should certainly last; and to deal with the problem of water he, the sailmaker, the bosun and the carpenter had contrived a system of really clean sailcloth, hoses and channels, easily shipped and designed to collect the rain that often fell in such prodigious quantities in the doldrums. The doldrums had behaved perfectly; the *Diane* had passed through the calms in little more than a week, picking up the trades well north of the line and running down for the forties touching neither brace nor sheet, hundreds and hundreds of miles of sweet sailing.

She had not reached them yet, though in thirty-seven degrees south she was on their edge. But, thought Jack, looking at the cliff that now stretched wide on either hand, unless he took measures fairly soon she would never reach them at all. There was no anchoring here: the bottom plunged to a thousand fathoms just off shore. And the swell was heaving the ship in, broadside on, at a knot and a half or even more.

He was extremely unwilling to wreck the people's Sunday, and they in their best clothes, particularly as no one had slept for a full watch these many nights past, all hands having been called again and again; but unless his prayers were answered by seven bells he would have to order out the boats to tow her clear — very severe work indeed, with this enormous swell.

'I beg your pardon, sir,' said Elliott, crossing the deck and taking off his hat, 'but Thomas Adam, sheet-anchor man, star-board watch, was here during the peace with another whaler: in a dead calm and in just such a swell their consort was heaved ashore and destroyed. He says the current sets east much stronger close inshore.'

'Pass the word for Adam,' said Jack, and Adam came aft at the double, a reliable mid-dle-aged seaman, now exceedingly grave.

He repeated his account, adding that the other whaler rolled her mainmast by the board as they were getting out a boat, and the ship was already in the kelp before they began trying to tow: he and his friends had watched from off the southern point, unable to help in any way. No one had been saved.

'Well, Adam,' said Jack Aubrey, shaking his head, 'if we do not have a breeze before seven bells we too shall lower down the boats; and I trust we may have better luck.' He looked at the sky, still full of promise, and scratched a backstay.

'Sir,' said Elliott in a low, strangely altered voice, 'I am very sorry — I should have reported it before — the carpenter found the garstrake and two bottom planks of the launch rotten under the copper, and he has taken them out.'

Jack instantly glanced at the boats on the booms. The jolly-boat was stowed inside the launch and the work was not at all apparent, but an informed eye saw it at once. 'In that case, Mr Elliott,' he said, 'let us get what boats we have over the side at once. And I should like a word with the carpenter.'

During all this time, that is to say from the end of divisions which as acting-surgeon he attended, Stephen had been sitting on a

209

paunch-mat, wedged between the foremast and the foretopsail-sheet bitts, gazing at the extraordinary wealth of life in, upon and over these waters: Port Egmont hens, Cape pigeons and four other kinds of petrel so far, the inevitable boobies, some prions, many terns and far, far greater numbers of penguins, some of which he could not identify at all. No great calm albatross hitherto, alas, but on the other hand the most wonderfully gratifying view of seals and fishes. The water was exceptionally clear, and as each unbreaking, untroubled wave of this prodigious swell rose and rose, towering above the ship as she lay in the trough, the inhabitants of the deep could be seen within it, seen with the utmost clarity, and seen *sideways*, going about their business, seen as though the observer shared their element. He sat there entranced, facing away from the island because the sun was now over the Tropic of Cancer and the light came from the north. Once Ahmed crept forward with a biscuit and said he would bring a covered mug of coffee if the tuan would like it; but otherwise there was no interruption at all.

He faintly heard the psalm; he was aware of the Sunday smells, pork and plum-duff, coming from the galley; and he had some notion that there were bosun's calls, vehement orders, the running of many feet. But piping, vehemence and running were commonplace in naval life and in any case his entire conscious attention was now wholly taken up with the most striking, moving and unexpected sight he had ever seen: as his eyes followed a penguin swimming rapidly westwards in the glassy wall rearing before him they met a vast shape swimming east. He instantly knew what it was but for a moment his mind was too astonished, amazed to cry out Whale! A whale, a young plump sperm whale, a female, slightly speckled with barnacles; and she had a calf close by her side. They swam steadily, their tails going up and down, the calf's faster than its mother's; and at a given moment they were on a level and even higher than his gaze. Then the ship in its turn rose, heeling on the crest, and they were gone, quite gone. Farther off he saw other whales spouting, but they were too far away; they belonged to the rest of the school.

Suffused with joy, he made his way aft through all the busy hands, their cries, their tight-stretched ropes, staggering on the roll and twice very nearly pitching into the waist. His expression changed when he saw Jack's face and heard him say privately, 'Stephen, you can do me an essential service: keep the civilians below, out of the way.'

He nodded and made straight for the companion-ladder. Fox and Edwards, his secretary, were just about to mount, but they stood aside to let him come down.

'I beg your pardon,' said Stephen. 'I have been banished. Apparently there is some manoeuvre toward for which the mariners require the deck quite clear.'

'Then we had better stay below,' said Fox. 'Would you like a game of chess?'

Stephen said he would be very happy. He was an indifferent player and he disliked losing; Fox played well and he liked winning; but this would keep the envoy quiet and in his cabin.

'It is curious that there should be little or no surf on that island with such a swell,' observed Fox, looking out of the scuttle as he fetched the board and men. 'We should surely see it from here. The island has come very much closer, in spite of the calm. Has the manoeuvre any connexion with it? Are we to confess our sins and make our wills?'

'I think not. I presume the activity has to do with our landing on Tristan. Captain Aubrey has promised a wind in the middle of the day, which is to waft us to the northern island. I look forward to it extremely; for among other things I hope to astonish and gratify Sir Joseph with some beetles unknown to the learned world. As to the surf, or rather its absence, the explanation, I am told, lies in a broad zone of that gigantic southern sea-wrack which some call kelp. Cook speaks of stems exceeding three hundred and fifty feet in length off Kerguelen. I have never been more fortunate than two hundred and forty.'

The game began, Stephen, who had the black men, following his usual plan of building up a solid defensive position in the middle of the board. Edwards, an obviously capable and intelligent young man, but unusually reserved, muttered something about 'a glass of negus in the gunroom' and sidled unnoticed out of the door.

Stephen's hope was that Fox, in attacking his entrenchments, would leave a gap through which some perfidious knight might leap, threatening destruction; and indeed after some fifteen moves it appeared to him that such an opening would come into existence if he were to protect his king's bishop's fourth. He advanced a pawn one square.

'Quite a good move,' said Fox, and Stephen saw, with real vexation, that it was fatal. He knew that if Fox were now to castle on his queen's side and attack with both rooks, black had no defence. He also knew that Fox would take some time before he made these moves, partly to check all the possible responses twice over and partly to relish the position.

Yet Fox delayed them three rolls too long. The board survived two unusually violent lurches as the ship entered the great kelp-bed, but at the third it slid off the table, scattering the pieces all over the cabin. As he helped to pick them up Stephen remarked, 'You are cleaning your Manton again, I see.'

'Yes,' said Fox, 'the lock is such a delicate affair that I do not like to leave it to anyone else. As soon as the sea grows more reasonable, we must go back to our competition.'

Fox had two rifles, as well as fowling-pieces and some pistols, and he was a remarkably good shot: better than Stephen. But although Stephen had little hope of improvement at chess he could outdo Fox with a pistol and he thought that with practice he might perform quite well with a rifle; hitherto he had used nothing but sporting guns and the usual smooth-bore musket.

'Do you think they have finished on deck?' asked Fox. 'There seems to be less trampling.'

'I doubt it,' said Stephen. 'Captain Aubrey would surely have sent a midshipman to tell us.'

Less trampling, no outcry, no sound but the furious working on the launch, the only voice that of the white-faced sweating carpenter with his 'I always said this coppering of boats was fucking nonsense. In course their fucking bottoms rot beneath it, never seen.' The whole being of all the others was fixed upon the boats, the ten-oared pinnace, the ten-oared cutter, the four-oared jollyboat and even the Doctor's personal skiff as they towed the ship, the rowers rising from the thwarts as they pulled, straining their oars to the breaking-point: the eyes of all but those who were labouring with such passionate zeal shifted now from the boats to the stark cliff of Inaccessible and now from the cliff to the ship's side to compare her forward progress with the sideways heave. The towing had begun quite well, but now that the ship had entered the binding weed, and now that the indraught of the current was stronger still it was clear that the boats were not pulling her ahead as fast as the swell was urging her inshore. There was only a quarter of a mile to go before the end of the cliff and the open sea beyond the island, but at this rate it was not possible that she should run that far before she touched. The anchors had been cleared away and they were hanging a-cockbill; but the lead gave no hope of a holding-ground — of any ground at all. And hands were stationed along the side with spars to boom off when the sheer rock was near enough; but that could not prolong the run more than a minute or so. Nearer; nearer with every enormous heave.

Jack gazed up at the top of the precipice. 'Mind your helm, there,' he called to the quartermaster with very great force, though the poor dazed man was within a few feet of him; and the nascent breeze he had seen stirring the grass up on that distant edge came breathing along the cliff-face. It moved the main topgallant and faded; it came again, nearly filling all three topgallants and the topsails; again, and they and even the courses bellied out. The ship distinctly gathered way, and cheering began.

'Silence fore and aft,' roared Jack. 'Man the braces.' And to the man at the wheel, 'Down with the helm.'

The carpenter came running from the waist. 'She'll swim, sir,' he said.

'Thank you, Mr Hadley,' said Jack. 'Mr

Elliott, get her over the side. Launch's crew away: jump to it, there, jump to it.'

They jumped to it indeed; but even pulling to crack their spines they could not make fast at the head of the tow before the ship, slanting away from that dreadful shore, had such motion on her that the hawser was slack.

'Mr Elliott,' said Jack, when the island was clear astern and the decks were filled with grinning men, laughing and congratulating one another as they worked in a general diffused sound of the most uncommon happiness, 'the course is north-east a half east. The hands may be piped to dinner as soon as the boats are in. Mr Bennett' — to a midshipman — 'pray tell Dr Maturin with my compliments that if he is at leisure I should like to show him the *north* side of Inaccessible.'

Jack Aubrey sat in what remained to him of the great cabin, contemplating not only the frigate's wake stretching away and away to the north-west, but also a variety of other things: the room, though now divided by a bulkhead running fore and aft for the accommodation of the envoy, was still a fine capacious place for one brought up to the sea, with enough space to contemplate a large number of subjects, and not only space but quietness and privacy in which to do so. Relative silence, that is to say, for the stays, shrouds and backstays were being set up again after the frightful stretching they had suffered off Tristan; and no one, least of all Jack Aubrey, could expect rigging to be set up without roaring and bawling: and Crown, the bosun, had a voice fit for a line of battle ship, a first-rate line of battle ship. Furthermore Fox and Stephen were still banging away at bottles, tossed overboard and allowed to go a great way astern; while at the same time Fielding, who had been allowed on deck in this easy quartering sea, stumped about on his crutches and plastered leg, making an odd resonant sound and calling out from time to time to any of the many hands aloft who might possibly spoil the blacking of his yards. But if things of this kind had worried Jack he would have run mad long since: he let them pass by his ears as the South Atlantic was now passing by the *Diane*'s gunports, in a smooth unnoticed flow, and he reflected upon the curiously hard fate of being unable to tell Sophie of their escape without at the same time letting her know of their danger. He had come upon this difficulty often enough in his correspondence with her, a correspondence that took the form of a serial letter that continued day by day until it could be sent, a fat bundle, by some homeward-bound chance encounter, or that was never sent at all but read aloud at home, with comments. Yet he had never come upon it so forcibly. The horror of that last cable's-length, with the ship moving with a nightmare inevitability to destruction, was still strong upon him, and he would so have liked her to share his immeasurable relief and present joy in living. He had written a watered version of the events, which he now looked over with no approval until he came to the words 'I was very pleased with the people; they behaved uncommon well' and to his praise of the ship. 'Of course, she is not the *Surprise*, but she is a fine responsive little ship, and I shall always love her for the way she took that breath of air off Inaccessible.'

She was not the *Surprise*: he had often taken the wheel and he had tried her with every conceivable combination of sails, and although she certainly proved a sound, dry, weatherly ship, carrying an easy helm, wearing and staying quick and lying to remarkably well under reefed maincourse and mizen staysail, she lacked that thoroughbred quality, that extraordinary manoeuvrability and turn of speed close-hauled. It was true that she also lacked *Surprise*'s vices, a tendency to gripe unless her holds were stowed just as she liked them, and to steer wild in any but the most skilful hands; the *Diane* was an honest, well-designed, well-built frigate (though he could not yet tell how she would behave in really very strong winds); but there was no doubt which ship he wholly loved.

That brought him to the second part of his contemplation. He had longed with all his being to be part of the Royal Navy again: now his name was on the list, and at this moment the familiar coat with its crown-and-anchored epaulettes was over the back of the chair by the scuttle, ready for his dinner with the envoy; and yet again and again he found himself regretting the *Surprise*. Not so much HMS *Surprise* but *Surprise* as a letter of marque, sailing where she pleased and when she pleased, carrying on her private and effective war against the enemy as she saw fit, with a ship's company of picked hands, some of them very old friends indeed, all of them thorough-paced seamen. With such men, with such a status, and with such a second-in-command as Tom Pullings, there had been an easiness that could never be found in a King's ship:

nothing approaching a democracy, God forbid, but an atmosphere that made the regular Navy seem formal, starched, severe, and in the article of pressing downright cruel. The foremast-hands were much too far removed from those in command; they were often very roughly treated by inferior officers; and one of the chief functions of the Marines was to prevent mutiny or on occasion to put it down by force.

The *Diane*'s crew were not very ill used in this respect, for upon the whole Jack was fortunate in his officers. By this time he knew them well: being perfectly able to afford it, he had reverted to the old and now declining naval custom of inviting the officer and midshipman of the morning watch to breakfast and those of the forenoon watch to dinner, often with the first lieutenant as well; while he usually accepted the gunroom's invitation to dine on Sundays. It is true that he did not invariably follow the custom, and that when he did his guests or hosts were unnaturally well-behaved, yet even so this contact, together with seeing them on duty, brought him acquainted with their more obvious qualities. Their defects, too; and tyranny was not one of them. Fielding and Dick Richardson were excellent seamen and they were both capable of driving a sluggish watch hard on occasion, but neither was in the least brutal; nor was Elliott, whatever other faults he might possess. Warren, the master, was a remarkable disciplinarian, a man of great natural authority, and he never had to raise his voice to be obeyed; while Crown, the bosun, was much more apt to bark than bite.

And in comparison with most captains he was reasonably fortunate in his men. At least half of them had been turned over from other ships before he came, and Admiral Martin had found him several quite good draughts; yet he had been in too great a hurry to sail for the news of his appointment to bring in many volunteers, and a quarter of the men had come by way of the press or some other form of compulsion, some having been bred to the sea, others never having set their eyes upon it at all. Still, this did give the *Diane* a better proportion of able seamen than most ships in her circumstances, and there were few really hopeless cases among the first-voyagers.

To begin with, naturally enough, the pressed men longed for their freedom, and during the enforced stay in Plymouth it had been difficult and in two cases impossible to keep the more enterprising or desperate from deserting; and even after the ship was well out in the ocean and there was no help for it many of them remained sullen and resentful. The landsmen and indeed some of the hands who had served under captains less taut than Aubrey particularly disliked his and the first lieutenant's insistence that hammocks should be exactly rolled, lashed up and stowed in the netting within five minutes of the bosun's pipe — an insistence implemented by the bosun's mates with sharp knives in their hands ready to cut the hammock-nettles and crying 'Out or down, out or down. Rise and shine, my beauties.' But by the Tropic of Cancer almost all of them, brought to it by degrees, could manage well enough; and by the Tropic of Capricorn they looked upon it as perfectly natural that a man should spring out of bed, whip on his clothes, roll his hammock and bedding into a tight cylinder lashed with seven turns, evenly spaced, and race up one or two crowded ladders to his appointed place. And by this time too each of the frigate's guns and carronades had a tolerably efficient crew, so that she could fire three quite well-directed broadsides in five and a half minutes. This was nothing like the *Surprise*'s deadly speed and accuracy, of course, but it was more than respectable in a newly-commissioned ship; furthermore, the thunder and lightning, the shattering din, the flashes and the smoke of real gunfire almost every evening at quarters which made this result possible were, in Jack's opinion, one of the main reasons that the ship's company had shaken down so well. The powder and shot over and above the Admiralty's absurdly meagre allowance had cost him a great deal of money, but he thought it very well spent; not only could the *Diane* now give a fair account of herself in any well-matched action but the costly, exciting and dangerous exercise brought first the gun-crews and then the whole body of the people very much together. The men delighted in the enormous noise, the power, the sense of occasion and of wild extravagance (it was said that two broadsides cost the Captain an ordinary seaman's pay for a year); they revelled in the destruction of targets and they cossetted their eighteen-pounders, squat iron brutes of close on two tons very apt to maim their tenders, with loving care, polishing everything that could be polished and painting their names above the port. One was called *Swan of Avon*, but *Belcher*, *Tom Cribb* and *Game Chicken* were more in the usual line. The ship's unvarying routine and the perils of the sea would have welded the Dianes into a right ship's company in time, no doubt, but the violent gunnery had certainly hastened the process, which was just as well in waters where a far-ranging enemy might be encountered any day. A decent set of men: they had behaved very well off Tristan. Yet even so there were still a good many who would run if they possibly could, and that was still another reason that he was glad to be going far south of the Cape.

The *Surprise* that he regretted had no pressed men, of course. Desertion never entered into consideration at all; in fact the only severe punishment he had ever had to inflict was turning men ashore for misconduct. And what was rather more to the point at this moment, she had no midshipmen either. The *Diane* had six young gentlemen in her midshipmen's berth, two of them, Seymour and Bennett, being master's mates. There were no really small boys, no squeakers under the gunner's care, but even so Jack's responsibilities — and he was a conscientious captain where his midshipmen were concerned, leaving little to Mr Warren the master — were quite varied. Since the ship did not carry a chaplain or a schoolmaster, Harper and Reade, the youngest, needed his help with spelling hard words and with fairly simple arithmetic, let alone the elements of spherical trigonometry and navigation; while Seymour and Bennett, near the end of their servitude, would pass, or try to pass, for lieutenants at the end of this year or the beginning of next and they were already growing anxious; they were very willing, even eager, to have the finer points of their profession explained.

It was they who were due at four bells, and as the second bell struck he heard them tap at the door, clean, brushed, exactly dressed, carrying the log-books and draughts of the journals they would have to produce, together with their captain's certificates of service and good conduct, at their examination.

'Sit down, both of you,' he said, 'and let me see your journals.'

'Journals, sir?' they cried: hitherto Captain Aubrey had been concerned only with their logs, which, among other things, contained their noon observations for latitude, their lunars for longitude, and a variety of astronomical remarks. Neither he nor any other of their captains had shown the least interest in their journals.

'Yes, of course. They have to be shown up at the Navy Board, you know.'

They were shown up now, and Jack

looked at what Bennett had to say about Tristan:

> Tristan da Cunha lies in 37°6'S and 12°17'W; it is the largest of a group of rocky islands; the mountain in the middle is above 7000 feet high and has very much the appearance of a volcano. In clear weather, which is rare, the snowy peak can be seen from 30 leagues away. The islands were discovered in 1506 by Tristan da Cunha, and the seas in their vicinity are frequented by whales, albatrosses, pintados, boobies, and the sprightly penguin, whose manner of swimming or as it were flying under water irresistibly brings Virgil's remigium alarum to mind. But, however, the navigator approaching from the west should take great care not to do so in a dead calm, because of the strong current setting east and the heave of the swell . . .

Seymour's journal, which had a drawing of Inaccessible with a ship scraping her yardarms against the face of the cliff, began:

> Tristan da Cunha lies in 37°6'S and 12°17'W; it is the largest of a group of

rocky islands; the mountain in the middle is above 7000 feet high and has very much the appearance of a volcano.

The sprightly penguin irresistibly reminded Seymour too of Virgil, and on reaching the remigium alarum Jack cried, 'Hey, hey, this won't do. You have been cribbing from Bennett.'

No, no, sir, they said with the utmost candour, for in spite of his stern expression they were perfectly convinced that he did not intend to mangle them. It was a joint production, with the facts taken from the Mariner's Companion and the style put in by — by a friend. But they themselves had worked out the position, and for the longitude they had had a particularly fine lunar according to the method he had shown them. There were several others, almost as good, in their logs, if he chose to look at them.

'Where is the style?' asked Jack, not to be diverted.

'Well, sir,' said Seymour, 'there is the sprightly penguin, for example, and the remigium piece, and later on there is the rosy-fingered dawn.'

'Well, no doubt it is very fine: but how in Heaven's name do you expect the examining captains to swallow two sprightly penguins, one after another? It is against nature. They will come down on you like a thousand of bricks and turn you away directly, for making game of them.'

'Why, sir,' said Bennett, the more ingenuous of the two, 'our names are so far apart in the alphabet that we cannot be called the same day; and everyone says the captains never have time to read the journals anyway, certainly not to remember them.'

'I see,' said Jack. The argument was perfectly sound. What really mattered in these cases was the severe viva voce about seamanship and navigation and then the young man's family, its status, influence and naval connexions. 'But still, the captains are not to be treated with disrespect, and in decency you must strike out the style when you copy your journals fair, make some changes in each, and keep to plain official prose.'

They turned to the moons of Jupiter, which might with profit be observed on St Paul's or Amsterdam islands, should they touch there, to fix their longitude with greater certainty; and when they had finished with the moons Jack looked at his watch, saying, 'I shall just have time to speak to Clerke. Pray send him aft.'

Clerke came within the minute, looking alarmed, as well he might, for Captain Aubrey's face now wore a look of strong and perfectly genuine disapprobation. He did not invite Clerke, a leggy youth with a still uncertain voice, to sit down but instantly said to him, 'Clerke, I have sent for you to tell you that I will not have the hands blackguarded. Any low scrub can pour out foul language, but it is particularly disagreeable to hear a young fellow like you using it to a seaman old enough to be his father, a man who cannot reply. No, do not attempt to justify yourself by blaming the man you abused. Go away and close the door behind you.'

The door opened again almost immediately and Stephen, equally clean, brushed and properly dressed, was led in by Killick, who had little notion of his punctuality or sense of fitness.

'Killick tells me that your dinner for the envoy is *today*,' he said. 'And Fielding is of the same opinion.'

'You astonish me,' said Jack, putting on his coat. 'I had the impression it was yesterday. Killick, is everything in hand?' He spoke with some anxiety, for he had had to leave his admirable cook Adi in the *Surprise*, and his replacement, Wilson, was apt to grow flustered when called upon for fine work.

'All in hand, sir,' replied Killick. 'Never you fret. Which I soused the pig's face myself, and one of the afterguard caught a fine great cuttlefish to start with, fresh as a daisy.'

Fielding came stumping in, looking pleased and well; he was immediately followed by Reade, the smallest, the least useful, but also the prettiest of the midshipmen, though now looking pale and drawn with hunger — he was ordinarily fed at noon — and they sat drinking madeira until Fox and his secretary arrived. Killick disliked the envoy and allowed him only four minutes before announcing, 'Dinner is on table, sir, if you please.'

Jack's dining-cabin was now also his sleeping-cabin, and sometimes Stephen's too, but naval ingenuity made little of stowing the cots and sea-chests on the half-deck, the Marine sentry perpetually on duty at the cabin door being shown how to cover them with a hammock-cloth in case of drifting spray. Six people, and more at a pinch, could be seated comfortably at the table, placed athwartships and gleaming with silver, Killick's pride and joy. Naval ingenuity was less able to deal with the two eighteen-pounder guns that shared the cabin, but at least they could be urged as far as possible into the corners, made fast and covered with flags.

It was one of these flags or to be more exact a long pennant kicked aside by Stephen as he took his seat on the envoy's right that was Killick's undoing. After the wholly successful soused pig's face, he brought in the monstrous cuttlefish, borne high on a silver charger, cried 'Make a lane, mates,' to Ahmed and Ali, standing behind their masters' chairs, and advanced to set it down in front of Jack. But his right foot trod on the pennant's end, his left caught in its substance, and down he came, flooding his captain with melted butter (the first of Wilson's two sauces) and flinging the cuttlefish to the deck.

'That was a lapsus calami indeed,' observed Stephen, when the dinner was in motion once again. It was a tolerably good remark, if taken on the bound, and like many of his tolerably good remarks it met with no immediate response whatsoever. But although Aubrey's coat, waistcoat and breeches were wrecked and Edwards had received a generous splash, Fox had been entirely spared by the melted butter; he had also gained a considerable moral advantage from the disaster and he could afford to dispense with a trifle of it. 'I do not think I quite follow you, sir,' he said.

'It is only a miserable little play on words,' said Stephen. 'This cuttlefish, which is a loligo, a calamary, has a horny internal shell like a pen, so very like that the animal is sometimes called a pen-fish. And as you will recall,' he added, speaking to his opposite neighbour, the midshipman, 'a lapsus calami is a slip of the pen.'

'I do wish I had understood at first,' said Reade. 'I should have laughed like anything.'

The dinner revived with an excellent saddle of mutton and reached its high point with a pair of albatrosses, stewed with Wilson's savoury sauce and accompanied by a noble burgundy. When they had drunk their port they returned to the great cabin for their coffee, and as they were sitting down Fox said to Stephen, 'I have at last routed out the Malay texts I spoke of. They are written in Arabic script and of course the short vowels are not shown, but Ahmed is familiar with the tales, and if he reads them to you please do not hesitate to mark the quantities. I will send them round as soon as our game is over.'

A little later Fielding took his leave,

leading Reade off with him: none too soon, for the boy's second glass of port, incautiously poured by Edwards as the decanter came round, was working in him: his face was cherry red, and he was growing unsuitably loquacious. The card-table was placed and their usual game of whist began, Jack and Stephen paired against Fox and Edwards.

Although they played for low stakes, Edwards being poor, it was severe, rigorous, determined whist; reasonably amiable too, with no ill-temper, no post mortems, for in this one instance Edwards, who was certainly the best player of the four, would not defer to Fox, nor was Fox overbearing; and since Jack and Stephen usually won more rubbers than they lost it was impossible for the other side to tell them what they ought to have done. They won no rubber this time, however. The first was in the balance, at one game all, when Fielding came in, looking grave, and said, 'May I speak to the Doctor, sir?' Macmillan, Graham's youthful mate, very much needed his advice in the sick-bay. Stephen went at once. He had taken Graham's place as a matter of course, Macmillan freely stating that his three months at sea did not fit him for such a charge; and although Stephen was reasonably well acquainted with seamen he was surprised to find how pleased they were. It was not only that Killick and Bonden had told them that he was not a mere surgeon but a genuine certificated physician, one that had been called in to treat the Duke of Clarence and that he had been offered the appointment of Physician to the Fleet by Lord Keith; nor only that he did not make them pay for medicines against venereal diseases (an unsound measure, he thought, one that discouraged a man from presenting himself at the earliest, more easily cured stage): it was the voluntary aspect of his labours that impressed them, and his wholly professional attention to his sick-bay and his patients. To be sure, he had inherited the former surgeon's cabin, which was convenient for his specimens and for nights when the Captain snored too loud; but that did not affect the matter at all, and they were touchingly grateful.

A message came back to the cabin: Dr Maturin's regrets, but he was unable to return; he was obliged to operate. If Mr Edwards wished to be present at an amputation, he should come at once, preferably in an old coat.

Edwards excused himself and hurried off. Jack and the envoy stayed, talking in a desultory manner about common acquaintances, the Royal Society, gunnery, the likelihood of heavy weather ahead, and of their private stores running out before the ship reached Batavia; and at the end of the first dog-watch (quarters having been put back for the Captain's feast) they parted.

The relations between Fox and Aubrey were curious; although their intercourse could no longer remain formal without absurdity (and clearly implied dislike) in so confined a space, with a quarterdeck sixty-eight feet long and thirty-two feet wide as the only place for exercise, it never reached cordiality, remaining at that stage of quite close acquaintance, governed by exact civility and small good offices, which it reached after the first fortnight or so.

It had not reached cordiality by thirty-seven degrees south in spite of the daily turmoil of clearing the ship for action at quarters; in spite of the gunfire, which interested the envoy to a remarkable degree; and in spite of more or less weekly dining to and fro, a good deal of whist and backgammon and a few games of chess; nor had it any immediate chance of doing so once the *Diane* reached 42°15'S and 8°35'W after a week of unexpectedly mild topgallant and even royal breezes.

The day broke clear, but when Stephen came on deck after having made his rounds of the sick-bay he noticed that Jack, Fielding, the master and Dick Richardson were looking at the sky in a very knowing manner.

'There you are, Doctor,' said Jack. 'How is your patient?'

Stephen had several patients, two with syphilitic gummata who were near their ends and some serious pulmonary cases, but he knew that to the naval mind only an amputation really counted, and he replied, 'He is coming along quite well, I thank you: more comfortable in his mind and body than I had expected.'

'I am heartily glad of it, because I believe all your people will have to go below presently. Look at the cloud just west of the sun.'

'I perceive a faint prismatic halo.'

'It is a wind-gall.

> Wind-gall at morn
> Fine weather all gone.'

'You do not seem displeased.'

'I am delighted. The sooner we are in the true westerlies the happier I shall be. They have been strangely delayed, but they are likely to blow most uncommon hard, we being already so far south. Ha, Mr Crown' — turning to the bosun, who stood smiling by the hances — 'we shall have our work cut out.'

The group broke up and Fielding asked whether he might look in on Raikes, the man whose leg Stephen had taken off. 'I have a fellow-feeling for him,' he observed as they walked along the lower deck.

'Well you may,' said Stephen. 'You were very nearly in the same boat, if I may use the expression.'

It was in fact the same injury, a broken tibia and fibula, caused by the same instrument, a recoiling gun, in Fielding's case when he was showing an inexperienced crew how best to handle their piece and the captain of the gun pulled the lanyard too soon, and in Raikes's because the forward breeching had parted, throwing the gun sideways. But Raikes's had been a compound fracture and after several promising days gangrene had set in, mounting with frightful rapidity, and the leg had had to go to save his life; whereas Fielding's was now quite well.

Jack had long since made his arrangements with the bosun and the sailmaker, and double preventer-stays, light hawsers for the mastheads and backstays were laid along, together with storm-canvas in large quantities; while Mr Blyth the purser and his steward had the Magellan jackets sorted in the sloproom, ready to serve out.

And Stephen had long since made his arrangements for a subsidiary sick-berth on the after-platform of the orlop deck, taking in part of the cockpit and part of the Captain's storeroom, which would be much less liable to flooding in the kind of seas to be expected in the high latitudes. It might seem less airy, and between the tropics it certainly would not do; but south of the fortieth parallel a trifling wind-sail would bring down all the air the most asthmatic patient could desire. He and Macmillan and their loblolly-boy William Low put the last touches to it that morning and then began transferring the patients, their messmates carrying them below in their hammocks with the utmost care.

He dined in the gunroom afterwards, as he often did, not as a guest but as of right. He liked most of the people: Spotted Dick Richardson was an old friend and Fielding a particularly agreeable companion; and once they had overcome a certain shyness of the Captain's guest the mess found he fitted in very well. It so happened that he was the only one among them who had been so far south — the others had served in the West Indies, the Baltic, the Mediterranean and even the African station, but never much below the Cape — and he spent much of the meal answering questions and describing the majestic seas of the fifties with a quarter of a mile, half a mile between their lofty crests.

'How tall would they be?'

'I cannot say the number of fathoms or feet, but very tall indeed — tall enough to hide a ship of the line; and we were becalmed between them. But when the wind blew even harder than usual their tops came curling over at the crest, sometimes tumbling down the slope in a white cataract, sometimes causing the whole prodigious mass to break in an utter confusion of shattered water, disrupting those that followed. It was then, I understand, that we were in the greatest danger of being pooped, and broaching to.'

'Dear me,' said the purser, 'that must have been a most uncomfortable situation, Doctor.'

'So it was too,' said Stephen. 'But an even greater danger was that of running into a mountain of ice. They are huge, in these waters, vast beyond all imagination, with what can be seen towering high and what can not spreading far out on either side, as perilous as any reef; they are invisible on a dark night, and even if they were not, one cannot steer as one chooses in such a preternatural blast.'

'But surely, sir,' said Welby, the Marine, 'they must be extremely uncommon, in the parts frequented by shipping?'

'On the contrary, sir,' said Stephen. 'We fleeted past scores, some of them an exquisite aquamarine blue in parts, with the surf raging against their sides, breaking mountains high; and we were partially crushed, almost sunk and quite disabled, our rudder torn off, by one that was reckoned half a mile across. This was in the *Leopard*, a ship of fifty guns.'

Twice that afternoon Stephen was called on deck, once to see a troop of grampuses, and once to be shown a startling change in the sea, which from a turbid, undistinguished glaucous hue had become clear, glass clear, and of that aquamarine colour which had come back to his mind when he spoke of *Leopard*'s iceberg: the rest of the time he spent in the cabin, speaking Malay with Ahmed or listening to him read from Fox's text. Ahmed was a gentle, good-natured, cheerful young man, an excellent servant, but far too deferential to be much of a teacher; he never corrected any of Stephen's mistakes, he always agreed with Stephen's stress on a word, and he went to infinite pains to understand whatever was said to him. Fortunately Stephen had a gift for languages and an accurate, retentive ear: Ahmed had rarely been called upon to exercise much ingenuity after the first few weeks, and by now they conversed with tolerable ease.

There was no beating to quarters that evening, which was unusual, and having attended to his patients in the last dogwatch, Stephen thought he would stroll on the quarterdeck and perhaps converse with Warren, the master, a well-informed and interesting man; but as he set foot on the ladder up from the orlop he was illumined by a flash of lightning so intensely vivid that its reflection pierced down hatchway after hatchway and along shadowy decks with such power that it dimmed the sick-berth lanterns. It was instantly followed by the most enormous and lasting clap of thunder, apparently breaking in the maintop itself. And by the time he had groped his way up to the gunroom bulk-head he could already hear the downpour, a rainstorm of prodigious violence.

'Come and have a look, sir,' cried Reade in great glee, checking his eager pace at the sight of the Doctor, 'I have never seen the like in all my time at sea. Nor has the master. Come along; I will fetch you a griego.'

Most of what Reade said was drowned by the thunder, but he urged Stephen up the ladder to the half-deck, fetched him a hooded watch-coat, and led him up to a total blackness filled with hurtling water, a blackness so thick that the bulwark could not be seen — nothing but a faint orange glow from the binnacle lights. But a moment later the entire horizon, clean round the ship, was lit by such lightning that everything stood out clear — sails, rigging, people, their expressions — the whole length of the ship, in spite of the rain. Stephen felt Reade pull his sleeve and saw his delighted face say something, but the continuous bellow of thunder covered the words.

Jack was standing by the weather rail with Fielding and he called Stephen over. Even his powerful voice, at close quarters, was somewhat overlaid, yet 'beats Guy Fawkes night' came through, and his smile, oddly cut by the intermittent flashes so that it appeared to spread in jerks, was quite distinct. They stood there with this stupendous display roaring and flashing for an indeterminate time and then Jack said, 'You are ankle-deep and in your slippers. I will give you a tow below.'

'Lord, Jack,' said Stephen, sitting and dripping in the cabin while Ahmed pulled off his stockings, 'a fleet-action must be quite like this.'

'Very like, but for the lack of smoke,' said Jack. 'Now listen, I shall be in and out till morning, waking you with my light, because it is likely to cut up rough, so you had better sleep below. Ahmed, see that the Doctor's cot is aired, and make sure that his feet are thoroughly dry before he turns in.'

Their Guy Fawkes night was as it were a gateway from one region to another totally different: in the morning the *Diane* was tearing away to the east-south-east at twelve knots through a confused tumbling sea with a great deal of white water on it but also an underlying pattern of long, consistent moderate swell, a cold, cold sea and a wind with a fierce bite to it; and there was enough north in the westerly gale to make her heel some twenty-five degrees.

A fair amount of water in the form of spray and odd packets came aboard, but nothing like enough to damp the galley fires or the appetites of the officer and the midshipman of the morning watch, Elliott and Greene, who breakfasted with the Captain. They were not Jack's favourite officers, but they had had a rough time of it since four o'clock when they relieved the deck, and in any case there must be no favouritism: he was perhaps a little less genial than he might have been with Richardson and Reade, but he plied them with porridge, eggs from his twelve worthy hens, with somewhat rusty bacon, toasted Irish soda-bread — Stephen's brilliant innovation — and marmalade from Ashgrove, the coffee coming in a succession of pots. Stephen watched them sitting there, all three haggard from their watch; and once again it occurred to him that it was not so much the iniquitous imposition of income tax that was causing the decline of this form of entertainment, but rather the boredom and the labour on the part of the host: by naval tradition Elliott could start no subject, and although as a well-bred man he made real efforts by way of response, he was no more gifted as a conversationalist than he was as a seaman; Greene, on the other hand, interrupted his steady eating only to say Yes, sir or No, sir.

'Now surely you will turn in, brother,'

245

said Stephen, when they had gone. 'You look destroyed.'

'Oh certainly: quite soon,' said Jack. 'But first I must take some readings for Humboldt; I have not missed a day yet, and it would be a pity to start now. Perhaps I will come down and tell you the temperatures at least. We can test the salinity later. Ho, Killick, there. Pass the word for my clerk, will you?'

Elijah Butcher had been expecting the call and he came prepared, muffled up to his ears, with an inkhorn in his buttonhole, the register under his arm, hygrometer, cyanograph and a variety of thermometers in his pocket, all cased, his bright black eyes and his bright red face eager for the fray.

'Mr Butcher,' said Jack, rising, 'good morning to you. Let us get under way.'

Jack did not come down. He sent Butcher to show Dr Maturin the temperature at the surface, and ten and at fifty fathoms, together with the hygrometrical readings and a message to the effect that Captain Aubrey was obliged to stay on deck.

Stephen had expected it, because he knew very well that this was the kind of sailing that Jack loved beyond any other; but he did not know how wholly the *Diane*'s captain would be absorbed in his task.

Jack had never really driven her before. The trades had been benign, regular, agreeable and steady, but always on the feeble side; they had hardly ever allowed him to log more than ten knots even with royal studdingsails abroad and the wind three points abaft the beam, which she liked best; and now he very earnestly wished to run off his easting as fast as ever he could make her fly. With the dear *Surprise* he knew exactly what sails would give her fifteen knots in these latitudes without straining, but he had little notion of what would suit the *Diane*. In winds of this force different ships behaved very differently on being driven; some would plunge their bows deep, shipping green seas that would tear aft; others would tuck down their sterns, and then the green seas, with a following wind, were worse by far; some might be sluggish, some might gripe, some might steer wild and even broach to with the very combination of sails that would make another fly.

As the *Diane* sailed south and south with even stronger winds, through even more tremendous seas, reaching forty-five degrees and then steering due east, he set about learning her true inner nature and her capabilities when she was pushed to the limit. This entailed many changes of sail, very exact trimming, very exact observation, and the closest watch on sheet and brace; but when the right set was found — they varied of course according to the amount of north or south in the great westerly winds, but they were variations on a single theme — there began a series of splendid days when she would run three hundred miles and more between noon and noon, and when Jack was rarely off the deck, appearing in the cabin only to eat or go fast asleep sitting in his elbow-chair.

This was splendid progress, the degrees of latitude passing in rapid succession; but for any but dedicated seamen the pleasure was intellectual only. This was the southern winter, the sky low and grey, the daylight sparse, the bitterly cold air filled with rain or sleet mixed with spindrift and atomized sea-water, the decks permanently awash. The cry of sweepers was no longer heard; there was no dust, there were no rope-shakings nor any hint of them, and the frozen afterguard could huddle in peace beneath the booms.

Stephen came up from time to time when neither rain nor flying spray was very severe to gaze upon the albatrosses that accompanied the ship, sometimes staying for days together. Most were the Diomedea exulans of Linnaeus, the bird he loved best of all that lived at sea, the great wandering albatross, an immense creature, twelve feet across or even more, the old cock-birds a pure snowy white with black, black edgings; but there were others that he could not identify with any certainty, birds to which the sailors gave the general name of mollymawks.

'Not nearly enough serious attention has been paid to the albatrosses,' he said to Fox, who had come to consult him about pains or rather general discomfort in his lower belly, difficulties with defecation, disturbed nights.

'Nor to the digestive system,' said Fox. 'If man is a thinking reed he is also a reed that absorbs and excretes, and if these functions are disturbed so is the first, and humanity recedes, leaving the mere brute.'

'These pills will recall your colon to its duty, with the blessing, and the diet I have prescribed,' said Stephen. 'But you will admit that it is whimsical to make distinctions between the lesser pettichaps and her kin, counting their wing feathers, measuring their bills, and to neglect the albatrosses, the great soaring birds of the world.'

'They are not the same pills as before?' asked Fox.

'They are not,' said Stephen with an easy conscience, for this time to the powdered chalk he had added the harmless pink of co-chineal.

Fox had consulted him quite often lately, and for a variety of disorders; but it had soon become apparent to Stephen that his trouble was loneliness. He was undoubtedly an able man — his account of the Malay rajahs and sultans, their intricate lines of descent, their connexions, feuds, alliances, past history and present policy was enough to prove that, without his profound knowledge of early Buddhism or current Mahometan law — but he had a strong, dominant personality and he had so crushed his retiring, unassertive secretary in everything except the matter of whist that the young man was no longer anything of a companion to him.

Yet although Fox might wish to be acquainted and even quite familiar with others, for his own part he did not choose to be known; he was unusually reserved. Then again there was a hint of condescension in his manner, a certain assumption of superior knowledge, status or natural parts, that prevented Jack and Stephen from looking forward to his company with very much pleasure.

Stephen had the impression that Fox thought the mission of very great consequence, in which he was probably right; and that the successful conclusion of it, the carrying home of a treaty, would gratify his ambition and self-esteem to the highest possible degree; but as well as this Stephen felt that he was more flattered by the office of envoy, and by its externals, than might have been expected in a man of his abilities. He never invited the officers, although they had been introduced to him; and if on the quarterdeck he asked them a question to do with the ship or gunnery he would listen to their explanation with a smile and a nod of his head that seemed to say that although he had not known these things the ignorance did not diminish him in any way — they were merely technical — an honnête homme was not required to know them.

In any case at this juncture neither Jack nor Stephen had any time to spare for social intercourse. Jack was taken up with sailing his ship and Stephen, quite apart from the preservation, classification and description of his Tristan da Cunha specimens, the rich harvest of extreme activity in a cruelly limited time on the lower parts of that scientifically unknown island, inhabited by numbers of nondescript cryptogams, probably several flowering plants (though this was the wrong season for them), a quantity of beetles and other insects, some spiders, and at least two peculiar birds, a finch and a thrush, and quite apart from his Malay, had his sick-berth to look after. A full sick-berth, for sailing a ship eastwards in the forties was a dangerous business at any time and more so in the winter, when numb hands had to grapple with frozen ropes high above the deck, while on the deck itself, in spite of the life-lines stretched fore and aft, a heavy sea might dash men against guns, bitts, the capstan and even on one occasion the belfrey. Strained, twisted joints, torn muscles, cracked ribs and yet another broken leg came down, together with rope burns, ordinary burns from the cook and his mates being flung against the galley stove, and of course disabling chilblains by the score — scarcely a watch without a majority of men who hobbled.

Yet it was not always foul weather. One morning after a day and a night of such a blast that the frigate could carry no more than a close-reefed maintopsail and forestaysail, Stephen, who had had little sleep until the changing of the watch at four, made his rounds late after a solitary breakfast in the gunroom. He was showing young Macmillan an expeditious way of fastening a cingulum for a hernia case when Seymour came in with the Captain's compliments, and when Dr Maturin was at leisure he might like to come on deck. 'You will need a watch-coat, sir,' he added. 'It is right parky up there.'

So it was; but the astonishment of the brilliant blue, the sunshine and the light-filled sails quite took the sense of cold away. 'There you are, Doctor,' cried Jack, who was wearing an antique Monmouth cap as well as a pilot-jacket, 'Good morning to you, and a very pretty one it is, upon my word. Harding, jump down to the cabin and ask Ahmed to give you a comforter to wrap round the Doctor's head: he will lose his ears else.'

'Heavens, what glory,' said Stephen, gazing about.

'Yes, ain't it?' said Jack. 'The wind hauled right aft in the morning watch, so we were able to spread more canvas. As you see, we have maintopsail, forecourse and spritsail; I hope for foretopgallant if it eases a little . . .'

The explanations continued, with some valuable remarks on scandalizing the foretopsail yard, but Stephen was taken up with piecing the elements of this stupendous scene into a whole. First there was the sky, high, pure and of a darker blue than he had ever seen. And then there was the sea, a lighter, immensely luminous blue that reflected blue into the air, the shadows and the sails; a sea that stretched away immeasurably when the surge raised the frigate high, showing an orderly array of great crests, each three furlongs from its predecessor, and all sweeping eastwards in an even, majestic procession. As each approached the *Diane*'s stern its high white-marbled face reared to the height of the crossjack-yard, threatening destruction; then the stern rose, rose, the deck tilting forward, the force of the wind increasing, and the crest passed smoothly along the side. A few moments later the ship sank into the valley between the waves, her view confined, her sails growing limp. To these there was added the sun, unseen for so long and unseen even now, since the topsail hid it, but filling the world with an almost tangible light. It flashed on the wings of an albatross that came gliding into the wind so close to the quarterdeck rail that it could very nearly be touched.

'There is our old friend,' said Stephen as the bird turned, heeling right over at ninety degrees and showing a gap in his right-wing primaries.

'Yes. He joined company just at daybreak. Lord, Stephen, such a sun-rise!'

'I am sure; and what a scene for the sun to rise upon! There are no less than six albatrosses and one giant petrel. Should we not tell Mr Fox and his secretary?'

'Oh, I sent to let them know and they came on deck for a while; but I am sorry to say a flaw in the wind brought a packet of sea aboard. It soaked them through and through, and they are gone below to shift their clothing. I doubt we see them again.'

Stephen observed a discreet general smile from one end of the quarterdeck to the other — discreet but for one ship's boy with a bucket of tow and sawdust for the helmsmen's hands who uttered a great horse-laugh and fled — and once more he reflected that the envoy had not succeeded in conciliating the Dianes' good will in spite of his admitted virtues: he had never at any time complained when the ship was cleared for action at quarters, really cleared, for Jack Aubrey was one of the few captains who insisted on a clean sweep fore and aft, which meant that his and Fox's cabins vanished, their contents being struck down below; and he had shown keen interest in the great-gun exercise, cheering the successful shots with real enthusiasm. But the seaman's traditional disregard for the landlubber, his scorn and even contempt, was here unmodified: possibly increased.

Cold it was, but he had known it colder south of the Horn; and presently the sun crept round the topsail, giving a perceptible warmth as well as the brilliance that transformed this blue sky and ocean into a perpetually renewed miracle. He watched the albatrosses as they glided effortlessly down the ship's side, crossed her wake, occasionally picking something from the surface, swept diagonally across the face of the advancing wave and so shot forward again at immense speed, breaking quarter of a mile ahead and turning to begin again. He stayed there entranced, sometimes beating his arms, sometimes exchanging a few words with the master, bell after bell, until the busy movement and the gathering of all the young gentlemen told him that the sun was about to cross the meridian and that those bearing quadrants or sextants were now going to take his height.

The ceremony followed its invariable course: Warren the master reported noon and 46°39'S to Richardson the officer of the watch; Richardson stepped aft from the bulwark, took off his hat and said, 'Noon and 46°39'S, if you please, sir,' his hair streaming forward in the wind.

'Make it twelve, Mr Richardson,' said Jack.

'Make it twelve, Mr Seymour,' said Richardson to the mate of the watch.

'Strike eight bells,' said Seymour to the quartermaster, who turned to the sentry at the cabin door and called out in a voice pitched to carry through the gale, 'Turn the glass and strike the bell.'

The Marine turned the half-hour glass, which he had been privately nudging from time to time to persuade the grains of sand to run faster, thus shortening his spell, and ran forward to the belfrey, helped by the wind. He struck the four double strokes and at the last Richardson said to Crown the bosun, 'Pipe to dinner.'

Now, from a silence as profound as the shriek of the wind in the rigging, the general omnipresent roar of the waters and the more immediate working of the ship would allow, there burst out a sound equal in volume to that of the lions in the Tower when about to be fed — loud coarse hoots of merriment, a rushing of feet to the mess-deck, a clashing of plates, kids and black-jacks on the hanging tables, and a bawling of mess-cooks waiting for their turn at the galley.

This Bedlam was so familiar to Jack

Aubrey that it acted as an aperitif, the more so as for the earliest, hungriest years of his naval life he, as a young gentleman, had also dined at this hour. His stomach gave a slight premonitory heave; his mouth watered: but these signs were cut short, abolished, by a cry from the lookout, humanely encased in a straw-lined cask at the masthead: 'On deck there . . .' The rest of his words were lost until the ship subsided into the trough of the wave, and then they came down clear: 'Mountain of ice on the starboard bow.'

Jack borrowed Richardson's telescope. As the ship rose he searched the south-eastern sea, and when the *Diane* was near the height of the rise he caught the ice quite near: nearer than he had expected and very much larger, a lofty mass with two peaks radiant green in the sun towering above the surf that broke to such an astonishing height on the western side.

He studied it for a while, altered course, not indeed to close the iceberg but to come within a mile, and passed the glass to Stephen, who, having stared hard for the space of three great upward heaves, most reluctantly handed it back again. 'I must go,' he said. 'I promised Mr Macmillan to be with him at noon; I am already late, and we have a delicate little undertaking in hand.'

'I am sure you will succeed,' said Jack. 'But even if you are delayed, I trust we shall meet at dinner.'

The only guest in the cabin that day was Richardson, and in his company Jack did not scruple to speak of the ship and her affairs. 'I believe we must edge away, once we have had a good look at the ice island,' he said. 'Perhaps I am mistaken, but it does not seem to me old ice at all. It may have come from behind Kerguelen, which is no great way off, and it may have a good many followers. We are well inside the northern limit. You have heard the drift-ice, Stephen, I am sure?'

'Would it be that rap, rap, rap?'

'Ay. There it is again.'

'I noticed it in the forenoon and I supposed it was the cooper or the carpenter or both; but then it occurred to me that they would hardly be working at dinner-time unless the ship were almost sinking, God forbid.'

'No. It is drift-ice. Fortunately we managed to ship a bow-grace, and it is not thick stuff. But even so it will do our copper no good.'

'Kerguelen is what some people call

Desolation Island, is it not, sir?' asked Richardson.

'So they do. But it is not *our* Desolation Island, which is smaller, farther south and east. And there is another in about fifty-eight south, to larboard just as you clear the Magellan Strait. I believe there are a good many places that have been called Desolation at one time or another, which is a pretty comment on a sailor's life. Not that our Desolation was so bad. I do wish you had been in the *Leopard*, Dick. Such fun we had, shipping a new rudder; and it was possible to make some capital observations — the prettiest triple fixing of our longitude by Jupiter's moons that you can imagine, each fix coinciding with the last and with a perfect lunar distance from Achernar.'

'And you would have been enchanted with the sea-elephants, leopard-seals, penguins, sheath-bills, blue-eyed shags, petrels and above all the splendid albatrosses on their nests. They were . . .' began Stephen, but he was interrupted by the changing of plates, the coming-in of the pudding, and he lost his thread.

'I fear this may be the last suet-pudding until we reach Batavia,' said Jack gravely. 'Killick tells me that the rats are grown outrageous bold in this freezing weather. So let us enjoy it while we may — damnably mouldy a hundred years hence.' A silence for the first slice of pudding, and then he said, 'But what I do not like about these ice-islands, quite apart from their sinking your ship under you, is that they seem to cause or at least to come before calms. When the poor old *Leopard* was stove we were in a fog, with scarcely enough air to stir the topgallantsails.'

After dinner they returned to the quarter-deck. The iceberg was now much nearer, and as the sun had moved westward its light was reflected from the many surfaces, showing not only the perfect green but also a broad band of that same pure light transparent aquamarine which Stephen remembered from the *Leopard*'s unhappy encounter. A wonderfully beautiful object, and now much more easily observable: but one to be observed from a distance. The vast mass was unstable; when both the ship and the iceberg lay in the same hollow of the sea, the ice a mile away on the frigate's beam, the watchers saw one of the peaks, the size of a spired cathedral, lean and fall and shatter, its huge component parts crashing down the slope to join the great blocks and minor bergs nearby and sending up vast jets of white seawater as they did so.

Stephen was standing just on the gangway, where a convenient stanchion allowed him to rest his telescope. He was not on the holy quarterdeck; and since all those who had ever been his patients felt that on neutral ground they were entitled to speak to him he was not surprised to hear a deep rumbling West-Country voice close to his ear saying, 'There you are, sir: just on the quarter you may see what we calls a Quaker.' Stephen looked, and there, poised on the wind like its betters, was a small undistinguished shabby brown albatross, Diomedea fuliginosa. 'We calls him a Quaker because he is dressed modest.'

'A very good name too, Grimble,' said Stephen. 'And what do you call the other one?' — nodding towards a giant petrel just beyond.

'Some says bone-breaker, and some says albatross's mate, but most says Mother Cary's goose. Goose, sir: not chicken. Her chickens you could put a dozen in your pocket.' A pause, and in a lower tone, 'If I may make so bold, sir, how does our Arthur come along?'

Arthur Grimble was one of the syphilitic gummata cases: Stephen and Macmillan had operated to relieve the pressure on his brain. 'The next few days will tell,' said Stephen. 'He is in no pain now, and he may recover. But do not tell his friends to be very hopeful: it was a last resort. And if he goes, he goes easy.'

'No,' said Captain Aubrey to the master, a few feet away. 'I am afraid it is not possible.' He had been looking hungrily at the blocks of ice, all pure fresh water, floating no great way off, sometimes half a mile from the parent island.

'Not in this sea, sir,' said Warren. 'But was we to lie to for a while it would surely moderate. The surf on the island is a good third less than it was before dinner.'

Jack nodded. He looked at the oncoming waves: their tall crests were no longer being torn off so that flying water raced before them. 'Mr Bennett,' he said, 'jump up to the masthead with a glass and tell me what you see. Take your time and report to me below. Doctor, will you join me in a pot of coffee?'

They were at their second cup when Bennett knocked on the door. 'I am sorry to be so dishevelled, sir,' he said. 'I had made my hat fast with a piece of marline, but it absolutely parted — white marline, too. I began right astern, sir, and made the sweep, but nothing did I see until one point on the starboard bow, where there was a mountain of ice, much the same size as this, about four leagues away; then three more smaller ones another point south. From the white water I thought there were some little islands after them, but I could not be sure of anything until I had come round to about due south, and there, stretching from the beam to the quarter, there were four, evenly spaced, three leagues off.'

'Thank you, Bennett,' said Jack. 'Have a cup of coffee to warm you.' And when he had gone, 'Alas, it will not do. I had hoped for a few more days of this glorious run. But it will not do. Although we are still too far west, I shall have to edge away. How I wish I had never spoken of calm: the wind has been dropping steadily ever since I said it.'

'Perhaps your unwilling mind had already perceived the signs but refused to acknowledge them. How often have I not said "Ha, it is six months since I had a cold", only to wake up the next day streaming and incapable of coherent speech?'

'What an unfailing source of cheer and encouragement you are, upon my word, Stephen. A true Job's muffler if ever there was one. And since you have now drained the pot I shall go on deck and change course. At least we shall be able to shake out a reef or two.'

A few minutes later Stephen heard pipes and the running of feet, cries of 'Belay, belay', and the frigate heeled as she brought the wind one point on her quarter, heading north-east.

The few movable objects in the cabin lurched across to starboard and Stephen, clinging to the arms of his chair, said, 'He may say what he pleases, but I am convinced the ship is travelling faster than ever: the water fairly shrieks along the side.'

Yet the next day the heel was less, though the *Diane* now had a fine spread of canvas abroad — indeed she had sent up her topgallantmasts in the hope of spreading more. It lessened progressively, strake by strake; and by the day young Grimble was buried the ship scarcely heeled at all.

Even so, for the convenience of his Tristan collections Stephen continued sleeping below, and on the Thursday after their meeting with the ice he walked into the gunroom for breakfast. 'Good morning, gentlemen,' he said, taking his place. 'Mr Elliott, may I trouble you for the pot?' And gazing about the table he added, 'I see we have come out in splendour once more,' for his eye had been caught, as it could scarcely have failed to be caught, by the mizenmast. In the *Diane,* as in almost all frigates, it was stepped on the lower deck, in the middle of the gunroom itself, the table being built round it; but in the *Diane*, and this was unique in Stephen's experience, some loving French hand had encased the mast with brass from the shining table-top to the beams, and had caused the brass to be covered with the best gold leaf. Ordinarily this glory was concealed by a sleeve, fitted to protect it from the lady of the gunroom, a very stupid, very obstinate, very deaf old man who always polished everything metal with a wire brush; and it blazed out only on Sundays or particular feasts.

'Yes,' said the purser. 'We killed our last pig the day before yesterday, and we have invited the Captain to dinner.'

Stephen was about to say that the Captain had a funeral-service that morning, but reflecting upon the Navy's attitude towards death — in battle the mortally wounded were often thrown overboard — he did not. Instead he observed that the ship's progression now seemed charmingly smooth, 'with little or none of the wild bounding about we have endured these many, many days, and unless I mistake almost no heel at all. I set my cup down with little anxiety.'

'Not above a couple of strakes,' said Fielding. 'But then, Doctor, we are out of the forties, you know.'

The gunroom was of course quite right. Jack Aubrey had been present at too many of these occasions to be deeply affected by the burial of a hand he scarcely knew; yet as they always did the words of the service moved him — *My soul fleeth unto the Lord: before the morning watch, I say, before the morning watch* — and so did the earnest attention with which the ship's company followed them, and the grief of the dead man's friends. '. . . *our dear brother here departed, we therefore commit his body to the deep,*' he recited in his deep grave voice, and Arthur Grimble's messmates slid him gently over the side, sewed into his hammock, with four roundshot at his feet.

He was not *deeply* affected, and he enjoyed his roast pork with the gunroom; yet even so the ceremony had cast enough of a damp on his spirits to make the modest conviviality of these dinners something of an effort. After it, having drunk the usual toasts and returned proper thanks, he paced out his usual moderate-weather three miles on the windward side of the quarterdeck, two hundred and forty turns fore and aft. Moderate weather, for they had quite suddenly passed into a new world, a world of smooth seas and uncertain winds. And their passage had been unfortunate: the *Diane* had barely reached thirty-nine degrees before the failing remains of the western breeze veered into the north-east and headed her; and now there was this most unlucky omen. Furthermore he had the gravest doubts about Amsterdam Island. His charts all agreed in laying down its latitude as 37°47'S but they differed by well over a degree in longitude: most unhappily his two chronometers had also chosen this moment to disagree, and as the covered skies had not allowed him to make a lunar observation since they met the iceberg he was now obliged to steer for the mean of the recorded longitudes with the help of the mean of the times shown by the chronometers. This would never have been a satisfactory pursuit or one calculated to soothe an anxious mind, and now the breeze made it worse by obliging the *Diane* to sail close-hauled. She was a good honest sea-boat going large, but close-hauled she was heavy, slow, inclined to gripe, and unwilling to come up closer than six and a half points at the best.

'I cannot possibly afford to run down the latitude,' he said to Stephen that evening, 'but at least I derive some comfort from the fact that the island's peak can be seen from twenty-five leagues away. But it is of no great consequence.'

'I am sorry you should think it of no consequence,' said Stephen sadly.

'I mean from the point of view of water. We are not very short, and even if we do not have the usual downpours under Capricorn, it would only mean going on short allowance for a week or two, provided the southeast trades blow with even half their usual force. Yet if we can but hit upon the island, why, I should be very happy to put you ashore for an hour or two while the boats make a few voyages. You did say there was plenty of water, did you not?'

'Certainly I did. Péron, my castaway, fairly revelled in it. He admitted it was a little awkward to come at, but I cannot suppose naval ingenuity likely to be baffled by awkwardness; and I am not master of words to tell you, Jack, the value of an exceedingly remote island to a naturalist, an uninhabited fertile volcanic island covered with a luxuriant vegetation, with no vile rats, dogs, cats, goats, swine, introduced by fools to destroy an Eden, an island untouched; for although Péron spent some time on it, he scarcely left the shore.'

'Well, I could wish the weather were less thick; but we shall keep the sharpest lookout and reduce sail at night. I have little doubt we shall raise it on Tuesday or Wednesday.'

On Wednesday they did raise it. At first light they were within five miles of that unmistakable peak: a spectacularly successful landfall after five thousand miles of blue-water sailing, even without the uncertainties of chart and chronometer. But most unhappily they were directly to leeward, carried past in the darkness by a brisk westerly breeze and a powerful current setting east, in spite of close-reefed topsails and the keenest looking-out.

'We shall never fetch it, sir,' said the master. 'It is right in the wind's eye, and with this current we could ply all day and never get any nearer. I will make my affidavit it is laid down at least a degree too far west even in the Company's chart.'

'Have you checked your water again, Mr Warren?' asked Jack, leaning on the taffrail and gazing at the distant cone, as clear as could be in the dying breeze.

'Yes, sir. Even without rain under the tropic I reckon we should do without much short allowance; and whoever passed under the tropic line without a deluge?'

'How I shall ever tell the Doctor I do not know,' said Jack. 'He was so set upon it.'

'So he was, poor gentleman,' said the

master, shaking his head. 'But haste commands all; and perhaps all these mollymawks and albatrosses will be some comfort to him. I never saw so many all together. There's a whale-bird. Two nellies; and a stink-pot.'

'Stephen,' said Jack, 'I am very sorry to tell you I have made a cock of your island. It lies astern, directly to windward of us. We cannot beat back with this breeze and current and if we were to lie to waiting for the wind to change we should lose days that we cannot afford to lose; we must pick up the south-east trades as soon as possible, if we are to reach Pulo Prabang with the tail of the monsoon.'

'Never grieve, soul,' said Stephen. 'We shall go there at our leisure in the *Surprise* once that Buonaparte has been knocked on the head. In the meantime I shall look at the master's birds: I should never have expected to see a stink-pot so far from the Cape.'

The *Diane* spread her royals for the first time since she reached this hemisphere and stood away to the north-east, studdingsails aloft and alow; but all day long the peak of Amsterdam Island remained in sight, a small cloud marking its top.

It had gone in the morning, however, and later in the day the sea-birds vanished with it. Jack, making his observations for Humboldt, noted so unusual a change of temperature at the surface and at ten fathoms that he checked his readings twice before calling them out to Butcher.

A new world: and now that they were thoroughly into it all the old pattern fell into place again; and the ship's routine, disrupted by the violent, perilous race eastward through sixty degrees of longitude, soon became the natural way of life once more, with its unvarying diet, the cleaning of decks before full daylight, the frequent call for sweepers throughout the day, the piping of all hands to witness punishment on Wednesdays (reprimand or deprivation of grog; no flogging so far in this ocean), the ritual washing of clothes and the hoisting of clothes-lines on Mondays and Fridays, quarters every weekday with a certain amount of live firing still, mustering by divisions on Sunday, followed sometimes by the reading of the Articles of War alone if the inspection had taken longer than usual, but more often by church. It was a comparatively easy life for those who were used to it, but literally and figuratively it was desperately slow: no more tearing along with everything on the point of carry away, the sea creaming along the side, filling the ship with a deep organ-noise, clear beneath the shriek of the harp-taut rigging, no more fifteen knots and better, with the reel almost snatched from the ship's boy's hand, no more of the wartime friendliness of shared excitement and danger. Now it was a matter of repairing or replacing everything that had been broken or strained, of painting, scouring, and above all sailing the ship north-east in light and variable airs, often contrary, so that jibs and staysails called for perpetual attention; and even when they did reach the south-east trades they were found barely to deserve their name, either for strength or constancy.

Day after day they travelled slowly over a vast disk of sea, perpetually renewed; and when, as the *Diane* was approaching Capricorn at four knots, Captain Aubrey ended church with the words 'World without end, amen,' he might have been speaking of this present voyage: sea, sea, and then more sea, with no more beginning and no more end than the globe itself.

Yet this mild, apparently eternal sameness did leave time for things that had been laid aside or neglected. Jack and Stephen returned to their music, sometimes playing into the middle watch; Stephen's Malay increased upon him until he dreamt in the language; and as his duty required Jack resumed the improvement of his midshipmen in navigation, the finer aspects of astronomy and mathematics, seamanship of course, and in these both he and they were tolerably successful. Less so in their weakest points, general knowledge and literacy.

Speaking to young Fleming about his journal he said, 'Well, it is wrote quite pretty, but I am afraid your father would scarcely be pleased with the style.' Mr Fleming was an eminent natural philosopher, a fellow member of the Royal Society, renowned for the elegance of his prose. 'For example, I am not sure that *me and my messmates overhauled the burton-tackle* is grammar. However, we will leave that . . . What do you know about the last American war?'

'Not very much, sir, except that the French and Spaniards joined in and were finely served out for doing so.'

'Very true. Do you know how it began?'

'Yes, sir. It was about tea, which they did not choose to pay duty on. They called out *No reproduction without copulation* and tossed it into Boston harbour.'

Jack frowned, considered, and said, 'Well, in any event they accomplished little or nothing at sea, that bout.' He passed on to the necessary allowance for dip and refraction to be made in working lunars, matters with which he was deeply familiar; but as he tuned his fiddle that evening he said, 'Stephen, what was the Americans' cry in 1775?'

'*No representation, no taxation.*'

'Nothing about copulation?'

'Nothing at all. At that period the mass of Americans were in favour of copulation.'

'So it could not have been *No reproduction without copulation?*'

'Why, my dear, that is the old natural philosopher's watchword, as old as Aristotle, and quite erroneous. Do but consider how the hydra and her kind multiply without any sexual commerce of any sort. Leeuenhoek proved it long ago, but still the more obstinate repeat the cry, like so many parrots.'

'Well, be damned to taxation, in any case. Shall we attack the andante?'

Fox too resumed his earlier way of life. A murrain among his remaining livestock put an end to their dining to and fro, since he would not accept invitations that he could not return, but they still played a certain amount of whist and ever since the weather had turned fair, set fair, he made his appearance on the quarterdeck twice a day, walking up and down with his silent companion in the morning and often shooting against Stephen, now a fairly even match, in the afternoon, especially when the sea was smooth and the bottle could be made out a great way off; and he returned to his frequent medical consultations.

On the Friday after they passed under Capricorn, for example — passing, whatever the master might say, without a drop of rain, although purple-black clouds could be seen far in the west, with torrents pouring from them — he sent a ceremonious note asking whether he might impose upon Dr Maturin's good nature yet again that afternoon. Stephen had long since decided that if they were to remain on reasonably good terms and co-operate effectively in Pulo Prabang they must see little of one another in these conditions of close confinement; he was also convinced that Fox's complaint was no more than intellectual starvation and a now very great hunger for conversation at a certain level — he must have been an unusually sociable or at least gregarious man on shore. But, he reflected as he now sat in the sun on the aftermost carronade-slide with a book on his knee, he could not in decency refuse his professional advice.

Both Jack Aubrey and Fox were taking their exercise before dinner, Jack on the windward side of the quarterdeck and Fox and Edwards, who had learnt the sanctity of naval custom early in the voyage, on the other; and from his seat Stephen could survey them both. Once again his mind turned to the question of integrity, a virtue that he prized very highly in others, although there were times when he had painful doubts about his own; but on this occasion he was thinking about it less as a virtue than as a state, the condition of being whole; and it seemed to him that Jack was a fair example. He was as devoid of self-consciousness as a man could well be; and in all the years Stephen had known him, he had never seen him act a part.

Fox, on the other hand, occupied a more or less perpetual stage, playing the role of an important figure, an imposing man, and the possessor of uncommon parts. To be sure, he was at least to some extent all three; but he would rarely let it alone — he wished it to be acknowledged. There was nothing coarsely obvious or histrionic about this performance; he never, in the lower deck phrase, topped it the knob. Stephen thought the performance was by now almost wholly unconscious; but in a long voyage its continuity made it plain, and on occasion the envoy's reaction to a real or imaginary want of respect made it plainer still. Fox did not seek popularity, though he could be good company when he chose and he liked being liked; what he desired was superiority and the respect due to superiority, and for a man of his intelligence he did set about it with a surprising lack of skill. Many people, above all the foremast hands of the *Diane*, refused to be impressed.

The frigate carried no trumpeter, but she had a Marine with a fine lively drum, and upon this, the moment four bells had been struck, he beat *Heart of Oak* for the officers' dinner. All those who were at liberty to go below hurried off, leaving Jack almost alone; he had no guests that day, and he paced on and on, his hands behind his back, thinking deeply. At five bells — for Jack dined earlier than most captains — he started out of this reverie, caught Stephen's eye and said, 'Shall we go down? There is the last of the sheep called Agnes waiting for us.'

'She was also the last of the flock,' he observed as Killick took the bare bones away and Ahmed changed the plates. 'We shall be down to ship's provisions tomorrow, salt horse and soaked over the side at that, because we must cut the fresh water ration. None to be spared for the steep-tubs, none for the scuttle-butt, none for washing. I shall tell the hands; and I shall turn them up for dancing this evening by way of consolation.'

When they were alone with their coffee Stephen, after a long brooding pause, said, 'Do you remember I once said of Clonfert that for him truth was what he could make others believe?'

Lord Clonfert was an officer who had served in the squadron Jack commanded as commodore in the Mauritius campaign, a campaign that had been fatal to him. He was a man with little self-confidence and a lively imagination. Jack spent some moments calling him to mind, and then he said, 'Why yes, I believe I do.'

'I expressed myself badly. What I meant was that if he could induce others to believe what he said, then for him the statement acquired some degree of truth, a reflection of their belief that it was true; and this reflected truth might grow stronger with time and repetition until it became conviction, indistinguishable from ordinary factual truth, or very nearly so.'

This time there was in fact something wrong with Mr Fox. Stephen could not tell what it was, but he did not like either the look or the feel of his patient's belly, and since Fox was somewhat plethoric he decided to bleed and purge him. 'I shall put you on a course of physic and a low diet for a week, during which you must keep your cabin. Fortunately you have your quarter-gallery, your privy, just at hand,' he said. 'At the end of that time I shall examine you again, and I think we shall find all these gross humours dissipated, this turgid, palpable liver much reduced. In the meantime I will take a few ounces of your blood; pray let Ali hold the bowl.'

Ali held the bowl; the blood flowed, fifteen ounces of it; and Stephen was touched to see its surface dappled by the young man's silent tears.

For the first few days Fox was in serious discomfort, sometimes in considerable pain, for the rhubarb, hiera picra and calomel worked powerfully; but he bore it well, and on his brief visits Stephen was surprised to find the plain uncomplicated Fox he had known only when they were shooting from the taffrail and he was wholly taken up with pointing his beautifully-made weapon and watching for the strike of his bullet. Nor was he at all fretful with his attendants, as invalids, particularly liverish invalids, were so apt to be. But Stephen had noticed his kind treatment of Ali, Yusuf and Ahmed long before this: there was of course a particular relationship where Ali was concerned, yet it appeared to Stephen that the Malayan context might be of more importance. For one thing the language required a very nice discrimination of status, there being whole series of expressions for the various ranks to use to one another, and those towards the top of the hierarchy were constantly kept in mind of it. 'But quite apart from that,' he reflected, 'perhaps he would be more at his ease in Malaya. It is, after all, his native heath.'

Edwards, the secretary, was free much of the time during Fox's physicking, and it was pleasant to see how he blossomed. He grew much more closely acquainted with the officers; he often dined or supped in the gunroom, where he was thought a valuable addition; and during Stephen's visits to the envoy's cabin he could be heard laughing on the quarterdeck. But his freedom could not last. At the end of the week Stephen examined Fox, pronounced him well, and said that he might walk for half an hour on deck, but that his diet must still be moderate. 'No beef or mutton,' he said automatically.

'Beef or mutton? Good Heavens, I am not likely to overindulge in either. I should have had nothing at all but pap if Ali had not preserved some aged fowls; and what I shall do when they are gone, I cannot tell.'

'The ship's salt beef is not unpalatable,' Stephen observed.

'It is scarcely human diet, surely?'

'Two hundred of our shipmates live upon it.'

'The iron guts of harvesters,' said Fox with a smile. 'No doubt they would prefer it to caviar.'

Remarks of that kind always irritated Stephen, a revolutionary in his youth, above all when they were applied to the lower deck, whose qualities he knew better than most men. He was about to make a sharp reply but he thought better of it and kept his mouth tight shut. Fox went on, 'I wonder whether this voyage is ever going to end. Do you know where we are?'

'I do not. But I should not be surprised if we were within a hundred miles or so of land. For these last few days I have seen increasing numbers of boobies, and on Tuesday two Indiamen were reported from the masthead, sailing from west to east. And I am told that we have succeeded in catching the tail of the monsoon, weak though it be.'

'What a satisfaction. And yet, do you

know, Maturin, after all these hours of lying here I have come to the conclusion that there is something not displeasing in this solitude, perpetual travelling, perpetual confinement, remoteness from all society, cares, activity . . . If reasonable food were forthcoming, I am by no means sure that I should wish it ever to come to an end. There is a great deal to be said for suspended animation.' He paused, staring at the bulkhead, and then he said, 'I wonder if you know the author of the lines I have ventured to translate

When the bells justle in the tower
The hollow night amid
Then on my tongue the taste is sour
Of all I ever did.'

From Fox's tone it was evident to Stephen that this was the preliminary to a confidence, a confidence prompted not by any high degree of friendship or esteem but by loneliness and a desire to talk. From the nature of the verse it was reasonably certain that the confidence would be of a somewhat scabrous nature, and Stephen did not wish to hear it. Restored to society, cares, activity and his usual environment, Fox would undoubtedly regret having made it; he would resent Stephen's knowledge of his intimate life, and that would make working together in Pulo Prabang far more difficult. Collaboration and indifference might agree; collaboration and resentment could scarcely do so. He said, 'I do not know the author. Can you remember the original?'

'I am afraid not.'

'It cannot be an ancient: the pagans, as far as my reading goes, were never much given to self-hatred or guilt about their sexual activities. That was reserved for Christians, with their particular sense of sin; and as "all I ever did" clearly refers to ill-doing, I must suppose it to be of a sexual nature, since a thief is not always stealing nor a murderer always murdering, whereas a man's sexual instincts are with him all the time, day and night. Yet it is curious to see how the self-hater often succeeds in retaining his self-esteem in relation to others, usually by means of a general denigration: he sees himself as a worthless creature, but his fellows as more worthless still.'

As a check to unwanted confidences this was effective, but Stephen had added the last words in another spirit, following his own reflection, and the effect was too harsh by far. He saw with regret that he had wounded Fox, who, with an artificial smile, said, 'Oh, I quite agree,' and went on to a very proper speech of thanks for Dr Maturin's great kindness in looking after him and for his great skill in curing a most disagreeable complaint. He was sorry to have been such an importunate nuisance.

'Where is the moral advantage now?' Stephen asked himself, walking along the half-deck to the companion-ladder. 'Heavy stupidity, incomprehension would have been much better.' He was just about to climb up it when a boy came hurtling down, took a great leap to avoid him, missed his footing and fell flat.

'Are you quite well, Mr Reade?' he asked, picking him up.

'Quite well, sir, thank you. I beg pardon for tumbling about, but the Captain sent me to tell you we have sighted Java Head. Java Head, sir! Ain't it prime?'

Chapter 6

It was quite true: within two days of being immersed in eastern ways, climate, food, languages, faces, expressions, and forms of civility Fox was a different man, a more agreeable one.

While the *Diane* was refilling all her water-casks except for half a dozen in the ground-tier at Anjer, and taking in wood, stores, livestock, arrack and tobacco, together with river-water to wash the salt out of their harsh and rasping clothes at last, he took Jack and Stephen to Buitenzorg, the country residence, and presented them to the Governor, Stamford Raffles.

Fox was proud of Raffles, and understandably so; he was a singularly accomplished and amiable man, and they both found their opinion of Fox change when they saw how the Governor valued him. Raffles at once invited them to stay, lamented the numerous dinner-party to which they were necessarily condemned that afternoon, but promised that they should sup in private; and perhaps between the two meals Dr Maturin might like to see a little of his garden and his collections. 'For if I do not mistake, sir, you are the gentleman to whom we owe Testudo aubreii. And, good Heavens, now I come to reflect, perhaps the Captain is that glorious reptile's godfather? What a delight to have two such famous names under our roof at the same time! Olivia, my dear . . .' But before Mrs Raffles could be made aware of her happiness urgent official messages came in, requiring the Governor's attention before dinner, and the visitors were taken to their rooms.

The dinner was indeed a very grand affair, the guests seated with exact regard to precedence, for the Javanese and Malays, of whom there were several present, were even more particular about rank than the Europeans. The Sultan of Suakarta was on the Governor's right, then came two major-generals, then Jack, the senior naval officer present, and a long way farther down Stephen sat between the captain of a recently-arrived East Indiaman and a civil servant. Fox was at the other end, on Mrs Raffles' right. Stephen's neighbours had been talking eagerly as they came in, and now, as they sat down, the civil servant on Stephen's right said to him, 'I was just telling my cousin here that he must not worry about the news from London. These things are always exaggerated by distance, do you not agree, sir?'

'Certainly truth is hard to come by, near or far,' said Stephen. 'But what is the gentleman not to worry about? Is it said that London is burnt again, or the plague broken out? And surely he would have noticed these things before leaving — he would have brought the news himself.'

'Why, sir,' said the sailor, 'the people here are all talking about the great losses on the Stock Exchange, the Funds falling to pieces and banks breaking right, left and centre, particularly country banks. It is all since I left Blackwall.'

'It may seem curious to you, Doctor,' said the civil servant, 'that we should have had the news before the Indiaman's arrival; but such is the case, for the Company sometimes has overland messengers travelling down at a great pace across the Arabian desert and Persia. The latest word is not three months old. But as it always happens, the latest word is much deformed by rumour. Rumour loves to make its hearers' flesh creep, and as soon as the Stock Exchange sinks a little rumour swears the bottom of the market has fallen out; yet it takes an even greater delight in breaking banks. In my time I have seen all the great houses brought down, Coutts, Drummonds, Hoares, the whole shooting match. Believe me, Humphrey, there is nothing in it; and I speak as the Governor's financial adviser.'

When they were drinking coffee in the long, cool, shadowy drawing-room, Jack came over and said in an undertone, 'By God, Stephen, how I hope you did not take my advice about money. I have just heard two damned unpleasant things: the first is about the City, and about a run on the banks. It seems that many have stopped payment, and that many country houses are broke: Smith's was particularly named. The second is that the French have already reached Pulo Prabang; they are there first, in spite of all our efforts.'

Before Stephen could reply his left-hand neighbour at dinner came to say good-bye, and on seeing Jack he claimed acquaintance; he had been aboard one of the Indiamen in whose company Captain Aubrey, commanding the *Surprise* even then, had engaged a French line-of-battle ship and a corvette and had obliged them to withdraw. By the time he had finished fighting the battle over again the room was almost empty, and the Governor claimed

Dr Maturin. 'It is rare,' he said, 'to have anyone who will look at my collections as anything but a raree-show.'

'Banks would enjoy this beyond anything,' said Stephen, stopping before an astonishing group of orchids growing from trees, crevices, baskets or the ground itself. 'He is very much more of a botanist than I. He showed me some of your drawings of the vanilla . . .'

'There is the very plant. A friend sent me a root from Mexico, and I hope to naturalize it. The insignificant green thing in a hanging raft.' Raffles broke off a piece of seed-pod and gave it to Stephen, who bowed, smelt to it, and continued '. . . with the utmost appreciation, and yet with a certain regret. He saw so little when he was here in the *Endeavour*.'

'I am afraid he must have been in a sad way; but even if he had been able to get about, he would have had to go very far to acquire anything like a true notion of the flora. There was nothing worth calling a botanical garden in those days. The Dutch looked upon the island with a commercial rather than a philosophical eye.'

'Certainly few Dutch naturalists come to mind. Apart from van Buren, of course, for the fauna.'

'To be sure, and he is a constellation in himself. I am so sorry he is no longer here; we were great friends. But you will no doubt meet him in Pulo Prabang, where, as I understand it, you mean to accompany Edward Fox.'

'I shall look forward to it. But am I mistaken in supposing that he withdrew from Java because of the British conquest of the island?'

'Quite mistaken, I am happy to say. We are excellent friends. He dislikes Bonaparte as much as we do, like so many of the Dutch officials who are now working with us. His removal was settled upon well before our arrival, primarily for the sake of Mrs van Buren, who is a Malay lady from those parts, but also for the sake of the orangutang and some of the smaller gibbons, which are to be met with there and not here, to say nothing of the gallinae or nectarineas. I have never been to Pulo Prabang, alas, but I understand it possesses all the advantages of Borneo without the drawback of headhunters.'

When they had finished the birds of paradise aviary, which was no small undertaking, and when Stephen had expressed his unqualified support for Raffles' projected zoological society and garden in London,

Raffles said, 'It can hardly be necessary for a man of your reputation, but if you should care for a letter of introduction to van Buren, nothing could be easier.'

'That would be very kind. Yet on reflection perhaps I ought to present myself at his door. If it were known that I had been introduced by the Governor of Java, my character as a wholly unofficial naturalist travelling with his friend Aubrey might suffer. On the other hand — I may assume that you know the conditions of my attachment to Mr Fox's mission?'

'Yes, sir.'

'On the other hand, then, I should be most grateful if you would recommend me to a considerable merchant here, capable of dealing with bills of exchange, who has dealings with a colleague in Pulo Prabang.'

'You would not object to a Chinese?' asked Raffles, having considered for a moment. 'They carry out almost all the banking business, bill discounting and so on in these regions.'

'Never in life. It was a Parsee or a Chinese I had in mind: I have always heard excellent accounts of their probity.'

'The better sort can put John Company to shame. Here in Batavia we have Shao Yen, who has interests out as far as the Moluccas and up to Penang. He is under some obligation to me. I will find out whether he has a correspondent in Pulo Prabang.'

'I may have occasion to disburse considerable sums, and it might be more convenient to draw them locally than to carry them about. But my chief reason is that I wish to appear in Pulo Prabang as a man of substance from the outset, not as a mere moneyed adventurer. If I go to Shao Yen with your recommendation he will treat me with respect; this respect will be conveyed to his correspondent; and an intelligent banker or merchant is often capable of giving valuable information. Yet obviously he is not going to do so for a stranger unless that stranger is uncommonly well vouched for; and although I can display quantities of gold and letters of credit, they would not serve as well as a word from you.'

'You flatter me; but I cannot pretend you are mistaken. I shall ask him to call tomorrow morning. What else can I do to be of assistance?'

'Could your people give me a list of the members of the French mission?'

'I am afraid not, apart from Duplessis and the infamous couple, whose names you know already. Their frigate only arrived a few days ago. It has already been removed from Prabang harbour, because the sailors made such a nuisance of themselves ashore. But Duplessis will not have audience of the Sultan until after the change of the moon. He is hunting with his cousin of Kawang, in the hope of a two-horned rhinoceros.'

'So much the better. Would it perhaps be possible to have a very brief sketch of the Sultan and his chief advisers?'

'Certainly. As for the Sultan, of course, Fox knows everything about him — his Javanese ancestors, his wives, mothers-in-law, concubines, minions — but the office may turn up something new about his council. How those dear gibbons hoot and howl, upon my word. Did you hear the bell?'

'I believe I did.'

'Then perhaps we should go in. My wife thought of beginning with a dish that might amuse you, bird's-nest soup; and she maintains that soup must be ate hot. But before we go, see if you can make out the big gibbon to the left of the casuarina tree, even though the light is so poor. He is a siamang. Ho, Frederick!' The gibbon answered with a melodious hoo-hoo-hoo, and the Governor hurried in.

'Pray, Captain Aubrey, tell us about your voyage,' he said, his soup-spoon poised half way.

'Well, sir,' said Jack, 'it was as uneventful as a voyage could well be until we were off an island in the Tristan group, and then it was on the point of becoming very, very much more eventful than we wished. There was a prodigious swell setting from the west, and as we lay there off Inaccessible, for that is the island's name, the breeze died away to a clock-calm: we were rolling so as to spew our oakum, and although we had sent up preventer-stays and swifted the shrouds — but I am afraid, sir, I use too many sea-terms.'

'Not at all, not at all. I believe, Captain, that I was at sea well before you.'

'Indeed, sir? Forgive me: I had no idea.'

'Yes. I was born aboard my father's ship, a West-Indiaman, off Jamaica, ha, ha.'

The rest of the evening was passed with voyages, passages to India and beyond, some extraordinarily fast, some extraordinarily slow, and with an account of Jack's friend Duval carrying the news of the battle of the Nile to Bombay by way of the desert and the Euphrates.

Shao Yen was a tall thin man in a plain grey robe, more like an austere monk than a merchant; but he grasped the situation at once. They spoke in English, he having had much to do with the East India Company's people in Canton in his youth and having lived in Macao during the two recent English occupations as well as in Penang. Raffles left them together after a few general remarks of a friendly nature and when the proper civilities were over Stephen said, 'When I go to Pulo Prabang it may be necessary for me to purchase the good-will of certain influential men. For this purpose I have a fair amount of gold. It appears to me that the best way of proceeding would be to deposit it with you and, subject of course to the usual commissions and charges, to carry a letter of credit to your correspondent in Pulo Prabang and to draw on him.'

Shao Yen replied, 'Certainly. But when you say a fair amount have you any approximate sum in mind?'

'It is made up of different currencies: it would weigh about three hundredweight.'

'Then may I observe that if either or both of my correspondents — for I have two — were to scrape the island bare they could not produce a tenth part of the amount you speak of. It is a very poor island. But in my opinion that tenth part, tactfully presented, would buy all the good-will that is to be had.'

'In this case there is likely to be some competition.'

'Yes,' said Shao Yen. He looked down for a few moments and then said, 'It might answer very well if I were to give you a letter of credit for what I believe my correspondent can produce and then notes of hand for various sums: my paper is good from Penang to Macao.'

'That would answer admirably: thank you. And may I beg you to impress upon your correspondent that I should wish any large transaction to be entirely confidential? Ordinary money-changing may as well be public as not, but I should be sorry if it were thought I could be squeezed for thousands.'

Shao Yen bowed, smiled, and said, 'I have two correspondents, both from Shantung and both discreet; but Lin Liang has the smaller house; he is less conspicuous, and perhaps I should direct your letter of credit to him.'

Having drunk tea with Shao Yen and eaten little cakes from a multitude of trays, Stephen looked for Jack Aubrey, but found to his disappointment that he had already set off for Anjer to bring the *Diane* up to Batavia, so that not a moment should be lost.

'Poor soul,' Stephen reflected. 'It will

take his mind off this foolish rumour.' For his own part he was satisfied by the financial expert's words, and he spent the first part of the day with Raffles' Javanese peacock, far finer than the Indian bird, a friendly binturong, the gardens, where he was joined by Mrs Raffles in an apron and leather gloves, and the enormous hortus siccus — such a pleasant forenoon.

Dinner was less agreeable, however. Before it Fox introduced him to three high officials who were to join the mission, almost caricatures of their kind, tall, red, thick, arrogant, with booming voices and an inexhaustible store of platitudes. Their conversation was dull almost past believing, and afterwards Fox said, 'I am sorry to have inflicted this upon you, but they are necessary properties on the present stage. We have to produce a show at least equal to what the French can offer — it appears that they have three gentlemen apart from the two traitors, who are not regularly accredited, and the servants — and these people the Governor has lent me are used to missions of this kind: they can stand there in their gold-laced uniforms for hours without suffering; they can give the appearance of listening to speeches; they never have to steal away to the privy; and at banquets they are capable of eating anything from human flesh downwards. But I admit that their company is a trial.'

'Vous l'avez voulu, George Dandin.'

'Yes. And I can bear it for the voyage and the time of the negotiations. I could and would bear a great deal more to succeed in this undertaking. Apart from anything else,' he added with a slight laugh, 'the Governor tells me that if I bring back a treaty and if he has the writing of the dispatch it might mean a knighthood, even a baronetcy.' For a moment Stephen did not know whether Fox was speaking seriously, but when after a reflective pause he went on to say, 'It would so please my mother,' the doubt was resolved.

The *Diane* came into Batavia with a leading wind and a making tide that afternoon, and Jack sent an official message to the effect that he hoped to sail at eleven the next morning. It was Seymour who brought the message, together with a private note to Stephen begging him to urge all those concerned to exact promptitude, to give an example himself, and to suggest that the Governor might like to visit the ship. 'And I was to say, sir, he was very sorry you were not aboard as we sailed past Thwart-the-Way island, because we were surrounded by those swallows that make bird's-nest soup.'

'I should like it of all things,' said Raffles, on hearing the suggestion. 'There is nothing, in its way, more beautiful than a man-of-war.'

'Nor anything, alas, more rigorously dominated by time and bells. I am so glad you are coming. Your presence will oblige the others to *show a leg*, as we say.'

They showed a leg, whether they liked it or not, for Raffles was as regular as a well-tempered chronometer, and a procession of boats, headed by the Governor's barge, set out for the *Diane* at a quarter to ten. She was looking beautiful, more beautiful than any ship that had been wooding, watering and taking in stores at such furious speed could be expected to look; but then her captain and her first lieutenant were perfectly aware of the effect of yards exactly squared by the lifts and the braces, the sails furled in a body, and of the quantity of unsightly objects that could be concealed under the hammock-cloths, drawn drum-tight and with never a wrinkle. And in any case the smoke of the thirteen-gun salute would hide a number of imperfections, while the ceremony of reception diverted attention from any that might be visible through the clouds. This ceremony had been rehearsed three times since dawn and it passed off perfectly well: the barge hooked on, the white-gloved sideboys ran down with baize-covered man-ropes to make the ascent almost foolproof, the bosun and his mates sprung their calls, the *Diane*'s forty marines, red as lobsters and perfect to the last button, presented arms with a fine simultaneous clash as the Governor and the envoy came aboard, welcomed by Captain Aubrey and all his officers in their best uniforms.

The day was hot and cloudless, and since the great cabin was divided up Jack had caused an awning to be stretched over the after part of the quarterdeck; here he and his guests sat, drinking sherbet or madeira and talking or contemplating the broad harbour with its great numbers of European ships, Chinese junks, Malay proas, and innumerable boats and canoes plying to and fro; and in the meantime the mission's additional baggage and servants came aboard on the larboard side. At a quarter past ten Raffles asked if he might be shown the ship: he walked round with Jack and Fielding, making intelligent, appreciative comments, and when he was brought back to the quarterdeck he called his people, said farewell to the mission, thanked Jack heartily for his entertainment and went down into the barge, once more with the usual honours, once more with the roar of guns.

Jack's eye followed the boat with great approval, and as soon as it was at a proper distance he said to Richardson, the officer of the watch, 'Let us get under way.'

With the bosun piping *All hands to unmoor ship,* the frigate sprang to ordered life: she was fast to the chain-moorings laid down long ago for Dutch men-of-war and it took her little time to cast them off and spread her topsails to the moderate westerly breeze. She made her cautious way through the merchant shipping, some of it wonderfully stupid, and as six bells in the forenoon watch struck she cleared the harbour.

'Now that is the kind of visitor I really like,' said Jack, joining Stephen in the cabin. 'A man who knows just when to come and just when to go. They are wonderfully rare. We will drink a bottle of Latour to his health.' He took off his massive gold-laced coat and tossed it on to the back of a chair: it slipped off as the *Diane* heeled to the thrust of her topgallantsails, and Killick, appearing as though from a mouse-hole, snatched it up and carried it away muttering 'fling it about like it was old rags — best Gloucester broadcloth — brushed all over again — toil, toil, toil.'

'You look worn, brother,' said Stephen.

'To tell you the truth,' said Jack with a smile, 'I *am* rather worn. Wooding and watering at top speed is a wearing occupation, particularly when the hands are all so eager for liberty, to kick up Bob's a-dying on shore after so many months at sea. We did lose ten, not having time to comb through all the bawdy-houses or the backsides of godowns. Still, that does allow us to shift hammocks forward to make room for all these new servants — preposterous numbers of servants. And then again I believe we can look forward to less anxious sailing now. We are directly in the path of the Indiamen bound for Canton until we have to steer east a little south of the Line, and although the waters are dangerous, I have Muffitt's very careful charts as well as his directions. And Muffitt, you know, made the voyage more often than any other man in the Company's service: a better hydrographer, in my opinion, than Horsburgh or even Dalrymple.'

Jack Aubrey, however, was reckoning without his guests. The three necessary properties, designed to give the mission greater weight or at least greater bulk, were called Johnstone, Crabbe and Loder, a judge and two members of the council, who had reached their present rank by outliving and outsitting all competitors; and when the *Diane*, having made her way through the close-clustered Thousand Islands and having crossed the notorious Tulang shoal with three fathoms to spare, was approaching the Banka Strait, Johnstone met Stephen on the half-deck, the one coming, the other going. Stephen had never known a judge he liked: those few he had met or seen in court had been self-important prating men, unequal to their great authority; and Johnstone was a particularly unfortunate example. After a few insipid remarks he said, 'I too am very fond of music; nobody loves a tune better than I do. But I always say enough is as good as a feast; do you not agree? And I am one of those curious people that are no good unless they have a good night's sleep. I am sure the Captain does not know how permeable the cabin walls are, permeable to sound, I mean; but I hope I may rely upon you to be good enough to drop a hint, just a very gentle diplomatic hint.'

'As to your position that enough is as good as a feast, Judge, allow me to point out that it is contrary to the views of all good men from the earliest recorded times,' said Stephen. 'Think of the feasts in

Paralipomenon, in Homer, in Virgil: they were neither prepared by fools nor eaten by them. As for the rest, it is clear that you cannot know that I am Captain Aubrey's guest, or you would never have supposed that I could give him hints on how he should behave.'

Johnstone flushed with anger, said, 'Then I shall do it myself,' and turned away.

He did not do so at dinner, though he was obviously nerving himself for it and although his friends kept looking at him, but the news reached Jack that evening, when the frigate was threading the strait between Banka and Sumatra, less than ten miles broad in places. The breeze was awkward, coming now from one shore, now from the other, and although the spectacle of forests on either hand, separated by a stretch of sky-blue sea, was agreeable for the passengers — Stephen, in the maintop with a telescope, was very nearly sure he had seen a Sumatran rhinoceros — the continual tacking, the continual cry of the leadsman in the chains, sometimes calling less than five fathoms, and the continual possibility of uncharted shoals made it an active and uneasy passage for the seamen. At one point Jack hurried below to check a warning in Muffitt's papers, and while he was doing so he heard Killick in the farther cabin giving Bonden a lively description of Those Old Buggers and the way they carried on about the music. Apart from calling 'Avast, there,' he took no notice, being too deeply concerned with his rocks, but it had sunk into the depths of his mind and it rose up again after quarters, when the cabins had just been reassembled and his violin-case came up from the orlop. 'Killick,' he called. 'Go and see if His Excellency is at leisure for a visit.'

His Excellency was, and Jack went round at once. 'My dear Mr Fox,' he cried, 'I am so sorry. I had no idea we made such a din.'

'Eh?' said Fox, looking startled. 'Oh, the music, you mean. Please do not feel the least concern. It is true I have no ear for music, no appreciation at all, but I cope with the situation perfectly well with little balls of wax: all I hear through them is a kind of general hum, which I find rather agreeable than otherwise — soporific.'

'I cannot tell you how relieved I am. But your companions . . .'

'I do hope they have not been making a fuss, after all your kindness in arranging their quarters and their stores. They have little sense of what is fitting: they have none of them travelled in a man-of-war, only in

Company's ships, where of course they are important people. I try to keep them in order, but they do not seem capable of understanding. One of them sent for Maturin this morning . . . Has the ship stopped?'

'Yes. We have anchored for the night. I dare not go through the strait in the darkness, not carrying Caesar, or at least Caesar's representative, and all his fortunes.'

Jack Aubrey rarely turned a compliment, but Fox's unaffected, generous response really pleased him, the more so as it was unexpected. In fact he would not have dared go through the strait in any circumstances. It was a slow and anxious navigation, with strong, varying currents to add to the difficulty. The Old Buggers remained perfectly indifferent to all this, however: they might have been travelling in a coach on a well-traced road. They none of them ever tackled Jack directly, but they made Fielding's life quite unhappy. Fleming was reported to him for having prevented Loder from talking to the quartermaster at the con: he was told that it was extremely inconvenient to have their baggage struck down into the hold every evening, and that last time it happened Crabbe's pencil-case and a valuable fan had not been put back in the right place

— it was at least half an hour before he could find them: and every evening in the strait, when the ship lay at anchor, Jack turned the hands up to sing and dance on the forecastle by way of a break after the arduous day, which was another cause for complaint. But the most usual grievance had to do with their servants, who were obliged to wait their turn at the galley and who were treated with coarse jocularity, even with obscene gestures and expressions.

In any case Jack was far out of their reach. He and the master spent much of their time in the foretop with azimuth compass and telescope at hand and a midshipman to hold their papers flat. They saw, noted and dealt with a number of hazards, and as the frigate was crossing the shoal that made leaving the strait so dangerous if the passage were missed — as she was in fact entering the South China Sea — they saw another peculiar to these waters. From an island to windward, laid down as Kungit by Horsburgh and Fungit by Muffitt, came two large Malay proas. They had outriggers, and with the wind on their beam they came up very fast: presently it could be seen that their long slim hulls were crowded with men, surprising numbers of men even for such an enterprise.

Their intentions were perfectly obvious, piracy being a way of life in these parts; and although ships the size of the *Diane* were rarely attacked it had happened on occasion, sometimes with success. 'Mr Richardson,' called Jack. 'Sir?' came the answer. 'Stand by to run out the guns as brisk as can be when I give the word. The hands are to keep out of sight.'

The proas separated, one on the frigate's larboard quarter, the other to starboard, and they approached cautiously, spilling their wind as they came. The tension mounted. The gun-teams crouched by their pieces, as motionless as cats. But no, it was not to be: the proas hesitated, decided that this was a real man-of-war, not a merchant disguised, hauled their wind and were gone: a universal sigh along the gundeck, and the handspikes were laid aside.

For some reason this stilled the Old Buggers' complaints for the following days, which was just as well, since just under the equator the *Diane* had to leave the Indiamen's course and sail into uncharted shallow seas, traversed only by proas or junks, which drew almost no water at all, whereas the frigate, with her present stores, drew fifteen feet nine inches abaft: perhaps they were dimly aware of the gravity aboard, an atmosphere in which querulous words might meet with a short answer.

Yet even so Jack was glad to be rid of them at the end of the voyage, a voyage indeed that ended in beauty. After a night of ghosting along the parallel under close-reefed topsails, the lead going all the time, dawn showed the perfect landfall, a large, unmistakable volcanic island directly to leeward, with a fine breeze to carry them in.

Jack kept to his reefed topsails, however. He wanted to give the Malays long warning of his arrival; he wanted the ship and the mission to have plenty of time for their preparations; he also meant to have his breakfast in comfort.

This he accomplished, together with Stephen, Fielding and young Harper; and when it was over they returned to the crowded quarterdeck, where Fox and his companions and all the officers were gazing at Pulo Prabang, now very much nearer. They gazed in silence, and apart from the sigh of the breeze in the rigging the only sound in the ship was the measured chant of the man in the chains: 'By the deep, twelve. By the deep, twelve. And a half, twelve.' To be sure, it was an arresting sight. The island stretched wide across the field of vision, most of it dark green with forest, the truncated cone of the central volcano soaring up in a pure line beyond the level of the trees; there were other peaks, lower, less distinct and perhaps much older, in the interior, but they could only be made out by attentive inspection, whereas the craters they were approaching, the crater in the sky and the crater at sea-level, could not conceivably be missed or mistaken. The second was an almost perfect circle a mile across, and its wall rose ten and even twenty feet above the surface; here and there a palm-tree could be seen, but otherwise the ring was unbroken except in one place, the gap towards which the ship was heading. Though it is true that on the landward side it was obscured by the long slow accumulation of earth and silt, the delta of the river on which the town was built.

On one of the horns of this immense harbour-wall stood a fort: ancient, perhaps Portuguese, obviously deserted. Jack fixed it with his telescope, saw grass growing in the empty embrasures, and shifted his glass to the farther side, where something not unlike a castle stood apart from the houses, commanding the approach to the shore, a shore lined deep with craft of various kinds and one that reminded him of Shelmerston, though the strand was black, the vessels often masted with tripods of bamboo, their sails made of matting; perhaps the common quality was a certain piratical air.

'By the mark ten.'

The water was shoaling gradually, and from the slight surf on the outer wall it was clear that the tide was making. Jack considered the rest of the harbour — a certain amount of activity among the fishing-boats and one of the big proas being careened — and the town — a mosque; another mosque; some houses built on piles along the river; a massive formless affair that must be the Sultan's palace.

'By the deep, nine. And a half, nine. By the deep, nine.'

Houses in large gardens or compounds round the town. Green fields beyond, some bright green: rice paddies, no doubt: all the flat ground cultivated: rising forest beyond.

He focussed his glass on the entrance to the harbour, a hundred yards wide, nodded, glanced at the boats, ready to be hoisted out, at the best bower a-cockbill, at Mr White with his guns; and turning to the master he said, 'The middle of the channel, Mr Warren, and round-to at eight fathom or a cable's length inside, whichever comes first.'

They came almost together. The *Diane*

rounded to, dropped her anchor, broke out her colours, and began her salute. Ordinarily in the unknown port of an unknown island Jack would have sent ashore to make certain that the salute would be returned gun for gun, the Royal Navy being very particular about its compliments; but Fox had assured him that the Sultan and his people laid great store by good manners and would never be found wanting in a matter of formal politeness. Even so, the prompt reply, well-spaced and correct in number, was a relief to him; so was the fact that the answering guns were little more than swivels. In case of disagreement it would not be pleasant to lie within range of a battery of eighteen-pounders.

With the last gun a canoe put off from the shore, a high-prowed tiger-headed canoe with an outrigger and a deck-house in the middle; it was paddled by twenty men and it obviously carried an important person.

'Mr Fielding,' said Jack, 'sideboys and manropes. But no piping the side, no Marines, I think.' He looked across at Fox, who nodded.

The canoe ranged neatly along; the important person, a slim brown man with a speckled orange-tawny turban and a kris tucked into his sarong, came aboard in a seamanlike manner and bowed gravely to those on the quarterdeck, putting his hand quickly to his forehead and his heart. At the same time the canoe-men raised some baskets of fruit on hooked poles to the hands on the gangway. Fox stepped forward, welcomed him in Malay, thanked him for the presents, and presented him to Jack, saying, 'This is Wan Da, sent by the Vizier. We should drink coffee with him in the cabin.'

The coffee-drinking went on and on. From time to time word came out, borne by Killick or Ali, once to lower down the launch, once to warn the gentlemen of the suite to stand by to go ashore, once to the mate of the hold to rouse their baggage up on deck; and during this time Ahmed, Yusuf and those Dianes who had any word of Malay conversed with the canoe-men through the gun-ports in the waist. At one point Killick darted up, seized the baskets with an angry suspicious glance all round, and disappeared again. Hope faded; the eager talk along the rail died away. But at six bells the word was passed for Mr Welby, and the large cutter was ordered over the larboard side, where it was filled with baggage, servants, five Marines and a corporal. And after another fifteen minutes Wan Da, Mr Fox and the Captain came out: Wan Da went down into the canoe and pulled off a little, while the launch advanced for the envoy and his suite. As the three boats pulled away for the shore the envoy's thirteen guns boomed out again; and when the triple echo of the last had died away Jack turned to Stephen and said, 'Well, and so we have delivered him at last. There were times when I thought we should never do it.'

Stephen, who could perfectly well see that Fox had been, or was just about to be set down on Pulo Prabang, frowned and replied, 'Would there be any of that coffee left, at all? I have been smelling it this last age, and never a sip sent out.'

'It appears,' said Jack as he led the way to the cabin, 'that we were expected, and the Vizier has set apart a fair-sized house in its own compound for the mission east of the river. The French have one on the other side. The Sultan will be back at the change of the moon, and then we shall both have our audience together.'

'When does the moon change?' asked Stephen.

Jack looked at him: even after so many proofs to the contrary it was hard to believe that a man could remain ignorant of these fundamental things; but such was the case, and he said, not unkindly, 'In five days' time, brother.'

As Shao Yen had told him, Lin Liang's house was comparatively small and inconspicuous. It faced on to a dusty lane that led from the street running along the east bank of the river and with its shabby warehouses it backed on to the outer edge of the town, not far from Fox's compound. The shop in front was crowded with goods, blue and white china, huge rice-jars, bales of blue cotton cloth, barrels, strings of dried squid and dark unidentifiable creatures hanging from the beams, but even so it looked run-down and poor. A Malay woman was buying a pennyweight of betel, lime and turmeric, and towards the back of the shop, idly fingering ginseng and shark's fins, stood Edwards and Macmillan, attended by Fox's younger servant Yusuf. When the woman was gone they pressed Dr Maturin to take their turn — they were in no sort of a hurry — but although Stephen saw that they were moved by something more than good manners he would have none of it. He stood in the doorway watching the sparse traffic while they changed some money with Yusuf's help and then murmured their enquiries; Yusuf was less discreet and his translation came shrill and clear: 'Two of these pieces for a short time; five for all night.'

When they had gone Stephen also changed a guinea and then said he would like to see Lin Liang. Calling another youth to keep the shop, the young man led him behind the two counters, through a store-room, out into a court between the ware-houses and so to an enclosed garden with a stone lantern and a single willow-tree: in the far corner there was a garden-house with a round door, as round as a full moon, and in it stood Lin Liang, bowing repeatedly. He advanced to meet Stephen half way, con-ducted him to the little house and sat him on a broad, outstandingly beautiful great chair made of Soochow lacquer, obviously brought for the purpose. He called for tea and port wine and cakes, which were carried in by a shabby one-eyed eunuch; and after perhaps a quarter of a pint of tea — Dr Maturin's liver, alas, would not allow port wine, though he was most sensible of the at-tention — Lin Liang said apologetically that he had not yet been able to bring together all the money named in the esteemed Shao Yen's note, even with the help of his col-league on the other side of the river, the re-spectable Wu Han. But Wu Han was calling in an important debt, and within a week the sum would be made up. Meanwhile Lin Liang had so arranged the available funds that he had an eighth part in pagodas, and three quarters in rix-dollars and taels, silver being much more current than gold in these regions, at Dr Maturin's disposal; and this, he said, shooting the balls of an abacus to and fro with extraordinary speed, represented certain proportions of the sequins, ducats, guineas, louis d'or and johannes deposited with Shao Yen. The numbers flowed past Stephen's ears, but he looked attentive, and when the calculation was done he said, 'Very good. I may make some considerable transfers quite soon, transfers that must remain confidential. Does Wu Han understand the importance of that? For I collect that he is associated with you in this undertaking.'

Lin Liang bowed: Wu Han was necessarily associated with him, and at half shares, the transaction being too important for either separately; but Wu Han was the soul of discretion, as silent as the legendary Mo.

'Is he not the banker for the French mission?'

'Scarcely. They have sent to change a little money into Java guilders for daily marketing, but the only real connection is between Wu Han's Pondicherry clerk and a man belonging to the mission, also from French India.'

'Then please let it be known to Wu Han and his Pondicherry clerk that I should like any information about the French that can properly be given — lists of names and so on — and that I am ready to pay for it. But, Lin Liang, you understand as well as I do that in these things discretion is everything.'

Lin Liang was wholly persuaded of it; many of his own affairs too were of the most private nature; and perhaps for the future Dr Maturin might like to come by the door actually named Discretion, behind the hovel in which he and his miserable family had their unworthy being. He led Stephen through another court, surrounded by verandas, some with truly astonishing orchids hanging from the beams and slim young women with bound feet tottering rapidly away. Still another, bounded by a high wall with a rounded projection whose spy-hole commanded the low iron door; and on the other side a lane, or rather a path, wandered along a neglected canal.

Stephen wandered with it; he had some time to spare before his appointment with van Buren and he looked with more than ordinary attention at the orchids in the trees along the water or on the ground between them, an extraordinary variety of flowers and vegetation. He took specimens of those he could not recall having seen in Raffles' garden or dried collection, and he gathered up some beetles for Sir Joseph — beetles that in some cases he could not even assign to a family, so far were they removed from his experience. By the time he reached van Buren's door he was somewhat encumbered, but in that house burdens of this kind were taken for granted. Mevrouw van Buren relieved him of the flowers and her husband brought insect-jars. 'Shall we carry on directly with our viscera?' he asked. 'I have reserved the spleen especially for you.'

'How very kind,' said Stephen. 'I should like it of all things.' They walked slowly across the compound — van Buren had a club-foot — to the dissecting house, where they were anatomizing a portly tapir. The garden gate happened to be open and as they passed it van Buren said, 'If you were to use this when you do me the pleasure of paying me a visit, it might save time, particularly at night, when the house is locked up and the watchman thinks all visitors are thieves; and time we must save, because in this climate specimens will not keep. Tapirs in particular go off as quick as mackerel, though one would hardly suppose it.'

His words were so true that they worked fast and silently, hardly breathing, sometimes shifting the mirrors that reflected strong light into the cavity, but communicating mostly by nods and smiles though once, pointing to the tapir's anatomically singular forefoot, van Buren murmured, 'Cuvier'; and when they had thoroughly examined the spleen in all its aspects, taking the samples and sections necessary for van Buren's forthcoming book, they sat outside to breathe the open air. Van Buren spoke luminously not only of this spleen but of many spleens he had known, the comparative anatomy of the spleen, and the erroneous notion of *force hypermécanique*.

'Have you ever dissected an orangutang?' asked Stephen.

'Only one,' said Van Buren. 'His spleen is on the shelf with the human examples, a pitifully meagre collection. It is very difficult to get a really prime cadaver in this country: nothing but the occasional adulterer.'

'But surely criminal conversation, illicit venery, even grossly over-indulged, will hardly affect a man's spleen?'

'It will in Pulo Prabang, my dear sir. The

incontinent person is peppered: that is to say a small sack or rather bag partially filled with pepper is tied over his head, his hands are bound, and he is delivered over to the aggrieved family and their friends; they form a ring, beating the sack with sticks so that the pepper flies. Presently it kills him and I have the corpse; but the prolonged and repeated convulsions that precede death distort the spleen most surprisingly and so change its juices that they are useless for comparison; they do not support my theory at all.'

'Does the ape's spleen differ widely from ours?' asked Stephen after a pause.

'Remarkably little. The renal impression above the posterior border — but I will show you both without naming either, and you will decide for yourself.'

'I should love to see an orang-utang,' observed Stephen.

'Alas, there are very few down here,' said van Buren. 'It was a great disappointment to me. They eat the precious durians, and they are killed for doing so.'

'Absurd as it may seem, I have never seen a durian either.'

'Why, my bat-tree is a durian. Let me show you.' They walked out to the far end of the garden, where a tall tree stood in a little enclosure of bamboos. 'There are my bats,' said van Buren, pointing to clusters of dark, almost black creatures about a foot long hanging upside down, their wings wrapped about them. 'When the sun reaches the far trees they will begin to squeak and gibber, and then they will fly off to the Sultan's garden and strip his fruit-trees, if the guardians do not take great care.'

'Do they not eat your durians?'

'Oh dear me no. I will find one if I can.' Van Buren stepped over the low fence, took a long forked pole and peering up into the tree he poked among the leaves. The bats stirred and muttered angrily and one or two flew out in a circle, settling again higher up — a five-foot wingspan. 'Some people eat them,' remarked van Buren, and then he cried, 'Take care.' The durian fell with a heavy thump, an object the size and shape of a coconut but covered with strong thickset spikes. 'The skin is far too thick for any fruit-bat,' he said as he cut it open, 'quite apart from the spikes. Ugly spikes: I have had several patients with dangerous lacerated wounds from a durian falling on their heads. The orang-utang opens them, however, spikes, coriaceous skin and all. This one is quite ripe, I am happy to say. Pray try a piece.'

Stephen realized that the smell of decay came not from their dissection but from the fruit, and it was not without a certain effort that he overcame his reluctance. 'Oh,' said he a moment later, 'how extraordinarily good; and what an extraordinary contradiction between the senses of smell and taste. I had supposed them to be inseparably allied. How I applaud the orang-utang's discrimination.'

'They are charming animals, from what I have heard and what little I have seen: gentle, deliberate, with nothing whatsoever of the baboon, the mandril, or even the pongo, let alone the restless petulant wantonness of monkeys in the general sense. But as I say there are almost none down here. To see a mias, for I believe that is the true Malay, you must go to Kumai.'

'I long to do so. You have been there, I collect?'

'Never, never: with this leg I cannot climb, and at the end of all possible riding there are innumerable steps cut into the bare rock of the crater's outward side. The path is called the Thousand Steps, but I believe there are many more.'

'I have an almost equal disadvantage. I am tied to this place until the negotiations are brought to an issue, I hope a happy issue. Today I learnt of a connexion that may prove useful.'

Early in their acquaintance or indeed friendship Stephen had found that van Buren was utterly opposed to the French project, both because he hated Buonaparte and what he had done to Holland, and because he thought it would ruin Pulo Prabang, which he loved. They had many friends in common, particularly the more eminent French anatomists; each knew and appreciated the other's work; and for once in his career as an intelligence-agent Stephen had laid aside dissimulation. He now told van Buren of his conversation with Lin Liang and of his hopes; and after that, as they sat on a shaded bench outside the dissecting-room, van Buren returned to his accurate, well-informed account of the members of the Sultan's council, their virtues, shortcomings, tastes, approachability.

'I am infinitely obliged to you, dear colleague,' said Stephen at last. 'The moon has risen and I can see my way back into the town, where I mean to walk about among the bawdy-houses and places where they dance.'

'May I hope to see you later? I usually start work again in the cool of the night, at about two; and if we do not finish some of the finer processes before tomorrow's sun, they may scarcely be distinguishable. But before you go let me tell you of a thought that occurs to me. Our Latif's half-brother is a servant in the house allotted to the French mission: he may be able to gather some small scraps of information about your man from Pondicherry.'

These days Stephen rarely saw either Fox or Jack Aubrey. He stayed ashore, usually sleeping in the favourite haunt of the small Javanese colony, a house where there were exquisite dancing-girls and a famous Javanese orchestra, a gamelan, whose rhythms, intervals and cadences, though entirely foreign to his ear, pleased him as he lay there through the night by his scented sleeping-partner, a young woman so accustomed to her clients' peculiarities — some very bizarre indeed — that his passivity neither surprised nor displeased her.

Here, in the main hall where the dancers performed, he sometimes met his shipmates, surprised, embarrassed, shocked by his presence. Mr Blyth the purser, a kindly man and older than Stephen, took him aside and said, 'I think I ought to warn you, Doctor, that this place is little better than a disorderly house; prostitution often occurs.'

Gambling often occurred too, very passionate gambling for very high stakes, sometimes going on till dawn. It was mostly monied people who came here, but he rarely saw any of the French and never Ledward or Wray, who had gone to join the Sultan in his hunting, Ledward having some acquaintance with the Raja of Kawang. Once however he played with four Spanish shipwrights in the French service who had brought their month's pay from the ship, anchored in a remote creek to keep her people out of harm's way. He took their money from them — he had always been lucky at cards — and a great deal of information; but on finding that they were most reluctant Frenchmen he let them win it back again. He also let them suppose that he was a Spaniard in the English service, which, as they confessed, was natural enough, Spain and England now being allies: for their part they had been impressed as long ago as 1807, when another face of things was seen, and they had never been able to get away since.

The rest of the time he walked about the countryside in a way that would be expected of a natural philosopher, the Captain's guest, sometimes with Richardson, sometimes with Macmillan, occasionally with

Jack, but more often by himself, for his companions objected to the forest-leeches that fastened upon them by the score in the wilder parts and the tormenting flies and mosquitoes in the irrigated fields. They were most profitable walks however, in spite of these disadvantages and even in spite of a shockingly aggressive kind of bee that built its comb in the open, hanging from a stout branch, and that attacked on sight, pursuing the intruder for a quarter of a mile or to the nearest very thick bush, sometimes itself inhabited by still more ferocious red ants or in one instance by an irritable female python, coiled about her eggs. Quite early he chanced upon a broad track where woodcutters had dragged their timber down with teams of buffaloes, and this clear tract in the deep forest gave him wonderful views of the arboreal birds, particularly the hornbills, and sometimes of a mouse-deer, while gibbons were far from rare. It was in this glade that Jack found him on the evening of a day during which he had had an unusually interesting conversation with Wu Han's Pondicherry clerk.

'There you are, Stephen,' cried Jack. 'They told me you might be here; but if I had known you was gone so far up the mountain-side I should have taken a pony.

Lord, ain't it hot! Where you get the energy from, after your nightly activities, I cannot tell, I am sure.' Like the rest of the ship's company Jack had heard of the Doctor's extraordinarily dissolute life, smoking and drinking until all hours, gambling; but he alone knew that Stephen could take the sacrament without confession.

'To be sure,' said Stephen, thinking of their work on the tapir, now a mere skeleton, 'I was very busy last night. But you too would walk far up the mountain-side without gasping if you did not eat so much. You were much better, physically, when you were poor and wretched. What do you weigh now?'

'Never mind.'

'At least another stone and a half, perhaps two stone. God be with us. You fellows of an obese and sanguine habit are always on the verge of an apoplexy, particularly in this climate. Will you not omit suppers, at least? Suppers have killed more than Avicenna ever cured.'

'The reason I came sweating up this infernal hill,' said Jack, 'was to tell you that Fox summons us both to a conference this evening. The Sultan returns tomorrow night, only a week after his appointed time, and we are to have our audience the day after.'

On the way down he told Stephen how the ship was faring, and how the stores laid in at Anjer, especially the great quantities of Manila cordage, were now being put to use, together with a detailed, perhaps a little too detailed, account of the restowing of the hold to bring her slightly by the stern. 'Just half a strake or so, you understand, nothing flash or outlandish or showing away. It pleased me very much indeed. But,' shaking his head and looking melancholy, 'there was something else that did not please me nearly so well. Having advised with Fox, I called all hands aft and told them that we were here to settle a treaty between the King and the Sultan, and that the French were here too for the same purpose: that the French fore-mast jacks had gone ashore in droves and had given great offence by getting drunk, fighting, offering to kiss honest young women, and touching their bare bosoms, and that they and their ship had been packed off to Malaria Creek. So, said I, the Dianes were not going to be given liberty except on promise of good behaviour, and even then only in small numbers at a time and with very little pay advanced. It was for their country's good, I said, only for their country's good. And I had thought of ending with God save the King or Three cheers for the King; but somehow by the time I had finished it did not seem quite suitable. A sullen, dogged set, upon my word: nothing but sour looks and wry faces. Even with Killick and Bonden it is nothing but Yes, sir or No, sir — never a smile. But then I am no orator. The Surprises might have worn it without oratory, because they know me; but not these swabs. They want to be ashore tumbling a wench and be damned to their country's good.'

'It is after all a very powerful instinct, perhaps the strongest of them all . . . I know your objections to having women aboard, but in this case, providing young Reade and Harper and perhaps Fleming were sent on shore, I cannot see that any very grave moral harm is likely to ensue.'

'Would you look after them?'

'I would not. But of Fox I have no doubt at all. He would sell his soul for this treaty, or tend to the needs of a whole orphanage.'

'I shall ask him.'

'Good evening, gentlemen,' said Fox. 'How kind of you to come. May I offer you some East India ale? It has been hanging down the well in a basket, and it is almost cold.' He poured it out and went on, 'As you know, we are to have our audience of the Sultan the day after tomorrow, and as it is possible that I may be called upon to address his council immediately after the formal proceedings, I should be grateful for any observations that may strengthen our case. You know the position. The French offer a subsidy, guns, ammunition and skilled ship-builders: we offer a subsidy, I hope larger than the French, subsequent protection and some trading concessions, admittedly of no great importance; and there is always the implicit threat of what we might do after the war is over. The trouble is that one single Indiaman taken would be exceedingly damaging to us and more immediately profitable than any subsidy I am empowered to offer: and in these parts the outcome of the war seems by no means as certain as I could wish.'

'Well, sir,' said Jack, 'as far as these ships are concerned — and this is the only matter on which I am qualified to speak — you could point out that although the Malays are capital hands at building proas and smallcraft — I have indeed ordered a new pinnace — they have not the slightest notion of what we call a man-of-war, a real ship capable of bearing the weight of a deck of guns and the strain of firing them. And although the French shipwrights may understand their trade, they must necessarily be used to working oak and elm; and they for their part would not have the slightest notion of these East Indies woods. Then you might tell them that although a proa can be run up in a week or so, a ship, a square-rigged ship, is quite another thing. In the first place it needs a proper yard, a dock, a slip; then, to take the example of a seventy-four, the hull alone needs the seasoned timber — the *seasoned* timber, mind — of some two thousand trees of about two ton apiece, with forty-seven shipwrights working a twelvemonth. Even a frigate like ours calls for twenty-seven skilled hands to build her in a year. And when the ship is built at last the men have to be taught to manage an unfamiliar rig and to handle the guns so that they are more dangerous to the enemy than to themselves — no easy task. The whole thing seems to me a scheme concocted in an office by a parcel of landsmen, if it is looked upon as one that will give quick returns.'

'Those are most valuable figures,' said Fox, writing them down. 'Thank you very much indeed. But Paris may also have had in mind the potential threat that would compel us to weaken our forces elsewhere. A potential threat often has effects far beyond . . . but I am not to be teaching you about strategy or tactics,' he said with a smile. 'Doctor, can you add a shot to my locker?'

'I have little definite to say at present and I do not propose to trouble you with surmises,' said Stephen. 'But I will observe that at least some of the shipwrights are impressed Spaniards, likely to run away to the Philippines as soon as ever they can; that at least some of the proposed French guns are said to be honey-combed: while at least some of the powder suffered extremely from wet during the voyage and from the gunner's negligence in omitting to invert the barrels in due sequence. That is all I have to report; but if I might be allowed a suggestion I should say that by way of setting off Ledward's undoubted advantage in already having met the Sultan — having hunted with him and perhaps prepossessed him in his favour — it might be useful to invite His Highness to visit the ship the very next day and see the great guns fired. A thundering discharge of whole broadsides and the visible destruction of floating targets would both divert him and give him some notion of our capabilities.'

'Yes, indeed. I shall certainly propose it to the Vizier at once: a very good idea in every way.' He poured out more ale, already flat and tepid, and said, 'Now, unless anything else occurs to either of you, let me say something about our clothes for the audience: splendour is everything on these occasions, and I have half the Chinese tailors in Prabang working on garments for our attendants. The officers are perfectly correct in their full dress and my suite and I are properly provided, while the Marines, of course, could not do better. But I was wondering, Captain, whether your bargemen might not escort you, carefully turned out, together with your officers and midshipmen of course. And then my dear Maturin, what about you? A black coat, even a very good black coat, would hardly answer the purpose here.'

'If it is splendour that is required, and if cloth and craftsmen are to be had, I shall go in my robes as a doctor of medicine, with scarlet gown and scarlet hood.'

And it was in a scarlet, or at least a Chinese red, gown and hood that he paced through the eastern gateway of the palace at Jack's side: a fairly rapid pace, because rain, furious tropical rain, was threatening, and the envoy had only one plumed hat. As fast as dignity allowed the mission and all belonging to it advanced across the open space before the moat and the inner wall, forty feet high and twelve thick, built by the Sultan's Javanese ancestors. They made a brave show, headed by the envoy on a state horse in silver-studded crimson harness led by grooms wearing sarongs and turbans made of cloth of gold; and the crew of the *Diane*'s barge in new white broad-brimmed sennit hats with ribbons, brass-buttoned blue jackets, snowy duck trousers, black shoes with genteel bows, and serviceable cutlasses by their sides were particularly remarked. On through another courtyard with the Sultan's men blowing trumpets and beating drums, and as the first warm heavy drops splashed down, into the palace.

Fox's attaché Loder might be indifferent company, but he was an excellent chef de protocole, and he and the Vizier's secretary had arranged the placing of the mission with the utmost precision, the most exact regard for precedence. Each man filed into his allotted place along the eastern wall of the great hall of audience with Fox and his immediate colleagues standing a few yards to the left of the empty throne. They stood there for some little time, listening not without satisfaction to the rain, and then they heard the drums and trumpets for the

French. Duplessis came first in a gliding run, followed by his suite, four men in official uniform and Ledward and Wray in bright blue coats with the star and ribbon of some order, then the French naval officers and the troop of attendants, all of them more or less soaked. For the first moments the French were wholly taken up with straightening their line, much upset by the last rush, and with their wet clothes, feathers, and papers; but as soon as they had settled in their due places Duplessis, on the far side of the throne, looked across the open space and gave Fox what could just be described as a bow: it was returned with an exactly matching degree of cordiality. At the same moment Wray caught sight of Stephen's scarlet robe and recognized first his face and then Jack Aubrey's with utter horror. He made a kind of harsh inward sob and grasped Ledward's arm: Ledward looked in the same direction; he stiffened, but betrayed no emotion and the appearance of the Sultan at the far end of the hall diverted the attention of all, yet not before Stephen had noticed the expression of cold hatred on Fox's white, closed face, one that he had rarely seen equalled.

The Sultan advanced, shaded by fan-bearers, supported on either side by his great feudatories and followed by the Vizier and the members of his council; he was a good-looking man, tall for a Malay, about forty-five; and he wore a famous ruby in his turban. He advanced slowly, looking from side to side with a civil expression; the French had the strange notion of clapping, as though at a theatrical performance, but he showed little surprise or displeasure, and when he turned to take his seat on the throne he bowed to each side with equal courtesy.

His attendants had all gathered in the space behind, but now the Vizier, a small dried man, stepped forward and stated in very respectful terms that two envoys had come, the first from the Emperor of France, the second from the King of England, and they begged to deliver their masters' messages. The Sultan said, 'In the name of Allah, the Merciful, the Compassionate, let the first comer speak first.'

Duplessis, with Ledward behind him, took up his station before the throne, and having bowed he began to read from his damp paper. A poor performance: the ink had run, the reader's spectacles were fogged with steam, and he himself was much oppressed by the heat and his wet uniform. Each paragraph was translated by Ledward.

A very fluent translation but also unconscionably free; and it was delivered in a hard voice, strangely at variance with its compliments and its expressions of good-will and earnest desire for an even closer alliance between the cousins of Pulo Prabang and the French Empire.

It had been agreed between the Vizier and the two envoys separately that since the Sultan intended to give a feast after the audience rather than hold a meeting of his council, the addresses should not exceed a quarter of an hour. To the astonishment of their party, Duplessis and Ledward did not speak so long; and Fox, who began badly, stumbling over the Sultan's titles 'Flower of Courtesy, Nutmeg of Consolation, Rose of Delight' so that he had to repeat them twice, scarcely reached ten minutes, in spite of a brilliant recovery and a much-admired evocation of the Sultan's illustrious descent. When he came to an end, bowed, and retired, the councillors exchanged covert looks of surprise, accustomed as they were to speeches that flowed on and on in self-generating eloquence; but the Sultan, realizing his good fortune after a moment's silence, smiled and said, 'In the name of Allah, the Merciful, the Compassionate, be welcome, gentlemen. Pray return our best thanks to your rulers, whom Heaven preserve, for their noble presents, ever to be preserved both in our treasury and our heart; and let the feast commence.'

It was now that the value of sterling insensibility became evident. Fox was still so affected by this encounter, although it had been long expected, that his social powers were much obscured, but Johnson, Crabbe and Loder talked away steadily, loudly and with frequent bursts of laughter, and the head of the English table kept up a creditable din. This table ran the length of the banqueting hall, and in compensation for their position during the audience the English were now placed on the Sultan's right, his table crossing the head of the room. Stephen was quite far down, and as he was one of the few who could carry on a conversation in Malay he had been placed between an elderly, morose and taciturn person whose function he never discovered and Wan Da, who had first received them. He was an agreeable neighbour: as a passionate hunter he knew a great deal about the forest, the jungle and the higher mountain. 'I saw you the other day above Ketang,' he said, laughing cheerfully. 'You were flying from the bees like a deer — such leaps! It is a dangerous corner, by the red rock: I had to run myself five minutes later, and I quite lost the track of my babirussa, a huge babirussa.'

'A severe pang, I am sure; but I hope it was mitigated a little by the reflection that swine's flesh is forbidden to Mahometans.'

'So is wine,' said Wan Da, smiling, 'but there are days when the Merciful, the Compassionate, is even more merciful and compassionate than others. No, in fact we kill them because they plough up the fields at night and because we use their tusks.'

The wine was real enough, however, a full-bodied perfectly drinkable red whose origin Stephen could not make out. Conceivably Macao? And although it was served not in glass but silver he was reasonably sure that several of the Malays as well as Wan Da were drinking it. The Sultan certainly was. His cup-bearer Abdul, a youth like a gazelle, made no pretence of hiding the dark red stream he poured.

So were the French. While Wan Da was giving a circumstantial account of his pursuit of a honey-bear, Stephen examined the faces opposite him. The sea-officers appeared to match the English reasonably well, and their captain had something of Linois' look, capable, efficient, determined, and cheerful. Duplessis was not a man to send to a hot climate, not a man to send abroad at all; and his official counsellors were not unlike Fox's. Wray had fallen to pieces since Stephen last saw him: flaccid, barely recognizable: the shock of recognition was still strong on him, and it was unlikely that he could sit out the meal — a greenish pallor increasing with every draught of wine. Ledward on the other hand, now that he had recovered his assurance, looked and sounded a formidable adversary, a man of quite unusual powers. Stephen watched him empty his goblet and hold it over his right shoulder to be refilled; and as he made this gesture he glanced towards the throne with a very slight but significant change of expression — a private look. Stephen's eye darted to the left and just caught Abdul's answering smile.

For some time Stephen could not believe that his first impression was not a mistake; but although from this point on Ledward was perfectly discreet, Abdul, behind the Sultan, was not; and the impression grew to a moral certainty. The possible consequences so filled his mind that he lost the thread of Wan Da's narrative until it ended 'So Tia Udin killed the bear, and the bear killed Tia Udin, ha, ha, ha!'

'Jack,' he said, as they walked along the

rim of the crater to a point where they could hail the ship, 'did you reflect upon Ganymede at all?'

'Yes,' said Jack. 'I was up with him all last night, and should be this night were it not for the Sultan's visit tomorrow. Such an endearing little pale golden body as he peeps out — he is easily my favourite. But I shall still have him almost all night, once the Sultan is done with.'

'Shall you, though?' said Stephen, looking at his friend's pleased, well-fed face, rather more florid than usual from the Sultan's wine; and after a pause, 'Brother, can we be talking of the same thing?'

'I should hope so,' said Jack, smiling. 'Jupiter is in opposition, you know. Nobody could have missed his splendour.'

'No, indeed: a very glorious sight. And Ganymede is connected with him, I collect?'

'Of course he is — the prettiest of the satellites. What a fellow you are, Stephen.'

'How well named. But I meant another Ganymede, the Sultan's cup-bearer. Did you notice him?'

'Well, yes, I did. I said to myself, Why, damn my eyes, there is a girl. But then I remembered that there would be no girls at a feast like that, so I returned to my excellent haunch of venison, no bigger than a hare's, but uncommon well-tasting. Why do you call him Ganymede?'

'Ganymede was Jupiter's cup-bearer; and I believe their connexion, their relations, their friendship, would now be frowned upon. But I use the name loosely, as it is so often used: I mean no reflexion upon the Sultan.'

Chapter 7

'Forgive me for bursting in on you at this time of day,' said Stephen, 'but I am in sad need of the Malay for mercury-sublimate, strontium nitride and antimony.'

'Pedok and datang for the first and last,' said van Buren, 'but I am afraid strontium is not yet known in these parts. Has it any therapeutic value?'

'None that I know of. Fireworks are what I have in mind, and it gives a noble red.'

'As for that, there are no less than three Chinese cracker-makers on the other side of the river, and they have the whole spectrum at their command. Lao Tung is said to be the best. I would come with you, but as I said in my note I am away at noon, and I must finish this creature before I go.'

'Of course. Lao Tung: many thanks indeed. We are to receive the Sultan this evening, on the occasion of Princess Sophia's birthday, and it occurred to me that a brilliant royal salute in her honour would not only give pleasure but would emphasize the mission's loyalty as opposed to

Ledward's open treason and make an evident contrast between on the one hand a set
of men who deserted first their king and
then their republic and who now support a
vile usurper and on the other a set who have
consistently supported the hereditary principle, which must surely appeal to a ruler by
divine right. Fox agrees. By the way, am I
right in supposing that His Highness is a
paederast?'

'Oh yes. Did I not mention it? Perhaps I
never thought of anything so obvious: such
things are as usual here as they were in
Athens. The present favourite is one Abdul
— I have rarely seen a man so besotted.'

'He is a pretty youth, sure. But that to one
side: I had a most satisfactory meeting with
the Pondicherry clerk in the night.'

'Duplessis' Pondicherry clerk?'

'Just so: Lesueur is his name. Wu Han's
young man, to whom he is deeply in debt,
brought him in the darkness, and we soon
came to an agreement. He has an importing
and exporting house in Pondicherry, where
his family still lives, and in exchange for our
good word with the Company, our protection for the future and a certain amount of
present money he undertook to give me
what information he could. He sent these
this morning. They are the rough draught of

Duplessis' official journal, which Lesueur writes out fair.'

Van Buren put down his scalpel, wiped his hands and took the sheaf of paper. He read intently, and after a page or two he said, 'I see that our contact is looked upon as purely scientific.'

'Yes. Fox wanted to come and see you to talk about the Buddhist temple at Kumai, but I pointed out that a visit by the envoy might compromise the position. Aubrey too was anxious to be introduced . . . which reminds me, I have an appointment with him for twenty minutes after nine o'clock,' said Stephen, looking at his watch. 'Jesus, Mary and Joseph, it is quarter to ten. He is a raging lion if he is kept waiting even as little as half an hour. I wish you both a very good journey — God bless. I will show you the papers again — forgive me. Oh dear, oh dear.'

Jack, with the purser, the purser's steward, Killick and Bonden were at Liu Liang's at Stephen's recommendation, laying in stores for the *Diane*'s reception that evening, served by Liu Liang himself. They had waited for Stephen eleven minutes at the landing-place and had then made their way to Liu Liang's by a route that led them through the hog-market, escorted by a cloud of ribald children, and they greeted him with a reserved severity, pursed lips and significant looks at their watches, or in default of watches, at a Chinese clepsydra by the dried medicinal serpents. Liu Liang, however, was as welcoming as could be, and once the stores were laid in, he sent an assistant to show the way to the firework-maker.

Jack and Stephen made the journey by themselves, Mr Blyth and the others returning to the ship. They crossed the bridge and followed the guide up a street leading away from the river, shops on one side, and open drains with many small black nimble pigs in the middle, the long wall of the French envoy's compound on the other; and a hundred yards ahead they saw Wray and Ledward walking arm in arm. As soon as he saw them Wray let go; he darted across the street, leaping the gutter and hurrying blindly into a clothes shop. Ledward walked on, his face set and tense. Stephen glanced at Jack: no apparent awareness, only a remote gravity. Ledward deviated slightly from his course, giving the wall, and they passed.

The pedok, the datang and substances warranted to give a brilliant red and a brilliant blue were weighed out and packed in small cotton bags, each labelled with a coloured twist. There was little conversation on the way down to the sea, but as they walked out along the crater-rim — charmingly fresh after the close, damp and very smelly heat of Prabang — Stephen said, 'What do you feel about those two?'

'Only disgust.'

'You would not kick Ledward, for example?'

'No. Would you?'

Stephen paused and said, 'Kick him? No . . . on reflection, no.' Some minutes of silent walking on the soft crumbled lava and then as they passed the stunted tree by which he had met Lesueur, the Pondicherry clerk, he said, 'Were there a white stone anywhere at hand, I should use it to mark this day. I brought off what may prove a useful stroke, in my own line.'

'I am heartily glad of it,' said Jack; and stopping to fill his powerful lungs he put up one hand as a speaking-trumpet and hailed '*Diane*, ahoy!' Watching the boat put off he added, 'No white stones — all as black as your hat — but at least we can break out a case of Hermitage: I am sure it will not mind the heat.'

Stephen, his heart and belly aglow with the Hermitage, spent the later afternoon with Mr White the gunner in the forward magazine and the filling-room, fairly cool below the water-line, measuring, weighing, and trundling the deadly little barrels to and fro.

'I do assure you, Master Gunner,' he kept repeating, 'it can do your guns no harm. The Captain has used the same mixture before, broadside after broadside — I saw it with my own eyes — from the stock of a pyrotechnician deceased, and sure it did his guns no harm. Besides, it is only for the salute. We shoot at the targets with your best long-distance red large-grain.'

'Well, I don't know, I'm sure,' said Mr White once more, privately conveying a little antimony out of the scales, 'but if chemicals, Chinese chemicals! don't honey-comb a gun, what does? And a gun honey-combed with chemicals — Chinese chemicals at that! — is liable to burst.'

He and his mates were the only dismal creatures in the ship, however. Most of the Dianes, sadly bored with lying at anchor, looked forward to the Sultan's visit with pleasure; they had of course scoured the frigate from truck to keelson, and now, having prepared four elegant lofty targets trimmed with bunting on staves as long as the carpenter could be brought to spare, they were carefully chipping their roundshot so that no unevenness should make the ball deviate from its mark. The ship was filled with the gentle sound of tapping hammers, interrupted from time to time by the crack of Fox's rifle as he shot at a tree-stump two cable's lengths away, hitting it with remarkable consistency, so that Ali, with a spy-glass, reported chips flying at almost every shot. He had his second piece at hand, waiting until Maturin should appear.

Everyone was perfectly ready well before the hour, but everyone was equally certain that the Sultan (a foreigner) would be late, and they settled down to enjoy the indefinite waiting in the calm luxury of doing nothing in their best clothes and enjoying the breeze that now blew across the anchorage. It was with real astonishment therefore that they saw a two-hulled proa with a large deck-house put off from the shore forty minutes before the appointed time and advance, blowing conchs and trumpets in a manner that would have been presumptuous in any but a ruling prince's vessel.

Fox, almost the only person not yet in full glory, hurried below for his uniform, and Jack observed to his first lieutenant, 'If some awkward sod had wanted the court to catch us with our breeches down, he could not have advised them better.'

Fielding glanced anxiously fore and aft, but everything seemed in order — the awning stretched just so, falls flemished, brass-work like that in a royal yacht, all hands shaved and in clean shirts, yards exactly squared — 'Touching wood, sir,' he said, 'perhaps the awkward sod may be disappointed: I believe we may receive all comers without a blush. But I will just step below and put the Doctor in mind of his coat and wig.'

The first comer was the Sultan himself, who like nearly all Malays came aboard in a seamanlike style, followed by his Vizier, many of his council, and his cup-bearer. They were welcomed with the roar of guns, the howl of pipes and the restrained splendour of a naval reception.

On occasions of this kind Fox and even his colleagues managed extremely well. They sat the guests under the awning, refreshed them with drinks judiciously laced with gin or brandy according to signals arranged beforehand, and helped Jack and Fielding show them round the ship. Jack was particularly struck by the Sultan's intelligent interest in all he saw, his grasp of the principles of naval architecture on the grander scale; for when Fox's perfectly fluent Malay ran dry on the subject of spirketting, hanging knees, brace-bitts and riding-bitts, the Sultan at once grasped Jack's explanation chalked on the deck and helped out with gestures. But it was the guns, the eighteen-pounders and the broad-mouthed carronades, the genuine short-range smashers, that really fascinated him and his followers: even the Vizier's benign, intelligent old face took on a predatory gleam.

'Perhaps His Highness would like to see them in action?' said Jack.

His Highness would indeed, and the whole party went back to the quarterdeck: the reception had gone very well so far and Jack was reasonably sure that it would go still better as soon as the ship was under way. Only Abdul would not be pleased. In spite of the fact that the envoy, now aware of the situation, had provided an unusually handsome present, Abdul had been froward from the beginning, and when drinks were being poured he snatched a decanter from Killick's hands with a rudeness that would have brought him a shrewd box on the ear in any other circumstances. And now, aware that the Dianes did not love him very much, he behaved with a petulant wantonness that made even confirmed old sodomites like the cook and the yeoman of the signals shake their heads. The Sultan himself had to stop him pulling the laniard of one of the quarterdeck guns, and while the targets were being towed out and the cables buoyed and slipped he capered about in a very offensive manner, openly despising Ali, Ahmed and the other Malay servants. Fox had left his two rifles on the capstan-head when he hurried below, and now Abdul picked up the Purdey. He was very urgent to fire it — he was perfectly used to guns — he was an excellent shot, the best in Pulo Prabang after the Sultan he said in a little boy voice — and to quieten him Fox loaded, showed him how to hold the rifle and where to point. Abdul did not listen, did not cuddle the butt close; and the recoil hurt his cheek and shoulder. He burst into tears of pain and mortification (Ahmed had laughed aloud), and the Sultan, ludicrously concerned, tried to comfort him; but there was nothing to be done until Fox, yielding to very strong hints on the part of His Highness, gave Abdul one of his fowling-pieces. The envoy put as good a face upon it as he could — the treaty was very dear to him — but his complaisance was not very convincing and it was a relief when the pipe of *All hands to make sail* brought the ship to active life, turning the general attention away from the nasty little scene.

The evening breeze at Prabang was reasonably predictable and at present it was behaving just as they had hoped, blowing across the west–east line from the seaward gap in the crater-rim to the town. The targets had been towed to their positions north and south of this line and four hundred yards from it, two to starboard, two to larboard.

The *Diane* let fall her topsails, sheeted them home and hoisted the yards, bracing them to the steady breeze just abaft the beam; she gathered way remarkably fast and Jack said to the master at the con, 'Pray keep her to five knots, Mr Warren.' She was to fire only the eleven forward guns of the main battery on either side, but here Fielding had concentrated all the frigate's talent, and he and Richardson, seconded by the four most responsible young gentlemen, were to supervise the firing. Not that there was any great need of supervision: the first and second captains of each gun thoroughly understood their business — Bonden, in charge of the starboard bow gun, had been pointing twenty-four- or eighteen-pounders ever since the battle of St Vincent — and by now the picked crews were all well above the average for speed and accuracy. Since the *Diane* was new, well-built and strong she could stand the shock of a simultaneous broadside, the most spectacular by far; but everyone concerned knew that this was an all-or-nothing affair, that no error could be corrected, and that they were being watched attentively by knowing eyes; most had taken off their shirts (their best shirts, embroidered in the seams), laying them carefully folded amidships or on the chain-pump brakes, and most were a little nervous. For this kind of exercise, where the new flintlock might fail, Jack always preferred the old-fashioned slow-match; and now its smoke eddied along the deck, awaking countless memories.

The frigate was almost abreast of the first target, the water rippling along her side. 'She bears,' murmured Bonden. 'Fire!' cried Fielding and the whole broadside went off in an immense long-thundering crash, eleven jets of flame with wadding dark in the brilliance; and before the smoke-bank rose to veil the sea those on the quarterdeck saw the target leap in an eruption of white water, with a few plumes beyond it and one shot that went skipping over the sea in great bounds until it hit the rocky shore. The Sultan's face was suffused with fierce delight; he pounded his right fist into his left palm in a European or perhaps a universal gesture and called out to the Vizier, his eyes sparkling with a most unusual animation. Meanwhile the teams were holding their guns inboard, sponging, reloading, ramming home the wad and running the piece up with a fine satisfying thump.

The *Diane* approached the second target in dead silence. The gunners glared out of their gunports with total concentration, making minute changes of bearing and elevation; the Sultan and his men lined the rail, motionless, wholly absorbed.

'She bears,' murmured Bonden again, and again Fielding, peering along the barrel behind him cried 'Fire!' This time there were no visible misses, and the Sultan laughed aloud.

'Hands about ship,' said Jack, and the frigate stayed in little more than her own length; the gun crews straightened for a moment, hoisting their trousers and spitting on their hands. They were now in perfect form, and bending to the guns again they destroyed the two remaining rafts with a deliberate certainty. The *Diane* picked up her moorings once again, by the two-hulled proa, twelve minutes after she had left them.

Jack and the returning first lieutenant exchanged private glances of relief. It had been a somewhat perilous caper, but they knew that the ship had performed it well, even by the most professional standards. 'Upon my word, sir,' said Fox at his elbow, 'that was a most impressive sight. The Sultan wishes you to know that he has seen nothing to equal it.'

Jack and the Sultan bowed and smiled to one another and Jack, glancing at the setting sun, said, 'Pray tell His Highness that in a few minutes I hope to show him something that may perhaps go beyond it, at least as an expression of loyalty. At one bell in the last dog-watch we are to fire a salute in honour of Princess Sophia's birthday.'

By one bell the tropical dusk had become tropical darkness, and Mr White stalked forth in his best uniform, a red-hot poker in his hand and a mate with a brazier behind him, and while the officers and Marines stood to attention and the hands to something faintly resembling it, he put the poker to the touch-hole of the first quarterdeck nine-pounder, which instantly shot out a vast tongue of crimson fire and a strangely shrill explosion. 'Oh!' cried the Sultan, in spite of himself; and repeating 'If I wasn't a gunner I wouldn't be here' Mr White paced on to the next: a jet of more than sapphire blue, and the whole court uttered a great 'Ah!' The brilliant white of camphor, the green of brass filings, a rosy pink, a most uncommon violet derived from orpiment, and so it went at perfectly regular intervals, timed by the gunner's ritual words, to the final prodigious blast from the aftermost carronade, crammed with a deafening, blinding mixture of pedok, datang and colophony.

Stephen saw the welcome light in van Buren's window, and stepping over the python that was travelling along the outer path he walked in by the garden gate.

'How pleasant to see you again,' they said almost simultaneously; and when van Buren had described his journey, safely performed but slow, tedious and unrewarding from the point of view of natural philosophy, and his treatment of the patient, Stephen said, 'By the way, there was a python in your lane.'

'Reticulatus, I suppose?'

'I imagine so. There was neither time nor light to examine his labial scales, but I imagine so. Twenty-five feet long, perhaps, and reasonably stout for a serpent of that length.'

'Yes. I see him from time to time. Pythons are said to be ill-tempered, but he has never proved objectionable; though perhaps it might not be wise to linger underneath his tree. Now tell me, how have matters come along?'

'As far as the official negotiations are concerned, they began well; but now they tend to become difficult, with endless restatements of the case.'

'Of course they will drag on for a great while; in these parts a rapid conclusion would be a loss of consequence. I put Cuvier's bones for the very small, very delicate red ants to clean, a long task for them, considering the tapir's bulk; but I am sure the bones will be perfectly white long before you carry them off to be sent to France.'

'Oh, I should be happy to stay. I have scarcely begun on the coleoptera, and I have never caught so much as a glimpse of an orang-utang, even in the summit of a very distant tree. But what distresses me is that although with your invaluable advice and the help of the amiable Wan Da I have won the good-will of the Vizier and the greater part of the council, particularly the Sultana Hafsa's relations, every time Fox makes real headway, the Sultan imposes his veto and the Vizier is obliged to overthrow everything, sometimes on pretexts that can hardly be attempted to be believed. And both Fox and I are convinced that this is because of Abdul. The Sultan has a strong, dominant character — his council is afraid of him — but as you said yourself some time ago, never was a man so besotted. It was embarrassingly obvious at the otherwise very successful reception aboard the frigate.'

'But what interest can Abdul have in the matter?'

'Have you met Ledward, the negotiator on the French side?'

'I have seen him two or three times, a fine upstanding figure of a man, though no doubt carrion.'

'He is not only a very able, persuasive negotiator, capable of out-talking Fox before the council and making him lose his temper, but he is also Abdul's lover.'

'Oh, oh,' said Van Buren. 'That young man is playing with fire. Hafsa *hates* him, and her family is powerful. She is a determined woman herself. And the Sultan is of an extremely jealous disposition.'

'It is my belief,' said Stephen, after a pause, 'that Ledward has made Abdul suppose that if they are put to their last shifts the French will give their frigate as well as the guns, the subsidy and the shipwrights they offered in the first place — they have nothing else left. Their money is all gone. They had no great matter to begin with, and Ledward lost much of it in play. He is a furious and uniformly unfortunate gambler; so is his companion Wray. Will I tell you the reason for my belief?'

'I should be very happy to learn it. But first let us drink a pot of coffee.'

'Do you remember how I exulted over the rough draughts of Duplessis' journal?' asked Stephen, putting down his cup and wiping his lips. 'It was the unwisest thing I ever did. Well, almost the unwisest. After a week however I did begin to feel that this was too easy entirely, too handsome to be honest. Now I did tell you, before you left, that I intended to arrange for your gardener's half-brother to bring me the waste paper from Duplessis' house?'

'Certainly.'

'The arrangement took some time, and the accumulation that eventually reached me when a discreet means of delivery had been contrived made a forbidding great heap. Still, I did flatten and class it all in time; and in time I came across some rough draughts of the mission's journal. Doubt had been growing in my mind and I was not altogether astonished to find that they were not the same as my alleged rough draughts of the same date; but I will confess that it vexed me extremely. Ledward is in charge of all the mission's intelligence, and I could see him laughing with Wray at my simplicity.'

'Galling. Oh very galling, I am sure.'

'So galling that I did not trust myself to act for some little while. Fortunately Wu Han, to whom I confessed some part of my disappointment, felt himself — I will not say responsible, but to some extent concerned, or engaged. I should add that he thinks of moving to Java, a more fruitful field for his talents, and he is very willing to be well-seen by Shao Yen and of course by Raffles. He questioned his clerk, whose good faith seems entire, bought his debt on my behalf, and made him invite Lesueur that evening. Lesueur came — I am not the only simpleton in Prabang — and he was summoned to pay. Of course he could not produce the money and so he was seized as a debtor — Wu Han has powerful porters for this kind of thing — and brought to me by night. He has no immunity of any kind. The Sultan gave safe-conduct and promise of protection to the members of the mission as it was constituted in Paris: Lesueur and other minor people were engaged in the East Indies. I represented to him that he had behaved very foolishly. He had not only ruined himself, since he would be kept in prison and scourged daily until he paid, but he had utterly wrecked the fortunes of his family and his mercantile house, all in British hands. He wept — he was exceedingly sorry — he had been forced into it by Mr Ledward who had found him abstracting papers after the first few days. I told him that his only hope of salvation was to say nothing whatsoever, to do what he had undertaken to do while at the same time sending me the false rough draughts as well: I had someone in the mission who would tell me if he did amiss, as I had already been told on this occasion. So far he has *not* done amiss, and I have the advantage of knowing both what they have done and what they wish me to think they have done or are about to do. And one thing that they or rather Ledward wishes me to think is that the French are prepared to throw their frigate into the scales in order to obtain their treaty.'

'How would your thinking that profit him?'

'I am not sure. It might be in the hope that the rumour would spread from our mission, eventually reaching the Sultan's ear from various sources and thus gaining in credibility. It might be in order to reduce Fox to despair, so that he should go away without any agreement. I do not know. But clearly it has floated into Ledward's mind and I am persuaded he has made Abdul believe it.'

The door opened and Mevrouw van Buren came in. She was little more than five feet tall, but she contrived to be elegant, slim, intelligent and above all cheerful, a quality Stephen valued highly — most Malays tended to be morose, and many, many married women to be glum. He was very fond of her: they bowed to one another, smiling, and she said to her husband, 'My dear, supper is on the table.'

'Supper?' cried van Buren, amazed.

'Yes, my dear, supper: we have it every evening at this time, you know. Come, it will be getting cold.'

'Oh,' said van Buren as they sat down, 'I was forgetting. There some post waiting for me when we came home. Nothing very interesting. The *Proceedings* are filled with mathematical papers, and in the *Journal* that charlatan Klopff vapours away about his vital principle. But I was sorry to hear that the City of London was in such a turmoil, and that there was a run on the banks: I do hope you are not likely to be injured?'

'Bless you, I have no money,' said Stephen. Then recollecting himself he went on, 'That is to say, for many years my life was solitary, poor, nasty, brutish, and it would have been short if I had not continued to live; so poverty and solitude became quite habitual — the natural state. I think of myself as penniless. Yet now in fact the case is altered. I have been blessed with an inheritance, which is, I may add, looked after by a banking-house of unquestioned integrity; and what is much more to the point I am no longer solitary. I have a wife; and by the time I return I hope to have a daughter too.'

The van Burens were touchingly pleased. They drank to Mrs Maturin and her baby, and when the subject had been thoroughly handled Mevrouw van Buren said, 'This brings in my news very happily: I have been bursting to tell you. The Sultana Hafsa is certainly with child, two months with child, and the Sultan is making a pilgrimage to Biliong to ensure that it shall be a boy. He promises to gild the dome of the mosque if he has an heir.'

'How long will the pilgrimage take?' asked Stephen.

'With the journey and all the proper lustrations, eight days: perhaps nine, since half the council necessarily go with him, leaving only the Vizier and a few others to keep the peace and try current cases,' said van Buren. 'I am afraid your negotiations are at an end for at least a week.'

'I shall go to Kumai,' said Stephen with a shining face.

On the way back to his bawdy-house he decided that in decency he must alas ask Fox to join him in the expedition; by the time he entered the lower, coarser hall he had composed a civil but not unduly pressing message, and as he was walking through to reach the upper, quieter regions where he could write it he noticed Reade and Harper sitting with a group of middle-aged women. Their short legs were resting on other chairs; each had a cheroot in one hand and a glass, probably of arrack, in the other; Reade's pretty, smooth, round, choirboy face was bright scarlet, Harper's something between grey and green. The sight puzzled him for a moment, but then he remembered they had been sent ashore so that their morals should not be damaged when girls were allowed on board. They did not see him, their gaze being fixed on a lascivious dance in the middle of the room, and he passed through to the stairs. Having written his note he came to their table and when their eyes had at last focussed on him they started to their feet. Harper flushed red; little Reade turned deathly pale and pitched forward. Stephen caught him as he fell and said, 'Mr Harper, you are all right, are you not? Then be so good as to deliver this note into His Excellency's hands as soon as possible. Halim Shah' — to the man of the house — 'pray have the other young gentleman carried to Mr Fox's residence without delay.'

The answer to his note came with the morning sun, and it was as welcome: Fox was désolé, désolé, but the Sultan had invited him to join the company going to Biliong, by way of compensation for Ledward's presence during his visit to Kawang, and the envoy saw that it was his clear duty to accept, for the sake of the treaty. He would go with death in his heart; never was a pilgrimage more inopportune. Yet if Maturin would do him the great kindness of breakfasting with him, Fox could at least give a brilliantly intelligent eye some notion of the things to look for and measure in the Kumai temple: Aubrey would be breakfasting too, which might be an added inducement.

'There you are, Stephen,' cried Jack, as he came in. 'A very good morning to you — it is days since we met. I am just going to flog those little brutes, and shall be back very soon. Here is His Excellency.'

'For all its mortifying effects,' said Stephen as he and Fox sat down to their kedgeree, 'you must admit that this invitation to Biliong is a great diplomatic coup. None of the French mission goes, I believe?'

'No, not one. I must draw what comfort I can from that.'

They talked for some little while about the journey, which, though by no means the great pilgrimage to Mecca, had many of the same strict ritual observances and much of the same austerity and abstinence. Would the presence of concubines or even of Abdul be proper? 'Oh no,' said Fox. 'At the time of vows of this kind chastity is absolutely required. Abdul will certainly not go.'

'Enter the righteous Sadducee,' said Jack, walking in. 'The trouble with flogging boys is that you may maim them for life, which is unkind, or not really hurt them at all, which is ridiculous. Bosun's mates never seem to have any trouble; they lay on as though they were threshing out a bushel of beans and then put the cat away as calm as you please. Nor did old Pagan, my schoolmaster. Plagoso Orbilio, we used to call him. But I tell you what it is, Excellency: you are no doubt a most capital diplomat, but you are a damned indifferent nursemaid.'

'I never thought such things would enter their heads,' said Fox sulkily. 'Public women! Lewd girls! I am sure they never entered mine, at that age.'

Jack and Stephen looked down at their plates; and after a while Fox begged Aubrey's pardon — his appointment at the palace was coming very close, and before he left he had to tell Maturin about this temple he was going to see — the particular features to be observed and if possible drawn and measured.

They saw him off, wished him a happy pilgrimage, and went back to finish the coffee. 'I wish I could come with you,' said Jack, 'but I cannot leave the ship. Yet since van Buren says there is at least a bridle-path to the crater-wall, may I not ride with you that far? And then Seymour or Macmillan or both could be there whenever you appoint, leading a pony for you to come back on.'

The road inland wound along the

Prabang river, right across the alluvial plain, and on either hand people were working their partly-flooded enclosures with buffaloes, or setting rice-plants. Weaver-birds flew in clouds, and down by the water various kinds of duck moved in surprising quantities: storks paced gravely in the paddies. 'I believe that was a real snipe,' cried Jack, putting his hand to his carbine. 'And another, by God!' But Stephen was deeply engaged in a discussion of the sago-palms that lined the road and filled the marshier parts with his guides, two sunny Dyaks belonging to that part of the Sultan's bodyguard detached to look after the British mission. They were armed with spears and their traditional blowpipes as well as krisses, and they were said to be quite fearless and deadly opponents; they were of course head-hunters; and they were full of information about sago and most of the creatures that passed. One of them, Sadong, was a remarkably good shot, and being an amiable, obliging soul he knocked down several of the more unusual birds for Stephen with his silent, accurate weapon, particularly after they had left the cultivated ground and had begun their long steady climb through the open forest, following the tracks made by the Chinese who brought down sandalwood, camphor and a number of the smaller trees used by cabinet-makers. Well before noon they sat under a spreading great camphor: Stephen skinned his birds and the Dyaks spitted them on twigs as an appetizer; then they ate a cold roast peacock, brewed a pot of coffee and set off in the hot, silent, shaded middle of the day. Nothing was moving; even the leeches were somnolent; but the Dyaks showed the recent tracks of two bears and the curious boar of those parts, and they pointed out a hollow tree in which the bears had obviously found honey, a tree with thirty-six kinds of orchid growing on it, some at a great height. The least spectacular was said to be useful in cases of female sterility.

On and steadily up; occasionally, when there was some exceptional thinning of the trees by lightning-stroke or whirlwind or bare rock outcropping, the volcano could be seen, coming closer and growing in height; and occasionally, in ravines or on open slopes, there were distinct traces of an ancient road, now reduced to a path where it was followed at all, but once broad, carefully planned and embanked. The Dyaks said that at its end there was a famous stand of durians, esteemed for their size, flavour and early ripening, and a heathen temple, just before the Thousand Steps.

'I have lost a stone,' said Jack, leading his pony up the deep-worn track.

'You can well afford it,' said Stephen.

On and on, up and up. Conversation drooped and eventually died quite away, Jack fairly aswim with sweat.

Then all at once the path ceased climbing and there was the durian grove on its fine stretch of flat ground: beyond it the grey wall of the crater soared up, the legendary steps catching the light, winding up and away like the Great Wall of China.

They walked slowly across the little plain under the wide-spaced trees, and there at the foot of the cliff, a cliff that now shut out half the sky, stood the Dyaks' heathen temple, almost entirely ruined and buried under rampant vegetation — figs, lianas and surprisingly a dense group of tree-ferns — but with part of one tower still standing. The rows of carvings on its outward face could not easily be made out; time had obscured them of course but even more the iconoclastic zeal of Muslim converts. As far as tall ladders could reach, noses, sometimes whole heads, bosoms, hands, arms and legs had been beaten off; yet enough remained to make it clear that this had been a Hindu holy place, and Stephen was trying to remember the name of the dancing figure with six arms — the remains of six arms — when he heard 'Oohoo, mias, mias!' from one Dyak and 'Shoot, tuan, shoot!' from the other.

He whipped round, saw Jack pulling the carbine from his saddle and the Dyaks pointing their pipes into a tall leafy durian. Following their direction he caught a fragmentary sight of a very large rufous shape high up and he called out 'Do not shoot, Jack.' At the same moment Sadong launched his dart. There was a violent movement above, a waving of branches, the tearing of leaves, and a heavy spiked durian shot out of the tree, passing between the Dyaks' heads. They fled, laughing, to a safe distance, and the orang-utang fled in the other direction, swinging from branch to branch, tree to tree, at a surprising pace. Stephen had two glimpses of him, reddish in the odd patches of sun, immensely broad-shouldered and long-armed, and then he was gone.

The Dyaks went to the tree and showed Stephen the empty remnants of fruit and the mias' droppings. 'There was a female here too,' said Sadong, pointing. 'I will see whether they have left anything at all.' He climbed into the tree, called 'Very few, the fiends,' and tossed down four of the ripest.

When the durians were done Stephen took his roll from behind the saddle, slung it over his shoulder and said, 'You must go back at once, brother, or you will be benighted in the forest. I shall have the sun much longer.'

'God help us,' said Jack, gazing up at the steps rising and rising for ever, 'what a climb. Just now I thought I saw someone a quarter of the way up, but either I was mistaken or he has turned the corner.'

'Goodbye, now, Jack. God bless. Dear Dyaks, goodbye.'

One hundred steps hollowed by a hundred generations of pilgrims, each step dreadfully high. Two hundred; already the forest was one vast green sheet spread out. And somewhere there was a full-grown male orang-utang moving about beneath the leaves. 'I should have given five pounds to have had time to see him properly,' he said; and then, remembering his present wealth, 'No. Much more; very much more.' Two hundred and fifty steps, and in a niche on the cliff side of the path the image of some god had been sadly disfigured. Three hundred, where the curve, always left-handed hitherto, became somewhat irregular, turned faster and showed not only a new stretch of country with the river shining silver a great way off but also another traveller far ahead.

A traveller wearing a shabby brown blanket, it seemed; a weary traveller, walking awkwardly, often on all fours where the steps rose steep, often resting. Three hundred and fifty. Stephen tried to remember Pope's lines about the Monument, and the number of the tall bully's steps. Whatever that number, four hundred of these had defeated Muslim zeal, since here, where a projecting spill of lava allowed the path to change direction, turning through a hundred and forty degrees, there stood a shrine untouched by violence, a dim, calm figure, almost effaced by wind and rain, but still conveying serenity and detachment.

The other traveller had rested by the shrine; now they were closer together, not two hundred yards apart, and now with a mingled incredulity and bubbling delight Stephen saw that the traveller was a mias, an orang-utang. The incredulity vanished when he had brought out his little pocket telescope, but the delight was tempered by a fear that the creature had not yet noticed him — that when it did so it would tear away. To be sure, this was no country for a great arboreal ape to make a sudden disappearance, there being nothing but bare lava and a stunted bush or two, but even so he kept his distance, watching the mias intently. He knew nothing of the ape's powers of hearing, sight or scent; and such a chance might never come again in a thousand years.

Up and up they went, still a cable's length apart; but slowly, for the ape was footsore and despondent. As for Stephen, by the sixth-hundred step his calves and thighs were ready to burst, and at each rise now they forced themselves upon his attention. Up and up, up and up until the ridge was no great way off at last. But before they reached it, the path took another turn; and when he too came round the corner he was on top of the ape. She was sitting on a stone, resting her feet. He scarcely knew what to do; it seemed an intrusion. 'God be with you, ape,' he said in Irish, which in his confusion seemed more appropriate. She turned her head and looked him full in the face; her expression was sad, weary, in no way hostile — remote. A falcon passed low overhead. They both watched it out of sight, and then she heaved herself up and went on, Stephen following. He took the most particular notice of her progression, her muscular movements, the paucity of the gluteus maximus, the odd disposition and contraction of the gastrocnemius, and on the other hand the prodigious breadth of shoulder and the very powerful great arms — clearly an animal made for moving among trees.

They were on the ridge at last, the crater's lip, and before going over and down she looked at him again with what he thought a happier, even a friendly look. He stayed for some moments, letting the pain ebb away from his legs and taking in this wholly unexpected scene: a vast bowl, miles and miles across, with a lake in the middle, a much gentler slope down the inside, trees almost to the top — a landscape of mixed forest interspersed with bamboo groves and wide stretches of grass, particularly by the lake. And down, far down on his left, the Kumai temple, a wisp of smoke rising from a building at its side. From where he stood there was only a path leading down, and a faint one at that; no steps were needed on this moderate fall. But the ape had left it; she was already among the low trees, swarming along with vast heaves, scarcely touching the ground and soon not touching it at all. He saw her shabby red-brown coat vanish among the leaves, travelling straight and fast towards the monastery, where someone was beating on a gong.

He arrived himself as dusk was falling. Much of the temple was ruined, but the severe broad front was whole as well as a large hall behind it, a hall from which a thin remote chant could be heard: across this front stretched what for want of the proper term Stephen thought of as a portico, a narthex, and in this narthex a monk in a worn old saffron robe was sitting by a brazier.

He stood up as Stephen emerged from the trees, reaching the open grass before the temple, and came forward to welcome him. 'Will you take a cup of tea?' he asked, proper greetings having been exchanged.

Ordinarily Stephen took no great delight in that insipid wash, but the Thousand Steps had reduced his pride and he accepted most thankfully. As they walked back and mounted the narthex steps (oh so painfully) he observed that the mias was sitting on the other side of the brazier, not indeed on a stool like the monk's but in a kind of tilted basket-work nest. Her feet had obviously been washed in a basin of warm water and there was blood on the cloth. Nevertheless the monk said, 'Muong, where are your manners?' and the ape rose high enough to bow.

Stephen returned the bow and said,

'Muong and I came up the Thousand Steps together.'

'Did she indeed go so far down as the durians?' asked the monk, shaking his head. 'I had supposed she was only walking on the higher slope for tilac berries. No wonder her poor feet are so torn. She too will be the better for a cup of tea.'

The ape had looked anxiously from face to face during this conversation; but at the word tea her visage brightened, and from the recesses of her basket she drew out a bowl.

While the monk, whose name was Ananda, was making the tea, and while they were all three drinking it, Stephen studied Muong's face; its varieties of expression were difficult to make out, but presently he could distinguish several, particularly the look of deep affection that she often directed towards the monk.

The chanting inside the temple stopped. The gong sounded three times. 'They are about to meditate,' observed Ananda.

Now night was coming fast. A final chorus of gibbons went hoo hoo hoo at great length in the forest below, and two of them hurried across the grass in front of the narthex, one with its hands clasped behind its neck, the other with its arms held high.

The monk brought a lamp, and at once it lit up a mouse-deer and her tiny fawn. Muong's eyes had closed; she was wheezing comfortably.

'I am sorry that she went so far,' said Ananda. 'It is too much for an ape of her age.'

'Perhaps she is very fond of durians.'

'She is; but there are plenty here, and some are ripe. No. She goes down there to see a male orang-utang; but she is old, and he scorns her. She comes back tired and sad, her feet torn, her coat quite matted.'

'Are there no orang-utangs here?'

'Oh yes, plenty, plenty; but they will not do. The only one for her is that animal below. She is friendly with her cousins here; they visit her quite often; but none can be looked upon as a mate.'

They talked about her for some time, and it appeared that more years ago than he could remember — the count of years was lost up here — when Ananda was a newly-arrived novice he had found her, a suckling, her mother dead, presumably from a snake-bite, and he had brought her up on ewe's milk. She could not actually speak, but he was quite sure that she understood at least two hundred words and could follow the drift of any ordinary conversation. She was very affectionate in a quiet, gentle way; and if she had not been so tired that evening, Stephen would have seen that she had pretty manners — she always wiped her mouth after drinking, for example, and she could eat with a spoon.

At moon-rise Ananda brought him a bowl of cold brown rice with salted green durian as a relish, and when it was eaten asked him — the first personal question since they met — where he would like to sleep. The room above this had once been called the pilgrim-chamber, but that was very, very long ago and now the bats might be an inconvenience; yet on the other hand sleeping down here exposed one to serpents, who loved to share one's warmth, and to porcupines.

'If Muong does not dislike it,' said Stephen, who had seen her busily and very exactly spreading a square of litter at the far end, 'I am sure I shall not.'

He had always understood that nothing in the vast and effectively sacred Kumai crater was ever killed by men nor had been so killed since the beginning of the Buddhist era, yet although he had had some small experience of this immunity during his time in Hindu India, where vultures would sit on the roof or squabble in the busy street and where monkeys walked in at the window, he

382

was astonished by what he saw. Before he went to sleep half the Ark, half the fauna of Pulo Prabang walked by in the moonlight or sat scratching themselves on the broad expanse of grass. Once in the night he was woken by a huge, sweet-breathed creature blowing on his face, but by that time the moon had set and he could not identify it; then in the early light, when first he raised his head, there was an orang-utang nonchalantly leaving the narthex, where it had presumably called on Muong. And the dewy grass was crisscrossed with innumerable tracks.

When next he sat up he observed that Muong had already left — her bedding was ranged neatly behind a row of stones — and that his legs were quite extraordinarily stiff. He rubbed them, listening vaguely to the chant within and watching the sun's light travel down the mountainside: the sky was already a full soft blue and the gibbons had been hooting this half hour and more. The light reached a noble tree that he took to be a liquidambar; the chant seemed to be moving to a close; he stood up, still bent, and felt in his roll for the offerings that Liu Liang (himself a Buddhist in the Chinese manner) had told him would be acceptable, a long thick silk-skinned sausage of delicate tea, a long thick leather-skinned sausage of benzoin. He washed his face in the remaining dew, pushed his roll into a shape at least as neat as Muong's, and sat on the narthex steps, eating a ship's biscuit.

The chanting stopped, the gong boomed and the door opened, a shaft of sunlight showing the great stone figure at the far end of the temple, a calm, harmonious figure with its right hand raised, palm outwards. The five choir-monks came out, led by their tall, lean abbot. Stephen bowed to them and they to Stephen. Ananda appeared with tea and several bowls.

Everyone sat on the ground, and Stephen proffered his silk parcel, saying, 'An unworthy offering to an ancient house,' and his leather parcel, 'To an ancient house, an unworthy offering.'

The abbot patted them with detached pleasure, returned thanks, and waited, drinking his tea, sip by sip. After a decent interval Stephen gave a short account of himself: he was a medical man, a naval surgeon, brought into these parts by the war between England and France; apart from medicine his greatest interest was living things and their way of life. He also had a friend who was deeply concerned with the first spread of Buddhism and the remaining early temples. Stephen therefore hoped he might be permitted to look at Kumai, measure it, draw it as far as his powers allowed, and to walk about the country for a few days to observe its inhabitants.

'Certainly you may look at our temple, and draw it,' said the abbot. 'But as for the animals, there is no killing here. We eat rice, fruit and such things; we take no life.'

'I have no wish to kill anything here; only to observe. I have no weapons at all.'

While the Abbot was considering this, another monk, who had been gazing at Stephen through his spectacles, said, 'So you are an Englishman.'

'No, sir,' said Stephen. 'I am an Irishman. But for the moment Ireland is subject to England, and therefore at war with France.'

'England and Ireland are small islands on the farthest western extremity of the world,' said another monk. 'They are so close together that they can scarcely be distinguished; birds flying at a great height may land on the one rather than on the other. But in fact England is the larger.'

'It is true that they are close together, and that it is not always easy to distinguish them from a great distance; but then, sir, the same applies to right and wrong.'

'Good and evil are so close at times,' observed the Abbot, 'that there is scarcely the breadth of a hair between them. But as for the animals, young man, since you undertake not to do any harm, you may certainly walk about among them; Muong will show you her friends among the mias, and there are quantities of swine, as well as all the gibbons and their kind, and medicinal plants in great variety. Yet like all pilgrims you are stiff and bent after the Thousand Steps. Ananda will take you to our hot baths, and then today you will draw the temple and measure it: tomorrow you will be supple and reposed.'

There were few carnivores in Pulo Prabang — no tigers at all — and fewer still at Kumai. Some pythons were to be found, and they had to make a living; but three months between meals were not unusual for them, and neither they nor the odd small cats, still less the honey-bears, created that perpetual half-conscious wariness and apprehension among the peaceful animals that made them so nervous and difficult to watch in most other parts. But above all they had not been persecuted by men for a thousand years and they took no more notice of human beings than of cattle; and Stephen found to his stupefaction that he could walk through a herd of rusa, pushing his way where they stood thick, as though he were one of themselves. He could offer the mouse-deer's fawn a green frond growing too high and it would not hesitate for a moment. Although the comparatively few birds were a little more diffident, no doubt because being airborne they were more experienced (very few other creatures could manage the bare, steep, shaley outer crater-wall, and it had only the single gap, by the Thousand Steps), but even so they sometimes perched on him; and the whole effect was very like being in a waking dream, of losing human identity, or even of being invisible as well as wonderfully supple and reposed after hours in the three basins hollowed in the rock and fed by three faintly sulphurous springs, each hotter than the last.

The grazing animals it was that took least notice of him; the swine — there were two kinds — were curious, sometimes embarrassingly so, and playful; but it was the primates, the golden and the proboscis monkeys and above all the orang-utangs that showed most interest. The orang-utangs were gentle, placid, rather lethargic creatures upon the whole, not particularly sociable and not at all gregarious — Muong never showed him more than five at once, two sisters and their young — but they often came down from the flattish nests in which they spent so much of their time and sat with him and Muong, looking earnestly into his face, their lips pursed and thrust forward, as though they were going to whistle, and sometimes gently touching him, his clothes, his meagre hair, his pallid, almost naked arm (their hands, though scaley, were quite warm). Once it was a perfectly enormous old male that came down by a liana as thick as a cable and sat at the foot of his tree with them: he was old, he had the expanded cheek-pads and the throat-pouch of the aged mias, but none of the peevishness and ill-nature so usual in the elderly. He positively caressed Stephen's shoulder before going up his liana again, with a swing as light and easy as a topman for all his prodigious weight. What communication there was between Muong and her friends he could not make out, though he tried hard: sound audible to him had little to do with it — a small vocabulary of grunts — and he could only suppose that it was a matter of the language of eye and minute change in expression. Whatever it was, she knew where they were and how, from a distance, to invite them to come down from their trees or through a bamboo-grove.

Those he most attentively watched were the two sisters, both rather a fine red, and their half-grown, playful, very active young. They spent much more time on the ground and he stayed with them for hours together, hoping he would remember all he observed. But Muong did not really approve of this frequentation, and gradually it was borne in upon him that she thought the children tiresome and the young mothers rather discreditable, even common.

Indeed it was his insistence upon going to see the group on his last day that led to their only disagreement. Muong knew perfectly well what he wanted and by now he knew perfectly well from her expression that she was not pleased; still, when both Ananda and he asked her to do so she did lead him to the far side of the lake, sometimes going along with her knuckles to the ground when they reached the open grassy slope, sometimes leaning on his arm.

The family band was there, where a tongue of trees ran almost to the water; and that was where Muong left him, obviously intending to go home alone.

The twins, lighter and more spidery than their one-at-a-birth cousin, were guarding the top of a boulder from him, a great rounded grey boulder at the edge of the water. With boundless energy the little apes attacked, repelled, fell on to the muddy shore or into the water, splashed and began again. Apart from some muted gibbering they were remarkably quiet for perhaps half an hour, but then in an excess of zeal one bit another's ear: they all fell into the lake, screeching; the mothers came rushing down — oaths, reproaches, blows, reddish hair torn out, and the game ended with the whole group shambling off over the grass and into the trees.

From his discreet observation-post, not a hiding-place at all but a comfortable tussock that gave him a general view, Stephen watched them disappear and then looked back to the boulder to estimate the orang-utang's ordinary unhurried quadrupedal speed over a moderate slope, but as it travelled his eye was caught by an object that stopped his breath, that almost stopped his heart and that banished all thought of calculation. What he had hitherto taken for another grey boulder was in fact a rhinoceros.

Rhinoceros unicornis. A male, by his long single horn and his size, something between sixteen and seventeen hands: though that was difficult to judge because of the huge bulk below its withers and the relative shortness of its legs. Three birds were perched upon its back.

Without moving from his tussock Stephen brought out his spy-glass — he was filled with a sudden illogical caution — and as well as he could with his shaking hands he focussed it upon the rhinoceros. Since the animal was not much above a hundred yards away this brought it very close indeed, so close that Stephen saw it close its eyes. It appeared to him that the rhinoceros had recently been wallowing — mud was drying on its massive back — and that on leaving the muddy shore it had gone to sleep there, facing up the grassy slope, a little way from the lake. The final outburst of the orang-utangs had woken it: now it was going to sleep again.

But this was a mistaken view. The rhinoceros was thinking. Presently it opened its eyes again, breathed in and out with enormous force, raised its head, sniffed the air from right to left, brought its ears to bear and set itself in motion, surprisingly buoyant motion for such a solid mass, going straight up the hill. And as he watched Stephen understood its reputation of shocking strength and savagery, disembowelling elephants, devastating thorn-brakes for hours on end out of mere blind fury and malignance, tossing bulls as though they were footballs. The speed increased; the thick short legs fairly twinkled as the creature ran, gathering impetus. Looking beyond, Stephen saw another rhinoceros at the top of the slope, quarter of a mile away; it too was male; it too was running at the same smooth, powerful, very rapid pace. At the half-way point they converged, and half turning met shoulder to shoulder in a blow that sent up a cloud of dust; but neither staggered, and each completing its turn they came down abreast, faster and faster still, straight for him. The ground trembled shockingly: Stephen leapt to his feet; and then with a great trampling rushing din they were past, racing towards the lake. Within a yard of its edge they wheeled together, wheeled as quick as boars, and raced up the hill again, shoulder to shoulder, their hooves twinkling in time as they crossed the ridge and disappeared.

Chapter 8

The way up the Thousand Steps had been wearisome but intensely happy both in anticipation and in the present; the way down was more wearisome by far, partly because an exceedingly heavy warm rain fell from the moment he crossed the crater's rim, so thick that he could not see fifty yards ahead and so violent that the drops splashed high, wetting him to the middle. It also obscured the worn, uneven steps, which made the descent anxious, tense, full of care; but beneath all the physical tension there was an even greater happiness than before, that of a fulfilment that had gone beyond any anticipation, and of something not far from the beatific vision.

It glowed within, under the sodden straw cloak the monks had given him, and it was glowing still when he staggered down the last steps and on to the level sward of the durian-grove. The rain stopped as suddenly as it had begun, and the forest was filled with the sound of running water.

He looked expectantly round, but seeing no one he felt in his bosom, the only moderately dry place about him, for the repeating watch that hung there by a string. It was as he inclined his head to hear its tiny bell state that he was an hour and a half behind his time that he noticed the horses' rumps glistening under the lee of the Hindu tower: beyond them a pyramid of tall palm-fronds, inverted to throw off the wet, and inside it Seymour, with two Malays smoking tobacco.

'Lord, sir,' cried Seymour, who had started up with a look of grave concern at his appearance, 'I beg your pardon. I thought you was an orang-utang.'

'Do I look like an orang-utang, Mr Seymour?' asked Stephen.

'To tell you the truth, sir, I believe you do.'

'Perhaps it is the effect of my straw cloak,' said Stephen, looking at his arm. 'Yet it was a fine stiff rain-shedding garment to begin with. I hope I have not kept you waiting?'

'Lord no, sir,' said Seymour. 'I think you are exact to the minute, or close on. We came rather early, as the Captain said.'

'How is Mr Aubrey?'

'When last I saw him, sir, he was in fine form. He ran up to the main-jack the other day — think of that, sir, at his age! But now he is gone off with the master to survey the coast. Should you like something to eat, sir? I have brought you a chicken. It was Mr Elliott that shot it.'

'I should like a chicken of all things,' said Stephen. 'A handful of rice was my breakfast at dawn.' He greeted the Malays, a glum, wet, cross-looking pair, very unlike the Dyaks; they bowed and answered politely, but said there was no time to be lost. The waters were out in the forest and in the plain; they must hurry if they were ever to get back at all.

'Well, I shall eat my chicken, however,' said Stephen, sitting down. 'How did Mr Elliott come to *shoot* it? This bird is far too big for a jungle-fowl.'

'Very true, sir, but he *thought* it was a jungle-fowl. He thought all these' — pointing to the stripped carcasses on the floor — 'were jungle-fowl, and he blazed away until the woman of the house came and threw a bucket of water over him and his gun. There was a great hullaballoo, and he had to pay. But that was nothing to the hullaballoo in the town the next day, sir — people running about and screeching and letting off muskets, like a revolution . . .'

'Come, tuan,' said the older, sourer, wetter Malay. 'The horses are saddled. We must go.'

Seymour's kindly chicken had been carried in a tarpaulin bag for hours through a tropical rain-forest and it tasted so very like physic that Stephen abandoned it without much reluctance and stumped out on to the sodden grass.

'Let me give you a leg-up, sir,' said Seymour, and Stephen, rising into the saddle under his impulsion, realized that for Seymour he too was an aged man. Several other marks of solicitude fell into line: he had been led across a busy street in Batavia; his boots had been pulled off at Buitenzorg; and a puzzling half-heard recommendation that Clerke should 'take care of the ancient' now lost its mystery. Did a very old, weatherbeaten, sun-bleached wig make its wearer look, if not decrepit, then at least past mark of mouth?

'Tell me about your revolution,' he began; but before Seymour could reply they had entered the homeward track from the durian-grove and the horses were slithering down what was now a muddy stream, in single file.

Before the rain began again Stephen did manage, in odd bursts, to extract what little information Seymour had to give: facts he had none, but he did convey an atmosphere of crisis. People said that there was an armed rising, that the Vizier had been dragged off to prison, loaded with chains, that the Sultan was on his way back. At another halt and in a completely different context Seymour also said that the French had heaved down their ship; they were careening her, and — raising his voice over the roar of the hurtling rain — they had chosen a damned bad moment for doing so, the lubbers.

It was a damned bad moment for travelling, too. The following hours, though not very great in number, seemed almost infinite in extent: the forest-leeches had never been so active, agile, enterprising; and when at last the troop reached the flooded plain, creeping in mud to their knees and often losing the way in the featureless landscape, the horse-leeches were worse by far.

During those halts when it was possible to converse Stephen tried to learn what was happening from the Malays, but they told him little. They may not have known; they may have been afraid; they certainly held him responsible for the perfectly horrible time they were having; and presently he saw that it was useless to insist.

When at last, at last, they reached it, the town was more informative. Prabang had been spared all but the fringe of the downpour, and although the river was tearing along, mud-coloured, covered with tree-trunks and branches, full from bank to bank, the streets themselves were now no more than damp, and even at this time of night they would ordinarily have been full of people. There was no one. Even Maturin's Javanese place was shut up and blind. The only light to be seen was a general orange glow over the palace roofs and the only sound, apart from the voice of the river, was a confused hubbub behind the palace walls.

The poor foundered horses were led back to their stable; the Malays paid and re-warded. Stephen, aware that the young, however kind and solicitous, had in fact less stamina than the old, took Seymour back to the ship, told Macmillan to remove every single leech before letting him lie down — the boy was sleeping as he stood — and then walked off to van Buren's house.

'How glad I am you are a night-bird,' he said, sitting down heavily. 'I should have been in a sad way else. My brothel is shut.'

'You must take off your clothes,' said van Buren, looking at him with close attention, 'and when we have rid you of all your para-sites you must rub yourself with a towel and put on a dressing-gown. Then with an omelet and a pot of coffee you will feel more nearly human.'

'Dear colleague,' said Stephen six cups later, 'never did you make a better prognosis. But I am interrupting your work.'

'Not at all. I am only arranging the skins you were so very kind as to send me. Many thanks indeed: there is a nectarinea I had never seen, and what I take to be a new subspecies of graculus. Tell me, how did your journey go?'

'Kumai was nearer Paradise than anything I am likely to see again in this life or the next; I cannot bless my fate enough for having been allowed it. I communed with orang-utangs; they held me by the hand. I saw the tarsier . . . immeasurable wealth. But allow me to tell you at another time and at immeasurable length. First, pray let me know what is afoot.'

'Before I do so,' said van Buren, holding up one hand, 'tell me whether you have brought the tarsier for us to dissect.'

Stephen shook his head, thinking of the simple-minded little creature that had gazed at him with its huge noctambulant's eyes, sitting just the other side of Ananda's lamp. 'I promised not to kill anything: and indeed, you know,' he said, 'a man would need a heart of brass to kill a tarsier.'

'Where primates are concerned, I have a

heart of brass,' said van Buren. 'And the tarsier is the strangest of them all. But to return,' he went on, looking at Stephen with his head cocked on one side, 'do you really wish me to tell you what is afoot?'

'Certainly I do.'

'Well' — still looking at him quizzically — 'Hafsa and her family took what I was going to call your advice but which I find I must call the advice arising from some outside source and at the third attempt their people seized Abdul in bed with Ledward and Wray. The Europeans pleaded the Sultan's safe-conduct and the Vizier let them go; but Abdul was hurried off and messengers were sent to the Sultan. Some of Abdul's friends made a commotion, but the Vizier's men and the remaining Dyak guard soon put them down, and now those who ran away are being searched for. That is why the houses are all shut up.'

'I see. I see.' A long pause. 'How do you think it will end?'

'I do not know. Abdul's pretty face may save his skin: it may not. I just do not know. By the way, I should have told you before: your Pondicherry clerk —'

'Lesueur?'

'Lesueur. Was murdered. Pray tell Mr Fox to take great care. He is likely to be here in the morning, well before the Sultan and his train. He would be well advised to go aboard the ship; so might you. Assassins are ten a penny in Prabang, and poison is by no means rare.'

'I might, too.'

'I will find you a pair of pistols and send Latif and the watchman with you.'

The boat put off, the boat pulled back; Stephen, limp with fatigue, was hauled up the side. Richardson led him to his cot, and before he sank into something not far removed from a coma he heard a voice say, 'The knocking-shop is closed, and the Doctor's come home to bed,' followed by a cackle of good-natured laughter.

Eight bells in the morning watch pierced through the very deep fog of sleep and Stephen raised his head, aware of an urgency though not of its nature. Some moments later the pattern fell into shape and he called aloud for Ahmed. After the first reviving cup he said, 'Ahmed, I must shave my face and put on my good black coat.'

At one bell in the forenoon watch he stepped on to the quarterdeck, smooth and decently dressed, stared at the washed, innocent sky, and said, 'My dear Mr Fielding, good morning to you. Please may I have a boat to take me ashore, with a couple of Marines as a guard? I am going to see Mr Fox, and the town is somewhat disturbed.'

Fox had arrived an hour before; he was in a state of intense but contained excitement and his greeting, though friendly and even familiar, was utterly detached. 'One of my informants has been murdered,' said Stephen, 'and as I dare say you know already, Ledward and Wray are still at large. There is the possibility not only of open murder but also of poison secretly administered: a most reliable source tells me that you should take very great care.'

'Thank you for the warning. I did indeed know that they were at large: I had scarcely reached the house before a note came from Wray, offering to bear witness against Ledward in return for protection and removal to any other country or island whatsoever. Here it is.'

'He must think you bear Ledward very great ill-will,' said Stephen, having looked at the note.

Fox grinned and said, 'I hope, I *hope* to have him put to the same death as Abdul. The only thing I am afraid of is the Sultan's notion of honour. He gave them his safe-conduct, and he is so very touchy about these matters that even the Vizier dared not arrest them: though to be sure they may have been taken up secretly, in case the Sultan should change his mind — they have not been seen in the French compound. Yet whether or no, I think we may say the treaty is in the bag, to use a low expression.'

'Let us not say anything of the sort,' said Stephen. 'My very best source tells me that it is the toss of a coin whether Abdul does not turn the scale, with his pretty face and his gazelle-like eyes.'

'Does he go so far? Does he indeed?' cried Fox, disconcerted. He searched Stephen's face. 'I must go.' He rang the bell and ordered a guard. 'I have an appointment with the Vizier. The Sultan comes back late this afternoon: there is to be a full council-meeting and there will be a decision tonight. Your balcony at the — at your lodging in the town looks over the palace courtyards. May I call on you this evening? I have not heard a word about your journey to Kumai — you went, of course?'

'I beg your pardon for appearing like this,' said the envoy, who was wearing the Marine officer's uniform and blue spectacles, 'but I thought . . .'

'A very sensible precaution, sir,' said Stephen. 'Nothing hides a man better than a red coat. Pray come in and sit on the balcony; there is a modest collation laid out. The sea-slugs are a speciality of the house; so alas is the luke-warm Macao wine, but we can always call for tea or coffee. And quite soon, shortly after sunset, you will see a blazing great star rise over there, by the Mosque of Omar. Jack Aubrey tells me it is Jupiter, and if he were here with his telescope he would show you the four little moons.'

'I beg your pardon,' said Stephen's sleeping-partner, opening the door and looking at Fox with intense curiosity, 'I forgot my drawers.'

'Before coming here,' said Stephen as they settled on the balcony, overlooking the busiest street, the open space in front of the Rasul mosque, and the wall and the outer courtyards of the palace beyond, 'I had like everybody else read about Malays running amuck, or amock, as I believe one should say, but never did I expect to see two of them doing so at once — my first sight of the phenomenon, at that. One came down this very street not an hour ago, cleaving his way in the midst of a frantic clamour, slashing right and left, a train of blood behind and a herd of people running away in front until he was brought down and killed by a Dyak with a spear. Then while the crowd was standing round the body, talking and laughing and pushing their krisses into it, another maniac came down that little side-street, screaming shrill and high, and they scattered again. He ran off out of sight right-handed, having wounded two men as he passed, and what happened to him I cannot tell; but five minutes later people were walking about, talking, buying and selling, and fanning themselves as though nothing had happened.'

'It is a strangely cruel and bloody country at times,' said Fox. 'Or perhaps indifferent is the better word.' They ate in silence, wandering among the array of dishes. The shadows lengthened. Fox was searching in a bowl of prawns when he raised his head and stood motionless. 'That must be the Sultan arriving,' he said.

The drums and trumpets grew louder, then suddenly louder by far as the procession turned the corner and filed in through the outer palace gate. More trumpets within and the sound of shouting wafted over on the seaward breeze so that it was almost at hand.

'Before the light fades, I should like to show you the drawings I made of Kumai,' said Stephen. 'They are inept, they suffered much from the rain, particularly the outer leaves, but they may give you some notion of what I saw.'

'Oh please do,' cried Fox, his whole attitude changing. 'I long to see what you have brought down.'

'This is my attempt at the great figure which dominates the temple. The stone is a smooth light-grey fine-grained volcanic rock. The drawing gives no sense of its majestic serenity nor any of that feeling of far greater size than its actual twelve feet which is so strong when you stand before it. Nor can you easily see that the raised right hand has its palm facing outwards.'

'Oh, I can make out the hand very well. A capital drawing, Maturin; I am so grateful to you. This is the Buddha in the abhaya mudra attitude, signifying *Fear not, all is well*. Oh, such an omen! As far as I know, no other has ever been recorded in these parts.'

'Here are my paced-out plans; and this is what I call the narthex, where I slept. These are the particular carvings of a sculptured frieze where the narthex roof joins the main body. The marks show where the beams have impinged upon the frieze, obscuring it in places: obviously the carvings are earlier than the roof.'

'Oh yes,' said Fox, studying the pages with great attention, 'these are very early indeed. Perhaps earlier than anything I have ever seen in Malay country. Lord, what a discovery!'

While there was still day enough he took Stephen over them again and again, and then he said, 'It would be a pity to call for a lamp. I have all the plans and drawings clear in my head, and I could follow you pace by pace if you would be so very kind as to describe everything you saw.'

'That would take us well into next year, but I will try to give some general impression. Will I begin with the nectarineas, which take the place of humming-birds here? Do nectarincas interest you?'

'Only moderately.'

'Orang-utangs, then?'

'To tell you the truth, Maturin, there are already so many orang-utangs among my acquaintance that I would not cross the street to see another.'

'Well, well: perhaps I had better start with the Hindu temple, and confine myself to holy things and their surroundings.' This he did, and as his tale rose up the Thousand Steps, shrine by shrine, so the sun sank to the western sea; and by the time he was describing his first sight of the temple, its former immensity and the disposition of its parts, Jupiter had appeared.

Stephen reached the narthex, the opening of the temple door, the sunlight showing him the figure within, and Fox said, 'Oh, I quite agree. I have had a greater sense of holiness — sanctity — detachment — un-worldliness in the severer Buddhist temples of the ancient rite than in any but the most austere Christian monasteries.'

Fox was making a long parenthetical remark about his travels on the border of Tibet and in Ceylon when there was a clash of discordant drums and cymbals from the palace, a volley of musket-fire, the sound of trumpets and of a great long roaring horn. This was followed by a more regular beating of drums, and the innermost courtyard was lit with great lanterns by the score. Then came the wavering orange glare of a fire, a fire that rose and rose so that sometimes its flames showed high above the outer wall. Its smoke drifted straight over them as they sat there silent on the balcony. The hoarse roaring horn again and the firelight turned blood-red as a powder was thrown on the blaze.

'Someone is going to catch it,' said Fox. 'I hope to God it is Ledward. I hope to God the sack is tying round his neck this moment.'

Now there was shouting from the palace,

loud shouting and laughter, perhaps some muffled screams. The fire leapt higher still, flame-coloured once more; the lights increased and the shouting — it was very like the sound of a rising or a hysterical mob. How long it went on there was no telling: once or twice Stephen saw great bats pass between him and the glare: and all the time Fox stood gripping the rail, dead still, hardly breathing.

At length the mob-noise diminished; the fire died down so that its flames could no longer be seen; the drums fell silent and the lanterns moved off, leaving no more than a ruddy glow behind the walls.

'What happened? What happened?' cried Fox. 'What happened exactly? I have no one inside the palace: I cannot make my visit until his fasting for an heir is over. I cannot even see the council straight away. To act on mere gossip or an inaccurate account would be disastrous; yet I must act. Can you help me, Maturin?'

'I know a person who will have the details within the hour,' said Stephen coldly. 'I shall call on him tomorrow morning.'

'Could you not go now?'

'No, sir.'

Stephen had in fact no need to call on van

Buren; they met in the buffalo-market. For a while they talked about the animals' wild relations, the banteng and the gaur, either of which might have breathed upon Stephen by night at Kumai — creatures of enormous size — and then Stephen said, 'My colleague is importunate to know what happened last night. Did Abdul's pretty face and gazelle-like eyes save him?'

'By the time Hafsa had finished he had no pretty face and no gazelle-like eyes, either. No. The sack was tied over his head and he was beaten round and round the fire until the pepper and the beating killed him.'

'Ledward and Wray?'

'Untouched. Some people thought they were going to be seized, immunity or no; but I believe the Sultan had a sickening of it all — Abdul's body was given to his family for burial rather than being thrown into the street — and they are only forbidden the court.'

It had always appeared to Jack Aubrey, ever since he was a little boy, that one of the purest joys in the world was sailing a small, well-conceived, weatherly boat: the purest form of sailing too, with the sheet alive in one's hand, the tiller quivering under the crook of one's knee and the boat's instant response to the movement of either, and to the roll and the breeze. A more stirring, obvious joy, of course, in a moderate gale and a lively sea, but there was also a subtle delight in gliding over smooth water, coaxing every ounce of thrust from what light air there was: an infinitely varied joy. Yet since he had left the midshipmen's berth he had done very little sailing in this sense, and almost none for pure pleasure; and as a post-captain, usually wafted to and fro in the glory of his barge, he could scarcely remember half a dozen occasions. Apart from anything else, the life of a captain, even with such a conscientious, intelligent first lieutenant as Fielding, was an uncommonly busy one: at least as Jack Aubrey led it.

He was fond of the *Diane*, that honest, stout-hearted though unexciting ship, but he was thoroughly enjoying his holiday from her. The survey of the coast of Pulo Prabang with Mr Warren, an able hydrographer, was a lively pleasure in itself, but the great charm of these days was the sailing, as varied as could be wished, the swimming, the fishing, and the hauling up on a lonely strand at sunset to eat their catch, grilled on driftwood embers, and to sleep in tents or in hammocks slung between two palms. They had sailed east, following the curve of the island, the almost round island, to its northernmost point, passing several villages on the way, including Ambelan, the little port to which the French frigate *Cornélie* and her over-enterprising crew had been exiled. Now they were on their way back, checking their recorded bearings and soundings and carrying on with Humboldt's programme of measuring temperatures at various depths, salinity, atmospheric pressure and the like, but none of this was very arduous and at present Jack was directing the *Diane*'s smaller cutter at the narrow pass between the cape right ahead and a small island just beyond it. He was sailing as close to the brisk west-south-westerly breeze as he could; the good clinker-built boat made little leeway and he thought he could run through the gap on the present tack.

Bonden, who though by right captain's coxswain had not had his hand on the tiller since the boat left Prabang, was sure he could. Warren, the master, who was unable to swim, thought he possibly could, but wished he would not attempt it; Yusuf, who had been brought along for the language and because he knew the difference between right and wrong, at least where fish and fruit were concerned, was convinced that it was impossible; but being a Muslim he took it in good part, since what was written was written and there was no arguing with fate, and in any case he was a sea Malay, as much at home in the water as out of it. There should have been a fifth opinion, that of Bampfylde Elliott. Jack had meant to bring him, because although young Elliott was no seaman and never would be, Jack liked him. As the *Diane*'s commander he had had to address harsh words to her second lieutenant oftener than was either usual or pleasant and he had hoped that this break would bring back kinder relations. It was not that Elliott had grown dogged, sullen or resentful; it was rather that his mind seemed oppressed by a sense of guilt and inadequacy and by the little esteem in which he was held aboard the *Diane*. But the day before they set out, when Fielding was having the frigate's yards reblacked, a hand busy high aloft dropped his bucket. It might perfectly well have fallen safely, there being very few people on deck — a hundred to one it would have done no more harm than a black stain to be scrubbed out by the afterguard — but in fact it struck Elliott on his wounded shoulder, he being unlucky as well as inept.

The headland, the gap and the island were coming closer, much closer. Jack, bending and peering forward, saw that the high land was deflecting the breeze so that it would head him in mid-passage: there was a slight cross-ruffle on the ebbing tide. His mind at once began computing speed, inertia, distance, most desirable course, and presented him with the answer in something less than a second, a hundred yards short of the rock. A few moments more and he bore up, gathered way, and with the greater impetus shot through the gap right in the wind's eye, his mainsail shivering, rounded the cape and ran down its farther side. The saving of five insignificant minutes was no very great triumph; indeed the caper had a faint, very faint air of showing away; but it was pleasant to feel the old skills unimpaired.

The coast in this part of Pulo Prabang was much indented, and the fjord they were now entering had a companion beyond it. These deep narrow bays were separated by Cape Bughis, and in his chart Jack called this one East Bughis Inlet and the next West Bughis Inlet, although in the *Diane* it was called Frenchmen's Creek, since Ambelan, with the *Cornélie* in its harbour, lay on the eastern shore. The road from a number of fishing villages and little towns to Prabang followed the coast wherever it could, and it crossed the bottom of both these inlets: Jack's idea was to land far down in the first, walk along the shore to the road and so round to the western side of the next, from which he could view the *Cornélie* over the water. In spite of all his swimming he felt in need of a walk, and he was by no means disinclined to see how the French were coming along. He knew they were careening their ship, a perilous business on a coast with such considerable tides, and he wanted to see their progress, if only from a professional point of view. On its outward voyage the boat had crossed the mouth of West Bughis Inlet, but Jack had not sailed down it, though the wind was fair. He wished to avoid any sort of indiscretion that might have a bad effect on Fox's dealings with the Sultan; but it seemed to him that his behaviour could not be thought improper if, in the course of a walk, he looked at the *Cornélie* from the other side of the bay, particularly as French officers had often brought telescopes to peer at the *Diane* from Prabang. Then, having gazed his fill and taken a fresh set of bearings, he would walk on, crossing the next promontory to the farther strand, where, touching wood, he would find the boat hauled up and smoke rising from the evening fire.

While the very word 'supper' was sounding in his head both Yusuf and Bonden caught a fish, a fine silvery fish, a two or three pounder with crimson eyes and crimson fins. 'Padang fish, tuan!' cried Yusuf. 'Good, good, very good fish!'

'So much the better,' said Jack, and he let fly the sheet, bringing the cutter gently to the shore: he stepped neatly out, his shoes and his ditty-bag slung round his neck, shoved thc boat off, called out 'This evening, then, in Parrot Bay,' and sat down on the warm sand to dry his feet.

Warren replied cheerfully, but Bonden, though back in his rightful place in the stern sheets, shook his head with a despondent look: he would have liked the Captain to take at least a hanger and a brace of pistols, if not a musket and a couple of well-armed hands as well.

The sand here was pinkish-white, quite unlike the volcanic black of Prabang itself, and delightfully firm. Jack, dryfoot and shod, stretched out at a fine pace, his eyes half-closed against the glare, and presently he reached the bottom of the bay and, above highwater-mark, the road. Five minutes after striking into it he was in the grateful shade of sago-palms; they stood deep on either side almost the whole way to the village, and they were completely uninhabited — no people, no animals, scarcely a bird — except for myriads of insects which he could rarely see and never identify but which kept up a continual din, so all-pervading that after a few minutes he was unaware of it except on those rare occasions when it suddenly stopped entirely. The sago-palms were not very beautiful, being thick and short, while their dull-green crowns were rather dusty, and presently he found their company and the loneliness oppressive. It was a relief to walk out of the shade at last and into the rice-paddies outside the village at the bottom of West Bughis Inlet; people were working in them, and some looked up as he went by, but without any particular interest, far less astonishment. Much the same applied to the village itself, sparsely inhabited at this time of day, and from here the reason for their indifference was evident, since the whole long bay was now open before him, with Ambelan on the eastern side, its harbour quite crowded and two Chinese junks lying just offshore. Of course these people were used to strangers.

Beyond the village the road mounted to the crest of the long rocky headland that formed the inlet's other arm, and at the top of the hill Jack, now in a fine state of sweat, turned off right-handed to walk out to a point where he would be opposite the little port. There was a path, he found, winding among the boulders and the low, wind-stunted vegetation, and soon he saw why: dotted along the edge of the sea below him there were great fallen rocks by the score, well out from the strand, and on many of them stood fishermen with long bamboos, casting beyond the moderate surf of the tide, now on the make; and each group of rocks had a corresponding side-path leading down to it.

When he had travelled something like a mile he took one of these and dropped down the slope, going rather more than half way, to the clearly-defined division between the zone where the wind was strong enough and steady enough to keep the trees and bushes short and the zone in the lee of the farther cape, where everything grew in its usual wild profusion, trees, rattans, screw-pines, and all along the shore itself coconut-palms soaring up in a thousand graceful attitudes. A few paces from where he stopped there was a little platform with a spring coming out of the cliff-face, a dense growth of soft fern, and an astonishing display of orchids growing on the rock, the deep moss, the trees and bushes, orchids of every size, shape and colour. 'Lord, I wish Stephen were here,' he said, sitting on a convenient mound and taking a small telescope and an azimuth compass from his ditty-bag.

He said it again some time later, when a large black and white bird laboured across the field of his glass, carrying a heavy fish in its talons. The glass was only a pocket telescope of no great power, but with the sun shining full on the opposite shore and the air as clear as air could be he had a brilliant view of the *Cornélie*. She had indeed been heaved down on a bank a little north of the town — her copper blazed in the sun — heaved down on her larboard side to a number of uncommon great trees, one of which, or perhaps the creeper that enveloped it, a mass of crimson flowers from top to bottom. 'Oh if only my roses would do that,' cried his mind in a parenthesis, running back to the mildewed, aphis-ridden, much-loved shrubs of Ashgrove Cottage.

But something was wrong. Something was amiss. There were all the frigate's belongings in neatly-squared tarpaulined heaps; there were her guns, intelligently placed to deal with any attack from land or sea; there were her people's tents; but where were the people themselves? A few were creeping about on her copper; a few were busy on a staging against a place where the sheathing had been removed far down under her starboard bow; but there was none of the feverish activity usual on such occasions, with all hands kept hard at it, calls piping, starters flying. Some of them could even be seen playing boules in a smooth bare place under the coconut palms, watched by scores of their shipmates. The others were presumably sleeping in the shade.

While Jack was considering this he heard the rattle of stones on the path above, and a man with a long rod went down past him. The man called out in Malay as he went by and Jack replied with an amicable hoot that seemed to satisfy both this fisherman and the one who followed him a little later; but a third man stopped and looked back. Jack saw that although he was as brown as an islander he was in fact a European, a Frenchman, no doubt.

'Captain Aubrey, sir, I believe?' he said, smiling.

'Yes, sir,' said Jack.

'You will not remember me, sir, but my name is Dumesnil, and I had the honour of being presented to you aboard the *Desaix*. My uncle Guillaume Christy-Pallière commanded her.'

'Pierrot!' cried Jack, his look of cold reserve changing to open pleasure as he recognized the little fat midshipman in the long-legged lieutenant. 'How very glad I am to see you. Come and sit down. How is your dear uncle?'

The dear uncle, in a ship of the line, had captured Jack and his first command, the *Sophie*, a small brig-rigged sloop, in the Mediterranean, as long ago as 1801; he had treated his prisoner very handsomely and they had become friends, a friendship ripening all the more easily since Christy-Pallière had English cousins and spoke their language well. His nephew Pierre had spent the peace at school in Bath, and he spoke it even better. They exchanged news of all their former shipmates — Uncle Guillaume was now an admiral (which Jack knew very well) but he was pining at an office desk in Paris — and it was clear that Christy-Pallière had followed Jack's career as closely as Jack had followed his. Dumesnil spoke, without the least animosity, of the dismay and admiration with which they had both received the news of Jack's cutting out the *Diane*, and went on, 'I saw you of course at the Sultan's audience, and I have seen you once or twice when I went to look at the poor *Diane* from Prabang: of course it would have been improper to make any gesture, but I did hope you might repay the compliment and come to look at the poor *Cornélie*. I know some of your people have done so, and from just this very place.'

'To be sure, it does give a most capital view,' said Jack, and there was a significant pause.

'Well, sir,' said Dumesnil, somewhat embarrassed, 'I don't know whether you have ever careened a ship with neither wharf nor hulk?'

'Never. That is to say never anything bigger than a sloop. Frightful things might happen — masts, futtocks . . .'

'Yes, sir. And frightful things have happened. I do not mean the slightest criticism of my captain or my shipmates — these things were more in the line of acts of God — but I may say that the ship cannot possibly float before next spring tide, is very likely not to float until the spring-tide after that, and in fact may not float until next year. I tell you this in the hope that you will not attempt cutting her out, so that we knock one another on the head to no good purpose: two line-of-battle ships anchored in the bay and heaving till their cables and their capstans broke could not bring her off that infernal bank. You might as well try to cut out the Cordouan light.'

Dumesnil was no more specific about the 'frightful things' than this, though Jack suspected a hopelessly wrung mainmast and several sprung butts at the least, but he did go on to speak of other miseries: the growing hostility of the people of Ambelan; the desertion, in two different Philippine vessels, of most of the Spanish craftsmen and many foremast hands; and of the frigate's extreme poverty: for weeks they had been living, cabin, gunroom and all, on ancient ship's provisions, because the money had been mismanaged and the purser could scarcely afford even the cheapest kind of rice. Credit had always been in indifferent health, and now it was stone dead; no bills on Paris could be attempted to be discounted with the Chinese merchants, even at ninety per cent. 'Fortunately,' he said, laughing, 'there are always these beautiful fish, the padangs. They cruise along in twos and threes just behind the break of the wave when the tide is making, and they take a feather or a shaped piece of bacon-rind, just like the bass at home. See how they are pulling them out!'

So they were. Four or five silver flashes along the line of rocks: and it was nearly high water.

'Pierrot, my dear fellow,' said Jack, standing up, 'you must run down, or you will lose your tide, and I cannot say worse to a sailor. I will send you over a little present by one of our Malays; but don't forget to sign the chit so that I know you have had it. There are a lot of goddam thieves about in these islands, you know.'

'Oh sir, that is extremely kind of you, but I cannot take anything from an officer who is technically an enemy. And I never meant to speak of our poverty in any sense of . . .'

'Quelle connerie, as your uncle would say. I didn't accept anything from him, did I? Oh no. By no means. Not at all. Only fifty guineas and a whole series of the best dinners I have ever ate. It was the same with the Americans when they took us: Bainbridge of the *Constitution* fairly loaded me with dollars. Don't be an ass, Pierrot. Send me word if you can think of a discreet neutral place where we can meet, or failing that, let me hear from you the minute peace is signed. Your uncle knows my address. God bless you, now.'

'Well, Stephen,' he said, 'there you are, back from your God-forsaken steps and all alive, I am happy to see. What luck to find you aboard. Have you abandoned your bawdy-house? Have the girls all proved poxed? Or have you turned evangelical? Ha, ha, ha, ha!' He sat down, wheezing and wiping his eyes. Stephen waited until he had had his laugh out, no small matter, since mirth in Jack Aubrey fed upon what it laughed at.

'What a rattle you are, to be sure,' he said at last.

'Forgive me, Stephen, but there is something so infinitely comic in the idea of you being a Methody, haranguing the girls, handing out tracts . . . Oh . . .'

'Control yourself, sir. For shame.'

'Well. If I must. Killick! Killick, there.'

'Which I'm a-coming, ain't I?' — this from a certain distance; and as the cabin door opened, 'This is the best I can do, sir. Lemon barley-water made of rice, and loo-warm at that; but at least the lemon is shaddocks, which is close on.'

'Bless you, Killick. That last three hours' pull in a clock calm was thirsty work.' He engulfed a couple of pints, broke into an instant sweat, and said, 'I had such a pleasant encounter yesterday evening. Do you remember when Christy-Pallière in the *Desaix* captured us in the year one?'

'Faith, I shall not easily forget it.'

'And do you remember his nephew, a

425

little round fat-faced boy called Pierrot?'

'I do not.'

'No. You were with their surgeon all the time, an ill-looking yellow-faced — that is to say a very learned man, I am sure. Anyhow, there he was, young Pierrot, all those years ago; and there he was again yesterday, a long thin lieutenant, much the same in essence — amazing good English, too. We talked for a great while, and he told me not to try cutting out his ship, because she could not swim until the spring-tide after next, if then. They have heaved her down, you know, and what has happened to her futtocks and top-timbers . . . however, since the spring-tide after next coincides with our second rendezvous with *Surprise* — the first is already past — that knocks my idea of waiting for her in the offing on the head. Though I do not suppose Fox will have finished his negotiations even by then, unless he and the Sultan spread more canvas: in any case, it was no more than a general notion.'

'As for the negotiations, my dear,' said Stephen, 'I believe you may be — how shall I put it? May be mistaken, laid by the lee. There have been some surprising developments since you sailed away. Shall we take a turn in my little boat? I will row, you being somewhat worn.'

'Now,' he said, resting on his oars, 'do you remember Ganymede, the Sultan's cupbearer Abdul?'

'The odious little sod I longed to kick off my quarterdeck?'

'The same. He was the Sultan's minion, not to use a coarser term; but he was unfaithful and he lay with Ledward. They were taken in sodomy. Abdul was put to death, but Ledward and Wray, who had been promised protection, were not. They are only banished from the court and the council and forbidden to take part in any discussions whatsoever. This has reduced Duplessis to helplessness; he cannot speak Malay, and the council, very strict about rank and precedence, will not listen, will not admit a plebeian interpreter. The French mission has very probably failed, but this cannot be known directly, since one or two days must still pass before Fox can wait on the Sultan. Ledward is of course ruined, and Wray with him, but Fox's hatred is by no more lessened: far from it. He was bitterly disappointed that Ledward was not put to the same hideous death as Abdul. There is a most inveterate, implacable enmity between them . . . What is more, it appears to me that Ledward's mind has become deranged. At one time assassination could have been seen as a perfectly reasonable move in negotiations of this kind and in this part of the world, and at a given point it was Ledward's only possible chance of success. But now, in the present posture of affairs, it can effect nothing. Yet Ledward has made two attempts.'

'A dirty business, Stephen.'

'Very dirty, brother; as dirty as can well be. But unless Duplessis can produce some fresh negotiator and some fresh inducement or obtain yet another postponement — and these are real possibilities, particularly the postponement — the negotiations may not drag on very much longer, and you may be able to keep your rendezvous with the *Surprise*.' He began to paddle back to the *Diane* in his awkward left-handed way, and after a while he said, out of a deep train of reflection, 'But, however, I am glad to hear what you tell me, about the French frigate's present state.'

'She will not move this many a day,' said Jack. 'It would not surprise me to see orchids growing in the mat on the mainmast, where the spar-shores meet it. Oh, Stephen, that reminds me: could it have been an osprey I saw, carrying a fish, slung fore and aft? An eagle-sized bird and quite a large fish?'

'I believe it might have been. I understand the dear birds to be almost universal. Some others are. I was amazed to find a barn owl at Kumai. A true barn owl. A robin would not have surprised me more.'

They were almost at the frigate's side. 'I hope you will sleep aboard tonight and tell me about Kumai,' said Jack. 'And then we might have some music. It is an age since we played so much as a note.'

'Tonight? I believe not: I shall almost certainly be engaged. But tomorrow, with the blessing . . .'

'Good night, dear colleague,' he said, opening the door, 'I hope I do not interrupt your work?'

'Not at all,' said van Buren. 'These are only notes for a paper on my usual subject for the Petersburg Academy.'

'I have brought you a cadaver. Wu Han's porters have it in a little cart in the lane. May I tell them to bring it in? And there is another, larger, if you would like a second specimen.'

'Oh, by all means — how very kind — how truly thoughtful, my dear Maturin — I will clear the long table.'

Wu Han's porters, though powerful, were adroit, exact in their movements; they put down their white-covered burden without disarranging so much as a fold. 'Pray wait by the cart a few moments,' said Stephen.

They padded out of the room, eyes cast down, their hands clasped before them, and van Buren drew back the cloth. 'This is a European,' he said.

'Yes,' said Stephen, trying the edge of a scalpel, 'an English renegado. I was acquainted with him in London, a Mr Wray.'

'An English spleen at last! An English spleen, the most famous of them all! And as fresh a cadaver as ever I have had the pleasure of opening. I am infinitely obliged to you, colleague. Death was caused by this bullet-wound, I see: a rifle-bullet. How curious.'

'Just so. That was also the case with his companion, the heavier one, whom you met once or twice; and the wound was equally recent. Perhaps they had been fighting. Will I send for him?'

Van Buren looked attentively into Stephen's face, and after a moment he said, 'Have you arranged this with the Vizier, Maturin?'

'I have, too. He said that the court was in no way concerned; that the protection had been publicly and specifically withdrawn and notified to Duplessis; and that we might do whatever we pleased. But he was sure that we would be discreet — that there would be no recognizable remains.'

'Then I am perfectly satisfied: oh what a blessed relief! Let us by all means send for the other, and in the meantime shall we start at the head?'

They worked steadily, with a cool, objective concentration: each had a clear understanding of the matter in hand — the relevant organs, those that might be useful for later comparison and those that might be discarded — and words were rarely necessary. Stephen had been present at many such dissections; he had carried out some hundreds himself, comparative anatomy being one of his chief concerns, but never had he seen such skill, such delicacy in removing the finer processes, such dexterity, boldness and economy of effort in removing superfluous material, such speed; and with this example he worked faster and more neatly than he had ever done before.

He had little sense of the passage of time; yet even so, when the long table was cleared at last and two fine fresh gleaming jars had been placed on van Buren's shelf of spleens preserved in spirits, when a certain number of organs — as impersonal as the wares in a butcher's shop — had been laid in brine for future use, and when the wholly unrecognizable remains had been shut away in zinc-lined wooden chests, he was surprised to find that it was still night.

They took off their long aprons, washed their instruments and their hands, and went to sit outside, in the light of a gibbous moon.

'What a charming breeze,' said Stephen. 'It must have been really hot and close in there.'

'Hot and close, I make no doubt; but it was the most gratifying dissection I have ever performed,' said van Buren, letting himself down on the bench with a groan. 'My hands and back are quite stiff; and tomorrow's patients may buy themselves dried salamanders in the bazaar — I shall not attend to them. But Heavens, how infinitely worth while! Do you know, I could scarcely overcome a feeling of extreme bitterness when I missed your Pondicherry clerk. On his mother's side he was a Hindu, and in common piety his co-religionists here — there are a score or so — felt themselves obliged to cremate him; and there, thought I, seeing the smoke ascend, was my very last chance of an at least partly European spleen. Lord, how little one knows!'

They sat in silence for a while, listening to the geckoes chuckling on the wall behind them, and then van Buren went on, 'Tell me again about your rhinoceroses. Had you not suspected their presence at all? No deep, well-worn paths, no droppings, no tracks?'

'I had not. All these things were there, and they were apparent to me as I went back to the monastery having seen the animals; but from some imbecility of mind, some lasting state of astonishment at the possibility of accosting a wild boar and scratching its back and of walking hand in hand with an orang-utang, I had seen nothing. In the very first place I had not liked to mention rhinoceroses to the monks, because of the alleged aphrodisiac virtues of the horn: I did not wish to arouse the least hint of suspicion. So they were not in my mind at all. In any case I have never thought of them as dwelling in mountains.'

'The Sultan attributes Hafsa's pregnancy solely to his use of the horn,' observed van Buren. 'But how very deeply concerned you must have been when they ran down the hill at you. I believe they weigh three tons.'

'I am sure they do. The earth trembled; I trembled with it. I had some fragmentary notion of leaping like a Cretan bull-vaulter, but before I could determine which foot, which hand would have been proper in Cnossus they were past me, thanks be to God. There was no malice in them, the creatures. Nor in any other living thing I saw at Kumai, except possibly for some tree-shrews which I heard quarrelling among themselves.'

They talked in a somewhat disconnected way about tree-shrews — the monks' imperfect Malay and how it increased Stephen's fluency and assurance — the anatomy of cheerfulness, what it is — plausibly said to have its seat in the spleen, perhaps in that curious set of minute granular bodies between the hilum and the gastric impression — only disordered spleens could have given the gland its indifferent reputation — spleens perhaps more frequently disordered in England than elsewhere, because of the climate — because of the diet — thoughts on the distribution of barn owls — and after a yawning pause van Buren said, 'We shall have to boil Cuvier's bones after all' in an artificially casual tone that would not have deceived a child.

Stephen knew that it was his duty to be amazed, and in spite of an almost insuperable weariness he cried, 'How? What are you saying?'

'I thought that would amaze you,' said

van Buren. 'We shall have to boil them because there will be no time for the ants to finish the cleaning. Your treaty is being written out fair at this moment, in gold letters upon crimson paper, four full sheets of it. Mr Fox, warned shortly after sunrise, will attend for the signature in the early afternoon.'

'Is a man to have no sleep at all, no sleep whatsoever, in this vile misshapen hulk?' cried Dr Maturin, striking at the hand that jerked his cot and pulling the clothes over his head. Ahmed had not dared persist, but Bonden was made of sterner stuff and the jerking continued, together with the words 'Captain's orders, if you please, sir. Now, your honour, rouse and bitt, Captain's orders, if you please, sir,' which had been mingling with his dream since the beginning of conscious time. At last he could bear it no longer; anger dispelled sleep and he sat up. Bonden handed him out of the cot with a most provoking mild solicitude, calling through the door 'Light it along, Killick.'

Ahmed appeared with a dressing-gown: between them they conveyed him to the dining-cabin, where Killick had laid out breakfast. A letter leant against the coffee-pot, and Bonden gave it to him: 'To be read directly minute, sir, if you please,' he said. 'Ahmed, pour away.'

Maturin was fairly wise in his generation when fully awake, but not so wise at present that he did not look earnestly at the back of the letter while he sipped his first reviving cup. 'It was brought by Mr Edwards, sir,' said Bonden. Killick, peering through the open door, said, 'Which he is down in the hold with the Captain and Chips this mortal minute, your honour,' and just overhead there broke out a shattering cry of 'Bargemen, d'ye hear there? Shave and clean shirt for six bells', followed by another set of orders and a sharp cutting pipe as the copper-bottomed launch, the honorary barge, was lowered down.

He broke the seal.

My dear Maturin

I give you joy. We have won! The Vizier has just sent me word that the treaty, in the exact terms we agreed upon, is ready, and I am to attend for signature at one o'clock, which the court astrologer declares a propitious hour. A propitious hour for us! I am only to take a small escort and suite, *because of the circumstances,* but I trust you will be of the number; and I trust you will also do me the honour of dining here afterwards.

In great haste
Yr most obdt humble servt

'Humble now I very much doubt,' said Stephen, and then, looking up, 'Good morning to you, gentlemen. You are both in a sad state of filth, I find. Jack, have you breakfasted? Mr Edwards, will I pour you a cup of coffee?'

'I am perfectly willing to breakfast again,' said Jack. 'We have been creeping about in the hold.'

'We have been rousing out the Sultan's subsidy,' said Edwards, joy radiating from him. 'You have heard the news of course, sir?'

'You were so kind as to bring it yourself,' said Stephen, nodding at the letter.

'So I did,' said Edwards, laughing happily. 'I am growing as forgetful as an old mole, or a bat.'

At five bells Jack stood up. 'Come, Mr Edwards,' he said. 'You and I and the Doctor must scrub ourselves from clew to earing and put on our birthday suits. Killick! Killick, there. You and Ahmed will help the Doctor to get ready to go to court:

he will wear his scarlet robe.'

It was in his scarlet robe therefore that Dr Maturin stood on the quarterdeck, as ready as severe shaving, a newly-curled, newly-powdered wig, and a good many other firm measures could make him. But in spite of them all — and the more savage kind of nursery-governess was nothing to Preserved Killick — his spirits rose with those of the ship. There was merriment all round him, laughter as the little heavy chests of treasure were lowered down one by one into the launch, lying under the larboard mainchains, much the same general happiness as if the *Diane* had captured a prize, and a rich one at that. The bargemen were already eating their dinner under the forecastle awning, holding it well away from their fine clothes.

Just before eight bells in the forenoon watch the last chest was stowed: the select guard of the Marines and their officer were all in place, together with Richardson, Elliott, Maturin and young Seymour. Jack appeared in full uniform, wearing his gold-hilted presentation-sword, glanced fore and aft, and came down the side, but with no ceremony.

And it was with little ceremony that he met Fox's people, who had come to the landing-place with a couple of shabby bullock-carts for the subsidy. Not much more attended the appearance of the envoy himself, riding a handsome little Javanese horse, sent by the Vizier. He called out 'Good morning, gentlemen,' dismounted, gave the reins to the attendant grooms, and in a low, confidential tone he said, 'Forgive me, Aubrey: I am several minutes late — the line is already formed, I see — but should this go as I hope and trust it will, would you have any objection to sailing at once? The news should reach the Ministry at the earliest possible moment, and India, of course. I could ask the Vizier to transport our impedimenta in that same double proa.'

While one part of Jack's mind was recording the impression of intense, barely contained excitement, not unlike a certain form of drunkenness, another ran over the state of the *Diane*'s water, wood and stores. 'It can be done,' he said. 'We may go a little short of fuel for the galley, but we can manage the evening tide.'

'I hoped you would say that, Aubrey,' said Fox, shaking his hand. 'I am *so* much obliged to you. I for one should be happy to eat my sea-pie raw to gain a day,' he added with a high-pitched laugh as he got on to his horse again and took the head of the procession.

It was a comparatively muted ceremony at the palace too: the Sultan was already on his throne when the mission entered the audience-hall, and although he greeted them with smiles and a proper complaisance his face was ravaged and during the long reading of the treaty it relapsed into an expression of very deep, settled unhappiness. After two speeches and the sealing and signing of both copies he retired, and the atmosphere became much less grave. The Vizier was in the highest spirits; he had formed a valuable, potentially an extremely valuable, alliance; he had filled the treasury; he had got rid of a most troublesome favourite; he had ensured the Sultana's good will; and it was not surprising that the presents given in the Sultan's name should reflect his chief minister's satisfaction. Fox had a coral-handled kris of great antiquity and a jade Buddha at least twice as old; Jack a star-ruby in a lacquer box, the fruit of some distant piracy; and Stephen a gift that for a moment put him out of countenance — a chest of the Honourable East India Company's best Bengal opium. As far as the baggage and servants were concerned, the old gentleman was delighted to be of service: Wan Da would attend to it immediately. And after fond farewells the envoy and his suite had the honours of drums and trumpets in each successive courtyard as they left, marching through a good-natured cheerful crowd to Fox's house to dine.

The dinner consisted almost entirely of fish, many sorts of fish, all fresh, all remarkably good, accompanied by rice and lukewarm bottled ale. But it might have been boiled beef or bread-and-butter pudding for all the notice Fox and his companions took of it. Like their chief, the Old Buggers were beside themselves with flow of spirits and elation; but unlike him they were extremely noisy and loquacious. At the palace their long training had kept them silent, but now they let themselves go; this was the sort of victory they thoroughly understood, and they celebrated it in their own way, with a flood of words, words that grew louder and louder as the meal progressed, voices often talking together. An odd, unbuttoned meal even in its material aspects, with servants taking things away to pack them — waiting in working clothes — disappearing themselves, leaving the room strangely bare, rather as if they had been bailiff's men.

'Let us have no ceremony, gentlemen,' Fox had said on walking into the dining-room, and they had sat down as they pleased: the officials were clustered round Fox at the head of the table, the sailors at the foot, with Jack and Stephen at the far end. Four aside, Fox at the head, Welby, rather lost, at the bottom. No ceremony: the civilians took off their coats, loosened their cravats and breeches. They talked openly about the events of the last few days, and Loder was particularly eloquent on the subject of the subtlety of their campaign, the way the information had been conveyed to Hafsa, the success after several failures; their talk became freer still, with a cross-fire of wit about sodomy. Both Jack and Stephen glanced at Fox as the noise increased, but he merely looked down at his colleagues on either side with an amused condescension. It was only when Johnstone cried 'And all the French are buggered too' that he said, 'That will do, Judge,' in an authoritative tone, unheard before.

Since discretion had flown out of the window, Stephen thought that he too would leave. It was deeply painful to hear all the fundamental rules of intelligence, all the rules of even common good sense disregarded; and the details of this particular intelligence coup, as it might be called, were more painful still. In any case he was determined to take a proper leave of the van Burens and his Chinese friends, whether the ship sailed that day or not: there was no urgency whatsoever about the treaty — the situation had already been dealt with entirely. While he was waiting for the roar of laughter that would cover his retreat he listened to the officials' conversation: their flattery had now become so gross that he wondered how a man of Fox's undoubted parts could swallow it; but the envoy smiled on, only shaking his head gently from time to time. The expected flash came ('peppering for adultery in England would lead to a run on the commodity: a fortune might be made by cornering the market') followed by the expected roar, and with a nod to Jack he slipped out. He passed Loder pissing on the verandah, gave his scarlet robe to one of the Marines on guard and walked off. 'But I am glad, right glad,' he said, 'that Jack knows just how the poor brutes were betrayed, and by whom.' He walked rapidly on, passing a herd of buffaloes, and then he said, 'Such mediocrity at such a level — a judge, members of the legislative council — they order these things better in France.' But honesty made him pause, and he went on 'They would order these things better in an independent Ireland, however.'

Jack was obliged to stay, though he did not much care for his company nor for the note in Fox's voice when he called down the table, 'Tell me, Aubrey, just when does the tide turn this afternoon? I wish there to be no time lost getting this document home: no time lost or dawdled away.' The matter was offensive; the manner more so; and both Richardson and Elliott looked extremely nervous. Captain Aubrey was not the most long-suffering of men.

Yet the feast was winding to its end at last, with many a hoot and jibe about the penniless Frenchmen's plight. 'Though now I come to think of it,' said Crabbe, 'since Duplessis does not have to produce his subsidy, he may be able to pay his way home.'

'If you have no remark more intelligent than that, Crabbe, you had better keep your mouth shut,' said Fox. 'Going home in disgrace is far worse than starving here.'

'His Excellency is quite right,' said Johnstone. 'Far worse.'

'Beg pardon, sir,' said Crabbe, sinking his face into his beer.

A truly glorious dessert of fruit on three battered tin trays covered this awkward moment: and then at last came the decanters, those fingerposts towards an eventual release. They drank the King with a certain return of gravity; and then Fox, taking the silk-bound treaty from Ahmed's reverential hands, said, 'I drink to the fruit of our joint efforts: I drink to what I have signed in His Majesty's name.'

'Huzzay! Hear him, hear him!' cried the suite, a confusion of voices in which the sailors joined with a decent zeal.

'What I drink to,' cried Loder, standing up and leering at Fox, 'is to the Bath. The Most Honourable Order of the Bath.'

'Huzzay, huzzay! Hear him! Bottoms up!' cried the others, and while Fox looked down in smiling modesty they drank the sentiment.

They huzzayed their way on to knighthood with three times three; and after that they drank 'Baronetcy, a governorship and five thousand a year on the Civil List.'

Jack looked at Elliott, saw that he was pallid-drunk, caught Richardson's eye instead, rose and said, 'You will excuse us now, Excellency. We must go and prepare your way. Mr Richardson will accompany you to the barge in forty-five minutes. Mr Welby, the new pinnace will come for you and your men in half an hour.'

He took the bewildered Elliott by the arm and guided him out. Seymour, at the landing-place, reported the departure of the big proa and some smaller boats full of servants. Jack told him what to expect, suggested that Bonden should spread sailcloth over the sternsheet cushions, and walked Elliott off round the crater-rim, hailing the ship from his usual point.

'Mr Fielding,' he said, looking into the crowded waist, 'are all the mission's servants aboard?'

'All aboard, sir; and the last baggage-boat will shove off in a minute or so.'

'I am delighted to hear it. The new pinnace for the Marines right away, if you please; then I believe we may unmoor and ride at single anchor — indeed, creep to a kedge, with such quiet water and so little breeze. The envoy and his people should leave the hard in half an hour. Salute, of course, and everything man-of-war fashion. Pray let me know when they put off. I hope to sail with the first of the ebb. I trust to God the Doctor has not wandered off looking for centipedes,' he added in a lower voice, going below.

He took off his coat and lay on his cot. Killick peered at him through a crack in the door and shook his head sympathetically. The *Diane* was unmooring, and her captain listened to the familiar sequence, the click of the capstan-pawls, the cries of 'Light along the messenger, there', 'Heave and in sight' and the rest, but his mind was elsewhere. In most men, in perhaps all he had ever known, victory made them benign, expansive, affable, generous. Fox had been arrogant and hostile. He had also betrayed a meanness that must always have been subjacent, since its appearance caused no surprise: there had been and there would be no feast for the young gentlemen, the warrant officers, the foremast hands, no drinks, no address, telling the good news and acknowledging their part in the successful voyage. To be sure, it was not a very pretty victory: it scarcely called for the ringing of church bells and bonfires in the street. He regretted his ale; he regretted his port still more; yet even so he dropped off for some minutes and when Reade came with 'Mr Fielding's compliments and duty, sir, and the barge has put off: he says the breeze and high water are all you could wish,' he felt surprisingly fresh.

'Thank you, Mr Reade,' he said. 'I shall be on deck in ten minutes or so.'

He let himself lie in that delicious state of complete relaxation for a while, rose up, plunged his face into water, squared his neckcloth and hair, and put on his coat. Killick instantly appeared, brushed him, arranged his clubbed pigtail and its bow, spread his best epaulettes wide and even.

On deck he saw that the breeze was indeed all he had wished: it was blowing right across the anchorage, and he had but to back his mizen topsail, make a sternboard with plenty of helm, fill, pluck up the kedge — Fielding had it almost atrip — and let the breeze and the turning tide carry the ship out while it was being run up.

He also saw that everything was exactly as it should be: yards squared by the lifts and braces, side-boys in white gloves, man-ropes just so, Marines all present, pipe-clayed and correct, officers and young gentlemen square-rigged, Mr Crown and his mates with their silver calls already poised, Mr White with his poker, the glow visible in the long evening shadow of the starboard bulwark.

He gauged the distance from the advancing barge still as rowdy as a boatful of Cockneys going down to Greenwich: nearer, nearer. 'Very well, Mr White,' he said, and the first gun spoke out, followed by the remaining twelve. The barge hooked on; the envoy came aboard followed by his suite looking squalid, frowsty, crapulous, old, and unclean, their coats buttoned to the wrong buttonholes, their hair astray and at least one flap or codpiece blowing in the wind. They were received with rigid, exact formality; and abruptly sobered, they fingered their clothes; Fox looked extremely displeased; the suite glanced uneasily at one another, and they all hurried below.

'Where is the Doctor?' asked Jack.

'He came aboard with the Marines,' said Fielding, 'carrying a hairy thing. He is in the gunroom, I am afraid.'

'Lord, what a relief,' murmured Jack, and in a strong official voice, 'Let us proceed to sea.'

As he spoke the Prabang fortress began to boom out a farewell salute; the *Diane* answered it, and they were still firing, gun for gun, with the smoke drifting away to leeward, as she passed through the channel into the open sea.

'Mr Warren,' said Jack, 'the course will be north-east by east a half east; and that, I trust, will bring us to our rendezvous with the *Surprise*.'

Chapter 9

The *Diane* had not run off two degrees of longitude before the old pattern of sea-going life was as firmly settled as if it had never been interrupted. It is true that she ran them off slowly, rarely exceeding five knots and never logging more than a hundred miles from noon to noon. This was not because she did not try, not because she was too early for her rendezvous: far from it: at present, with the balmy air coming in one point abaft the beam, she had a magnificent display of canvas spread, with studdingsails aloft and alow, royals and even skyscrapers, and a variety of rarely-set objects on the stays; yet the balmy air was so languid that she only just had steerage-way.

Jack Aubrey, having done all that could be done, paced fore and aft on the windward side of the quarterdeck according to his habit before dinner with his mind perfectly at ease on that point if not on all others; the greater part of a lifetime afloat had convinced him that railing at the weather only spoilt one's appetite, which

450

was always a pity and which would be even more of a pity today, when he and Stephen, alone for once, were to eat some particularly fine fish, bought from a proa that morning.

'What is it that you wish me to see?' asked Stephen, coming up the companion-ladder with his usual precautions, although there was scarcely any movement at all under his feet.

'You cannot see it from here, because of the awning,' said Jack. 'But come with me along the weather gangway, and I will show you something that perhaps you have never seen before.' They went forward, and some of the hands in the waist nodded and smiled significantly. The Doctor was going to be stunned, amazed, taken aback all standing. 'There,' said Jack, pointing upwards. 'Abaft the topsailyard, right up against the trestletrees. Have you ever seen that before?'

'The thing like a tablecloth pulled out at one corner?' asked Stephen, who could be sadly disappointing on occasion.

'Well, it is a mizen topgallant staysail,' said Jack, who had expected little more. 'You can tell your grandchildren you saw one.' They walked back to the quarterdeck and resumed the pacing; Jack accommodating his long-legged stride to keep in step.

'As I understand it,' said Stephen, 'we keep our appointment with Tom Pullings off the False Natunas and then drop Fox in Java to take an Indiaman home; but is it not a strangely roundabout way, as if one should go from Dublin to Cork by way of Athlone?'

'Yes. His Excellency was good enough to point that out to me yesterday — perhaps he showed you the same map — and I will make the same reply to you as I did to him: as the prevailing winds lie at this season, it is quicker to go back to Batavia by the False Natunas than by the Banka Strait. And then' (lowering his voice) 'which is more to my purpose though not perhaps to his, there is our rendezvous.'

'Well, I am content. There is, I presume, a convenient harbour in the False Natunas? And, by the way, why False? Are the inhabitants unusually treacherous?'

'Oh no. There is no harbour. That is only a sea-going expression, a hyperbole, as I believe you would say: they are only a parcel of uninhabited rocks, like the Dry Salvages. It is understood that we cruise for a week in their latitude or in fact a trifle south of it. Their longitude has not yet been fixed with any certainty, but as you know we can be reasonably sure of our latitude; and so we cruise along it, a glass at every masthead, and at night we may lie to, with a lantern in each top. As for their being false . . .'

The ship's bell stopped him in mid-stride, mid-sentence, and together they hurried below, their mouths watering steadily.

'. . . as for their being false,' said Jack, after a long and busy pause, 'that arose when the Dutch were first making their conquests in these parts. The master of some ship bound for the real Natunas but who was sadly out in his dead-reckoning, raised them one foggy morning and cried, "I have made the perfect landfall! Ain't I the cheese!" The *Dutch* cheese of course, ha, ha, ha! But, however, when the mist lifted they proved to be these mere God-damned barren rocks, looming large in the thick weather; so he put them down in his chart as the False Natunas. The South China Sea is full of places like that, imperfectly fixed, mistaken for one another; and vast areas outside the Indiamen's track are not charted at all — just hearsay of islands, reefs and shoals picked up from proas or junks that can only give the vaguest of bearings for the places they are talking about.'

'I am sure you are right. Yet it does seem strange to a landsman. These are populated waters: at this very moment I can see . . .' He was looking out of the stern-window, his eyes narrowed against the brilliance of the day. '. . . six, no, seven vessels: two junks, one large proa, four small things with outriggers paddling fast, whether fishermen or pirates on a modest scale I cannot tell.'

'It is just as occasion offers, I believe. In the South China Sea, by all accounts, the rule is to take anything you can overcome, and avoid or trade with anything you cannot.'

'I am afraid it was much the same with us until very recently. I have read strange accounts of Maelsechlinn the Wise, son of Erc, and he the kindest of men by land. But these are populated waters, as I was saying, and the Chinese who sail them belong to a very highly civilized, literate community, while the Malays are by no means ignorant of letters, as we know very well. Why, then, do we swim in this cloud of uncertainty?'

'Because junks never draw more than a few feet of water — they are flat bottomed — and proas even less. Whereas a ship of the line, a seventy-four, draws 22 or 23; even our light draught aft is close on fourteen foot, and with stores and all very much more: I am never happy unless we have at least four fathoms under our keel even in smooth weather. A shoal that a junk would scarcely notice, much less mark down, might rip our bottom out as easy as kiss my hand. These are the very words I shall use when I explain sailing in uncharted waters elsewhere, after dinner,' he said with the significant look that often passed between them in this sounding-box of a divided cabin.

Stephen nodded, put his perfectly clean skeleton on to the dish in the middle, took another Java sea-perch, looked at Jack's unseemly heap of bones, and observed, 'You have to be a Papist to eat fish, I find. Pray tell me how you arrange private meetings at sea, half the world apart.'

'They cannot be at all precise, at such a distance, but it is remarkable how often they answer. The usual thing is to give three or four cruising-grounds, always if possible near some island where a message can be left after the agreed cruising-time is over; and then if circumstances call for it we set a final rendezvous where one or the other can lie at anchor until a stated time. Ours is Sydney Cove.'

'So if we should not meet this time, we have another chance?'

'I will not deceive you, Stephen: we do have another chance. In fact we have three other chances — a week each side of the next two full moons, and then of course in New South Wales.'

'What joy. I long to see the *Surprise* and all our friends again — I long to tell Martin of my dear ape, my tarsier, that rarest of primates, my enormous beetle, whole unknown genera of orchids. What is amiss, brother? Have you a flogging to deal with?'

'No. Just a disagreeable little matter to clear up.' Killick and Ahmed came in, the one bearing a roly-poly pudding and the other a sauce-boat of custard. 'Killick,' said Jack, 'just jump round to the other side, will you: my compliments, and will His Excellency be at leisure for a few minutes in half an hour.'

Fox had never been liked in the *Diane*, but until Batavia he had given little active offence, while his secretary, Edwards, was positively esteemed, in a quiet way, by both officers and foremast hands. But since the envoy's behaviour at Prabang, his ignoring of the people belonging to the ship that had taken him there, his total indifference to their pleasure at the signing of the treaty, his treatment of the Marine guard — 'airs and graces and all turn out to present arms every time the bugger puts his nose out of doors and not so much as a half bottle to drink the King's health even at the end when him and his friends was as pissed as Davy's sow' — and of the seamen who rowed him to and fro, this absence of liking had grown into strong reprobation. His suite, of course, and their servants, had been unpopular from the beginning; but they were only passengers, and of passengers, landsmen at that, nothing could be expected. The present dislike of Fox was on another plane altogether; it was personal, not directed against a class, and it was so marked that a man far more insensitive than Fox must be conscious of it.

'You may say what you please,' said Jack, 'but I have eaten roly-poly within the Arctic Circle, damned nearly within the Antarctic, and now under the equator, and I am of opinion that it has not its equal.'

'Except, perhaps, for spotted dog.'

'Ah, you have a point there, Stephen.'

They drank their coffee and presently Jack said, 'I hope to be back in five minutes.'

He was not back in five minutes, and Stephen sat there by the pot — how the coffee retained its heat in this climate! — reflecting. He knew that last night some one of the mission had mounted to the dark quarterdeck, had approached Warren, the officer of the watch, just as the ship was wearing on to the larboard tack, had been intercepted by Reade, had cuffed the boy aside and had told Warren that he should make more sail, that the Captain would certainly wish it for the King's service, that this miserable pace was dawdling away precious time. But hc hoped that Jack would not take the matter up before Fox had to some extent recovered from his present state of over-excitement: a foolish hope, perhaps, since a thing of this kind had to be taken up at once to prevent any recurrence (the offence in naval eyes was very grave) and since there were no signs of Fox's restless enthusiasm declining at all.

As he listened to the indistinct but certainly angry voices on the other side of the thin bulkhead he reflected upon a whole variety of things, his mind relapsing into a contemplative after-dinner state in which it swam between dreaming and waking; and at one point he found himself recalling an eating-house by the Four Courts — an extraordinarily clear detailed visual image of the place. He was sitting at the far end and he saw a man open the door, look at the long, crowded room (it was term-time), and, after a moment's hesitation, walk in with exaggerated nonchalance, his hands in his pockets and his hat on his head, taking one of the few vacant places not far from Stephen. There was nothing in any way remarkable about him except that he was ill at ease; he felt conspicuous, regretted it, and made himself more conspicuous still by sprawling in his chair with his legs stretched out. But soon it became apparent that he was an ill-conditioned fellow as well. On being shown the bill of fare he questioned the waiter about every other item: 'Was the mutton well hung? Had the parsnips no wood in their middle? Was it bullock's beef or cow's?' and eventually he called for colcannon, a cut off the sirloin and half a pint of sherry. By this time he was aware that he was an object of dislike and he ate his meal with deliberate coarseness, hunched there with his elbows on the table, fairly exuding hostility and defiance.

'If this is my inner man providing me with an analogy,' he said, his mind moving into the present, 'I cannot congratulate him at all. He has left out the essential factor of triumph and intense excitement. The only valid aspect is the man's suspecting that he is unpopular and then going to great pains to make certain he is loathed.'

Stephen had never liked or wholly trusted Fox, but until the actual signature of the treaty they had got along smoothly enough. During the negotiations, in which Stephen had enabled the envoy to outflank Duplessis again and again and in which, as Fox knew very well, he had acquired the support of a majority in the council, without which the execution of Abdul would have had no diplomatic effect, they had worked well together; and he had been touchingly grateful for Stephen's help in the matter of Ledward and Wray. But a kind of lasting drunkenness or exaltation had come upon him at the ceremony of signature, the consummation of their voyage; and since that moment he had treated Stephen very shabbily indeed.

It was not only his inattention to his guest at that discreditable meal: it was a quantity of minor slights and an insistence upon his sole unaided personal success. And although even in the most unreserved flow of indiscretion during that interminable dinner Fox had not betrayed Stephen's real function, it was no very ungenerous reflection to suppose that this was because he meant to arrogate all the merit to himself. What would Raffles make of that? What would Raffles make of the present Fox? What would Blaine have to say to him?

It was altogether a very strange state of affairs. Here was a man of real abilities, one who had despised the Old Buggers — had apologized for them — but who was now revelling in their company and their by no means delicate flattery. It was known that the governorship of Bencoolen would soon be vacant, and they all asserted that Fox must be the obvious choice. This pleased him, but it was a knighthood that Fox really longed for; he was convinced, or very nearly convinced, that his treaty would earn him one, and nothing could exceed his desire to get back to England for it as soon as conceivably possible. He even contemplated the extremely arduous overland journey.

'There is some flaw there, some radical disturbance,' said Stephen. 'Was it always present? Should I have detected it? What is the prognosis?' He shook his head. 'I wish I could consult Dr Willis,' he said aloud.

'Who is Dr Willis?' asked Jack, opening the door.

'He was a man of great experience in disorders of the mind: he looked after the King in his first illness. He was kind to me when I was young, and if he were alive now I should importune him with my questions. May I ask any of you, or would that be untimely, indiscreet, improper?' He could see from Jack's face that the visit had not been pleasant, but he did not think that Fox, even with all his present glory and his elevated state of mind, was of such moral weight as to cause Jack Aubrey much uneasiness, and he was not surprised at the reply, 'Oh, it was a disagreeable little interview; I had thought it might be. But at least I believe the matter is dealt with — there will be no repetition.'

Later, speaking in a disconnected, dissatisfied voice, he said, 'Why, I cannot tell, but this has been preparing ever since we left Pulo Prabang. Still, I had hoped to get through the next few days without a collision; it is so unpleasant to have bad blood aboard. I shall be heartily glad to be shot of them. Nutmeg of Consolation, maybe; Rose of Delight, perhaps; but Flower of Courtesy . . . the scrub. Apart from anything else I cannot play easy with ill-will just at hand — we have had no music since we sailed. Yet even with this wind we should reach our cruising-ground by something like noon tomorrow, and then it is only a week of going to and fro if Tom is not already there or has left no message, and then the couple of days' run to Batavia. Perhaps there will be news from home waiting for us there. Lord, how I should love to know how things are going.'

'Oh so should I,' cried Stephen. 'Though it is not yet possible that there should be word of Diana and our daughter. Sometimes when I think of that little soul I grow quite lachrymose.'

'A few months of roaring and bawling and swaddling-clothes will soon cure you of that. You have to be a woman to bear babies.'

'So I have always understood,' said Stephen.

'Oh very well, Dr Humorous Droll: but there is also that damned uneasy talk about banks breaking that I should like to see denied.'

And later still, when he was floating in the warm South China Sea by Stephen's skiff, his hair spreading like a mat of yellow seaweed, he said, 'I shall ask them to dinner for the day after tomorrow, in return for that remarkable feast. I do not wish to look pitiful; and I know what is due to his office.'

'Jack, I beg you will watch your step, however. Fox is an extraordinarily revengeful man, and a lawyer; and if he can carry home any substantial grievance it may do you harm, in spite of your position. For a short while he is likely to have the ear of those in power.'

'Oh, I shall not commit myself,' said Jack. 'I have seen too many post-captains, good seamen too, denied another ship for flying out under provocation.' The breeze had dropped entirely, as it often did for an hour before sunset, and the ship lay motionless.

But the sun was not far from the rim of the sea; the breeze would return when it dipped; and Jack, calling upon Stephen to 'lay over, there,' heaved himself into the little boat, gliding his seventeen stone over the gunwale so that it remained just free of the surface.

'I believe you once said you were taught Greek when you were a little boy,' said Stephen as he paddled gently towards the frigate.

'To be sure I was *taught* it,' said Jack, laughing. 'Or rather I was attempted to be taught it, and with many a thump; but I cannot say I ever *learnt* it. Not beyond zeta, at all events.'

'Well, I am no Grecian either, but I did get as far as upsilon; and there I met with the word hybris, which some writers use for insolent pride of strength or achievement, open unguarded triumph and exultation.'

'Nothing more unlucky.'

'Nor in a way more impious, which is perhaps close kin. Herod was probably guilty of hybris, before being eaten by worms.'

'My old nurse — back astern, there. T'other oar. Look alive.'

Jack's old nurse had had a capital remedy for worms, or rather against worms, but it was lost in the dismal collision, the rescuing of Maturin from the bottom of the boat, the recovery of his sculls. Jack, when he at last got there, was received at the gangway by Killick, screened by Richardson, Elliott, the young gentlemen and two quartermasters, and wrapped in a large towel. All hands knew perfectly well how the wind was blowing, and though utterly indifferent to his state themselves, they did not wish Fox and his Old Buggers to see their Captain mother-naked.

After quarters that evening, when for the first time since the Sultan's visit the *Diane*'s guns spoke out in earnest, achieving their three broadsides in a fairly creditable four minutes and twenty-three seconds, and after the bulkheads had been replaced, Jack said to his steward, 'Killick, I am asking His Excellency and the suite to dinner: not tomorrow, because I mean to spread out, but the day after. Five gentlemen, Mr Fielding, the Doctor and myself. You had better get the sherry and claret over the side, towing deep, right early; and let us have a fine blaze of silver. And I should like a word with my cook and Jemmy Ducks.'

By a logic clear to all seafaring men, turtles came under the heading of poultry as far as their care and well-being were concerned, and Jemmy Ducks said that he had never seen a brisker nor so likely a creature than the larger of the two in his charge; the other seemed 'timid, rather bashful like'. As for the little Java geese, he had four prime birds, fairly yearning for the spit; and four birds would be plenty for eight gents with quite enough over for manners. The Captain's cook, a one-legged black man from Jamaica, said with a flashing smile that if there was one thing he really could send up to table fit for King George himself, it was a goose; and turtles of course came as natural to him as kiss my hand, he having been weaned on calipash and calipee.

'That was very satisfactory,' said Jack. 'I should have been sorry to keep the matter hanging for any length of time.' And having written the invitation and sent it off he said, 'Since we cannot have our music, what do you say to a hand at piquet? It is years since we played.'

'I should be very happy.'

Happy in a sense, since he always, invariably, with the utmost regularity skinned Jack Aubrey, as he skinned most others at this game, and although the money was now of no significance, it was still a pleasure to see his point of five outdo Jack's by a single pip, his tierce major triumph over a tierce minor, and Jack's eagerly announced

septième beaten down by the almost un-
heard-of huitième; yet in another sense unhappy — uneasy at the sight of all this luck
slipping away in trivialities. For although
there was skill in the game for sure, this kind
of success was all luck; and if a man had
only a given amount for his whole share, it
was a shame to fritter away so much as a
pugil.

'What is a pugil?' asked Jack, to whom he
had made this observation.

'It is a physical term, a fair and just return
for all your poops and garstrakes, and it
means as much as you can pick up between
your thumb and first two fingers: dried
herbs and the like. Jesuits' bark, for example.'

'I have always heard that a Jesuit's bark is
worse than his bite,' said Jack, his blue eyes
slits of mirth in his fine red face. 'Come in,'
he called.

It was Edwards, extremely unhappy.
'Good evening, gentlemen,' he said, and
then, addressing Jack, 'His Excellency's
compliments, sir, and would it be possible
to diminish the noise on the forecastle? He
finds it break in upon his work.'

'Does he, indeed?' said Jack, cocking his
ear forward. 'I am sorry to hear that.' This
was the last dog watch, and the hands had

been turned up to dance and sing: not that they needed any encouragement, not that they would not have danced and sung without the pipe, but the pipe made the whole thing legal, not to be checked for any ordinary reason. 'That must be Simmons's tromba marina,' he said, catching the distinctive note, a note that could scarcely be missed, an immensely loud deep brassy hoot marking the end of a measure in the dance and followed by a confused cheering and two more hoots. 'Have you ever seen a tromba marina, Mr Edwards?' he asked, to ease the young man's woe.

'Never, sir.'

'It is a very singular instrument, a kind of prism of three thin planks about a fathom long with a string stretched over a curious bridge — it is played with a bow, though you would never think so from the sound. If you would like to see one, go along forward with the midshipman. A carpenter's mate knocked it together the other day.' He rang his bell and to Seymour he said, 'My compliments to Mr Fielding and the merriment on the forecastle is to diminish by half.'

'I would have sworn that was an answer to my note,' he said, returning to his disastrous game.

In fact the answer did not appear until

well on in the next forenoon watch, when he came from the masthead in a long controlled glide down the maintopgallant backstay. The *Diane* had been on her cruising-ground for some hours now, and each mast had its lookout; in this clear weather they could survey seven hundred square miles of sea, but so far they had seen nothing at all, not so much as a proa or a drifting palm-trunk: a pale cobalt dome of sky, darkening imperceptibly as it came down to the sharp horizon and the true azure of the great disk of ocean — two pure ideal forms, and the ship between them, minute, real, and incongruous.

'Sir, there is a note for you in your cabin, if you please,' said Fleming.

'Thank you, Mr Fleming,' said Jack. 'Pray let me have it, together with my sextant.'

While they were coming he looked at the log-board: between four and five knots with this rather stronger breeze, just one point free. 'Very little leeway, Mr Warren,' he observed.

'Almost none at all, sir,' said the master. 'I paid particular attention each time the log was heaved.'

The note and the sextant came. He slipped the paper into his pocket, stepped over to the starboard hances and brought the sun down to the horizon. The corrections for the time short of noon were clear in his mind; he applied them to his reading and nodded. The *Diane* was certainly on her true parallel.

He found Stephen in the cabin, working over a musical score by the strong light of the stern-window. 'We are on our true parallel,' he said, and opened the note. 'Well, I'm for ever damned alive,' he said in quite a surprised tone of voice and passed the unfolded sheet.

Mr Fox presents his compliments to Captain Aubrey, whose invitation to dinner on Wednesday he has received but which pressure of work prevents him and his suite from accepting.

'Well,' said Stephen, 'I had not thought a man of his education could be so gross. Tell me, brother, were you very severe?'

'Not at all. The only time I spoke a little sharp was when he asked me whether I knew I was addressing His Majesty's direct representative, and I told him that though he might represent the King by land, I represented him by sea — that under God I was sole captain aboard.'

A pause. 'Killick,' called Jack. 'Killick, there.'

'Now what?' cried Killick with real indignation. He was wearing a frock and gloves that shed powdered chalk at every movement; and there was a long pause before he added the necessary 'Sir.'

'Killick has been polishing the silver,' observed Stephen.

'And only half done and my mates always needing an eye on them, heavy handed hoaves liable to scratch it something cruel.' Killick took a passionate delight in silver and for this dinner he had brought out the rarely-used best service, much tarnished in spite of its green baize.

'Pass the word for Mr Fielding,' said Jack: and to his first lieutenant, 'Mr Fielding, pray sit down. I have a damned awkward request to make of you and the gunroom. The position is this: I had invited the envoy and his colleagues to dine with me tomorrow: foolishly I took their consent for granted and here is poor Killick in a cloud of powdered chalk, while my cook is working double tides at two or even three courses and God knows how many removes. But this morning I find that I had counted my geese without laying their eggs — that I had killed my geese — that is to say, pressure of work prevents Mr Fox and his people from dining with me tomorrow. So what I should like to do, with your permission, is to invade the gunroom and feast among friends. It is a damned left-handed kind of an invitation, yet . . .'

Left-handed it might have been, but it was an unusually happy and successful one. The gunroom table blazed from a great gilt tureen at its foot to the golden mizenmast in the middle and then to another gilt tureen at its head, and they standing in a spring-tide of silver, exactly squared and set so thick that there was scarcely room for bread between. No direct sun reached it, but in the diffused light the general effect was extraordinarily rich, and the hands brought aft on various pretexts felt that it did their ship the utmost credit.

The splendour had the curious effect of doing away with the stiffness and solemnity that usually and perhaps necessarily attended the Captain's ordinary visits to the gunroom: from the beginning it was clear that this was not going to be one of those many, many *Yes, sir, no sir* dinners through which Jack Aubrey had sat since his very first command, labouring in an occasionally successful attempt at making official entertainment somewhat less forbidding. It had not needed as much as a single bottle of wine to set the table in a pleasant hum of conversation, though the stream that flowed throughout the meal certainly helped. Nothing particularly brilliant was said, but all the officers sitting there were pleased with their company, pleased with their fare, and pleased with the glory. Another point was the servants. Every man had one behind his chair, sometimes a Marine, sometimes a ship's boy, and although they were well turned out, clean and attentive, they were not highly trained; even the comparatively rigid Marines took a certain part in the feast — much more than usual on this glittering occasion, which pleased them even more than the guests — and the attendants' smiles, nods, becks (for there was no pretence of not listening to what was said at table) and cheerful faces added to the general gaiety. At one point they added too much. Welby, the Marine officer, was almost as inept a teller of anecdotes or jokes as Captain Aubrey, but he did have one story in which he could scarcely go wrong: it was true, it was decent, he had told it many, many times, and it had no pitfalls. Now, in very fine form after his second helping of goose and his sixth glass of wine, he launched upon it. He caught Jack's eye during a momentary lull in the conversation, smiled at him and said, 'A curious thing happened to me, sir, when I was acting as recruiting officer in the year eight. A young fellow, a fine upstanding young fellow though rather ragged came to the rendezvous: I was sitting there at a table with the clerk, and my sergeant behind me, and I said to him, "You look as if you might suit us. Where do you come from?" "Ware," says he. "Yes, where?" says I, and the sergeant says rather louder, "the Captain asks where you come from — what is your parish?" "Ware," says he. "No," says I, louder still, "Where was you born?" "Ware," says he in a shout, looking dogged, and the sergeant was going to learn him his duty when the clerk whispered, "I believe, sir, he means Ware, the town of Ware, in Hertfordshire." '

At this Macmillan's servant, a ship's boy more used to the midshipmen's berth than the gunroom, burst into a half-strangled hoot of laughter, a hideous adolescent crowing that set off two other boys. They could not look at one another without starting again and they were obliged to be put out: they missed the rest of Welby's tale, a fictitious addition that had just occurred to him in which the recruit's name was Watt.

'A glass of wine with you, Mr Welby,' said Jack when at last the laughter had died away. 'Yes, Mr Harper, what is it?'

'Mr Richardson's compliments and duty, sir, and there is land bearing north-north-east about five leagues.'

The news of land spread through the ship, and after dinner the mission came on deck to gaze at the horizon on the larboard bow, where the False Natunas, already clear from the tops, might soon be seen by those that did not choose to climb. Stephen met Loder, the least objectionable of the Old Buggers, on the companion-ladder.

'You seem to have had a very cheerful time in the gunroom,' said Loder.

'It was most agreeable,' said Stephen. 'Good company, a great deal of mirth, and the best dinner I remember ever to have eaten at sea — such a turtle, such Java geese!'

'Ah,' said Loder, meaning by this that he regretted the turtle and the geese, that he thought Fox's refusal for his colleagues an abuse of authority, and that he for one dissociated himself from the barbarous incivility: a considerable burden for a single 'ah', but one that it bore easily. Stephen had in fact already noticed a decline in the suite's excitement, something of a return to everyday sobriety, though Fox's exaltation was still at the same high and surely very wearing pitch. 'May I consult you, Doctor, when you have a spare moment?' asked Loder in a discreet voice. 'I do not like to speak to the ship's young man.'

'Certainly. Come to the dispensary tomorrow at noon,' said Stephen, and he went on to meet Macmillan himself. They made their round together — the usual port diseases had made their appearance — and when they, for want of an intelligent reliable loblolly boy, had rolled their own pills, prepared their own draughts and triturated their own quicksilver in hog's lard for blue ointment, Stephen said to Macmillan, 'Among your books, do you have Willis on Mental Derangement or any of the other authorities?'

'No, sir. I am sorry to say I have not. All I have in that line is an abstract of Cullen: shall I fetch it?'

'If you would be so very kind.'

He returned to his cabin, carrying the book, by way of the quarterdeck, and there he saw Fox at the lee hances, staring intently at the Natunas, the False Natunas.

All the species and degrees of madness which are hereditary, or that grow up with people from their early youth, are out of the power of physic; and so, for the most part, are all maniacal cases of more than one year's standing, from whatever source they may arise, he read, nodded, and turned the page. *Another remarkable circumstance is, that immoderate joy as effectually disorders the mind as anxiety and grief. For it was observable in the famous South Sea year, when so many immense fortunes were suddenly gained, and as suddenly lost, that more people lost their wits from the prodigious flow of unexpected riches, than from the entire loss of their whole substance.* 'That is something to the point,' he said, 'but what I really want is a case of the sudden onset of folie de grandeur.' He glanced at the measures recommended: diet low but not too low, bleeding of course, cupping, saline purgatives, emetics, camphorated vinegar, the strait waistcoat, blistering the head, chalybeate waters, the cold bath; and closed the book.

Presently, heavy with turtle soup, goose and a number of side-dishes, he closed his eyes as well.

The *Diane* stood off and on all night, just south of the False Natunas, and quite early in the morning Captain Aubrey stood tall

477

and shadowy by Stephen's cot. 'Are you awake?' he asked in a soft voice.

'I am not,' said Stephen.

'We are going ashore in the new pinnace, and I thought you might like to come too. There may be a whole colony of nondescript boobies.'

'So there may — how truly kind — I shall be with you in a minute.'

So he was, unwashed, unshaved, tucking his nightshirt into his breeches as he tiptoed across the twilit deck, now being flogged dry after a thorough swabbing. They helped him down into the boat: 'Why, it has masts,' he exclaimed as he sat in the stern-sheets. 'I had not noticed before.' The faces of the boat's crew lost all expression: they gazed into vacancy.

'We take them down when she is hoisted in, you know,' said Jack. 'It makes stowing one inside the other so much easier.' And turning to the coxswain's seat he asked, 'How does she handle, Bonden?'

'Fine and stiff, sir, and answers very quick. So far I should say she is a rare pretty job, for a country-boat.'

She *was* pretty — fine-grained teak, carvel-built, as smooth as a dolphin's skin — but Stephen's eyes were fixed on the island ahead, as black and jagged a mass of tumbled rock as could be desired and surely uninhabited, but by no means as barren as he had supposed. There were coconut-palms growing at odd angles here and there, with a curious grey vegetation between the naked boulders: at midday it might look as repulsive as a slag-heap, but now in the perfect clarity of growing daybreak it had a severe beauty of its own, a moderate surf white against the black and the whole bathed in an indescribably soft and gentle light. Furthermore, so exceptional a mass of rock, largely earthless, baked by a tropical sun and soaked by tropical rains, was likely to have an exceptional flora and fauna.

'Bear a hand with the lead,' said Jack; and sounding as they went they coasted along to a little bay, dropped a grapnel and pulled in to the low-tide shore, one part white where the currents laid down coral sand, the other the unredeemed dull black of the mother-rock. Two hands leapt out with a gang-plank. Jack and Stephen went ashore, followed by Seymour and Reade, Bonden and a young foretopman called Fazackerley: they carried a compass, tools, a bottle, and a pot of paint, and as they walked up the damp sand to the tide-mark the sun rose behind them. They turned to look: pure sea, pure sky, and the sun, at first an orange arc in the faint haze, then a half-disk, still to be borne with narrowed eyes, and at last a blinding sphere, heaving clear from the horizon entirely and providing them with long dark shadows.

Jack took the bearings, stared inland for some while, and then, nodding towards a crag he said, 'I am afraid there is no paint upon it, but that is probably the most conspicuous rock, do you not agree, Doctor?'

'Certainly it stands well above its fellows; but why should there be any paint upon it, at all?'

'It was agreed that the first to come should leave his message twenty-two yards north of a conspicuous rock marked with white.'

'Twenty-two yards, for all love?'

'It is the length of a cricket-pitch.'

They left their message in its bottle, they left their mark, and they sailed back to the ship, carrying a collection of plants and insects that would have been very much larger if at last the Captain had not cried 'Come: we shall miss our tide. There is not a moment to lose.'

All these things were handed up the side, and some of them, in pill-boxes, accompanied Stephen to breakfast. 'It would have been worth getting up before dawn merely for the splendid appetite it engenders,' he said, 'but when to the appetite you add anomalous annelids and some of these plants . . . When I have finished my kedgeree I will show you the isopod crustaceans I found under a fallen branch. They are almost certainly close kin to our own woodlice, but with some most unusual adaptations to this climate. How Martin would love to see them!'

'I hope he will, before long. We are on our true parallel, and as we sail to and fro upon it we may meet with them at any time. Today we shall stand to the east, perhaps lying-to at night; and tomorrow to the westward, and so on for a whole week.'

'You have been out in the new pinnace, I hear,' said Loder, who had kept his appointment in the dispensary to the minute but who now seemed unwilling to state his symptoms. 'How does she handle?'

'Very well, I believe. You are a sailor, sir?'

'I have always loved it. We had a yacht in England, and I have a little yawl here, a country-boat like yours, but clinker-built. I sailed her right round Java last year, with a couple of hands. She is half-decked.'

'Pray take off your clothes and lie on this

couch, or padded locker,' said Stephen: and some time later he said, as he washed his hands, 'I am afraid you were right in your surmise, Mr Loder; but we have caught it early, and this ointment, these pills, will probably check it in no great length of time. You must apply the one and swallow the others with exact regularity, however: the Prabang infection is particularly virulent. Come tomorrow at the same time and I will see how you are getting on. You will strictly observe your diet, of course: no wine or spirits, very little meat.'

'Of course. Thank you very much indeed, Doctor: I am extremely obliged to you.' Loder dressed, put the remedies in his pocket, and went on, 'Extremely obliged, both for these and your great care, and for not being lectured. There is no fool like an old fool, as I know very well; but the old fool don't like being told of it.' He paused and then said rather awkwardly, 'By the way, I suppose you cannot tell me when we shall be back in Batavia? I should love to see how my English lettuces are coming along; and of course Fox is in a tearing hurry.'

'As I understand it we are to sail up and down for a while in the hope of meeting another ship and then *sheer off* for Java or possibly New South Wales; but I may well be mistaken. If Mr Fox were to ask Captain Aubrey, the fount of orders, directions and all proper information, I dare say he would be told with greater certainty.'

But Fox did not ask Aubrey. They moved their hats to one another and sometimes exchanged a 'Good morning, sir,' when they took their exercise on the quarterdeck, the Captain on his holy weather side, the envoy and his suite on the other, but it went no further and what communication existed was carried on in an oblique, rather furtive way by means of Loder's conversations with Maturin and Edwards's with the gunroom, his friendship with the officers being unaffected.

The ship sailed east with a steady breeze on her larboard beam, still in this fine clear weather and in a springing cheerful atmosphere of hope. The hope was not fulfilled that day, but it was with no real disappointment that she wore round on the starboard tack a little after sunset and proceeded slowly westwards under close-reefed topsails and a blaze of lanterns.

Westward to the night of Thursday, and turn again, the lookouts eagerly making the whole deliberate sweep of the horizon from their mastheads: they could see fifteen miles of ocean in every direction before the curve of the earth carried it below their range, but even then a ship sailing on the hidden surface as far as fifteen miles beyond would still show the far white fleck of her topgallant-sails to the watchful eye.

At noon the officers on deck took the altitude of the sun once more: their course was exactly true. Far below, Stephen, having finished with his patient and having prepared the physic while the patient babbled on — nervousness made Loder talkative — said, 'In answer to your first question, yes, your informant was perfectly in the right of it. Captain Aubrey is member for Milport, a family borough; he is a wealthy man, with estates in Hampshire and Somerset, and he is very well with the Ministry. And in answer to your second, or the implication of your second, no, I will not act as a go-between.' He said this rather loud, to be heard through the din of the hands being fed. It was wonderful how a mere two hundred men could fill the entire ship with noise; but once each mess had been provided with Thursday's salt pork the sound died away, and by the time Stephen came on deck to ask for another wind-sail in the sick-bay there was quietness enough for him to hear the run of the water along the ship's side, the familiar creak of rigging, the sound of blocks and the general continuo of the wind blowing across a thousand cords, lines and ropes of varying tautness.

Jack and Fielding were looking down into the new pinnace, whose foremast was having its step moved four inches forward, but after a few minutes' earnest conversation Jack turned, and seeing him called out, 'There you are, Doctor. Should you like to go into the top and view the False Natunas again?'

'Few things would give me greater pleasure,' said Stephen, lying in his heart: he had never overcome his dread of height, his distrust of these insecure swaying rope ladders, ill-adapted for their purpose, more suitable for apes than rational beings. Yet as he climbed he reflected that the distinction was unsound; Muong was an ape; Muong, though slow-witted at times and occasionally stubborn, was a rational being.

'There,' said Jack, passing his telescope. 'I can make out our white streak, where young Booby spilt the paint-pot. But I am afraid the answering flag ain't there. They have not passed by yet.'

He said the same on Friday: just such a day, just such a course, still with lively expectations aboard, hope not disappointed but only deferred. And again Stephen, before beginning his horrifyingly inept descent, remarked upon the total absence of ships, vessels, smallcraft — an ocean strangely deserted, even by the sea-birds themselves. 'It was perhaps unreasonable to hope for the Philippine pelican; yet this is supposed to be an archipelago.'

It was during these days that Stephen, who usually took up his after-dinner station by the taffrail, sometimes gazing at the wake, sometimes gazing forward, noticed signs not exactly of disaffection among the envoy's suite but rather of an increasing lack of the first eager enthusiasm and deference, even toadyism; Fox seemed unaware of it however and his own excitement was undiminished, his voice loud and confident, loud and high-pitched, his eyes unusually bright, his step elastic. On Saturday he met Stephen walking along the half-deck and cried, 'Why, Maturin, how do you do? It is a great while since we exchanged more than a good day. Will you indulge me in a game of backgammon?'

Fox played with a great want of attention, and having quite unnecessarily lost the second game — a downright backgammon, with one on the bar and one in Stephen's home table — he said, 'As you may imagine, I am extremely eager that our triumph should be known in England as soon as possible, because . . .' He had emphasized the *our*, but with Stephen's cool, thoroughly informed eye upon him he felt unable to produce any of the high political and strategic reasons he had mentioned to Loder, and after a pause for coughing and blowing his nose he went on, 'So naturally I should very much like to know what Captain Aubrey has in mind — whether he still intends to pursue the course we spoke of earlier, or whether this more or less mythical ship I hear of has suddenly assumed great importance.'

'I am sure he would tell you, were you to ask him.'

'Perhaps so. But I do not choose to risk a snub. He spoke to me in a most intemperate manner the other day, enlarging upon the powers of the captain of a man-of-war, his unaccountability to any but his own superiors in the service, and his complete autonomy afloat — an absolute monarch. He spoke with a masterful, domineering authority and dislike that shocked me extremely. And this was not the first example of ill-will by any means, an ill-will that I find absolutely incomprehensible, gratuitous and incomprehensible.'

'I do not believe it exists. A brief, strongly-expressed vexation about the incident some nights ago, certainly, since for a sea-officer it was a most heinous offence; but as to any settled ill-will, no. Oh no, no, not at all.'

'Then why did he not have the ship dressed, with flags everywhere and the sailors standing on the yards and cheering when I embarked with the treaty? I pass over many other slights, but an insult so deliberate as that could only be the effect of deep ill-will.'

'No, no, my dear sir,' said Stephen smiling. 'There you must allow me to correct a misapprehension. Manning the ship occurs when a member of the royal family visits her; sometimes when two consorts meet or part; and above all in honour of an officer who has won a famous victory. Captain Broke of the *Shannon* was so honoured in my sight. But the victory has to be won in battle, my dear sir, not at the council-table: it must be a military, not a diplomatic victory.'

For a moment Fox was staggered, but then his face resumed its look of complete, knowing assurance. He nodded and said, 'You are obliged to support your friend, of course. And of course your motives are quite clear. There is no more to be said.' He stood up and bowed.

★ ★ ★

Stephen's intense irritation lasted all the time he was climbing into the maintop, and this so took away from his dread and his habitual caution that Jack said, 'What a fellow you are, Stephen. When you choose you can go aloft like' — he was about to say 'a human being' but changed this before it quite left his gullet to 'like an able seaman.'

A league away to the north, over a sea that seemed as devoid of malice as it was of ships, birds, cetaceans, reptiles or even driftwood, a sea of the second day of Creation, rode the white-fringed False Natunas, their generous streak of paint as certain in the glass as the absence of any kind of flag.

'This is not unlike polishing Cape Sicié on the Toulon blockade,' said Jack, closing his telescope. 'Day after day we saw that God-damned headland, always looking much the same. We used to stand in — but of course you remember it perfectly well. You were there. Yes, Mr Fielding?'

'I beg pardon, sir,' said his first lieutenant, 'but I quite forgot to ask you whether we were rigging church tomorrow. The choir would like to know what hymns to prepare.'

'Well, as for that,' said Captain Aubrey

with a resentful look at the False Natunas, 'I think the Articles would come better before the salute. You have not forgotten it is Coronation Day, I am sure?'

'Oh no, sir. I was having a word with Mr White just now. Should you like the board put out, sir?'

'I know them pretty well by heart; but even so it would be as well to have the board. Two precautions are better than one.'

It was before this folding double-leafed object, like a log-board but with a large-printed text of the Articles of War pasted on the wood and varnished, that Captain Aubrey took up his stand at a little after six bells in the forenoon watch on Sunday. He had already inspected his ship, and now its well-washed, shaved, clean-shirted people were ranged before him in attentive groups rather than regular lines; though the mission, the officers and young gentlemen gave the assembly a more formal appearance and the Marines provided their usual geometrical red-coated perfection.

The Articles did not possess the terrible force of some parts of the Old Testament, but Captain Aubrey had a deep voice with immense reserves of power, and as he ran through the catalogue of naval crimes it took on a fine comminatory ring that pleased the hands almost as much as Jeremiah or the Great Anathema. It seemed to Stephen, who attended this ceremony as he did not that of the Anglican rite, that Jack slightly emphasized Article XXIII, 'If any person in the fleet shall quarrel or fight with any other person in the fleet, or use reproachful or provoking speeches or gestures tending to make any quarrel or disturbance, he shall, on being convicted thereon, suffer such punishment as the offence shall deserve, and a court-martial shall impose', and XXVI, 'Care shall be taken in the conducting and steering of any of His Majesty's ships, that through wilfulness, negligence, or other defaults, no ships be stranded, or run upon any rocks or sands, or split or hazarded, upon pain that such as shall be found guilty therein be punished by death . . .' He did not stress the notorious XXIX which laid down that any man guilty of buggery or sodomy with man or beast should also be punished with death, but a good many of the foremast hands, particularly those who had rowed Fox to and fro across that blazing anchorage without so much as a good day or a thank you, did so for him, with coughs and pointed looks and even, far forward, a discreet 'ha, ha!'

491

Jack clapped the boards to and called out in an equally official voice, 'All hands face starboard. Carry on, Mr White.'

Fox and his suite sat there, looking uncertain, but as the royal salute boomed on and on in its deliberate splendour, the loyal smoke-bank rolling away to leeward, the envoy's face cleared, and after the last gun he stood up, bowing right and left, and said to Fielding, 'I thank you for a very handsome compliment, sir.'

'Oh no, sir,' said Fielding, 'I must beg your pardon, but no thanks are due. It was in no way personal: all ships of the Royal Navy fire a royal salute on Coronation Day.'

Somebody laughed, and Fox, with a furious look, walked rapidly to the companion-ladder.

The laughter had come from the waist or the gangway: no one on the quarterdeck took the least notice of the painful little incident, and while the *Diane* was returning to her usual occupation Jack took a few turns fore and aft, fanning himself with his best gold-laced hat. He said to Stephen, 'Somewhere in these waters Tom will have done the same. How I hope they heard us! That would bring them tearing down, indeed, clapping on like smoke and oakum.' They reached the barricade, and Jack, looking forward, noticed a ship's boy seated on the fore-jear bitts rising and bowing graciously right and left. 'Mr Fielding,' he called, 'that boy Lowry is cutting capers on the fore-castle. Let him jump up to the masthead as quick as he likes and learn manners there until supper-time.'

All the seamen who had seen action were of their Captain's opinion about gunfire: nothing would bring another man-of-war over the horizon quicker than the distant thunder of a cannonade, even one so far away that it sounded like swallows in a chimney; and if possible those aloft looked out with even greater zeal — so great a zeal indeed that a little before Jack's guests arrived for dinner a message came below: from the main masthead Jevons, a reliable man, had almost certainly sighted if not a sail then something very like it far to lee-ward, two points on the starboard bow, now dipping below the horizon, now nicking it again. This was not confirmed either from the fore or the mizen, but then they were both considerably lower.

'I believe there is just time to have a look,' said Jack. 'Stephen, be so kind as to entertain Blyth and Dick Richardson for a moment if they should come before I am down.' He tossed his coat on to a chair, seized his telescope and made for the door: opening it he found himself face to face with his guests. 'Forgive me for two or three minutes, gentlemen,' he said, 'I am just going aloft to see what I can make of this sail.'

'May I come too, sir?' asked Richardson.

'Of course,' said Jack. On deck he hailed the lookout, telling him to move down out of the way; and while Richardson was shedding coat and waistcoat he sprang into the shrouds and so up and up into the top, where the lookout had just arrived. 'Oh Lord, sir,' he said, 'how I hope I was right.' 'I hope so too, Jevons,' said Jack: he grasped the windward topmast shrouds while Richardson took those to the lee, and very soon they were at the masthead, the look-out post, standing on the crosstrees and breathing a little quicker in the heat; and with one arm round the topgallantmast Jack swept an arc of the western horizon. 'Where away, Jevons?' he called. 'Between one and two points on the bow, your honour,' came the anxious reply. 'It came and went, like.' He looked again, hard and steady: sea, sea and nothing more. 'What do you make of it, Dick?' he asked, passing the glass.

'Nothing, sir. No. Nothing, I am afraid,' said Richardson at last, most reluctantly.

The *Diane* was one of the comparatively

few ships that had royal masts; they allowed her to set true royals and even skysails above them on occasion; and these royal masts rose above the topgallant, being secured by jack-crosstrees high above, by a pair of shrouds and of course by stays. But the *Diane*'s main royal mast was not six inches across at the thickest, while the topgallant itself was not much more, its shrouds and stays correspondingly frail; and Captain Aubrey weighed at least seventeen stone.

'Oh, sir,' cried Richardson, seeing him grasp the topgallant shrouds with his powerful hand. 'I will jump up in no time at all. Please may I have the glass?'

'Nonsense,' said Jack.

'Sir, with respect, I am only just nine stone.'

'Bah,' said Jack, already clear of the crosstrees. 'Keep still. You will wring the mast, leaping about like a goddam baboon.'

Richardson said, 'Oh sir,' again, then fairly clasped his hands in prayer as he saw Jack's massive form mount the meagre spider's web. The leverage of that revered bulk on so great a length of slender mast with the ship rolling fifteen degrees and pitching somewhere near five hardly bore thinking about, and he had put his hand on the topgallant-cap for signs of movement or yielding when Jack, firmly perched up there, one arm hooked into the royal shrouds, called, 'I have them, by God. I have them. But only proas. Three sail of proas, standing south.'

They reached the deck by the backstays, gravity lending them wings or the equivalent. 'I am very sorry to have kept you waiting, Mr Blyth,' said Jack to the purser, 'and I am very sorry not to bring you good news: they were only proas.'

'Only proas. Ruined his Sabbath nankeens to see them, and delayed the fucking poached eggs in red wine till they was fucking grape-shot in horse-piss,' said Killick to his mate, his harsh, shrewish voice perfectly audible in the cabin.

'As far as I could make out,' continued Jack, 'they were on a bowline, so perhaps our courses may converge.'

Converge they did, and with surprising rapidity: at pudding-time the word came down that they were hull-up from the deck; and when the dinner-party moved up to drink their coffee under the awning in the open air, the proas, three of them, were within gunshot — remarkably large craft, and with their outriggers remarkably stiff and fast, sailing on a wind. They were crammed with men.

'There is not much doubt of their calling,' observed Mr Blyth. 'All they lack is the Jolly Roger.'

'Perhaps their presence explains the emptiness of these waters,' said Stephen. 'Perhaps they have swept the ocean clean.'

'Like pike in a stew,' said Richardson.

In his glass Jack could see their chief, a little wiry man with a green turban, high in the rigging and staring at the *Diane* under a shading hand. He saw him shake his turbaned head, and a minute later the proas hauled their wind, skimming away at thirteen or even fourteen knots on the moderate breeze.

Divisions, Articles, plum-duff, proas had marked that Sunday; but there was still another event to set the day apart. As the sun went down into the sea, a great red-golden ball, so into the eastern sky there rose the moon, a great golden-yellow ball, as full as a moon could be. It was not a rare phenomenon; indeed it was a very usual one; yet this time, for purity of sky, the particular degree of humidity and no doubt a host of less obvious, rarely coinciding factors, it had an extraordinary perfection, and all hands, even the ship's boys and the loquacious, thick-skinned Old Buggers, watched it in silence. All hands, including the *Diane*'s captain and most of his officers, held it to be an omen; but there was no agreement about what it foretold until the next day, when they sailed westward, passing the False Natunas within a quarter of a mile. There was no flag, no flag whatsoever; but on the conspicuous rock, at the very top of its white streak, sat a large black bird, a cormorant with its black wings open and dangling.

It was in vain that Stephen asserted that a cormorant's presence was perfectly natural — they were usual in the southern parts of Asia — the Chinese had tamed them these many ages past. Everyone knew from that moment on that there was no chance of a meeting at this rendezvous; and although they looked out most dutifully that night and the next day, no one was much surprised when their eastward passage, their last, proved as fruitless as the first.

Jack sailed along the chosen parallel until the end of the chosen time for conscience sake, and then, sad at heart, he gave the order to steer south-west, following the course he and the master, working throughout the afternoon on all the available charts, all Dalrymple's and Muffitt's notes and observations, had plotted as the best for Java. Sad at heart and angry too, or rather deeply vexed: he and his clerk had been making their usual readings of temperature, salinity and so on for Humboldt before sunset; he had all his tubes, pots and instruments by his open book in the cabin, but before recording the figures he had retired to the quarter-gallery, his privy. Sitting there he heard a crash and a confused tumbling, and when he came out he found that Stephen had fallen off the chair from which he was trying to catch a spider under the skylight and had not only flung sea-water all over his records but had broken an improbable number of instruments — hygrometers, seven different kinds of thermometer, Crompton's device for measuring specific gravity: practically everything made of glass. He had also contrived to shatter the hanging barometer and tear down a sword-rack: all this in a very moderate sea.

By the time the cabin was in order darkness was at hand, and after quarters Jack climbed into the maintop to watch the rising of the moon; but for once the eastern sky was barred, promising rain by night, and he sat there on the folded studdingsails, feeling tired and discouraged. It had been a distinct effort heaving himself aloft and he had felt his weight: going much higher on Sunday he had not been aware of it at all. 'Is this age?' he wondered. 'God help us, what a prospect.' For a while he leant back against the sailcloth watching the stars right overhead and the truck of the mainmast weaving among them; without giving it any conscious attention he also heard the quiet steady working of the ship, the occasional orders, the mustering of the watch: Richardson had taken over; Warren would have the middle and Elliott the morning watch. He found that he must have dropped off, for two bells woke him: 'This will never do,' he said, stretching and looking at the sky — the moon was well up now, slightly out of shape and veiled by low cloud; the wind was much the same, but it was likely to bring up showers and thick weather.

In the cabin he found that Stephen had retired to the lower deck, so he called for toasted cheese and a long, heavily lemoned glass of grog, wrote a note in which Captain Aubrey presented his compliments to Mr Fox and had the honour of informing His Excellency that the ship was now heading for Java; that wind and weather permitting she might reach Batavia on Friday; and that it might be thought proper for the mission s servants to begin packing tomorrow, as it was not contemplated that the *Diane* should make any prolonged stay in harbour, sent it round by the duty-midshipman, and turned in early.

His cot moved with the ship's easy roll and lift, and the few other hanging objects moved with it, their rhythmic sway just visible by the light of the small dark-lantern at his side. He felt sleep coming, and as he turned on his side to welcome it the gleam of the epaulette on his best coat caught his eye: how he had longed for it all through the time he had been struck off the Navy List! Once in those days he had dreamt he saw it, and the waking had been indescribably painful. But now there it was in fact, solid, tangible: a deep happiness flooded through his heart and he went to sleep smiling. He woke again to the distant cry of 'Do you hear the news?' the traditional facetiousness at four o'clock in the morning to tell the watch below that they must relieve the watch on deck; then the voices, closer at hand, of Warren saying to Elliott, 'Here you have her,' together with course and orders, and then Elliott's formal repetition. And there was the voice of the ship, which told him that the breeze was steady: nothing could be more regular. And out of nothing came the thought that of course Stephen would have learned acquaintances in Batavia — the instruments could all be replaced or made by skilful artisans: the chain of careful measurements carried half way round the world would be broken only by a day or two — three at the most.

A little before two bells the idlers were called and at two bells itself, by pale moonlight, the ritual cleaning of the decks began, although they had been thoroughly washed by showers throughout the middle watch. The grinding of holystones that reverberated through the ship did not wake Jack Aubrey; but the first rasping shudder as the keel scraped on rock brought him out of his cot, wholly alive and present. The moment he was upright the *Diane* struck with shocking force and flung him down. Even so he was on deck before the messenger had reached the companion-ladder.

'Man the braces,' he shouted in a voice loud enough to carry over the all-pervading sound of the ship crashing on over the reef. 'Lay all flat aback. Bear a hand, bear a hand. Cheerly there, forward.' The way was coming off the *Diane*, and now a last heave of the sea set her high on an unseen rock, motionless.

The men of the watch below were pouring up in the half light: almost all the officers were already there. Jack sent a carpenter's mate to sound the well. 'Mr Fielding,' he said, 'let us get the Doctor's skiff over the side.'

'Two foot, sir, and rising moderate,' said the carpenter himself. 'I went down directly.'

'Thank you, Mr Hadley,' said Jack: and the news spread along the deck — only two foot, and rising moderate.

A few more urgent measures and now Richardson was calling from the skiff. 'Three fathom under her stern, sir: two and a half amidships: two under her forefoot. No bottom with this line a cable's length ahead.'

'Clew up all,' said Jack. 'Stand by to let go the best bower.'

The half-light was changing: the sun sent a brilliance into the low eastern cloud and then showed above the horizon. Four bells struck. Jack walked forward to see the best bower dropped — a precaution in the event of a very violent squall but taken chiefly by way of general comfort: not all present were heroes — and when he walked back it was day, a day that showed a fairly heavy but declining sea, a sky promising fair weather, and a mile to the north an island, a green-covered sloping island of no great size, perhaps two miles across.

'What of the well, Mr Fielding?' he asked.

'Two foot seven inches, sir, and now we may be gaining. Mr Edwards would like to speak to you, if he may.'

Jack considered, looking over the side. The ship felt dead, as though she were in dry-dock; she had not stirred, much less hammered, since that last terrible heave. And she was unnaturally high in the water. In an aside to the quartermaster and the two helmsmen he said, 'You may leave the wheel,' and then he returned to his contemplation, while the chain-pumps whirred and flung out their stream. The water by the frigate's side confirmed his instinctive guess: she had struck at the last moment of spring-tide high-water; the ebb was already moving fast. Turning he saw Killick, mutely holding up a watch-coat, and beyond him Stephen and Edwards. 'Thankee, Killick,' he said, putting it on. 'Good morning, Doctor. Mr Edwards, good morning to you.'

'Good morning, sir,' said Edwards. 'His Excellency desires his compliments and can he or any of the mission be of service?'

'He is very good: for the moment nothing but keeping those people out of the way' — nodding towards a group of servants huddled in the waist. 'But no doubt he would like to hear of the position. Pray join us, Doctor: this is for your ear too. We have struck an unknown, uncharted reef at high water. We are now aground. I cannot yet tell what damage the ship has suffered, but she is in no immediate danger. There is a strong likelihood that by lightening her we may float her off the reef at the next high tide. It may then be possible to make her seaworthy enough to take us to Batavia to be docked. In any event we are about to lower down the boats, and it would be as well if Mr Fox with all his people and as much baggage as possible were to go ashore under a proper guard and leave us to our task.'

Chapter 10

Their task, their arduous, complex task: very severe and often highly-skilled labour day and night with peaks of intensity at full tide as extreme as anything Jack had known in his long experience.

All day they lightened ship: perpetually rousing out stores and carrying them to the shore in boatloads; lowering all uppermasts and spars over the side, there to be formed into rafts; starting the ship's water, though none had yet been found on the island (an island inhabited only by ring-tailed apes), and pumping it away by the ton together with the sea-water that still came in almost as fast as they could fling it out. And as they worked they saw the ebb, the most surprisingly rapid ebb, bare the reef on either hand, so that there was white water all around: moderate white water, since there was no considerable sea and the breeze was neither here nor there: but as the ebb proceeded so the ship took more and more of her own unsupported weight, and her timbers groaned again. And now from the boats they could see her plain, standing there unnaturally high, showing her copper, supported by three dark weed-grown heads of rock, two under her quarters and one beneath her keel about as far forward as her belfry, where that last surge had set her down, almost upright, before she could grind her way over the rest of the reef and into deep water.

So upright and so solid was she at low water that once Jack had placed some shores by way of precaution all hands had their dinner aboard, by watches, and with extra allowance to recruit them for the heavy work past and to come. The pumping went on all the time of course, and to its steady churning the carpenter and his crew, with lanterns and with all the hatchways wide open for the help of what reflected sun might get down, crept about the encumbered hold and orlop dealing with what damage they could reach and making out the nature of the rest, the Captain being with them most of the time. Meanwhile the bosun and his mates, together with the most experienced forecastle hands and tierers, roused out the best cable the *Diane* possessed, the most nearly new and unfrayed, a seventeen-inch cable that they turned end for end — no small undertaking in that confined space, since it weighed three and a half tons — and bent it to the best bower anchor by the wholly unworn end that had always been abaft the bitts: the bitter end. There was thought to be good luck attached to the bitter end, as well as greater strength.

The best bower, backed with the smaller stream anchor, they lowered carefully down into the launch, and at last the boat, moving over the longed-for grateful rising tide, dropped the two into what Fielding and the master, after prolonged sounding in the skiff, considered the best and cleanest holding-ground in a most indifferent and rock-strewn anchorage.

All this while the other boats had been plying to and fro, shifting great quantities of stores, lightening the ship as fast as ever they could. And much of the time Stephen and Macmillan had been sitting not in their usual action-station far below where they would now have been a great hindrance, but in the after cabin. This was a time of great hurry and even greater effort and they had already treated many falls, sprains and twists and even one most unfortunate hernia — a good man who had undone himself in his zeal. Now their patient was Mr Blyth. A hen-coop flung from the waist had struck him down in the small cutter and he was bleeding profusely from a scalp-wound:

they sewed him up, staunched the flow, and asked him how the ship was doing.

'I hope, oh how I do hope, she will be afloat in half an hour,' he said. 'It is very near high-water; the leak is not much worse, though she sat right down; and the Captain believes he may pluck her off. If she leaks extremely when she is in deep water, then he means to beach and careen her; she will certainly last as far as the island, and there is a good berth there. The breeze is on the land and we shall drop our courses while the boats tow as well. But I do not believe it will come to that: he thinks she will swim. The lower futtocks have suffered, in course; but he thinks she will swim, with the pumps going and maybe a sail fothered over the bottom, until we reach Batavia. But the first thing to do is to pluck her off. Hark!'

'All boats,' came the powerful cry. 'All boats repair aboard.'

Their hands came tearing up the side, for they too had been watching the tide rise to its height with infinite attention: a fine height — perhaps not quite so fine a height as could have been hoped for, but at least the barky's copper was well out of sight: she sat there like a Christian ship, and if there had been anything of a sea running she would almost certainly be lifting and bumping. And all the seamen knew that this was their best chance, with a tide not much lower than the last and the ship lighter by God knows how many tons, most of them manhandled over the side.

'Ship the capstan-bars,' said Jack. 'And Mr Crown, pray swift them long.' Then after a pause while the swifting-line joined the outward ends of the bars, leaving a loop at each extremity for extra hands to clap on to, 'Carry on, Mr Fielding.'

More orders, but no running of feet, for the men were already there, and the fife shrilled out loud and clear, cutting high above the tramping feet. Tramping fast as they ran in the first few turns, then slower, slower, much slower.

'I think we may go on deck,' said Stephen. 'We might find a place at the bars. We must go by the waist, or we shall be trodden down and destroyed.'

They skirted the lower capstan, crowded with almost motionless men straining against the bars: half a step and a single click of the pawl at the cost of huge grunting exertion. They ran up to the quarterdeck, to the upper part of the same capstan, equally crowded, equally unmoving, or nearly so. The fife screamed, the little fifer standing on it; the capstan-head blazed in the sun.

The men heaved, pale with extreme effort, breathing in quick gasps, their expressions entirely inward and concentrated. 'Heave and rally, heave and she moves,' came Jack's almost unrecognizable voice in the middle of the press. From the starboard hawsehole right forward the cable could be seen squirting water, stretched to half its natural width or less, rigid, almost straight from bow to sea.

'Rally, oh rally,' he called again. Stephen and Macmillan each found a handhold on one of the swifter-ends — there was no room at the bars — and heaved with all their might: thrust on and on and on with no gain.

'Oh sir,' cried the carpenter, running aft, 'the hawse-pieces will never bear it.'

'Vast heaving,' said Jack, after a moment, and he straightened: it was a little while before some of the others did the same, so set were they.

'Surge the messenger,' he said, and the strain came off. He walked stiffly to the rail, then along the gangway to the forecastle and the bows, considering the tide, the ship, the reef, all with the extremity of concentration.

'There is only one thing for it,' he cried. 'Pass the word for Mr White. Mr White: I am sorry, the guns must go overboard. All but the carronades.'

The gunner, pale from his labour, went paler still. 'Aye aye, sir,' he said, however, and he called his mates and quarter-gunners. This was the cruellest blow of all, a deliberate self-castration: there was not a man who did not feel it when the cherished guns went out through their ports, splash after deeply-shocking splash, the inversion of all natural order.

'The chasers, sir?'

These were Jack's personal brass long nine-pounders, wonderfully accurate, very old friends. 'The chasers too, Mr White. We keep only the light carronades.'

After that last double splash — he was ashamed of the pang it caused — he called 'Mr Fielding, let us splice the main-brace.'

This was greeted by a confused cheer, and Jemmy Bungs darted down to the spirit-room, returning with a beaker not of rum, for that was all gone, but of the even stronger arrack, a quarter of a pint for every soul aboard. This was mixed on deck with exactly three times its amount of water from the scuttle-butt, with stated proportions of lemon-juice and sugar, and so served out, Jack taking the first full pint.

It seemed to him that whatever might be said against the custom there were times when it could not be faulted, and this was one: he drank his tot slowly, feeling its almost instant effect as he watched the still water over the side. 'Now, shipmates,' he said at last, 'let us see if we can shift the barky this time.'

It seemed to him that he had felt some life underfoot since the loss of the guns, as though she were on the edge of being waterborne: if there had been anything of a sea she would surely have lifted on her bed, and it was with rising hope that he took his place at the capstan-bar. He nodded to the fifer and all hands walked steadily round to the tune of Skillygalee-skillygaloo and the invariable cries of *nippers, there* and *light along the messenger* and *side out for a bend;* steadily round, and then the strain came on, stronger and stronger; the cable lifted, jetting from its coils and stretching thinner, thinner. 'Heave and rally,' cried Jack, setting his whole weight and great strength against the bar, grinding his feet into the deck. 'Heave and rally,' from the deck below, where another fifty men and more were thrusting with all their might.

'Heave, heave, oh heave.' The ship made a grating motion beneath their feet and they flung themselves with even greater force against the bars: at this everything gave before them and on both decks they fell in a confused heap.

'Wind her in,' said Jack. 'A man at each bar will be enough.' He limped forward — some heavy foot had trodden on his wounded leg — and watched the cable come home alone. Bitter end or not, it had parted. 'A bitter end indeed, for us,' he said to the bosun, who gave a wan smile.

All that night they lightened ship, and at low tide, a calm low tide, they saw her guns all round her in the shallow water, catching the light of the moon. After an early breakfast they carried out the small bower with two carronades lashed to it, choosing a slightly truer line, more nearly a continuation of the ship's keel; and having done so they waited for high water, shortly after sunrise.

The sun came up at six, and it shone on clean, trim decks: they had not been holystoned but they had been thoroughly swabbed and flogged dry, particularly under the sweep of the capstan-bars; and now all hands were watching the tide as it rose. It crept up the copper, the ripples gaining and losing, but always gaining a little more than they lost until the sun was a handsbreadth clear of the horizon, when the rise came to an end, leaving a broad streak of copper above the level of the sea.

Can this be all, they asked, can this be true high water? According to the ship's chronometers it was, and had been for some time past. Of course, as every seaman knew, each succeeding tide after the spring mounted less and less until the neap was over; but so great a difference as this seemed unnatural.

However, this was all the high water they were going to have to float the ship, so they manned the bars and they heaved till sweat poured off them on to the deck. But it was clearly hopeless and presently Jack cried 'Belay,' then directing his hoarse, cracked voice below, 'Mr Richardson, there, avast heaving.' And walking away from the capstan he said in an involuntary whisper to Stephen, 'It is no good heaving out both her guts and our own; we must wait for the next spring-tide. Shall we have our breakfast? That good fellow has the coffee on the brew, by the smell. I should give my soul for a cup.' But with his foot on the ladder he turned and called, 'Oh, Mr Fielding, when the gunroom has breakfasted and when you can summon enough hands able to pull, I think we should weigh the small bower with the launch. I do not like to keep the cable chafing on this rocky ground until next spring. And then perhaps after a pause we can carry some more of the envoy's baggage ashore.'

The first boat to carry anything to the island brought back the secretary, Edwards, with the envoy's compliments, and should it be convenient for Captain Aubrey to come ashore, Mr Fox would be happy to have an interview, as a matter of some urgency.

'Please put my reply in the proper form,' said Jack, smiling at the poor young man. 'I am far too stupid to do so this morning. Something in the line of happy — delighted — earliest convenience, if you please: compliments, of course.' And when Edwards had gone he said to Stephen, 'I shall go, when I have had a cat-nap; but what a time for standing on ceremony, for God's sake. He might just as well have come here in the same boat.'

Fox seemed to have some sense of this when he greeted Aubrey at the landing-place — a haggard, ill-looking, dead-tired Aubrey, in spite of his cat-nap. 'It is very good of you to come, sir, after what I am sure was a trying day and night; and I should not have troubled you if I had not felt it urgently necessary to consult you on the King's service. Shall we walk along the shore?' They turned from the miscellaneous heaps of files, tape-bound papers, baggage, bales and stores, with disconsolate people sitting about among them, and paced slowly towards the farther end of the little bay, where the sand curved away to rocks that thrust far into the sea.

'I speak under correction, sir,' began Fox after a few steps, 'but as I understand it, in spite of your heroic efforts the ship has remained on her reef and must there remain until the next spring-tide.'

'Just so.'

'And even then it is not quite certain that she will come off, or that having come off she can sail to Batavia without more or less prolonged repairs.'

'There is almost no absolute certainty at sea.'

'Yet in all this we do have one firm unquestioned fact: she cannot float until next spring-tide. Now I do not speak in the least sense of criticism, far less of blame, but I do put it to you, Captain Aubrey, that this delay would be most prejudicial to His Majesty's service, and that it is therefore my duty to ask you to have me conveyed to Batavia in one of the larger boats. The loss of more time may have incalculable effects on the general strategy at home — as you know, the balance is so fine that the detachment of a single ship can make an enormous difference — and it may have more immediate and obvious effects on the East India Company's actions. The Directors must know as soon as possible whether or not they can risk this season's Indiamen on the China voyage; and all this has the greatest influence on the country's prosperity and its power of waging war.' And after a pause in which Jack was turning this over in his weary mind, 'Come, it is barely two days' sail with the steady breeze of this time of the year; and the Governor will instantly send ships and artisans in case the *Diane* needs extensive repairs.'

'It is close on two hundred miles to Batavia,' said Jack. 'And these are dangerous waters. I am not familiar with the South China Sea or what its sky foretells, and my instruments are out of order. There is the weather; there are the Malays, the Dyaks and the Chinese.'

'I have known these waters for thirty-five years; and Loder, who has sailed right round Java in just such a boat as the pinnace, has known them almost as long. He foretells fair weather; our Malays foretell fair weather; and well-armed we should be quite at our ease. I put it to you again: this is a matter of duty.'

They walked on in silence, and when they reached the end of the cove Jack sat down on the rock, reflecting. 'Very well,' he said at last. 'I will let you have the pinnace with a carronade in her bows and a couple of hands to work it — muskets for all your people — an officer to navigate, and a coxswain.'

'Thank you, Aubrey, thank you,' cried Fox, shaking his hand. 'I am deeply obliged . . . but I expected no less of you, sir.'

'I shall send the pinnace in at eleven o'clock, manned and rigged. There are provisions, water and firing already ashore. I wish you a quick and fortunate passage: my best compliments to Mr Raffles, if you please.'

Returning to the ship he said to Fielding, 'The envoy is away for Batavia in the pinnace, armed with a twenty-four-pound carronade, a dozen muskets and proper ammunition. They have all they need in the way of stores. I shall need three volunteers, one fit to act as coxswain, and an officer to take them there.'

To Stephen he said, 'Fox cannot wait for the moon. He is off to Batavia with his treaty: I have agreed to let him have the pinnace.'

'Is this a sensible man's undertaking, Jack?' asked Stephen in a low, troubled voice. 'It is not a mad, disproportionate venture?'

'Mad? Lord, no. Batavia is only a couple of hundred miles away. Bligh sailed close on four thousand in a smaller boat, much less well-found than our pinnace.'

'Your pinnace,' observed Stephen; and in fact it was Jack's private property.

'Well, yes. But I hope to see it again, you know.'

'He will be accompanied by competent people? He will not give wild improper orders?' Stephen went on, willing to soothe his uneasy conscience.

'He may give wild improper orders,' said Jack, smiling wearily, 'but no one will take any notice. One of our officers will be in command.'

The officer in question was Elliott, who had had the watch when the *Diane* struck. He knew very well that if he had remembered his orders and had reefed topsails when the breeze increased the ship would have been making no more than three or four knots at the moment of impact rather than a full eight. A cruel blow in any case, but probably not a disastrous one. Jack knew it, since he had seen the full topsails laid aback; and Elliott knew that he knew it. Neither had said anything, but Jack at once agreed to his request that he should take the pinnace, led him through the charts and observations and checked his instruments, lending him a better azimuth compass.

Elliott left the ship in what was in fact his first command a little before eleven. He was at the landing-place at the stated time; and then followed one of those intolerable delays typical of landsmen — packages forgotten, fetched, exchanged for others, confused; arguments, screeching, counter-orders; arrangements changed — and Jack, who had intended to remain on deck until the pinnace sailed by into the offing, went below and slept for twenty minutes: he had not turned in all night.

Hauled back into the present world, he stood on the motionless quarterdeck, taking off his hat to the distant Fox, equally erect, equally bareheaded, as the pinnace, quarter of a mile away, went about and headed south-south-west.

'Well, Mr Fielding,' he said, having gazed for a while at the decks and the distant shore, 'they have left us looking not unlike Rag Fair: decks all ahoo, and the beach like a gypsy encampment after the constables have taken them all away. Is that Mr Edwards I see over there, in the black breeches?'

'Yes, sir. He told me he was to be left behind with a copy of the treaty, in case of accident.'

'Oh, indeed? After dinner, then, let all hands make things look a little more ship-shape here — I should like my joiner and his mates to put the cabin back as it was — and then repair on shore and put that mass of objects into some kind of an order before we lighten the ship any further. We cannot go on living indefinitely with a disused pawn-shop just at hand: furthermore, we must set about finding water.'

A real sleep before his own dinner, and above all dinner itself did wonders for Captain Aubrey. 'I once ate my mutton at an inn called The Ship Aground,' he said to his guests, 'but I never thought to do so in sober earnest: a very whimsical idea, upon my word. Mr Edwards, a glass of wine with you, sir. Captain Welby, I know I must not speak of service matters at table, but pray put me in mind of the word that has been on the tip of my tongue this last half hour — the sub-ject I must consult with you when we go ashore — the learned word for setting up tents and so on.'

'Castramentation, sir,' said Welby,

beaming with decent triumph — it was rare that a soldier could triumph aboard a man-of-war — 'And there is more to it than might be supposed.'

Certainly there was more to it than Jack had supposed. 'To begin with, sir,' said Welby, 'it is always wise to be both on rising ground and to have a good supply of fresh water within your lines if it is at all possible; and it would be strange if this sloping stretch of grass did not kill two birds with one stone. By that, sir, I mean it might on the one hand house all our people on its upper right-hand face, and on the other, give them a well at no great depth — there has certainly been a watercourse in the middle, long ago. The position would not answer against artillery, but for an ordinary surprise you could hardly ask better. A square with a moderate breastwork and a stockade would leave a fine open space between itself and the forest on three sides, and command the landing-place on the fourth. With a carronade at each corner it would make a very neat little post, even without re-entering angles or ravelines or anything ambitious like that.'

Jack could best survey the broad sweep, a green triangle thrust uphill into the swarming forest, from a central mound, now covered by the *Diane*'s livestock, sheep, goats, pigs, geese, poultry, grazing on a particularly sweet grass shoulder to shoulder. 'Baker,' he called, 'drive them over to the far side.'

'I can't, sir,' replied Baker. 'They won't follow anyone but Jemmy Ducks and young Pollard; and the hogs bite, if shoved.'

It was the old story. Even the most recent animals, influenced by the older inhabitants, were already too tame to be driven; they could only be led by those they liked. The next step would be their conversion into holy cows that could not possibly be slaughtered, cut up and served out. 'Then pass the word for Jemmy Ducks and Pollard,' said Jack, making a mental note to tell Fielding to move Pollard to other duties; detachment was easy enough where poultry was concerned, but the four-legged stock required a frequent change of keeper.

'Yes, I think it should do very well,' he said, when he could see the whole extent. 'I was not really thinking so much of defence as of neatness, so I believe we scarcely need a breastwork or stockade, far less covered ways or outworks; but we must have a well, and we should like a trim square for tents and stores, where purser, bosun, carpenter and gunner can lay their hands on what they need. So if you would be so good as to sink your well and then trace out the lines according to the rules of the art, I will have a word with the sailmaker and set tents in hand.'

'Perhaps just a little ditch for drainage, sir, in case of rain, with the earth thrown up outside?'

'As you please, Captain Welby,' said Jack, walking off. 'But nothing elaborate.'

'The sergeant and I will pace it out and break ground as soon as we can get out picks and shovels from the ship, sir,' called Welby after him.

At the landing-place he learnt that Stephen had last been seen making his way into the extraordinarily tangled forest with a cutlass sharpened for him by the armourer and a large pair of tendon-cutters, so he took Bonden and Seymour in the skiff to survey what he could of the island before nightfall. Richardson was engaged in sweeping for the lost anchors or Jack would have taken him too, an excellent surveyor's mate.

It was as well that the skiff was light, for their voyage was pulling all the way; the breeze had dropped away shortly after Fox and his company dipped below the horizon, and although an unusually strong current swept them along the southern shore, from the western point right along the island's high straight north face they had to pull very hard indeed, and as Bonden observed, if the tide had been running with the current they could not have stemmed it at all. The island was more or less rectangular, like a battered book set down on the sea at an angle, the southern side awash, the northern an almost sheer rise, a couple of hundred feet high in places, with caves in it, some of them deeply recessed, with small beaches to them.

As they rowed along they heard a shrill hallooing from one of the cliffs, and looking up they saw Dr Maturin, waving a handkerchief. He called out when he saw they had seen him, but although the air was so still and the sea so calm all they could make out was the word soup.

Between taking his angles and recording depths, Jack turned this over in his mind, but he could make nothing of it until after sunset, when they reached the ship, her great stern window glowing its full width and Stephen sitting there in the restored cabin, his cello between his knees. He smiled and nodded, carried the phrase, part of his own Saint Cecilia's Day, through to its end, and said, 'Did you see our streeted camp?'

'Only a glimmer of white from the sea.

Surely it is not finished already?'

'Finished to Welby's satisfaction, no; but much is standing and even more is marked out to the exact inch and degree. I have rarely seen a man take more pleasure in what he was about. Though I may say I believe I took even more delight in my afternoon than Welby. I found the edible-nest swallow! Hirundo esculenta, the bird's-nest soup swallow! Colonies of them, several thousand strong, on those cliffs from which I saw you. In the depths of those caves their nests lie in rows. Little small grey birds they are, not three inches long, but true swallows and even swifter than ours; and their nests are almost white. I hope you will come and see them tomorrow.'

'Certainly, if work permits. Was it very difficult to get through the forest?'

'Tolerably so, because of the lianas; yet there are boars in plenty, and by crouching one can follow their paths fairly well. There are some other paths too, though much overgrown; people must come here from time to time — the animals are by no means tame.'

Jack fetched his violin and while Stephen gave him a short account of the island's flora and fauna he tuned it lovingly. 'So much for the ring-tailed ape,' said Stephen at last, and with one accord they swept into his Saint Cecilia. After that, and after a visit from Fielding to report, they ate their customary toasted cheese and played on and on, the music echoing the length of the almost empty ship with quite another resonance.

Jack turned in late and he slept deep, although his cot moved no more than if it had been slung in the Tower of London; yet he woke uneasy. Of course any man commanding a King's ship that is poised on a reef with several days before he can hope to float her off must wake uneasy, even when expert opinion has told him that the fine weather will continue and when he knows for certain that Thursday's high-water will be as high as that during which she struck, while the full spring-tide on Sunday will be higher by far — will necessarily raise her free. But this was an uneasiness of another nature, closer to superstitious or instinctive dread.

Washing, shaving, and then a hearty breakfast dispelled some of it; a most encouraging tour of the hold with the carpenter — Mr Hadley's repairs meant that now the pumps were in action for only half a glass in each watch — did away with more; and after a visit to Welby's encampment he was almost himself again. The encampment, with its exact earthwork (for Welby had interpreted ditch very freely), its trim lines, its store-tent in the middle, and its well with three and a half feet of water already, was a joy to behold; and so was the pleasure of the Marines, now for once the experts, aware that they had astonished the foremast jacks.

But at low tide he took a small party to buoy the guns; the men were the ship's few swimmers and three or four were competent divers too; he went in, and down, with them, and there was something indefinably wrong about the water: not only too warm to be at all refreshing but also in some way unclean. They buoyed the guns neatly, but the uneasiness returned, and although at dinner he told Stephen how reasonable it was to expect the ship to lift off on Thursday without any cruel dragging over the remaining length of reef and how nearly certain it was on Sunday, with the sun and the new moon both pulling the spring tide to its fullest height, at least half a fathom more, he had no appetite, and leaving both wine and pudding he went on deck to look at the sea and the sky.

Neither pleased him. It was slack water — a very low tide indeed — and there was an odd heave and shudder on the surface, a motion not unlike twitching. The sky had been somewhat veiled before dinner. Now it was hazy and low: no breeze at all, and the exposed rocks smelt disagreeable in the oppressive heat. A large pale fish, a shark of a kind he had not seen before, passed slowly by.

He watched the sea; and even before the turn of the tide he saw an unnatural swell set in: unnaturally sudden, unnaturally strong. His uneasiness increased, and after half an hour he turned to the master.

'Mr Warren,' he said, 'the signal for officers and all boats, if you please; and meanwhile let the people get ready to lay out the small bower as before, but with two cables.'

Over on a level stretch of green outside the camp he saw the ordered pattern of a game of cricket break up and the players run down to the landing-place; and already the surf was sending its long lines of white along the shore.

'Mr Warren,' he said again, 'I did ask whether you had a barometer, did I not?'

'Yes, sir, you did; and I had to say I gave it to Dr Graham to have adjusted in Plymouth. It is still there, in course.'

Jack nodded and walked up and down, looking eastward at each turn, for not only was the swell coming from that direction but the horizon and the sky for ten degrees above it was taking on a dark coppery glare rarely to be seen.

'Mr Fielding,' he said as soon as the first lieutenant was aboard, 'is the Doctor on shore?'

'Yes, sir: he is under the impression that you may go for a walk in the forest with him, and perhaps climb down the farther cliff. He has a coil of stout, supple line and Sorley, a cragsman from one of the Scotch islands.'

'Not today, I am afraid. Let all hands turn to and lighten ship: carronades, small arms, ammunition; whatever purser, carpenter, gunner, armourer, sailmaker and bosun think most important in their own line; then the hands' bags and chests, officers' personal property. And beg the Doctor to come aboard for his own things and the medicine-chest.'

Doctor Maturin came by the first returning boat, and though the tide of flood was not yet a half hour old, surf was breaking high on the rocks that closed the little bay on the west, breaking at unusually long and solemn intervals. He found Jack in the cabin with his clerk, assembling the ship's documents, registers, signal-books, the enormous and sometimes most secret paper-work of a man-of-war. 'Mr Butcher,' said Jack, 'do not for Heaven's sake let us forget Mr Humboldt's readings: they are on that locker over there. Let them be packed up with my hydrographical remarks.'

'I will take them at once, sir,' said Butcher, who had suffered from these hundreds of hours of accurate measurement and who valued them at their true worth.

'Brother,' said Stephen, when the clerk had staggered off with the files clutched to his bosom, 'what is afoot?'

'I am not sure,' said Jack, 'but it may be your St Cecilia:

> *And when that last and dreadful hour*
> *This crumbling pageant shall devour,*
> *The trumpet shall be heard on high,*
> *The dead shall live, the living die,*
> *And Music shall untune the sky.*

Look out to the east, will you?' They gazed through the stern window, where deep purple was massing beneath the coppery glare. 'I only remember to have seen a sky like that once,' said Jack after a long considering pause, 'and that was when we were in the South Sea, standing for the Marquesas. You saw precious little of it, because a lee-lurch tossed you into the waist and you hit your head on a gun, but it came before a most stupendous blow, that same blow that wrecked the *Norfolk*. I do not like this sudden swell, neither. So I am clearing the ship as much as ever I can and I beg you will have everything you value taken ashore, and all your physic and saws and pills. If I am wrong, there is no great harm; they can only call me an old woman.'

It was perfectly clear that by now none of the seamen belonging to the frigate were going to call their Captain an old woman; they were all of his opinion, and their total conviction infected the afterguard, the landmen and the first-voyage Marines, vexed at first by the loss of their game of cricket but now silent, casting anxious glances at the eastern sky.

The boats plied to and fro at racing speed, but with the making tide the much fiercer surf ran farther up the beach, much farther every voyage, however fast they pulled; and soon it was very hard to work the boats out through it to the ship. Worse: the ship being stern-on to the swell gave no shelter and coming alongside grew more and more perilous, so that chests, stores, cases had to be lowered or often tossed from the head-rails.

It was now that Jack called his first lieutenant below and said, 'Mr Fielding, if this develops as I fear it may, let each officer be prepared to get his division ashore when I give the word. There will be no piping *abandon ship*, no calling out or excitement, just a plain going ashore in due order.'

For nearly an hour longer the swell grew without a breath of wind, and the great solemn crash came echoing back from the rocks; and towards the end of this hour the ship first began to shift on her bed. Jack had already given the word and little by little the ship had emptied until now there were only four men of the final boat-load still aboard, the Captain, his steward, the sentry guarding the spirit-room and a hand who was not quite right in the head. The purple had spread over half the sky, the coppery light over almost all the rest, reaching the far horizon here and there. From the darkness far astern there was a low constant thunder and the reflexion of lightning all along the eastern sky. Then with a howl the wind came racing across the sea in a white squall: one moment the air was calm and the next the full blast was on them, flying shattered water cutting their breath and blurring their sight. The launch, crammed with its last cargo, was hooked on to the forechains, only just holding, and Fielding roared with all his might, 'Come on, sir. For God's sake come on.'

Jack was at the break of the quarterdeck with the others. 'Get along forward,' he said to them and darted into the cabin to check: nobody. A last look and he raced along to the ship's head and strode into the boat as it rose to the level of the rail. The moment Bonden and the bowman let go the boat shot away, flying before the terrible wind, rising and falling enormously; and away ahead Jack saw the large cutter pooped by a breaker, turn and roll over and over in the killing surf. But before the launch was half way to the shore the wind brought rain, a great black hurtling mass of warm rain; and now they were in the very midst of the thunder, stunning, ear-splitting thunder just overhead and lightning all about them.

'Back water all,' roared Bonden above the uproar, poising the launch on the back of a towering wave. 'Give way, oh Christ give way.'

The heavy boat rose, rose, and sped for the beach, grounding high in a smother of foam. The whole crew was lining the shore and those who could find a hold ran her up the streaming sand and then by skids far up beyond the highest tide mark, close to the remaining cutter. The skiff was nowhere to be seen.

Jack had often noticed, and now he noticed it again, that in time of extreme emergency men often seemed to go beyond dread, pain and fatigue; and for noise, danger and the overturning of all natural order this was as extreme as a great fleet-action fought yardarm to yardarm. As they waded up the yielding slope and through the unbelievable rain, carrying their burdens, a line of trees on the edge of the forest blazed blue-green, and the lightning leapt back from them into the sky with a hiss. He bent to shout into a quartermaster's ear, 'Look after Charlie,' for the half-wit was crying, his knuckles to his eyes, and it looked as though he might lose his senses altogether. 'Aye aye, sir,' replied the quartermaster, as though it were the most natural thing in the world, 'I'll change him directly we're under cover.'

They made their way up, and the enormous force of the wind diminished, for they came into the lee of the trees, the roaring trees; and through what light there was — for it was still day — they saw that the tents were standing. Welby's ditches were gushing a thick muddy stream, tearing up the sward below their outlet, but the camp

536

was not waterlogged and when Jack reached his quarters he found the ground quite firm. Not that he took notice of this not even the shelter from rain for some time: there was Fielding's report of seventeen hands lost in the cutter and six much injured; four lost in the skiff; one hand struck by lightning, and Edwards had to be told that there was not the least hope for the pinnace: it was not until an indefinite period of time had passed and that he was sitting there with Stephen, with the tremendous beating of rain grown habitual and only the more extravagant crashes of thunder or strokes of lightning close at hand exciting attention, that he perceived the dryness of the ground underfoot, the presence of his sea-chest and other possessions laid on trestles, and his chronometers and their case enclosed in a bladder.

Now that there was no longer the stimulus of action, now that there was in fact nothing to be done, they both felt numbed by the mass of events, by their own exertions and by the enormous and continuing noise, which made even common interchange a matter of more effort than they could afford; they sat there companionably enough however, nodding to one another occasionally, at some outrageous thunderclap or the crash of a forest tree nearby; but beneath it all Jack's ear strained to make out the horrible sound of his ship hammering on the reef.

This he was spared: the general uproar was too great for even a broadside to pierce through from the distance; and from time to time he closed his eyes, bowed his head, and slept. Waking at about three in the morning he noticed a new strain in the universal and all-pervading sound: a tearing, rushing noise like a torrent in spate. And when he had been listening to this for some time, while the lightning flashed overhead, giving an almost continuous light in the tent, sometimes so bright and prolonged that he could see Stephen telling his beads, there came another: not a continuous sound this time but a long deep roar lasting four or five minutes.

'What was that?' he cried.

'A landslide, my dear.'

Torpor again; extreme weariness. But during this stretch of the perpetually roaring, flashing night Stephen did not really sleep; and although at times his mind wandered off to something not far from waking dream it often came back to dwell on the Prabang treaty: Edwards's copy was now lying in Dr Maturin's particular metal-lined medicine-chest, as the safest, driest placc in the camp. Its accompanying letter was much what Stephen had expected, except that it was longer, more vehement and less able by far; and its animosity against young Edwards surprised him. Yet since it did not betray his own role even by implication — the envoy made no mention of any source of intelligence whatsoever — the letter would have to go as it stood. At times, when his mind clouded over with fatigue, he was tempted to make it ludicrous for Edwards's sake by adding still another name or two to those who had plotted to lessen the envoy's consequence, to make his task even more difficult and to take away from the merit of what had been accomplished. But in this context such a thing would not do at all; and even if it had been possible it would be pointless, for clearer reflection showed him that the list was already so long that it defeated its own end — the product of a mind unhinged.

The typhoon passed over somewhat after dawn, the rain moving westward and leaving a clear sky, so that Jack waking thought for a moment that this was an immensely-prolonged lightning-flash. The wind was much less, yet the volume of noise was even greater, partly because the tremendous surf was no longer tempered by the downpour but even more because the raging torrent that poured out of the forest and down what had been the grassy triangle was checked by Stephen's landslide, so that it made a series of cataracts. The mass of sward, trees and earth had partly diverted the stream from the encampment, which had lost only its southeast corner, but had turned it full upon the grassy slope above the landing-place. The grassy slope was gone; the landing-place was wholly overlaid; the launch had been shattered and swept out to sea, though the small cutter and some of the spars were still there, caught in the tangle of uprooted trees and bushes on either side of the torrent's mouth.

Jack stepped quietly out of the tent, for Stephen had dropped off in his turn; he looked up at the clean, washed sky and then over the white water to the reef. No ship, of course; but his eye travelled along the line to the island's westward point, where the anchor might possibly have brought her up if she had been heaved over into the deep water without too much damage: a vain hope, only very faintly held.

Several people were moving about the camp, talking in low voices or not at all: Jack had the impression that they were stunned, but glad to be alive. Fielding and Warren were among them, looking to the westward with a little pocket-glass.

'Good morning, gentlemen,' he said. 'What do you see?'

'Good morning, sir,' said Fielding, flattening his hair with one hand. 'We believe it may be a substantial piece of wreck.' He passed the glass, and Jack, having peered for a while, said, 'Let us go and see.'

Down the ravaged slope, now steaming in the sun, across the torrent by the tangle of fallen trees with their treasure of boat and spars, and out along a firm, hammered low-tide strand, littered with coconuts, presumably from Borneo, and with many drowned ring-tailed apes, certainly from here. Several people joined them: Richardson, the bosun, the carpenter, all the midshipmen and many foremast hands. The Captain and the first lieutenant walked ahead and Fielding said in a low voice, 'I am sorry to have to tell you, sir, that the tent which carried away in the south-east corner was the powder-store.'

'Was it, by God? Is there none left?'

'I have not checked that yet, sir: there may be a few barrels set aside as spoilt or damaged, but there cannot be many.'

'Let us hope there are some, at all

events.' They walked on without speaking for a while, a radiant day with the long surf booming on the left hand and rushing up the shore in vast fields of white; but nothing like as far as it had rushed in the night — that high-water mark was deep in the forest; and the forest-edge was all hung with weed. 'I believe you were right about the wreck,' said Jack at last, and they walked faster with their shadows long before them on the sand.

'Yes. Yes,' he said, gazing on that familiar side, the frigate's starboard bow and hull as far aft as half way along her waist, something like a quarter of the ship there on the perfect sand, her top-timbers buried but the rest quite free, remarkably unmutilated, the paintwork fresh. 'She must have parted where the floors cross the keel,' he said after a long considering pause.

The others, who had all come up, stood looking at the piece of ship in silence, with a curious respect. At last the carpenter said, 'These floor-timbers were never honest work, sir; not like the futtocks or the rest.'

'I am afraid you are right, Mr Hadley,' said Jack. 'But there is plenty of sound wood, as you observe. Enough for a fair-sized schooner, I make no doubt.'

'Oh yes, sir,' said Hadley, 'plenty enough and to spare.'

'Then, shipmates,' said Jack, smiling at his people, 'let us build one as quick as we can.'

We hope you have enjoyed this Large Print book. Other Thorndike, Wheeler or Chivers Press Large Print books are available at your library or directly from the publishers.

For more information about current and upcoming titles, please call or write, without obligation, to:

Publisher
Thorndike Press
295 Kennedy Memorial Drive
Waterville, ME   04901
Tel. (800) 223-1244

Or visit our Web site at:
www.gale.com/thorndike
www.gale.com/wheeler

OR

Chivers Press Limited
Windsor Bridge Road
Bath BA2 3AX
England
Tel. (01225) 335336

Or visit Chivers Web site at
www.chivers.co.uk

All our Large Print titles are designed for easy reading, and all our books are made to last.